A Moment Before Midnight

A Naverro Vampire Tale

Aziza Sphinx

Published by Aziza Sphinx, 2017.

<u>Publisher's Note:</u>

This literary piece is a work of fiction. Any references to historical events, to real people, living or dead; or real locales are intended only to give the fiction a setting in historic reality. Other names, characters, places, and incidents either are the product of the author's imagination or are used fictitiously, and their resemblance, if any, to real-life counterparts is entirely coincidental.

Learn more information at:

www.authoranagiawright.com

First Edition: February 2013

CHAPTER ONE

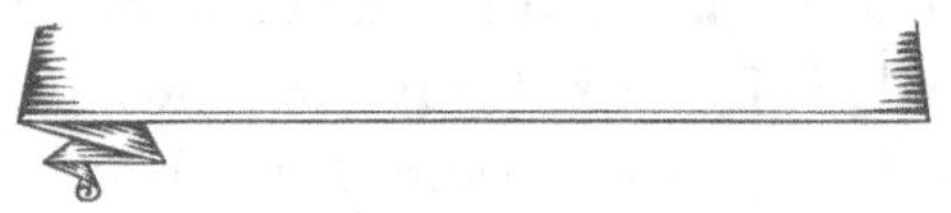

PAIN SNATCHED NICOLAY from the darkness, his hands immediately going to his throat. Frantically he searched for any marks, any sign that what he had just experienced was real. For centuries nothing had disturbed the Dark Slumber. The intricate part of him inherited when he became the undead engulfed him in security, allowing him a time of peace when he faced so much turmoil.

Lately though, something crept into the darkness. The sleep no longer offered comfort; instead it bred fear, deception, and death. Dreaming was forbidden by the Dark Slumber, and yet for the past two weeks dreams slithered their way into his mind's sanctuary.

"It must have been a dream," he said, shaking his head.

His shoulders relaxed and relief overcame him as he realized he was safe in his lair. Initially searching the room with eyes, he only saw the dark outlines of the few items in his sparsely furnished home. The silhouettes of the unlit candles hung in the distance as well as the shadows of the contemporary chair and desk set and the armoire that occupied the other side of the room. He then searched the room with his power, spreading it first in one direction, then in another and ultimately in a circle surrounding his sarcophagus.

"Nothing. Nothing at all."

The rays of the setting sun beat on the walls of his lair, trying desperately to cook the flesh of the corpse Nicolay had become, but he was well hidden and safe. Centuries had passed since his rest had been interrupted, and even then, the dreams had been nothing like the one he'd just experienced.

This one had been more than just some light images dancing around in his mind distracting him from the solution to an unknown problem. This one was laced with hatred and violence and had the makings of a child's nightmare hours after watching his first horror movie and consuming gobs of sweets. Never before had the images been so vivid, so lifelike.

Even when Kaida had called him, it was a subtle nudging, just enough to get him to explore the possibilities of the situation. But not this time. This time the message was very clear; someone wanted to get to him. Someone was reaching out to him, urging him to take action, to follow some pre-ordained path. Whatever it was wanted more than just to make him choose, it was forcing him to react.

He lay back down, trying to calm his mind into clarity, attempting to recall the details of the haunting dream. He closed his eyes and concentrated, searching through the still vivid images. Just as if he'd stepped back into the dream, the vision of the temple surrounded him. He stood before a bloodstained altar in the center. The place seemed all too familiar to him, but he couldn't quite figure out why. In all of his six hundred years, he didn't recall ever visiting a temple.

He visually searched the walls, admiring the engravings. The engravings were also familiar. Looking down at his arms and then back to the walls, he noticed the markings were identical to the tattoos covering his body.

He'd never known life without the tattoos, and from what he was told, he'd probably had them even before he was old enough to remember. His adoptive mother had told him they'd adorned his body from the day he came to her as an infant. As he grew, so did the tattoos. They never distorted. Like magic, the images were always in direct proportion to the changes his body experienced.

For years he had searched, trying to find someone, anyone, who could tell him the meaning of the pictures, but to no avail. He'd searched libraries in over a hundred countries, reading book after book of modern and ancient civilizations, passionately searching for another who may have shared his plight, knowing he couldn't possibly be the first to be blessed, or cursed, with the markings.

In his days as a young man, the days prior to the change, he'd contacted archeologists, hoping someone had discovered markings similar to his on the walls of some hidden tomb. Each letter he received painted the same picture: no one recognized the markings. No one was able to shed light on where he had come from, who his people were, or why had he had been sent away.

He'd finally come to realize the images were those of a people long lost, long forgotten. Images of a people who'd chosen to remain hidden in the depths of history. He had given up after three hundred years, accepting the markings as a part of him, a detail defining who and what he once was.

Once again, Nicolay attempted to remember any additional details of the dream. The images momentarily eluded him, but then *she* came to him, appearing in his mind like the light of a firefly in the pitch-black night. He couldn't see her face, but her scent filled his nostrils, soothing his mind. Even as he relived the memory of the dream, her scent surrounded him in his lair, following him from the depths of his mind into reality.

She wore a long cloak made of animal skin which covered her from head to toe. The hood draped carefully over her face, hiding even the slightest of silhouettes. She held something out to him, something square, quite possibly a book of some sort. Initially hesitant, although not quite sure why, Nicolay finally reached out and took the object from her. It was then he noticed she was adorned with many of the same tattoos as he.

Who was she?

He dared not ask for fear of how she might react. As she released her hold on the object, she turned and began to walk towards the entrance to the temple. She spoke softly to him, the pain of parting with the gift tearing away at her existence. Though just a whisper, her voice echoed as if it wasn't just one voice but the voice of a chorus, one that had not quite mastered the art of singing in unison.

She turned to face him one last time and spoke clearly, decisively signifying the importance of his understanding her words:

"I have returned what is rightfully yours. So it begins." Then, turning abruptly on her heels, she was gone.

Opening his eyes to once again return to his reality, Nicolay rose from the confines of his sarcophagus. He hadn't slept with the cover open in years and yet, as he had retreated to his humble abode to escape the rise of the fiery sun, he'd decided the darkness of the lair was enough. He felt the need to be exposed to the world, to test fate, to leave himself all the more vulnerable to true death.

Propped up on one end, the sarcophagus resembled those of any ancient Egyptian ruler. The exterior was trimmed in gold, a picture of his face engraved in the cover, the eyes made of jade, the nose a perfect replica of his own as if someone had poured a mold and attached it to the coffin's exterior. He'd paid the carpenter and artist well for the custom-made sarcophagus and it had all been worth it.

As he stepped from the interior, he heard something hit the floor. The sound of the impact echoed against the smooth walls of the lair. With a wave of his hand, the candles awakened from their long slumber, bursting to life, flames stretching, glad to be free. He reached down and picked up the object, the soft fur tickling the tips of his fingers.

His voice was but a whisper, "No, it couldn't be."

Lifting the book from the floor he ran his fingers over the rough leather bound edges of the cover. The top of the cover was animal skin, soft and furry under his touch. The pattern was familiar, but he couldn't quite place it. The edges had been sewn together with strips of what appeared to be cowhide. He didn't recognize the hieroglyph on the front, although the flow of the lines reminded him of his tattoos. Opening the book, the sound of the leather stretching pierced his ears, paining his keen sense of hearing.

The first few pages held drawings of the outside of the temple in his dream. He followed the stair-like exterior to the peak. He wondered how they had been built all of those years ago with no technology, but somehow, inside he knew. He felt a connection to the temple, like it had been his home at some point in time. It was the strangest feeling, to know somehow you had a connection to a place you had only visited in a dream.

The next pages contained drawings of totems, identical to two of the images drawn facing each other on either side of his heart. He traced the pattern in the book and then on his chest. Although he had yet to feed, the outline felt warm to the touch. He knew the warmth was impossible. His mind was probably just playing tricks on him, but it felt so real, the warm tingling sensation encircling his chest at the exact spot where his hand rest.

Oddly enough, the book seemed to have some effect on his body. The image on the page began to cast a soft glow. As the images began to illuminate more, he felt the images on his body begin to heat with some unknown flame lying just below the surface, warming the flesh from the inside out. He placed his hand over his heart, willing the burning to cease. And it did. The fierce heat reduced to just a tingle below the surface of the skin.

Nicolay's eyes turned down to the image on the page. It too had returned to its original state, a dark amber color brushed lightly across the paper.

"But what does it all mean?"

As he spoke the words, he turned the page. He ran his hand over the drawing of a dagger. If the picture had been drawn to scale, the dagger was only a few inched longer than his hand. The butt of it appeared to be jade fashioned into a perfect sphere. The blade was engraved from the handle to the tip. He couldn't understand the writing, but he was sure the dagger had once belonged to him. He placed his hand over the picture and closed his eyes, but as hard as he tried, he couldn't remember.

None of this made sense, not the woman in his dream, not the book, not the dagger, none of it. He just couldn't figure out the connection.

Turning another page, images of villagers celebrating danced around the paper. Two men and a woman stood in the entrance way of the temple, the larger man holding what appeared to be an infant child, presenting it to the other villagers.

A page later, he saw a cloud of darkness surrounding the village. Drawings of those running for their lives dotted the page covering every corner, every open space. Horror masked each face. The terror in their eyes was unmistakable. Something sinister had occurred in the village that pages before had been celebrating the addition of a new life.

But it was the next page that was the most troublesome. A figure covered from head to toe by a cloak stood at the home of one of the villagers. The picture depicted the couple handing a baby covered in strange markings to the cloaked figure.

"A woman."

Now that he took a moment and thought about it, the figure did seem familiar to him. By the look of the well-groomed hands, the fragile curve of her fingers, the figure was definitely a woman. Then he saw them, the markings, the same markings covering his body, and the same markings the woman in his dream had.

Once again the hood of the cloak hid her face, but the markings couldn't be mistaken, the woman the couple was handing the baby to had to be the same woman who'd visited him in the dream. It was her, had to be her, but who was she?

He started to flip the pages, searching for the answers. Page after page depicted his life. Each picture illustrated a significant event. The day he came to the Hopi village as an infant, the woman who cared for him as a child, days he lived as a boy in the house of an elder, and the first time he killed an antelope were all depicted.

The first pages were happier times. But for every happy time, Nicolay knew the book would show him the desolate times. When he reached the page he dreaded seeing, the day his life had been stolen from him, he almost cried. The day he had been attacked and morphed from a mere human man into the monster he was today stared back at him.

Who had known the attack was going to occur? How had they known? And if they did know, why didn't anyone stop it from happening?

The questions mocked him. They urged him to turn the page adding hope that maybe their answers lay just on the other side. Nicolay turned the page hoping to get a glimpse of the answer to the questions that had been burned into his mind for centuries. However, to his surprise, the rest of the pages were empty. He turned page after page after page, but each time the nothingness stared back at him, taunting him until he could bear it no longer.

He slammed the book closed.

"Who are you? Why do you haunt me so? What does it mean?" he bellowed the words, knowing no one was there to answer his pleas. No one was there to explain the mystery his life had been for so long. He was, as he always was, alone.

Trapped in more despair than any one person should be allowed to suffer, he threw the book in the armoire, quickly dressed, and exited his lair to feed the everlasting thirst that plagued him.

CHAPTER TWO

BACK AND FORTH. BACK and forth. Kaida sat in a plush chair in the office of The Apache, filing her nails and watching her friend walk a permanent groove into the floor. She'd chosen to spend her night off in the presence of the most powerful creature she had ever crossed paths with, Nicolay Constantine.

Sometimes she'd sneak to the club and hide in the shadows just to be close to Nicolay. Something about him mesmerized her. His closeness was comforting; at least that's what she kept telling herself.

Tonight though, things had been different between them. She found it odd he'd sought her out instead of the other way around. Only under the direst of circumstances would he have approached her to feed.

Over the years Nicolay had begun to care for Kaida, but not in the way she cared for him. He took every possible chance to make it clear their relationship was nothing more than platonic. If he ever asked, she'd vow her complete and utter devotion to him. She was in love with him, or so she thought. He knew how she felt about him, she had told him a number of times, but he was always the perfect gentleman, carefully teetering on the line between employer and employee.

"If you keep pacing like that, there'll be a trench in the floor within the hour," Kaida continued to file her nails, not hesitating even for a moment to glance up at her friend.

The pacing vampire stopped. With his back turned to the beautiful woman he remarked, "I suggest if you intend to remain welcome in my presence, you'll keep your criticism to yourself."

"Touchy. Touchy. You should be nice to your meals. It keeps them willing to offer more. Remember, you summoned me back to the forbidden chambers, not the other way around." She feigned curtness with her comment, keeping her snickering under control, but she obviously found his irritation amusing.

All of the employees called Nicolay's office the forbidden chambers. Of those who went in, only Kaida and Xavier appeared to return with their jobs.

"And I am beginning to regret that very action," he spoke the words through clenched teeth.

"Look, your pacing is giving me a headache. Is there something you want to talk about or was I just a quick meal?"

Kaida was being sarcastic and it did not please Nicolay at all. He could hear her laughing under her breath. This was neither the time nor the place for her mockery and he intended to let her know just that.

"If my pacing bothers you so, you are welcome to leave. But do not mock me, child."

Although his back remained turned to her, she could imagine the scowl on his face the moment he spoke the words.

"Child! Oh, so I'm just a child now!" Kaida stood, her action so swift it pushed the chair she had been sitting in squarely across the floor, "How dare you call me a child! You may be six hundred years old, but I will not allow you to treat me like I mean nothing to you. Should you need another meal, don't come looking for me."

Before she could make it across the room to storm out of the door, he appeared to block the doorway, a task only those of his kind had the ability to achieve.

"Get out of my way," the words were spoken through gritted teeth.

"Kaida wait, I apologize."

Things had been hard enough for him lately. He hadn't intended to offend her.

"My rests have not been peaceful for the past few days. As much as I have tried, I have not been able to hunt. You know how hard it is for me to ask you to satisfy the bloodlust, to nourish me."

He turned from her, lowering his head and resting it against the door. He didn't want her to see the hurt in his eyes. Kaida was always his last resort. He truly did hate feeding from her, but desperate times called for desperate measures.

"I should not have asked you here under these circumstances, but I trust no one else."

What Nicolay said was true; he had not been able to hunt. For the past three nights, each time he ventured any distance from his lair, the air became thick. He tasted sulfur in the air. It burned his nostrils and throat. It was an unmistakable scent. The scent and taste of pure evil. Something was lurking about, he was sure of it, and whatever it was, it was like nothing he'd ever felt before.

The past few nights he'd been uneasy. He feared for his life as well as the lives of those he had vowed to protect.

The fact he couldn't hunt wasn't the only thing bothering him; it had been nearly a century since he'd dreamed during the hours of the day. The darkness was usually peaceful for him. His lair was sufficiently hidden, so he had no need to fear attack, and yet lately he had an overwhelming sense that something out there was searching for him. By day, he had a constant nagging feeling of being sought out only to have it disappear at sunset.

The darkness hadn't trapped him in over three hundred years as it did those newly turned. The newly cursed had no control over the

Dark Slumber. The moment the sun began to creep above the horizon they were sucked under, becoming utterly helpless.

But Nicolay was, by all accounts, old. When the Dark Slumber came he rested, his limbs heavy, his body lethargic, but his mind always remained fully aware of any and everything around him. This time though, something evil, something magic, was seeking him out, and for what purpose he wasn't sure. Whatever this thing was, it was disturbing his peace of mind and he was growing weary of it.

Nicolay let out a deep sigh. It was time he stopped hoping this thing would go away and face the fact there was something out there he couldn't control, and sooner or later this thing was going to find him if he didn't find it first. He turned to face Kaida again.

"Please, sit down. I guess it is time I explain. Much has happened in a short period of time. I'll try to explain what little I understand of what is going on."

He gestured for her to be seated. He hoped she would hear the sincerity in his voice and give him a chance to explain.

Kaida hesitated. She took a moment to study him, his body language, trying to decide if she should accept his apology. He did appear to be at his wit's end. She had never seen him so distraught. That, and the fact he hated feeding from her made for a convincing argument for forgiveness.

As much as she hated to admit it, she was his last resort when it came to satisfying the bloodlust. That little bit of knowledge hurt her sometimes, mainly because she wanted him to think of her as more than just a meal. Even so, she owed him her life and much more.

"Are you sure you're ready to talk?" she wasn't completely convinced, but she'd give him the benefit of the doubt. He had apologized, but Kaida knew Nicolay was a very private person. It took a lot for him to open up. She wondered for a moment why he had chosen her tonight instead of Xavier.

Nicolay nodded his confirmation, "Yes. I am sure."

At least she wasn't yelling at him anymore. Accepting his apology was a good sign.

Still fuming from his comments, but knowing there was something larger than her pride at stake, Kaida abruptly turned and made her way back to the chair she had forced across the room. She sat down, facing him, watching as he composed himself before he walked back over to where she sat. Kaida laid her head back against the chair and closed her eyes to wait.

Lately, hiding his emotions had become more difficult for Nicolay. When they first met, she would have sworn he felt nothing for anything or anyone. She'd secretly watch him sometimes. He'd just stand there, still as the Lincoln Monument, not a glimpse of emotion present on his face or in his body language. He'd just absorb all surrounding him, process the information in that mind of his, and no one would ever know what he was thinking.

Lately, things had been different. His emotions shone like a lone jack-o-lantern in a pumpkin patch on All Hallows Eve. He was losing his temper, being short with the employees, and most of all he'd once again started that accursed pacing.

Nicolay composed himself and joined her, taking a seat on the couch. He stared at the painting of the Margay above her head. The animal was beautiful, poised in a tree, ready to pounce on its prey. The artist had perfectly captured the mischievousness in its eyes. Looking at the picture, Nicolay felt as if the creature was staring back at him, wanting him to see and understand the secrets it hid.

He shook the thoughts from his head and turned back to Kaida. Not quite sure where to start, Nicolay began with the first thought to enter his mind.

"It's been a long time, but once again someone haunts me."

Kaida took a moment to comprehend what he had just said.

"I'm not following you. What do you mean someone haunts you?"

How to make her understand? Nicolay thought for a moment, and then it came to him.

"Remember the day I came to you? The day we met?"

"Yeah, as clear as the sunset," Kaida saw the dagger she had just thrown pierce his heart, "Sorry."

"Forgiven. Remember when I told you that a few days before I came to you, you haunted me? Even though we had never met, I could not get you out of my mind. Each waking moment you called out to me. I heard your screams each time that tyrant touched you. I shared in all that happened to you."

Nicolay stood and made his way to the wall hanging. The painting always eased his mind and calmed his spirit.

"Your torture became my torture," he continued, "It was nearly unbearable for me, so I could only imagine what it was for you. It started out as just hearing your screams, and the more I tried to ignore it, the more in tune with you my mind became. I began to feel your pain, to suffer as you were suffering."

He turned back to face her. She had not turned around, so her back was to him.

"I had to stop it as much for you as for myself. I found myself in Japan, searching for you, to rescue you from whatever harm was to come your way. Now, the feeling has returned. But it's different this time, like a subtle hum. It's growing in depth and intensity, but the urge to take action is still the same."

They'd had this conversation before. He'd told her years ago the inclination to protect her had overwhelmed him, not because of what she was, but because she was female and neither man nor creature had the right to treat her the way she had been treated. Kaida assumed this was currently the case.

Needing confirmation, she asked, "Do you have any idea who she may be?"

"No. I do not know," he turned away again, staring into the eyes of the margay, "That is not my only concern."

Kaida knew things were bad and something told her things were about to get worse. When he had come to rescue her, he fought for her life. He'd risked his own for her. She knew when the calling came he could not fight it for long. Eventually, it would overcome him and he would go to her, whoever she was.

She hadn't responded to his last comment, so he continued to speak.

"I fear for all of our safety," he turned back to her, "I have felt something cursed lurking not far from here."

"You too?" Kaida asked. She faced him now, a surprised expression on her face, "I was beginning to think I was hallucinating. I thought it was just a figment of my imagination, but if you've felt it too then something must be out there. Whatever it is, it's been here a while. I've felt it for some time. The last few days, it has been growing stronger."

Kaida was glad she wasn't the only one detecting something distinctly supernatural near their home. Nicolay had never told her he had the ability to detect the magic of others; if she had known sooner, she would have informed him of what she had felt.

"I am not sure what it is, but I am sure it is here to do us all harm," Nicolay was firm in his conviction. Kaida detected the underlying fear of the unknown in his voice.

"So what's the plan?"

"For now we wait," he intentionally stressed the word "we," indicating he wanted her to stay at a safe distance, "I will find whatever this evil is and deal with it myself."

"And what about the woman?" Kaida asked.

"That, my dear, is my problem. So will you be joining us in the club tonight?" he quickly changed the subject, not giving her the opportunity to object.

Nicolay did not want to discuss the woman with Kaida. Although they had remained friends, she had made it perfectly clear she wanted more. He did not, so he thought it safer he not discuss the woman in his dreams with her. She already knew too much.

"After what you've just told me, I think not. I will leave you to your business."

She rose from her seat and, once again, Nicolay was there beside her. He knew she was angry. In so many words he had just told her to mind her own business. He didn't have time to nurse her ego, so he let it go.

"I will escort you out. It is late and not safe for a woman to be out alone."

"Now you know good and well I can take care of myself," she replied smugly.

"Will you not let me be a gentleman, just this once?"

She thought about his comment for a moment. Since she had known Nicolay, he had always been the perfect gentleman. He needed to feel like he could protect someone tonight. He was vulnerable, and she knew it.

"I guess. Just don't make a habit of it." Kaida gave him a sneer and allowed him to do for her just this once since he really wanted to.

CHAPTER THREE

DAKOTA NAVERRO CALLED out to her brother from the bottom of the immense staircase in the plantation house they shared.

"Dayton! Dayton! You up there?"

When she received no reply, she decided to investigate. She needed to make sure he was packing, otherwise he might miss his flight.

"Dayton!" she called as she searched.

As she walked past each open door, the fury inside of her began to boil over. He wasn't in any of the rooms, and she wasn't even sure now if he was even in the house. And if he wasn't in the house, she was pretty sure she knew where he was. He'd been trying to talk his way out of the trip for days, but she wasn't going to let him, and if it was the last thing she did, he was going to be on that plane.

Dakota picked up the phone and dialed the number to the shop.

"Paradise. How can I help you?" the voice on the other end of the phone spoke.

"Kelsy?" Dakota asked.

"Yeah."

"Is Day down there?"

Dakota was really getting irritated with her brother. She was about fed up with chasing him down to go on this trip. True enough, it was her fault that he had to go, but they were both adults now and she could take care of herself. Dayton thought he was being slick by avoiding her, but she wasn't going to let him get away with it.

"Yes, ma'am. Wanna talk to him?" Kelsy replied. He'd detected the anger in her voice and wanted off the phone as quickly as possible. He'd been at the other end of one of her thrashings before and it hadn't been pretty.

"Yeah, I wanna talk to him all right. Don't let him leave. I'll be down there in ten minutes."

"Whatever you say, you're the boss."

Dakota slammed the phone onto the receiver. If he wanted to play hardball, then she was going to play hardball and he wasn't going to like it. She grabbed her purse and car keys and went to get her brother.

Ten minutes later, she skidded to a halt in front of the tin building. Slamming the car door, she stomped her way toward the door marked "Paradise, Inc."

"What the hell are you doing out here? You know you still need to pack."

Dakota swung the door wide open as she entered the auto body shop she and her brother had started a few years back. She wasn't surprised to see her brother just standing over the last set of company invoices without a care in the world when she knew he hadn't finished packing for his trip.

"Just wanted to make sure there weren't any loose ends I needed to tie up before I left."

Dayton was just stalling. He didn't want to leave his sister, so he was looking for any excuse not to take this trip.

"That's bullshit and you know it, and don't even fix your mouth to say what you're thinking," she walked over to him giving him a deadly stare and then a loving hug, "Look, I know this is hard, but Dayton, I can take care of things around here. I've been doing it for years, in case you've forgotten."

He looked up at her with tired eyes, "No, I haven't forgotten. I just don't want to leave any mess in your hands. I know how you hate it when the guys leave the distraught client for you to deal with after they've missed a deadline."

She smiled at her brother. He was right. On a number of occasions she had come into the office to find ten voice mail messages from a not so happy customer. Instead of the guys calling the client to tell him or her that the job was going to be late, they just convinced themselves everything was going to be all right. Meanwhile, no one dared answer the phone, so Dakota always had to play nice to the client, show a little compassion and understanding, and accept the chewing out she inevitably received. In this case, she knew the truth to be far different from the line Dayton was feeding her.

"You mean you're trying to find an excuse not to go. It ain't gonna happen, buddy," Dakota dragged Dayton to the front doors and pushed him out, "I'm going to grab some paperwork off of my desk and I'll be out in a minute. You want to wait or meet me back at the house?"

"I guess I'll wait."

Dayton didn't care either way. When his sister had her mind made up about something then that was it. She'd made up her mind about him going on this trip, and there was nothing he could do about it. He finally decided to just give in and go.

"Then I'll be right back," Dakota said slipping back into the shop.

Dayton could only laugh as he watched Dakota go back inside and close the door behind her. His sister had jumped right in and taken charge of the books when things first started going bad for the business. By the second month, they were so booked with business that none of the employees had taken a vacation since. Now, it was getting close to winter and business would be slowing down, so there was no excuse. Winter was always their slow time, so when his friend had called saying he was sick and needed someone to stay with him, Dakota quickly volunteered her brother. Now, Dayton was trying to find any reason he could not to go. It wasn't that he didn't want to help his friend out; it was because he didn't want to leave his sister.

"Ready?" Dakota yelled in her ever so chipper voice.

Dayton jumped. He had been daydreaming and hadn't noticed her come back out of the shop.

"I guess," his tone was solemn, unhappy, but he knew she wasn't going to let him weasel out of this.

"Dayton, look at me."

He raised his head and turned so that he stared at a female version of himself.

"What do I have to do to convince you that I'll be fine?"

"I don't know. I guess there isn't anything you can do. I just have to acknowledge you're a grown woman and you can take care of yourself and the business alone," he looked and sounded like a wounded puppy. Dakota hated to see him like this, but it was time they had a break from each other

"I won't be alone, Dayton. The guys will be at the shop if I need anything, and you know Lysette is not going to let me stay in that big old house of ours by myself," she patted him on the knee, reassuring him things were going to be okay.

Dayton let out a small sigh of defeat, "Let's get me to the house so you can ship me away."

Dakota turned and planted a chaste kiss on her brother's cheek, "I'm not shipping you away, at least not permanently; I'm just sending you on hiatus."

She started the engine and they began their journey back to the house.

DAKOTA, DAYTON, AND Dakota's best friend Lysette rode to the Savannah International Airport in silence. The only sounds in the vehicle came from the engine and passing cars. They'd even turned

the radio off. They all seemed content with sharing the silence with each other. Lysette drove so that Dakota and Dayton could spend just a little more time together. They huddled together in the back seat like a couple of puppies. Dakota rested her head on his shoulder, which gave him plenty of access to play with her hair. Dayton always played with Dakota's hair when he was nervous.

Lysette walked a few steps behind them in the airport, giving them as much privacy as a busy airport would allow. When they finally reached his gate, Dakota turned to her brother and spoke, "I hate to see you go."

Dakota took a long look at her brother. She smiled weakly, "You realize this will be the first time we have been separated for more than a few hours."

"Yeah, I know. Come here and give your big brother a hug," Dayton hated to leave her as much she hated to see him go, but his back was against the wall, his friend was depending on him. They knew it would eventually come to this. They knew sooner or later they would be separated, but it still felt too soon for the both of them.

"Big brother, huh? Only by thirty four seconds, and as the story goes if I hadn't kick your butt out first we'd have never been born."

They both giggled at the accusation. The running joke between them revolved around why Dayton was born before Dakota. The Naverro twins were born nearly a week late because Dayton refused to turn.

"Knock it off, you two," Lysette always enjoyed the banter between the pair, but she needed to assure them both that Dakota would be alright while Dayton was gone.

"I'll take good care of her," looking at the concern in Dayton's eyes, she pulled Dakota into her arms, "I won't let anything happen to her. I promise."

Dayton looked away from his sister and gave a weak smile to Lysette, their oldest friend.

"I know you will," leaving her was eating away at him. His heart was beginning to hurt.

"Last call for flight 221 to Seattle."

"Well," Dayton's words were solemn and painful, "that's my flight. I'll call soon as I get there."

"Make sure you do."

Dakota wanted to hold on to her brother just a little longer, but she knew she had to let him catch his plane. Seattle was a long way away from Georgia. As Dayton boarded the plane, he took one last long look back at his twin and their friend and knew everything would be ok.

Dakota felt numb. She didn't quite know what to do. All of this was so new. Since birth, she and Dayton had never been separated for very long. They still lived in the same house they were raised in. After graduating from high school they went to the same trade school and worked at the same job. The more she thought about it, even when Dayton and the guys went camping and planned to be gone for a few days, she was always invited. If they went without her, Dayton was on the cell phone every half hour making sure she was okay. They'd never been apart for more than a couple of days, and now he was going for who knows how long to the other side of the country.

Dakota and Lysette watched with somber faces as Dayton boarded the plane.

"So now what?" Dakota turned worried eyes to her only friend. She'd kept the tears from falling while Dayton boarded the plane, but she was about to fall apart.

Lysette saw the tears about to flow and had to think fast. She hated to see Dakota cry and refused to let this time apart from her brother put her in a solemn mood.

"Now, we go home and get ready for tonight. I know you don't think I am going to let you sit in the house and mope because your brother had to skip town. We're going to pick out our finest club wear and prepare to Salsa the night away."

Lysette knew this was a stretch. She had been trying to get Dakota out of the house for weeks, but she always had some excuse; she and her brother had a client to meet, or she needed to clean the house. Well, not tonight. Tonight, her brother was on a plane to the other side of the United States and they were going to party.

CHAPTER FOUR

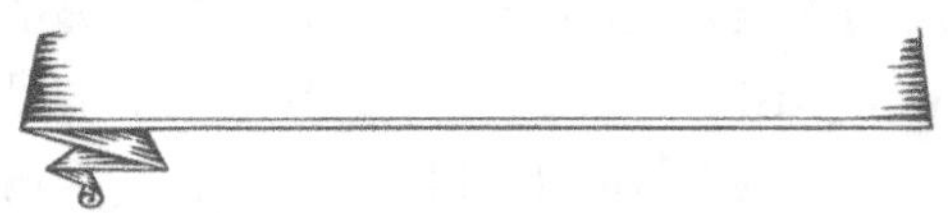

"SOOOO, WHAT DO YOU think?" Dakota twirled around holding a black leather skirt and tangerine halter-top.

"About what, that outfit or that tired hair style? Girl, get out of that closet and let me see what you've got. After I have found the perfect man finding outfit for you, we'll work on your hair. I refuse to let you walk out of this house with your head looking like Mrs. Doubtfire meets the bride that Frankenstein rejected."

As Lysette stepped into Dakota's closet, she felt like she had stepped into a Lord and Taylor department store. Clothes hung from racks in every nook and cranny of the walk-in closet. Lysette knew the closet was as large as some of the smaller rooms in the house, but she had no idea of the extent of Dakota's wardrobe until that moment. Overwhelmed with the possibilities, she smiled at herself and began to pull outfits off of the racks. She sifted through the closet, pulling some items off the hangers while she frowned at others and hung them back.

Dakota watched Lysette with awe as she rambled through the closet. She had known Lysette Angelique LaRedoute since the first grade. Her family had moved to Savannah from Florida after a long battle with her mother's relatives. Right off the bat, Lysette took to Dakota. They'd spent hours as little kids playing with dolls and cooking with Lysette's mother, or playing hide and seek with Dayton and the few other children in the neighborhood.

Dakota remembered one summer she, Lysette, and Dayton followed a cotton-tailed wild rabbit into the woods. Not paying attention to where they were going, they all tripped over a fallen tree. Lysette fell first, hitting her head on a large limb protruding from the trunk. Somehow she managed to get one of its branches stuck into her forearm. Blood gushed continuously from the wide open wound. Although Dayton and Dakota had fallen over the same tree, Lysette was the only one to sustain any significant injury. Dayton ran back to the house for help while Dakota and Lysette took turns applying pressure to her arm to slow the bleeding.

Lysette lost a lot of blood during the short time in the woods. During her time in the hospital, she needed multiple transfusions and it was then Lysette came to know her parents weren't her biological parents. Luckily, Dakota was a perfect match so she was able to give Lysette the blood she so desperately needed. Since then she and her best friend shared more than just the bond of friendship.

Although Lysette took the news of being adopted quite well, Dakota was traumatized to find out the truth about her friend's parents. From Lysette's reaction, it was apparent she had suspected the people who raised her for all of these years were not her biological parents. Dakota never asked how she had known, but she really didn't need to. Lysette always paid close attention to the details others simply dismissed as coincidence. Deep down, Dakota knew that was how her friend had known. Lysette's situation at home was the only taboo subject between the two friends.

Other than avoiding the discussion of Lysette's adoption, Lysette and Dakota didn't keep secrets. Actually, Dakota couldn't remember an event in her life she hadn't told Lysette about. From her first kiss to her first period, Lysette knew everything. Now that she thought about it, she knew just as much about Lysette as Lysette knew about her.

Startling Dakota from her memory, Lysette stepped out of the closet, arms full, and dropped everything on the bed. She made three trips in and out of the closet, not able to carry all she wanted to coordinate with in one trip. Clothes flew in every direction as she searched and arranged until she had the perfect outfit for Dakota.

"This is it!" Lysette held a dress out for her friend to examine, "this dress and these shoes are going to get you a man."

Although she wasn't too sure about the man part of Lysette's plan, Dakota had to agree, the lilac dress and three inch stiletto heels would be perfect for salsa dancing. She had to give it to Lysette; her girl knew how to coordinate. Even if the dress wasn't quite what Dakota had anticipated for tonight, she'd take her friends advice and wear it anyway.

"Now go get dressed while I change," Lysette quickly shooed her friend to the master bathroom while she grabbed her overnight bag and headed for the bathroom down the hall.

Ten minutes later, Dakota stared at her reflection in the antique floor length mirror in her bathroom. *Who would ever want me, a plain Jane?* Personality wise she was never what the old folks referred to as a typical girl. Other than playing with dolls with Lysette when they were younger and the occasional cooking with Lysette's mother, she had done very few "girlie" things in her life.

Dakota preferred spending time with the boys over going to the mall to shop or attending dances. That's probably why while all of the other girls in school went off to modeling school, colleges, or the corporate world, she went to a small local trade school and learned sheet metal fabrication. She loved what she did. She never had to worry about trying to be cute or getting a guy to notice her. She worked with them all day. The guys at the shop were impressed with her knowledge. She learned how men think, so all she had to do was approach one with her knowledge and they welcomed the challenge.

She again focused on her reflection in the mirror. Over the years, she had changed her outer appearance a number of times, growing from the little girl Naverro to the lady Naverro. The last couple years, she had made the most dramatic changes to her outer appearance. She'd let her hair grow to shoulder length only to cut it all off in the last few months. Lysette convinced her to spend more time presenting herself as a lady rather than a grease monkey. Dakota had been pleased with the way the changes had made her feel. She was still deeply rooted in her naturalism, but with just enough flare to boost her self-esteem. But even after all of the experimenting with the exterior changes, Dakota still felt she needed more change in her life, and this night out would be a new start for her. Though she wouldn't lose sight of who she was or where she came from, Dakota decided to put all inhibition aside for the night and be who she wanted to be now, not who she was when Dayton boarded his plane.

The Naverro family was descended from a long line of slaves on their father's side. The land under Dakota's very feet belonged to the master who once owned her family. When slavery became illegal, most of the slaves left this place as quickly as possible, but not her great great grandfather. Thaddeus Naverro stood his ground. The master of the house had been relatively kind to him, so he never felt the urgency to leave as many of the others did. Thaddeus was a blacksmith, and his job was essential to the plantation. The guys at the shop always teased Dakota, suggesting she was Thaddeus reincarnated as a woman.

In the end, when the old master was on his death bed, he called Thaddeus into the house and gave the land to him. The money the old man had made on the plantation long before had alienated him from his family. They'd all leeched off of him for years until he'd gotten so fed up he cut them all off. His family dismissed him as a lost cause, so with no family the land was his to do with as he pleased, and giving it to a man well deserving was what he wanted to do. Her family had been here ever since, choosing to embrace the memories of the past instead of running from them.

Thaddeus Naverro had six children and eight great grandchildren. Dayton and Dakota were the only children of the youngest great grandson and a gypsy woman their father met on one of his travels out of the country. Most of their family had fled north in search of employment, but the twins' father chose to remain here. For some reason, he felt attached to the land, as did Dayton and Dakota. Neither of them ever felt the need to venture far from the plantation. This place was their home, and they intended to keep it that way. They setup an automotive repair shop at one end of the property so they were close to work and home. It was fairly successful so they had no need to leave. Besides, they loved this place and couldn't imagine living anywhere else.

Dakota continued to study her facial features. She inherited the wide nose of her father, but it was perfectly proportioned to her other features. Her almond shaped eyes were definitely her mother's, as were her naturally perfectly arched eyebrows. Also inherited from her father were her full lips, the bottom one protruding just a little further out than her top, giving her the image of a permanent pout. Though small in frame, thanks to her smart wit and her Springfield Armory .45 caliber pistol, she could hold her own against any adversary. Her caramel complexion was a perfect combination of both of her parents. She missed them so much sometimes, but she wouldn't think of them now. She dressed quickly and went back to the bedroom so Lysette could do her hair.

"You know, for your father's hair to have been the nappiest hair I have ever seen, yours is thick but still manageable," Lysette sat on the bed curling Dakota's hair with a hot iron.

"Don't start."

"Whatever."

"Whatever is right."

They both burst out laughing. Lysette always made fun of Dakota's hair. She never took the comments to heart though. Dakota had gotten her mother's hair and Lysette knew it, but it never stopped her from teasing.

It didn't take long for Lysette to finish curling Dakota's hair. Dakota added just a touch of makeup: a little eyeliner and some lipgloss, and she turned to face Lysette.

"How do I look?"

Lysette joined her in front of the mirror. They looked at themselves and could't help but admire their style.

"Girl, that outfit is slammin'. We're going to be the two best dressed sistas in the spot."

Dakota reached for her hair, wanting to touch the masterpiece Lysette had created.

Lysette smacked her hand away, "Don't you dare ruin it."

Dakota stared at her hair, "You're really going to have to teach me how to do this on my own. You know how much I love this hairstyle and you keep rubbing it in my face every chance you get."

"In due time. In due time," Lysette replied.

"I've heard that before."

"Yeah, yeah and you'll probably hear it again. So you ready to go?" Lysette was anxious now. She had waited months for a night like this, a chance to get Dakota out of the house. Dakota was just stalling, and Lysette had no intention of letting it continue.

"As ready as I'll ever be. I still can't believe you talked me into this."

"And why not? You know I have my ways of being very persuasive. Besides, it's about time you took some time away from the shop and met some real men."

"Hey, the guys at the shop are real men."

"Yeah, but they treat you like a sister, not how a man treats a woman."

The look Lysette gave Dakota said it all. Tonight was going to be about one thing and one thing only. Dakota hated it when Lysette got on her match making missions. If she hadn't figured it out by now, Dakota wasn't interested. But tonight, she decided to play along. Tonight, she'd let the Dakota Lysette wanted her to be lead the way.

"There is one last small detail we must tend to before we can go."

"I know. I know."

The two young ladies faced each other and lay their hands palm to palm. "Ready?" Dakota nodded and they began the invocation that had protected her most of her life.

"Cardea we invoke thee. Cast a shield of protection around your children. Shield us from harm in all ways. Protect our minds, bodies, and spirits so we may continue to worship you."

They both felt the warmth wrapping around them, bathing them in protection. Since Dakota had discovered her gift of clairvoyance, they performed this ritual on almost a daily basis. Dakota had probably had the gift since birth, and in their secluded environment it was easy to control. But when they became school aged, everything changed. Initially, school was difficult for Dakota. Everything she touched gave her an image of the past. She never told her parents of her gift, so she had to find ways of dealing with it on her own.

After failing miserably at finding a solution, Dakota approached Lysette for a shielding spell. Lysette practiced witchcraft since before Dakota could remember. Her mother was a witch and had taught Lysette all she knew about being at one with nature and invoking natural power for good. After the first day of using the spell, Dakota returned home from school energized instead of drained.

In many cases, their gifts, Dakota's clairvoyance and Lysette's talent for casting spells, solidified their friendship. The other kids just thought them weird, and that was all right by them. They helped each other through hard times with their gifts and they would continue to do so as long as they could.

They both bubbled with excitement as they jumped into Dayton's cherry red '69 Chevy Impala, opened all of the windows, turned the system to full blast playing Sade's *Paradise* and pulled out of the driveway on the road to adventure. The incantation and shield of protection always made them feel invincible, like the world was there for the claiming; all they needed to do was reach out and grab it. Dakota decided that tonight, she'd allow fate to determine her destiny.

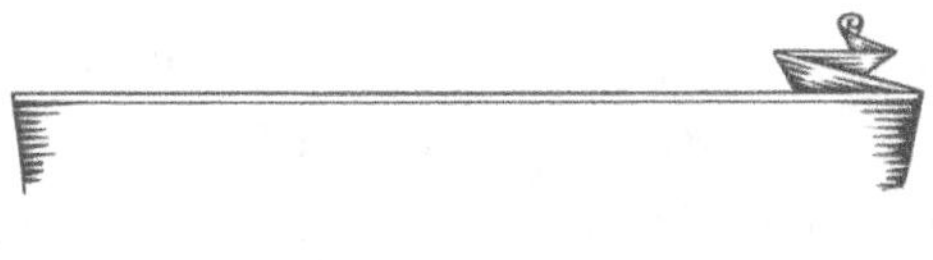

CHAPTER FIVE

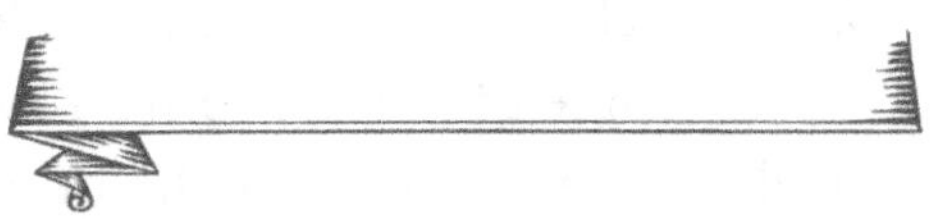

THE BRIGHT NEON LIGHTS read "The Apache" and the waves of Soca music could be heard from a block away. The outside of the place looked like it belonged on an Indian Reservation. At one time, the building had been an old abandoned warehouse. About a year or so earlier, renovations had begun, and within two months the place had become a club.

"No line? That's unusual. If it's like this every Friday night, we may have to come here more often."

Those few words were the most Lysette had spoken since they had left the house. She'd spent much of the time holding on for dear life. One day, she was going to have to teach Dakota how not to drive like a complete maniac.

Dakota couldn't believe her eyes. Never had she been to a club downtown anywhere without there being a long line. True, it was just 6:30 in the afternoon, but on a Friday night no place was immune to a line. She took a moment to study the totems on either side of the entrance. She reached out to touch one and then thought better of it. Although the spell allowed her to more easily control her gift, if she touched an object with some sort of strong psychic ties to it, she'd still get pulled in and she'd have to relive the experience until all that the universe wanted her to know had been passed on. After they had paid the cover charge, Dakota followed Lysette into the establishment.

The place was more of a dinner club than a traditional dance club. It was dim inside, just enough of a romantic setting for a couple to have a private conversation, but also enough atmosphere that the dance party never stopped. Candles strategically placed on the tables and the pillars around the club illuminated the inside. There was an enclosed room towards their left in the far corner that opened to the outside. Whoever had designed the room took into account that patrons might want to enjoy the outside without having to deal with the insects. Dakota thought it was a great idea. The area had its own bar to accommodate those sitting on that side of the club.

The parquet dance floor was located in the middle of the room surrounded by dinettes for two. The larger main bar was against the far wall and tables and booths were located throughout. The table settings were quaint with what appeared to be hand woven place mats and table clothes. This place felt really homey to Dakota.

The owner took care to place wall hangings of various animals throughout the club. Dakota saw wolves and jaguars and a number of other creatures resembling miniature versions of leopards. Dream catchers hung from the rafters and the candlelight illuminated handmade pottery. The place was breathtaking. She'd never seen anything like it. Lysette appeared not to be fazed; she liked new places and was always more comfortable with the unknown. Dakota just stood in awe of the place.

"So, where should we sit?" Lysette asked. She could tell Dakota was taking in the surroundings. She had to admit, the place did have a uniqueness all of its own.

"Well, there's a full moon tonight, and you know how I love to be bathed in the light of the moon."

Lysette knew where this was going. They had spent many a night lying in the garden of the Naverro plantation house under the full moon. As a witch, the full moon gave Lysette many opportunities to focus her craft, but Dakota seemed to gain a sort of peace when under its light.

"Ok. Come on. There's an empty table over there just waiting for you."

They chose a table in the far corner of the room. From where Dakota sat, she could watch the moon rise into the night sky. She was mesmerized by the view. Tonight was a perfect night to be out. Not a cloud in the sky. She was glad Lysette had convinced her to come.

"Want something to drink?" Lysette startled Dakota out of her daydream.

"Club soda for me."

Dakota wasn't sure what the night held, but she was sure she wanted to be sober for the entire experience. She couldn't remember the last time she had gone out, much less to a club even remotely like this one. She did miss Latin dancing; it was one of the few pastimes she took part in and she couldn't imagine what could have kept her from this joy for so long. Not in her seat five minutes, she was reminded at least a dozen times why she had stopped coming to the club to dance.

NICOLAY LOUNGED BEHIND the bar watching the night's crowd. He recognized a number of the patrons. Many of them had come into his humble establishment over the past couple of weeks. It wasn't often that he ventured out to the main part of the club. Most nights he hid in the office. The few nights he did venture out, his disappointment sent him crawling back to his humble abode. The crowd he was watching right now reminded him why. It was still early, the same faces dotted around the club, but something inside of him beckoned him out tonight. An energy he couldn't quite place brought him from the shadows to mingle with those who patronized his establishment.

He loved this place. It reminded him so much of his home on what was now a reservation. That was his intention when he designed The Apache. Nicolay remembered the time when he was young and the land in the Americas belonged to the Mother Earth, to the people who respected it. His people occupied the land. It didn't belong to them. They took only what they needed, used all that they took, and always respected Mother Earth.

As a boy he'd learned archery to hunt for food. Since he was the sole provider in his home, he'd spent most of his time hunting, but on those rare occasions when the kill came early in the day, he'd take the time to watch his adoptive mother make pottery, weave baskets, and cook. Although he never tried any of the women's tasks while at home, he had picked up quite a bit of it by watching her toil.

Looking around the club, he admired his work. He had made all of the table settings, candle holders, and pottery. He studied the craftsmanship of the place. Almost everything surrounding him, including the totems in the entry way and the carvings in the rafters, he had made, and the pride showed on his face.

Nicolay turned his attention back to the crowd. He watched as people entered the club. No one really caught his attention. There were some beautiful women who came in, mostly with their girlfriends, probably out on the town to get away from their men. They were short, tall, plump, and small. Some had on too much makeup, others not enough. Watching the women, no one in particular warranted his need to be out amongst the crowd.

How he longed for the days when he was mortal. He'd had some wonderful years before he was cursed. Life wasn't always perfect, but it was his life, and he missed it. His life had been filled with sweet summer sunrises, games of hide and seek, and the thrill of the daytime hunt. But it was a life that would now forever elude him.

Although not by choice, he had been quite the ladies' man. He had even fallen in love once, and vowed to love, cherish, and honor her until their parting days. But, that was to never happen. Before their life together began, his was stolen. He wondered what his mother had told her after his disappearance. Not able to bear the thought of losing control and hurting anyone he loved, Nicolay left his tiny village to hunt the first night he had awakened with the bloodlust. The night before that was the last time he ever saw his mother or the love of his life.

Now, watching all of these people coming in, he was once again reminded of all he had lost. The people who were here to relax from a hard day's work, the ones that came out at night to escape the heat of the sun, had no idea of the things that they took for granted. How he missed the days of hiding inside his home to escape the blazing heat of the noontime summer sun. He longed to feel the rays against his skin, to experience the blinding brightness of the day. It had been centuries since he had seen the fiery God. Centuries since he had felt warmth that didn't come from another being, warmth he stole from unsuspecting victims each and every night.

Just as the thought of warmth crossed his mind, the most beautiful ray of sunshine entered the room. Now this woman was enchanting enough to have drawn him out. She was striking, breathtaking. She possessed a beauty he had not seen since his last sunset. In that moment it all became clear. The woman who haunted him had just entered his club and his life. He knew, before the night was over, he was destined to meet this woman. She had to be the reason the magic had called to him tonight, beckoning him from his resting place; he was called to meet her, and meet her is what he would do.

He watched with wonderment as she absorbed her surroundings. He slid into the shadows, making himself invisible, so he could watch her without being noticed. He couldn't take his eyes off of this woman. Her dress molded perfectly to her curves. The coloring highlighted the caramel undertones in her skin. Her nervousness was endearing. It made her all the more attractive.

"Maybe all is not lost?"

He wanted to make her comfortable. He wanted to hold her, feel her breath against his body, rock her gently in his arms until she relaxed in and became one with him.

Nicolay reached out to her with his power. He wanted to touch her, to feel each and every part of her. She seemed to notice a change in the atmosphere almost immediately as the wave of magic rubbed against her skin and then passed through her. He watched as goose bumps formed on her arms, making the tiny hairs stand on end. She rubbed her arms vigorously trying to ward off the cool, eerie feeling. She turned in his direction as if she'd sensed she was being watched and the culprit was in that direction. But she only saw the bar, just as he had intended.

"Amazing," was all he could say.

Although she couldn't see him, she had sensed him there. She'd followed the wave of power back to its source. He would have to be careful with this one. She was mortal, that he was sure of. He detected something different about her, but it wasn't the typical impression of deeply rooted power that constantly surrounded other creature of magic.

One thing he did know: she was like no other women he'd ever crossed paths with. The others were easy to sway. Most of them had wanted him anyway; the lust emanating from them sometimes sickened him. A man of his stature and breeding was considered a great catch for a single woman looking for a handsome face to father her children.

The others were just looking for a pretty face to show off to their friends. Somehow he didn't get that from this one. As a matter of fact, now that he thought about it, he didn't get anything from her. He could usually read the mind of any mortal. Maybe she wasn't mortal? He shook the thought from his head. She was mortal, but she was in some other way different. He needed to find out what else there was.

He reached out to her again, using more of his power, reaching beyond the physical. He searched for her mind, for any emotions, or any change in her breathing that might indicate what was special about her. In return he received nothing, nothing at all, no sense of who or what she was. Now he was confused, but more so intrigued. It was as if there was a wall around her, protecting her from his power, from him. He meant her no harm; he just wanted to know her, to know everything about her.

"Well, guess I'll have to do this the old fashioned way."

It had been a long time since he had had to charm a woman, a very long time. He hoped he hadn't lost his touch.

"Before the night is over beautiful lady, I will at least know your name."

His gaze followed her every move as she and her friend entered the exterior room. Her movements were as fluid as a gymnast. Each step, each sway of her hips... hypnotic. The flow of her muscles...enchanting. Her beauty pulled at him. Each moment he watched her sucked him further into her web. He lusted for her, wanting to touch each and every part of her. Even more, he was fascinated by her every move, her every breath, her complete existence.

Just watching her, he felt a connection with her he had never felt before. It was as if she was somehow a part of him. He didn't understand what he was feeling. He was sure he'd never met her before. Her beauty would not be easily forgotten. Maybe he was experiencing a moment of deja vu; whatever it was, it made him need to be close to her, to feel her warmth against his body.

Nicolay shook his head, willing himself from the trance she had put him under, but it was no use. Again he found himself watching her intently as she and her friend chose the table in the far corner. She was even more breathtaking with the moonlight dancing upon her.

Her hair shimmered like silk. It framed her face perfectly. Her skin had a healthy glow, the glow of youth. He could imagine her portrait hanging in a museum, bathed in natural light for all to enjoy.

He watched curiously as her friend got up from the table and walked to the bar. Now was his chance. Laughing at himself, he took in a few deep breaths to calm his nerves. Here he was, a six hundred year old vampire, acting like a teenage boy gathering up the courage to ask the head cheerleader to the senior prom. Nicolay brought himself out of shadows. Pacing himself, he weaved his way through the crowd.

With each step he watched her. Something just wouldn't let him take his eyes off of her. It was as if she had cast a spell over him. That kind of power was dangerous. He had swayed many women over the years, not that they hadn't been willing to share his bed. Now he felt what he was sure those women had felt, an undying need to be one with another. With each step, his anger escalated as he watched man after man approach her. His jealousy turned to rage so much so that he had to stop himself from knocking down one of the rejected men.

He continued to watch as she turned away each anxious suitor with a curt nod or a wave of the hand. She was going to be a difficult catch. He'd win her over though. He could have her if he really wanted to. All he needed to do was have her look into his eyes and she would be his for the taking. But for reasons unknown to him, he felt the need to approach her with his real self. If she was as special as he thought she was, he wanted to win her over. He wanted her to be his of her own free will. He didn't want to scare her off, and he would not attempt to cloud her mind. He wanted her to know him for who he really was, not some memory he planted in her mind. He would be as polite as possible. A quick dance is all he would ask of her, then, he'd take his time to court her properly. But before the night was over, he had to know her name.

Only two tables away, Nicolay was surprised to see her friend returning so quickly. Composing himself, he stopped and spoke with a couple that frequented the club at a table directly across from the dance floor. Never once did his gaze retreat from the woman's face. Now that her friend had returned, the tension previously filling her as each suitor approached dissipated. She appeared much calmer. She seemed more comfortable now. This could prove to be to his advantage He still had to tread carefully. It only took a moment to make a total fool of himself or scare her away, and that was definitely not what he wanted tonight.

CHAPTER SIX

LYSETTE PLACED HER drink on the table and handed Dakota her club soda.

Dakota leaned over to her friend so she wouldn't have to yell.

"Now I remember why I stopped coming to the club. I swear, in the five minutes you've been gone, I've heard every pickup line in the book."

Lysette was about to respond when she caught a glimpse of this bronze Adonis approaching their table out of the corner of her eye.

"Every line in the book huh? What do you think this one's line is going to be?"

Lysette was trying to hide her smile but it was no use. She had picked out Dakota's outfit to intentionally attract attention, and by the looks of the gentleman approaching their table, her plan was working just fine. She didn't intend on telling Dakota she'd been watching this guy staring at her the entire time she was at the bar. He definitely had his eye on Dakota.

Besides, her friend needed a man in her life. Lysette didn't count Dayton or the guys at the shop. None of them saw her as anything other than just one of the fellas. But this one, Lysette was sure would see Dakota for who she really was: an attractive single woman in need of the gentle caring of a man.

He looked decent enough. Lysette was quite pleased with his physical appearance. He seemed to be well groomed with not a hair out of place. His outfit complemented his complexion and it fit him perfectly. He'd do quite nicely. Now, the biggest challenge facing her was how to get Dakota to dance with him.

Though a little confused, Dakota soon caught the hint. She turned her head just as Mr. Dark and Lovely reached for her hand and asked, "May I have this dance?"

This man's voice mesmerized Dakota. His cream colored linen pantsuit fit him in all of the right places. The color offset his deep caramel skin; it was perfect for his skin tone. One look at that dazzling smile and she was hooked. She hadn't seen a smile so white, so perfect, in all of her life. His high cheekbones and nearly straight hair gave him an exotic look. She was sure somewhere in his family tree there had to be Native American or some sort of Spanish descent. He'd pulled his hair back into a neatly braided ponytail tied back with a rubber band on the end. Dakota could only imagine what it would feel like to have his muscular arms holding her. He was toned, but not overly bulky, just enough to make a woman feel safe.

Aside from all of that, his eyes drew her in to him; she couldn't get past the eyes. They were like two auburn pools with depths unknown to man. It wasn't just the coloring surrounded by a small white ring, it was the way the lights flickered off of the dark flakes in them that made his eyes so striking. They held a hidden sadness. His eyes showed that life had not been kind to him, and yet they seemed to have a twinkle that the hard life had not yet extinguished.

Dakota pulled herself away from gawking at this gorgeous man long enough to say, "I'd love to."

"Then it is settled."

He gently raised her hand to his lips and laid the softest kiss on the back of her hand. He then escorted her to the dance floor.

From the moment they touched, they seemed to be in sync. It had been a long time since Dakota had been dancing, but all of the time away from the club had not diminished her dancing skills as she thought it might. The music enveloped her, and in this man's arms she felt as if she were floating above the ground. The music pulsed through her veins, willing her body to respond to the rhythm. Losing conscious control of her body, she allowed the music to dictate her movements.

The first couple of songs were up-tempo, and they moved across the dance floor with ease. The other couples on the floor seemed to be oblivious to their movements. Each place they gravitated was open for the taking. Dakota thought it creepy, like the other couples knew where she and this stranger would be. The others parted like two halves of a Georgia peach whenever they were close.

As the music slowed, Dakota felt her body being pulled closer to this unbelievably gorgeous man. He wrapped his arms around her waist, leaving just enough space between them to ensure proper etiquette. Everything around them faded into the background. The lights, the people, everything else became irrelevant. Her body felt light, weightless. She was sure her feet were planted firmly on the ground until she glanced down and realized they were levitating ever so slightly above the parquet floor. Startled, she lost her footing and had it not been for this angel's embrace, she would have collided with the floor.

"Are you well, beautiful lady?"

Nicolay witnessed the fear in her eyes. It was then he realized he had lost control and allowed them to hover above the floor.

"How? How is this possible?"

Dakota held on to this man like her life depended on it, even though he was the reason they were above the floor instead of on it. Her head jerked frantically from one side to the other trying to make sense of the situation. Her breath quickened. Her pulse raced, the blood flowing to swiftly through her veins. She began to feel warm, then nauseous, and finally lightheaded. In any moment she was sure she'd faint.

"I apologize, my little one."

Nicolay felt the change in her body. His slip had caused her distress, and distress was the last thing he wanted for her. He needed to get her to a table before she passed out. He tightened his hold on her, then loosened some. Her reaction confused Nicolay. Since reintroducing himself to the modern world, he had yet to meet a mortal that hadn't detected his power. Surely this one knew what he was.

"May I ask you a question?"

The color was returning to her face and her heart rate was stabilizing. Maybe he wouldn't have to carry her off of the dance floor after all.

"Can you put us down first?"

"Sure."

Nicolay obeyed her request and slowly lowered them to the floor. The expression on her face said it all. He'd frightened her. She looked like a gazelle that had just spotted a lioness two paces behind her. His only consolation was that she still clung to him. He hoped she'd give him a chance to explain.

"Do you not know the capabilities of my kind?"

"What do you mean by your kind?"

Nicolay smiled to himself.

"Well, most people pick up on what I am as soon as I walk into a room. Please accept my apology, I thought you knew."

He'd tried all night to avoid scaring her away only to lose control with her in his arms. This was not turning out as planned.

"So, are you going to tell me what you are?"

Dakota fought an internal battle, trying her best not to show fear or become distraught. She looked up at him and her brow furrowed. Her mind screamed for her to get as far away from him as fast as possible, her heart and her body refused to respond to the request.

"Can I first offer you a drink?"

Dakota looked up into his eyes. She was drawn to them, like they were the gateway to his core. She had just had the scare of a lifetime.

She had experienced some really strange things in her life, but nothing like what had just happened. She wasn't sure what to do at this point. What she had just experience was beyond even her comprehension. She'd only read stories of the powers of mystical creatures. She had her suspicions of what he may be but it had never occurred to her that she'd ever be this close to someone or something that had the power to kill her in the blink of an eye. In the back of her mind, she was sure that is what he meant by what he was. Something about this man though had her intrigued. Something at the center of her existence wanted to know him, to understand him.

She'd promised herself tonight would be a new beginning and she intended on keeping that promise. Besides, sitting at home waiting for Dayton just so they could watch movies all night long was getting a little old. Lysette was right. She'd spent too much time without the companionship of a man. A man who saw her for the woman she had blossomed into. At that moment, Dakota thrust all inhibition aside and gave in.

Lowering her head she said, "Sure."

Relieved, Nicolay escorted her to the bar. He guided her to the two empty seats at the corner farthest away from the other patrons.

"Now, beautiful lady, what would you like to drink?"

Dakota looked shyly at her hands. She hoped her nervousness didn't show. Nicolay slid his finger under her chin and raised it up so she had no choice but to look at him.

"I see that is a habit I am going to have to break you out of."

He had watched her as each man approached. Each time, she lowered her chin before she declined the offer. He was now glad her friend had returned prior to him reaching the table. He would not have allowed her to lower her eyes to him before rejecting his offer to dance. That probably would have been the end of him approaching her without using his powers to cloud her mind.

"Now, I'll ask again, what would you like to drink?"

Tension filled her neck as Dakota fought to drop her chin, but Nicolay refused to let her look down. She took a deep breath before she spoke, "Club soda would be nice. I'm the designated driver for the night and my friend and I are a long way from home."

"Then club soda it is," Nicolay turned to the bartender. "Xavier, would you be so kind as to get a club soda for the lady and a red wine for myself."

"Sure boss."

As quickly as the request was made, the bartender immediately took to preparing their drinks.

Nicolay watched Dakota struggle not to look at him. She seemed so sure of herself on the dance floor. Now, she was as timid as a baby bird facing its first flight. Xavier placed their drinks in front of them and returned to tending to other customers.

"Shall we find a more private table?"

Nicolay wanted to talk with this woman, but he wanted her all to himself. He wanted to sit with her under the moonlight and watch the clouds play shadows across her face. He searched the crowd and located an empty table in the back room that would be perfect. Turning to Xavier, he whispered for him to send a drink to a young lady sitting alone, compliments of the house of course, and then he led Dakota to the table.

An awkward silence hung between them. Nicolay watched with amusement as Dakota carefully nursed her drink. Even when she was nervous, she was beautiful. Shadows from the clouds crossing the bright moon danced on her face. He studied her full lips, oh how much he wanted to kiss her. Her body called out to him. He could almost taste the sweetness pulsing though her veins. The longer he sat there taking her in, the more difficult it was becoming for him to concentrate. He closed his eyes and inhaled her scent. She smelled of Patchouli. The intoxicating aroma made him yearn for her. He desired to be close to her in ways he had never felt before. It was then he knew she was destined to be his.

Carefully choosing his words, Nicolay broke the uncomfortable silence.

"I guess I should start by formally introducing myself," he covered her hand with his own, tracing the ligaments just below the surface, "My name is Nicolay Constantine and I guess you now know my little secret. I am the undead."

He paused watching her grasp what he had just said. When he felt she understood and accepted it, he continued, "I lived the first three hundred of my six hundred years as Vampyre in utter seclusion, battling with what I am."

It was his turn to lower his head, but he did it in shame. Nicolay had denied himself the simple pleasure of the company of a woman who truly knew him for far too long.

"I did not choose this curse, but after three hundred years, I finally realized that I could hide until someone killed me, or I could try to put together some sort of life. It took some time, but I have been able to slowly find where I belong in this world."

Dakota didn't know what to say. She had always imagined vampires as vicious creatures with no human emotions. The movies always portrayed them as evil. And here she was, sitting across from one, who seemed unhappy with the power bestowed upon him. She never imagined being a vampire was forced upon someone. She always thought it was a choice. She wanted to cry for him, to reach out to him and take away all of his pain. She knew he spoke the truth, yet she didn't understand his sorrow.

Dakota calmed her voice long enough to ask, "What made you decide to try to live among those who would only try to destroy you?" Dakota had first-hand knowledge of how people treated those they deemed abnormal.

"I have watched as mankind's beliefs of my kind have evolved from fear, to obsession, to hatred, and then to understanding. Many of the patrons here come with hopes of getting a glimpse of me. Sometimes it's hard being a freak show, but it is my life."

Nicolay could not believe he was sitting here telling a complete stranger his most embarrassing secret, that he had hidden like a coward for three hundred years because of who and what he was.

"I purchased this warehouse a few years back, before anyone in this town knew what I was, and decided to open a club. I figured this new venture would allow me to get back my life while allowing little suspicion to arise about my daytime whereabouts. I am still not totally comfortable with being out in public, but hey, what can you do? I will admit, since I have denied who and what I am for so long, I am not sure what it all entails. There are some aspects that are fairly obvious, such as the levitating but I may have abilities I have yet to discover."

He didn't want to tell her about him trying to read her earlier. He had given her enough of a scare for one night.

"But enough about me and my issues, tell me about you, beautiful lady."

Dakota didn't know where to start. Since he had revealed a more personal side of who he was, she chose to provide him with the same courtesy.

"This may sound strange, but before I tell you about me, I want to try something, with your permission of course." He had referred to himself as a freak show, something Dakota could definitely relate to. She had been one all of her life. She couldn't run from her abilities, so she embraced them, learning to nurture and control them.

"What kind of something?" it was Nicolay's turn to be curious.

"If I tell you it may not work. I promise it won't hurt."

Nicolay thought for a moment. He looked at the beautiful goddess in front of him. He could not think of one thing she, a mere human, could do to harm him.

"All right, I'm all yours," he tried not to show fear, but his voice still quivered when he spoke.

Dakota took a moment to calm herself. Closing her eyes, she visualized herself in the woods on a cool fall night, the breeze gently caressing her face. She stilled her soul, focusing on connecting with her psychic power. She separated herself from the loud music, the many conversations, and the noise of the club. She opened her eyes and could only see the man in front of her. She reached for his face and he jerked back, apparently startled by the magic. She looked him in the eyes, reassuring him with her smile she'd cause no harm.

As her hand lay gently along his jaw line, she searched. She opened herself up to the part of her that read images. Lysette had called this gift a form of psychometry. Dakota didn't care about the scientific name for it; she accepted that she could read people and things with just a touch. She looked for the ghost she knew haunted the dead. She tried to feel any remnant of his soul. She searched for his history, for any impressions indicating his past experiences. All she saw were shadows and darkness. She picked up remnants of death and an overwhelming sense of darkness, but he didn't feel dead to her. He felt like nothing she had felt before.

Dakota remembered feeling the bodies of her dead relatives, the ones who had truly been at peace with death. She remembered when a person died, if that someone had truly accepted death, they would feel cold. She knew the souls of those people had fled to wherever it was that souls went after escaping the flesh. But this one, this gorgeous man in front of her felt not cold, but not alive either.

Dakota opened her eyes, not knowing when she had closed them or how long she had sat there. She didn't recall her hand moving from his face or his hand being laid upon hers.

"Did you find what you were seeking?"

Nicolay looked perplexed. He had never experience what he had just felt her do. She had been searching inside of him. For what, he didn't know. It was strange to have someone else's magic inside. He wondered if that was how others felt when he used is power to search them.

"Yes and no. It's the strangest thing. I sense that you're dead, but not yet truly dead," Dakota's didn't know how to explain it. She felt some source of life to him, but it was hidden so deep inside that it was beyond her reach. She felt the warmth of it radiating from his core, but it was too far hidden for her to touch.

"And how did you do that?"

"That's my story, my deeply rooted secret," Dakota took a moment to adjust to being back in her own body and reorient before she spoke. She knew she didn't want to talk here, among this crowd, but this man intrigued her, and she needed to know that he could deal with who she was before she could even consider being his friend or anything more.

Dakota sighed; the least she could do at this moment was tell the man her name.

"My name is Dakota Naverro. Garden City has always been my home, but my life has never been normal. We both have our secrets, and I'd very much like to tell you more about me. I'd also love to know more about you, but not here," as she spoke the last words, her voice became that of a seductress. She wanted to know as much about this man as he wanted to know about her.

"What did you have in mind?"

Nicolay definitely picked up on the change in her demeanor. He was relieved that his loss of concentration on the dance floor had not scared her off. He was enjoying this game of cat and mouse. It had been a long time since a woman had captured his attention, and Dakota was definitely making the wait worth it.

"It's late, and I need to find my friend. Perhaps we could get together tomorrow night? That is, if you're available."

Once again Dakota lowered her head. She had just asked this guy out, a personal first for her, and she didn't even know if he had a significant other. She'd be heartbroken if he wasn't available. She couldn't bear to look at him, afraid that he'd reject her.

"Available? That's interesting. If you are asking if I am involved, the answer is no, and I can't think of anything I'd love more than to see you tomorrow night. If it's all right with you, I'll send a car to pick you up just before dusk."

He watched her relax as he accepted her date. He was sure the words had slipped out before her mind could stop them, but he was fine with that. This night was turning out better than he could have hoped.

"Are you sure you can get someone to come out my way? I mean, I live in the middle of nowhere, and most people would prefer to not drive down a dirt road to get to the house," she said shyly, "I can meet you here tomorrow night. It's really not a problem."

Although she tried desperately to hide her excitement, the smile on her face told him exactly what she was feeling.

"No. I cannot ask that of you. Besides, it wouldn't be gentlemanly of me to ask you to make a trip here knowing that you will be out most of the night. It's not safe for you to be out unescorted during the early hours of the morning. The least I can do is send my driver to come pick you up. Believe me, it's not a problem."

"If you say so," Dakota grabbed a cocktail napkin and scribbled the address and phone number to the house on it.

"Here's the address. It's clearly marked at the street, but like I said, the driveway is long and unpaved."

"I'll make sure I pass that along to my driver. Now that we have settled that, let us find your friend."

Scanning the club, Dakota spotted Lysette sitting at the bar and talking to the bartender.

"There she is."

Lysette and the bartender seemed to be deep in their conversation and Dakota hated to interrupt, but it was getting late and she had to drive. From what she could tell, it looked like Lysette had had a good time without her, so maybe they'd both have juicy details to share.

CHAPTER SEVEN

XAVIER WAS MORE THAN happy to send the drink to the lovely woman sitting alone. He had been secretly watching her all night. He remembered her coming into the club with another woman, but she had been alone for the last couple of hours. She seemed to be having a good time and she had no shortage of suitors, but none of them kept her attention long. He watched her on the dance floor, her dress billowing around her legs as she and a number of men in the club danced.

This woman was endless legs. He imagined his fingertip wrapped around her slender waist, her smile lighting up the room. She was definitely experienced in the arts, her movements flowing gracefully as the men twirled her around and slid her body against theirs. Xavier secretly studied her face. Her cheeks were flushed from the exertion of the dancing. The bridge of her nose was slightly crooked, giving her other facial features a softer undertone. Butterscotch was all that could describe her complexion. After she had returned to her table from her last dance, she seemed content with nursing her drink and watching the crowd. He stared at her, watching intently as each drop of liquid poured down her throat. He wanted her to drink him in, savor him just as she did each drop of her drink.

Since he wasn't sure what she was drinking, he sent over a Shirley Temple with a note just as Nicolay had requested.

When the waiter appeared, Lysette gave him a confused glance. She hadn't ordered anything, and yet here he was delivering a drink

to her table. She looked around before she read the note, trying to figure out who had sent it. No one in particular seemed to be paying her
any attention. She opened the note and slowly read.

*A simple drink for a beautiful lady. Please accept this drink, compli-
ments of The Apache. If it is not to your liking, please return it to the bar
for the drink of your choice.*

Xavier

GLANCING IN THE DIRECTION of the bartender, Lysette
smiled. She had been secretly watching him all night, and she found
him quite attractive. Not wanting to get him in trouble by hanging
around while he was working, Lysette had kept her distance. She
wondered, could this little surprise have come from him?

"Only one way to find out," she answered her mind's question
aloud as she rose from her table, the Shirley Temple in hand, and
sashayed over to the bar. Xavier greeted her with a warm smile.

"Is this from you?" she then took a seductive sip of the drink, savoring the taste as the cool liquid slid down her throat, quenching her
nervous thirst.

"As the note states, it is compliments of the house. It was my pleasure to make you smile."

She didn't need to know it was Nicolay who had requested the
drink be sent over. Besides, Xavier had been plotting to send one to
her anyway, even if it meant he had to pay for it out of the night's tips.
Nicolay just made it easier. Now that he thought about it, Nicolay
didn't make a habit of sending drinks to anyone's table. He wondered
why he had chosen to send one to this woman.

"Maybe he was reading my mind again?" Xavier said aloud.

"Did you say something?" Lysette looked curiously at him.

Xavier quickly recovered, realizing he had spoken the words instead of just thinking them.

"No, no. So, will this beautiful woman grace the likes of me with her name?" Xavier quickly changed the subject. He didn't want her to think he was crazy.

Lysette looked this man over; he was handsome in his own way. His light brown eyes were bright and full of life. Freckles covered his cheeks and nose, but didn't overpower his other features. His lips were full and his smile revealed a perfect set of white teeth. His goatee was neatly groomed, and although he worked with alcohol most of the night, he smelled mysteriously like the islands.

"Like what you see?" Xavier folded his arms and leaned against the bar while this beautiful woman scrutinized his every detail.

"I'm sorry, I didn't mean to stare," ashamed at being caught staring at this man, she quickly recovered by telling him her name, "My name is Lysette and I take it you are Xavier. It's nice to meet you."

She offered her hand for him to shake. Wiping his hands off before he dared touch her smooth butterscotch skin, he instead placed a gentle kiss on the back.

"The pleasure is all mine," he smiled at her, his eyes never wavering while he kissed her hand, "So, is the drink to your liking or would you prefer something else?"

"Definitely to my liking, just as you are," Lysette was just as surprised as Xavier when the words exited her mouth. Never had she been so bold, "Sorry, don't know what came over me."

"No need to apologize. I've had to catch myself tonight as well. There were things that have crossed my mind since you sat at my bar I dare not even tell my best friend," he smiled sheepishly at her. He had been thinking devilish thoughts about her, thoughts of things they both would take pleasure in.

Stimulating conversation held them captive for the next hour or so. Occasionally someone would interrupt them for a drink, but it was near closing time, so the crowd had thinned quite a bit. Xavier told her of his time in various countries, trying to find himself as a young man. They talked about his excursions to Brazil and adventures in Australia and the many cultures he'd experienced over the years.

Lysette spoke of her life and how she had always been an outcast. Everyone always thought her strange because she wasn't Christian like the rest of the community. He didn't judge her. He listened intently as she shared the few details of her life that she chose. When she spoke of her home, she seemed to drift off to a place filled with happy memories. The way she spoke of this beautiful place, he could tell she missed her home. He wasn't sure why, but he had the feeling she hadn't been there in far too long.

The night was coming to a close as Dakota and her new friend approached. The crowd had thinned considerably and the club would be closing soon. Now was his chance. Xavier wanted to hear more about Lysette and her life, so he asked for her phone number.

"Would you mind if I call you sometime? I work weekends, but I am usually free on weeknights."

Lysette wasn't so sure about giving her number to this guy. He seemed nice enough, but she'd learned early on to never judge a book by its cover.

"How about you give me your number, and I can call you."

"Ah, I see someone's going to play hard to get. Very well," he removed a pen from his pants pocket, grabbed a cocktail napkin, and scribbled down his number.

Lysette thought his handwriting fairly neat for a guy. She watched as he formed each letter with just a little too much loop. He meticulously dotted the "I" in his name. She giggled, thinking how cute that was. Just as she was folding the napkin and placing it in her purse, Dakota was at her side.

"DIDN'T MEAN TO DESERT you."

Although the words fell from Dakota's mouth, the look on her face said otherwise. She gave a look to her friend only a girl would understand, and Lysette definitely got the hint.

"No problem. You know I know how to have a good time. I wasn't in need of a chaperone, but I must say, I probably didn't have nearly as good a time as you did."

The huge grin on Lysette's face said it all. She wanted to get her friend home as quickly as possible. The sooner they got home, the sooner she could hear all the juicy details about this guy, and she could tell her about Xavier.

"Nicolay, this is my best friend in the whole wide world, Lysette. Lysette, may I introduce to you Mr. Nicolay Constantine."

Lysette offered her hand and just as Xavier had done, Nicolay placed a gentle kiss upon the back.

"The pleasure is all mine," Nicolay said.

"Two gentlemen in one night, I don't know what to say. And who says chivalry is dead?" Lysette chided.

It didn't take long for the two women to strike up their own conversation. Nicolay stood there for a moment and watched the banter between the two old friends. He could tell they were really close and probably shared everything. He wondered what Dakota would tell her about him.

"I hate to interrupt you two catching up on the events of tonight, but I have some business to tend to," Nicolay turned to Dakota and handed her a business card, "Here is the number to the club in case you need to cancel our date tomorrow night."

He'd said date on purpose. If her friend wanted dirt, that one word should be enough to give them both a lot to talk about.

Placing a quick kiss on Dakota's cheek, he whispered in her ear, "I shall see you again when the sun tiptoes beneath the horizon."

He then turned to face her and her friend, "Now, I will bid both of you ladies goodnight," with that, Nicolay turned and blended back into the crowd, but not before Dakota could get a good look at his behind.

"Stop drooling."

Lysette saw the look on her friends face and she couldn't blame her for ogling, but they were still out in public and it was best she tried to keep a low profile.

"What?" Dakota asked.

She shook her head with disbelief. How could a man that gorgeous want to be with a plain Jane like her? Not only that, a plain Jane who is clairvoyant. Of course she hadn't told him that part yet. She hoped he could see past her abilities, however, she'd learned not to get her hopes up on that.

"You think too much."

Lysette observed the emotions on Dakota's face. She was sure her friend was thinking all of this was too good to be true. Sad thing about it was she felt the same way. She really wanted to make sure Dakota didn't get her hopes up too high, but she didn't want to just flat out crush her dreams, either.

"I know, I know. Let's get back to my house so I can tell you the dirt on Mr. Lovely," Dakota was about ready to spill her guts, but she wasn't going to do it in front of Xavier.

Lysette turned to Xavier, "So I'll give you a call later today."

"I'd like that very much. Good night," he replied.

"Night."

And with that, they picked up their purses and jackets and headed back to the car.

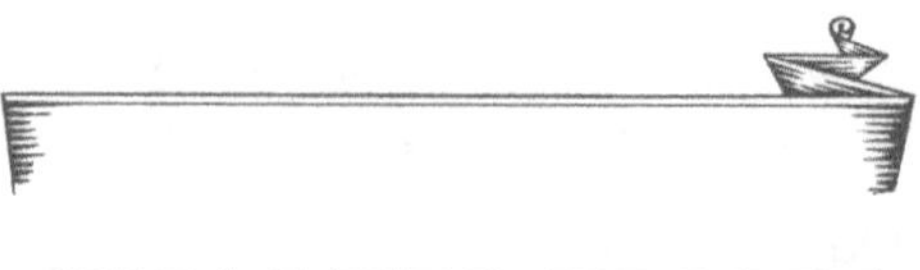

CHAPTER EIGHT

THE DRIVE HOME WAS quite nice. The ladies let the top down on Dakoat's brother's "Ghetto Mobile," and enjoyed the wind whipping through their hair. The Isley Brother's *Atlantis* was the perfect song to end this perfect night.

"Thanks for convincing me to go out tonight. It felt good to just get out of the house."

The more Dakota thought about it, the more she realized how sheltered she'd allowed herself to become. Her gift had hindered her for far too long, and she promised herself she would not sink back into the same pattern of staying home with Dayton. Even he had more dates than she did. If he could overcome the obstacle of his gift, then so could she.

"I don't think just getting out of the house is the only reason you're glad I dragged your butt down to that club. You know you have to give me all of the juicy details on dream boy."

"I will, I will. But in due time."

"In due time? What about giving a sister a little hint?"

"Um, no."

Dakota always liked to make Lysette wait. She'd always been impatient, so this was Dakota's way of balancing out the universe. Lysette needed to learn that the best things come to those who wait.

"Oh, you gonna do me like that? And after all I've done for you tonight?"

"Yep."

"You wrong, you know that don't you?"

Lysette loved teasing Dakota. Yeah, she thought she had the upper hand making her wait, but the reality was Lysette could get any information she wanted out of Dakota whenever she wanted, she just chose not to push those buttons too often.

"What? What'd I do?" Dakota said with a surprised voice.

"I finally get you out of the house to meet a real man and you keeping all of the juicy gossip to yourself," Lysette crossed her arms feigning hurt.

"Oh, isn't that the pot calling the kettle black. When's the last time you had a man in your life and told me about it?"

"I don't tell your butt nothing because you don't ask. I'm asking and you still holding out."

"So now I'm asking. You all up in my business so it's about time I get up in yours. What's up with you and the bartender?" Dakota decided if she was going to give up some info, she wanted some of her own.

"I asked first," Lysette was not about to let Dakota change the subject.

"Well, I asked second and if you want to get any information out of me, you're going to have to give up some."

"You know I'm going to remember this?"

Dakota cut her eyes over at Lysette, "Ask me if I care?"

"What's with the attitude?"

"What are you talking about? Why I gotta have an attitude just because I want to know some of your business before I go blabbing about mine. Turnabout is fair play. If you gonna have dirt on me, then I gotta have dirt on you."

"You already have enough dirt on me."

Dakota thought for a moment before she replied, "Yeah, I guess knowing about Austin Johnson is enough."

She stuck her tongue out at Lysette, knowing she'd just committed what they considered to be the ultimate sin.

"I thought we agreed to never to mention his name."

Dakota had struck a nerve with that one comment.

"Awww. I was only playing."

"Well, your game is no longer funny," Lysette crossed her arms over her chest and looked away. Dakota had crossed the line by mentioning the ex-boyfriend from hell.

Lysette turned back to face Dakota, but before she could fire off her next smart remark something darted across the road, causing Dakota to slam on the brakes. The force of the sudden stop forced Lysette back into the seat. She only had a split second to brace herself before she was jerked forward as the car skidded to a halt in the middle of the street.

"What'd you do that for?"

Lysette had no idea what was going on. One minute they were riding along joking about the new men in their lives, and the next they were skidding down the road and she was holding on for dear life.

"Tell me you saw that?" Dakota franticly asked.

"Saw what?" Lysette's head jerked from side to side, trying to see whatever it was that had caused Dakota to stop in such a hurry.

"Something just ran across the street."

Lysette looked over at her like she was crazy.

"You slammed on the brakes, nearly cutting my head off with the seat belt over something that ran across the street. Hello! We are on a road out in the middle of nowhere, surrounded by trees. How many times have you driven down this same road at two or three in the morning and had some deer dart across the road in front of you?"

Dakota was not amused, "That wasn't a deer. Last time I checked, deer ran on four legs, not two. Whatever that was, it was on two legs and fully clothed."

"And you saw that much as this 'thing' ran across in your high beams?"

"I know what I saw and it wasn't no damn deer."

"Well, what are you going to do about it? No wait, don't answer that. I know what you think you're going to do, but I'm not having it tonight. Now put the car back in drive and get us to the house. We'll call the police and have them send someone out here to investigate. I think we've just past mile marker sixteen. We're only a mile or so from the house. If there is someone out there, I don't want to know. Now let's go."

"But..."

"Think about it. If there is someone out there do you really want to take the risk? Here we are, two females riding alone on a deserted country road with the roof open, blaring music, fully exposed, and you want to go investigate? True, you are a good shot and you never go anywhere without your weapon, and I'd trust you with my life any other time, but this is too freaky."

Lysette began to get nervous as all of the possibilities began to cloud her mind.

"But what if it's someone who's hurt?"

"If the person was that hurt wouldn't they have tried to flag us down?"

"I guess so."

"And what if the 'person' who ran across the street was just a decoy to get us to stop, there could be others out there right now waiting for us to get out so they can jump us and make off without car or worse."

"But..."

"No more buts. Let's go."

There really wasn't need for further arguing. Dakota knew that Lysette was right. It wasn't a good idea for them to be out there alone trying to play hero for what could turn out to be a trap. So, following the advice of her trusted friend, Dakota put the car back in drive and headed straight for the house.

CHAPTER NINE

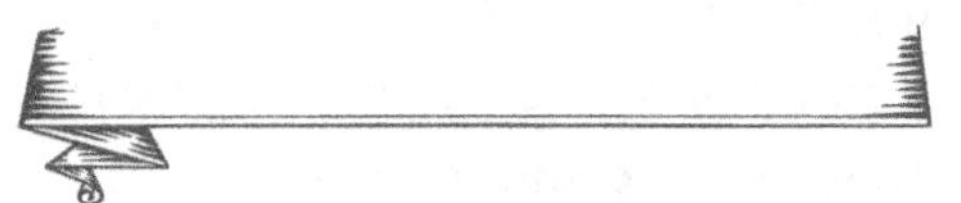

DAKOTA PULLED INTO the garage attached to the two-story plantation house and closed the aluminum door behind them. She rushed into the living room and dialed the local police department.

"Chatham County Police, how can I help you?" said the officer on the other end of the phone line.

"My Name is Dakota Naverro and I live off of route twenty. I want to report a suspicious person near mile marker sixteen," she paused as the operator asked her a question, "I didn't see much. Me and a friend were returning home when a man ran across the road in front of our car. He was thin, maybe six foot three or so, wearing a light colored shirt and dark pants."

Dakota leaned on the couch as she finished the conversation, "No. There weren't any other cars on the road and I don't remember passing any stalls on the way," she proceeded to give the officer her address and phone number before ending the call.

"All the doors and windows locked?" Lysette asked.

"Getting scared?"

"Oh, real mature. Just remember we are miles from the main road and help," it was nights like this when Lysette wished Dakota live within reach of civilization.

"We always have the phone."

"Unless the perpetrator cuts the line."

"You watch too many movies. Besides, between Dayton and I we have enough weapons and ammunition to supply a small army. If it'll make you feel better, I'll arm the alarm so no one can open a window or door without us knowing."

"What about in the other wing of the house?"

"We have sensors attached to the windows and doors there too. We've got nothing to worry about."

Dakota couldn't believe her friend was freaking out thinking someone was going to come and in try to attack them. She was the main one saying it was probably just a deer that ran across the road, now she acting like there was a serial killer stalking them.

"Wanna go upstairs and barricade ourselves in my room?"

Dakota took great pleasure in watching Lysette show signs of being human. Her friend was always the calm one, never letting anything get to her. It was nice to see her react to fear just like everyone else although Dakota did wonder why this was bothering her so much.

"No. I don't think that will be necessary," Lysette needed to change the subject. She grabbed Dakota by the arm and dragged her to the couch.

"Soooo?" Lysette asked.

"Soooo what?"

"I know you aren't just going to leave me hanging after what I just saw of you and dream boy on the dance floor. I was watching your eyes go all googly. Plus, I saw you getting all mushy over him at the bar."

"Not much to tell, except he's the owner of the club."

"Really? I'd heard someone had purchased that old warehouse, but no one seemed to know the details or wanted to talk about them at least. He had a great idea turning that dilapidated place into a dinner club. So that hunk is the new owner of the hottest Latin club in this place? Sounds like a keeper to me."

"Whoa, slow down sister, there is a lot more than just what you've seen. Don't have me married off to this guy with a dozen kids and a white picket fence."

Dakota could tell by the look on Lysette's face her friend already had her future planned out with this guy. They both had a hardy laugh at the idea. However, Dakota secretly hoped for just that, at least the part about married with a white picket fence. She knew the stories of vampires, and every one she had ever read had said they couldn't have children.

"There may be one small complicating factor," Dakota fidgeted with her dress.

"What's that?"

Lysette tried hard to think of anything that might keep Dakota and Nicolay apart. He was handsome enough, had a good job, took great care in his appearance, and he was polite. What more could a girl ask for?

"How long were you watching us on the dance floor?" Dakota was pretty sure now her friend hadn't noticed that they were dancing above the floor, not on it.

"Long enough, I thought, but by the tone of your voice I'd say I missed something."

"Yeah, you missed something all right. You missed the ten ton boulder I am about to throw at you."

"Pease Dakota, enlighten me. Tell me what I missed," Lysette was getting irritated now. She hated it when Dakota held out on her.

"What you missed was he and I levitating above the floor." Dakota watched Lysette's face. She knew this was going to be a Kodak moment.

"You're kidding right?"

Lysette mouth dropped. She sat there stunned for a moment, then she took an additional moment to determine if her friend was kidding or not. Her expression said it all, but Dakota wanted to make sure that she understood the complete ramifications of what she was telling her.

"He's a vampire."

Those three simple words shattered Lysette's fantasy of her friend living happily ever after. She didn't know what to say, so she didn't say anything at all. The only thing she could think of was all of the dreams she had for her friend now lay in limbo. She was beginning to feel bad for getting her friend's hopes up only to have them come crashing down.

Dakota understood the predicament Lysette was now in. She'd tried to do everything right. Pick out the perfect outfit, encourage her friend to dance with the gentleman, only to have it all turn on her with three simple words. Dakota reached out and hugged her.

"It's no big deal. I'm cool with it. I mean, who am I to throw stones in a glass house? Actually, I'm looking forward to our date tomorrow night. My first real date, and it's with a vampire. Wonder what else fate has in store for me? "

"Uh, I knew you were holding out on me. So where are you two going? Are you driving or meeting him back at the club? Do you need a chaperone?"

"One question at a time, and *no*! I do not need a chaperone. To be honest, I have no idea where we're going. He said he'd send a car for me tomorrow. It's supposed to be here around dusk."

"So, you mean you're going out with a guy you just met and you have no idea where you're going?"

"That's the jist of it."

"Look, you're new to this dating thing, and people out here are crazy. Are you sure it's wise for you to go out with this guy alone at night?"

Dakota rolled her eyes, "He's a vampire, what other time could I see the man?"

"I'm just saying," Lysette threw her hands up, trying to remain non-threatening, "you can never be too careful."

"So, what do you want me to do? First you encourage me to go out with him, now you act like you don't want me to go."

"Look, I just want you to be careful that's all. Ok?"

"I will, I promise. So, you staying tonight?" Dakota asked, changing the subject.

"Might as well. We'll have us an old fashioned sleep over."

"Yeah, except we'll both be sleeping in beds instead of on these hardwood floors. You know we're both too old for that."

"You, maybe," Lysette teased.

"Okay, now. Just know, if you sleep out here on this floor, I don't want hear a word in the morning talking about 'my back hurts.' And don't even think of trying the puppy dog eyes, 'cause it ain't gonna work."

They both laughed. Climbing the stairs, they entered Dakota's bedroom to get ready for bed.

"You think your brother will mind me sleeping in his bed?" Lysette yelled into the master bathroom. Dakota had gone in to change out of her club wear and into a sleep shirt.

"Nah. Sometimes I crash in there myself. He doesn't care about the bed. Just don't mess with his music. He'll have a fit. It's like he has some kind of radar or something. I played a CD in his CD player one time, and I made sure that I put it back into the case and back onto the shelf where I found it but 30 minutes later he was storming into my room talking about: 'Why you all in my stuff?' You could probably go in there and paint the walls fuchsia and put pink butterflies on everything and he wouldn't notice, but touch one CD and he'll have your hide. I don't know how he does it, but somehow he just knows."

"Well, I'm going in there to crash. I'll see you in the morning."

Lysette left Dakota to finish her hair. She lay on Dayton's bed and next thing she knew, sleep had enveloped her.

CHAPTER TEN

DAKOTA STARED AT HER reflection in the mirror. She still found it hard to believe Nicolay had chosen her over all of the other women in the club. She wasn't special in any way on the outside, a little hippy if you ask her. Otherwise, she was as plain as could be. Her hair was shoulder length today, although tomorrow maybe she would remove the weave and go natural.

She remembered seeing all of the women in the club with their skintight dresses and high heels. Most of them had on so much makeup their faces looked painted. Some of them were breathtakingly beautiful, and yet he'd forsaken them all and chosen to dance with her. Although she normally put on a little eye shadow and lipstick, she had decided tonight she didn't feel like being bothered with having to take it off, so she had opted only for the eyeliner and gloss.

Dayton always told her she was beautiful. He was her brother though, and the only family she had left. It was his job to make sure she had high self-esteem, so she always dismissed his comments as Dayton being Dayton. But tonight, with Nicolay approaching her and showering her with those same comments, maybe her brother had really seen something in her only a man could see.

She inched her way back to the bed, never taking her eyes off of her image in the mirror. She laid her head on the down pillow and stared up at the ceiling. There was so much going in her head. She tried closing her eyes and counting sheep or visualizing herself in dreamland, but all she could see was the face of Nicolay Constantine.

It was as if his image had been burned into the front of her mind with no other thought being able to penetrate. It didn't take her long to realize she'd never be able to sleep, so she decided to get up and find something else to occupy her thoughts.

Since sleep eluded her, Dakota decided to try to get some work done. She went across the hall to the bedroom Dayton had converted to an office some years before. The room was sparsely furnished. A drafting table and matching chair occupied the space in front of one of the large windows. This bedroom was located at the corner of the house, so there were windows on two sides of the room. There was a smaller desk in one of the corners she used to pay bills and write letters when she brought work home from the shop, which wasn't very often. Dayton always said work needed to stay at work, but sometimes she'd sneak away with a project that needed her midnight inspiration to complete. Tonight, she was sure, was going to be just that, a night for midnight inspiration.

She pulled out the blueprints and pictures of a restoration project Dayton had left for her. As Dakota reviewed the notes and pictures, she realized the automobile was in pretty bad condition. Most of the panels were rusted and would have to be totally replaced. The roof had seen better days as well as the car's interior. She definitely had her work cut out for her. She'd need to cut the new panels, order the new interior, not to mention get with the guys to find out what kind of engine work needed to be done. She looked at all she needed to complete, but she still couldn't concentrate.

Giving up on work, she returned to the master suite. She lay in the bed again, this time staring out of the picture window across from her bed. She had a perfect view of the nearly full moon. As she gazed out into the night sky, she replayed the feel of Nicolay's body against hers as they danced. She could almost hear the salsa music playing in her head. Slowly but surely she began to float. It was almost startling, but soon, she was sound asleep.

AFTER TYING UP SOME loose ends, Nicolay retired to his office. As he stood in front of the picture of his last sunset, he replayed the last few hours he'd spent with Dakota. While hiding in the shadows, a feat he'd become extremely good at, he had secretly watched her and her friend leave the club. She was just as breathtaking from behind as she had been from the front. He felt her watching him as he had walked away, and even then he secretly smiled to himself. As they left, she once again turned in the direction in which he stood. Nicolay was sure she couldn't see him. It was possible though she'd felt him staring at her. He'd made it across the first hurdle. He promised himself he wouldn't rush things with her. He'd take things as slowly as she wished. He knew he'd love her for all eternity if she'd only allow him to. The soft knocking on his door pulled him from his thoughts.

"Boss, everything's closed and locked up tight. You need anything else before I head out?"

Nicolay turned from the painting of a sunrise, just as the office door swung open. He looked at his trusted friend and saw pity. Xavier was the only person working at the club who knew his secret. True, the other employees as well as most of the patrons knew he was a vampire, but none knew how old he was and what his heart ultimately longed for. He had confided in Xavier a time or two about his longing for knowing who he was, but those talks had been few and far between.

"Boss... you..." Xavier didn't have to say the words. He saw the distant look in Nicolay's eyes.

Nicolay wasn't ready to reveal what he was feeling about the mysterious Dakota, and he hoped his friend would understand and just let things be.

"Yeah, just thinking how I will never see another sunrise. You would think after all of this time, it would be easier."

Nicolay sighed. He was disappointed. He did miss the sun rising. As a kid, he used to wake up hours before dawn just to watch the sun rise, a joy he would never again know. This was a believable enough excuse, considering Xavier had caught him engrossed in the paintings. He just hoped his friend wouldn't pry, that he'd just accept the explanation.

"You sure that's all it is? I saw you dancing with that little lady tonight. Seems to me like something more than just missing the sunrise."

Xavier knew if his friend wasn't ready to confide in him, he would not press the issue. He just wanted to let him know he was there to listen if he wanted to talk.

"Not ready," was all Nicolay said.

Xavier took the clue and made his exit, "Night, boss."

"Goodnight, Xavier."

After he heard the door shut and the lock turn, Nicolay returned his gaze to the painting. The longing returned to him as well. The sadness almost overwhelmed him. All he could think of was he would never watch a sunrise with Dakota. At this very moment, the sun was rising on the other side of the wall. He felt the rays beginning to force away the darkness. Finally, filled with enough sorrow to last a lifetime, he retired to his lair.

CHAPTER ELEVEN

DAKOTA AWOKE TO A RINGING in the hallway. She didn't know how long she had been asleep or how long the phone had been ringing. With a groggy hello she greeted the person on the other end of the receiver.

"Where the hell have you been?" the voice over the phone yelled.

"Hold up. We're going to try this one more time. Hello?" the grogginess immediately left her voice as she corrected the obviously unhappy person on the other line.

"Don't act like you don't know who this is. I am gone less than a day and you stay out all night and don't return my calls. What have you and Lysette been up to? Answer me!"

At that moment, Dakota realized it was Dayton on the phone.

"Well, good morning to you, too."

"Morning? Morning? It is four in the freakin' afternoon there and you have had me worried sick. I have been calling all day with no answer."

Dakota looked at the phone and realized the ringer was turned off.

She calmly explained to her brother, "First of all, if you would stop turning the ringers on the phones in the bedrooms off I would have heard the phone the first time. Secondly, I'm grown and I don't have to answer to you for anything."

After she'd said it, Dakota wished she hadn't. She knew she'd just hurt her brother's feelings. He was only trying to make sure she was safe. Just as he was all she had, she was all he had. He'd looked out for her all of these years and this is how she repaid him.

"Fine. Don't expect me to be concerned about you anymore, Ms. 'I'm grown and I don't have to answer to anyone.'"

"I'm sorry, Day," she sincerely meant it, "It's just that I had a long night and you know I'm cranky when I wake up. You forgive me for snapping at you?"

"Only if you forgive me for yelling. Being away from you has been hard and when I couldn't get an answer at Lysette's place or home, I didn't know what to think. All I could do was imagine you and her in a ditch somewhere in the middle of nowhere, dead."

"She stayed here. We got back late and I didn't want her driving out there by herself. Plus, you would have known if something happened to me, you would have been able to feel it."

"Actually, I wouldn't have."

Dayton spoke the words solemnly. He had never told his sister that when they cast the shielding spell and it had not completely worn off, he would sometimes lose the connection with her.

"What are you talking about?"

She and Day had always been able to feel each other. Even hundreds of miles away, she could still feel his presence in her head. It used to creep her out. Now the feeling was comforting.

"We'll talk about it when I get back. So what time did you guys get home?" he held the word 'time' out a little too long.

"None of your business."

"Fine, I'll leave it alone, but we're going to discuss the hours Lysette is having you keep when I get home. I do have a little bad news though. Looks like I won't be back as soon as I thought."

An uncomfortable silence lingered between them. The conversation was getting awkward. Neither knew what to say to the other.

"Well, I'll let you go. Are you going to be all right while I'm gone?"

Dakota considered telling Dayton about the guy she met and the incident with the person running across the street. They had few if any secrets between them, but she decided to wait a little longer to see what became of her and Nicolay. Besides, she didn't want to worry Dayton any more.

"Yes. Lysette is keeping me quite entertained."

"You know what, I'm not going to touch that with a ten foot pole," by the sound of Dakota's voice, he didn't really want to know what Lysette had been doing to entertain her, "I'll call again if the plans change, otherwise I'll see you in a day or so. Call me if you need anything. I love you."

"I love you too. And I promise if I need anything, anything at all, you will be the first to know."

They both hung up the phone, neither saying the word good-bye. They both thought it bad luck. Imagine the daughter and son of a gypsy believing in luck!

"Who was on the phone?" Lysette dragged into Dakota's room looking like she hadn't slept in days.

"My brother. Who else?"

Lysette made a face and quickly changed the subject, "What's the plan for today?"

"I need to go down to the shop and get some of the invoices. After that, I don't have any plans until I have to get ready for my date."

"You make me sick," Lysette said.

"Oh, don't hate because I have a date and you don't."

"Whatever. I'll ride down to the shop with you, but I need to make a run to the house first."

Though similar in size, Lysette and Dakota's body shapes were entirely different so it was nearly impossible for Lysette to wear any of her friend's cloths.

"That's cool. It'll give me time to take a bath and grab something to eat."

Lysette grabbed Dakota's keys and headed down the stairs. Once she got back, they'd go to the shop then come back to the house and hang around until Dakota had to leave.

Getting up out of the bed, Dakota decided that Nicolay would get to know another side of her tonight. She entered her walk-in closet and wondered where to start to look for an outfit. She had no idea where they were going, so choosing an appropriate but comfortable outfit presented quite a challenge. She had about an hour and a half before dusk, more than enough time to make her decision. She puttered around for nearly twenty minutes with no ideas. At this rate, she'd never get down to the shop in time to get the invoices and be back.

She glanced over to the digital clock on the night stand. It read 4:50pm.

"Guess work will have to wait until tomorrow," her frustration mounted, "Lysette is so much better at this than I am."

As she continued to try to make a decision, the phone ringing interrupted her thoughts. She didn't have an inkling as to who might be calling.

"Hello?"

"Well hello my precious flower," the voice on the other end of the receiver said.

"Nicolay?" what a surprise! The sun was still shining brightly outside. She was sure he wouldn't awaken until the sun had completely descended below the horizon.

"Expecting a call from someone else?"

"Why no, but how is this possible?"

"We shall speak of it tonight. I am calling to confirm you will still grace me with your presence tonight."

"Yes," she smiled, though he couldn't see it, "I'm having trouble deciding what to wear?"

"I'll make it easy for you. We'll be outside most of the night, and where we are going it can get relatively cool, so dress warm."

"Is that supposed to be some sort of hint?" Dakota asked him.

"Take it as you like."

"So I guess that's all that you're going to tell me?"

"Then you have guessed correctly. As I said before, my driver will be there to pick you up at dusk. Is that still suitable for you?"

"Sure."

"Then I will see you in a couple of hours."

"I'm looking forward to it."

Dakota placed the receiver back on the cradle and grabbed all of the clothes she had taken out. None of them would do. She piled them on one of the shelves in the closet and walked to the other side. It was here she found the perfect outfit. She had just enough time to slip into a nice warm bath and relax before Lysette returned.

CHAPTER TWELVE

WITH HER ROBE TIED tightly around her waist, Dakota descended the stairs to answer the door. She peeped through the curtains to make sure it was Lysette ringing the doorbell like a mad woman.

Dakota swung the door open, "What's your problem? Ringing that doorbell like you crazy."

Lysette rushed past her, "Close the door quick!"

"What?"

"Just close it!"

Dakota closed and locked the door.

"Ok, spill it," she turned to her friend, her arms crossed over her chest.

"Someone's out there," Lysette was panicked. She never let anything get to her, but for the second time in twenty-four hours she seemed scared senseless.

"How do you know?" Dakota peaked through the curtains. She didn't see anyone.

"When I pulled up, I got a creepy feeling. You know, when you can feel someone watching you even when you're sure no one's there. I've been sitting out there for ten minutes. The feeling finally subsided and I thought that was my chance to get to the door. That's why I was ringing the doorbell like that."

"What do you think it was?"

"I'm not sure, but whatever or whoever it was is gone now."

"Think I should cancel my date?"

"No! You are going on this date if it's the last thing I do. Did you get a chance to go down to the shop?"

"Nope."

"Still need to go?" Lysette secretly hoped she'd say no. She really didn't want to go back out there, but if Dakota needed to get some things for work she figured they'd be safer together.

"Uh-uh. I don't think I have time. Guess who I got a call from?" Dakota gave Lysette an ear to ear grin.

"Who?"

"Nicolay. He said the driver will be here promptly at dusk."

"He called? But the sun's still up?"

"I know. I was just as surprised as you. He said he'd explain tonight."

The two friends started their ascent of the staircase to the upper floors of the house. When they reached the top, Lysette glanced out the large gothic-styled window. She still sensed something out there lying in wait, but she had no idea who it was or what they wanted. She'd make sure Dakota made it out safely, and then she'd use her magic to try to get some answers.

"So, what are you wearing?"

Lysette wanted to make sure her friend was properly dressed for her first official date. No doubt, Dakota had good taste, but tonight could be the beginning of something special and Lysette wanted to make sure that Dakota was prepared.

"I'll show you."

They first entered the sitting room attached to the master suite, then the main bedroom. On the bed, Dakota had placed a long sleeved lilac chenille mock turtleneck sweater with a pair of lilac and black slacks.

"Where are you two going?"

Lysette plopped down on the bed and examined the fabric of the sweater while she waited for Dakota's reply.

"I still don't know, but he said we'd be outside and it would probably get cool. Any ideas?"

"Maybe the river front? I can't think of anywhere else unless he has some private retreat somewhere."

"Yeah, that's what I was thinking too. I'd love to go on a boat ride tonight. I can't recall the last time Dayton and I took a ride on one of the ferries. This should be okay for tonight, shouldn't it?" she picked up the pants to make sure they were lined. She'd hate to be out somewhere and be freezing her butt off all night.

"Of course. It's sexy and yet sophisticated, but most of all comfortable, and warm. It's perfect. So, are you excited?"

"More nervous than excited."

Dakota's stomach had been doing somersaults all day. The bath had calmed her nerves some, but this was all new to her and her body was having a field day with the new feelings.

"There's nothing to be nervous about. I think he really likes you."

"He liked what he saw last night, and that was more your doing than the real me. I plan to tell him about my gift tonight."

"You think that's wise? I mean, you two just met."

"I think it's best to be honest."

"Well, if he, of all people, can't understand and accept you for who you are, then you don't need him," Lysette got up and gave her friend a hug, "It's going to be okay."

"I know. I just don't know what to expect. How am I supposed to act?"

"You're not supposed to act, silly. You're supposed to be yourself. Just be true to Dakota, and everything will fall into place."

"Easier said than done. I just want everything to be perfect."

"Baby, nothing's perfect. I thought you knew that by now."

"I do, I'm just trippin.'"

"So, you gonna get dressed or what?"

"Yep." Dakota grabbed the sweater and pants and headed to the bathroom.

"Let me know if you need help with your hair."

"You know I do. I don't even know why you fixed your mouth to ask me that," Dakota yelled back at her.

Lysette lay on the bed, staring out the window and watching the sun set. She thought about all she and Dakota had been through over the years. Dakota had been there for all of the significant events of her life. Now her friend was all grown up, and although it was strange she was going on her first real date at the age of twenty seven, it made this night all the more special that she could share this milestone with her. As the sun slipped below the horizon, Dakota returned to the room.

"What do you want me to do with your hair?" Lysette didn't have any ideas. If they went to the river, anything she did would be ruined in a matter of minutes.

"I don't care."

"How about we just wrap it then? If you end up on the water, you won't have to worry about it frizzing on you."

"That's cool. I've got a scarf that will match this perfectly," Dakota pulled the lilac scarf from one of the dresser drawers and handed it to Lysette. It only took a couple of minutes and she was done.

"What do you think?" Dakota twirled around so that Lysette could make sure nothing was out of place.

"You look wonderful. Nice touch with the eye shadow and gloss."

"Thanks. Are you going to wait with me downstairs?"

"You know I am. I've got to check out this driver. Make sure he's not going to run off with my best friend. Got everything?"

"Think so."

They headed out of the bedroom, down the long hallway that led back to the stairs.

"How do you think Dayton's going to feel when he finds out he missed out on your first date?"

Dakota hadn't even thought about that, "I don't know. I am pretty sure he wouldn't approve of my choice of men. I mean, my date is dead. And don't even think of telling Day about Nicolay. I don't intend for him to find out until I am good and ready. Understand?" she gave Lysette a serious look.

"Fine. Not that I had planned to tell him anyway. I was just curious. So what should I tell him if he calls?"

"Don't answer the phone, then you won't have to make up anything."

"But what if you need to reach me?"

"You've got your cell right?" Dakota knew she didn't go anywhere without that phone. If she didn't know any better, she'd swear that girl slept with it attached to her ear. With her friend's confirmation, Dakota continued, "Well then, I'll call you on it. You know Dayton's cell number, if it shows up in the caller-id, don't answer it."

"Got'cha."

As they reached the bottom of the stairs, the doorbell rang. Dakota looked down at her watch. It was nearly six thirty.

"Guess that's my ride. I don't feel too well." she grasped her stomach as she began to feel queasy.

"Just calm down and take a couple of deep breaths. I'll get the door."

Dakota was so nervous, and this was just the driver. She couldn't imagine how she'd feel once she was greeted by Nicolay himself. With the driver waiting patiently at the door, Lysette turned her attention back to her best friend.

"Come on. You can do this. Stop worrying about impressing him. He'll see you for who you are. Just be yourself and you'll be fine."

Dakota's eyes began to tear over, "I-I can't."

Lysette hugged her friend, "Yes, you can. Just think positive and it'll be okay. Besides, if Nicolay doesn't see what a beautiful, talented, caring woman you are, then I promise to curse him for all eternity."

Dakota smiled back at her, "Thanks. But I think, in a way, someone has already beaten you to the punch. So I'll see you when I get back?"

"I'll be here waiting to hear all of the dirt."

"Good night," she followed the driver to the black Lincoln town car and within minutes they were driving down the road

LYSETTE WATCHED FROM the bay window in the living room as the tail lights of the Lincoln slowly disappeared through the pecan trees as it headed for the street. She'd accomplished her main goal for the night, making sure Dakota got off to her date safely. Now it was time she focused on her second task. When she could no longer see the tail lights, she opened the door and stepped out into the night.

Taking a seat at the bottom of the wooden staircase, she waited patiently for the eerie feeling to return. While she waited, she opened her mind to the night. The song of the crickets soothed her soul while the gentle breeze massaged her skin, causing tiny goose bumps to form up and down her arms.

Lysette didn't know how long she'd sat there meditating, but she knew the moment the unknown creature entered her domain. She waited, giving it a chance to make the first move. She felt it moving from one side of the house to stand in the cloak of the trees directly across from where she sat. When she opened her eyes she'd expected to see it, but nothing was there. She didn't know if the creature was waiting for her to react to its presence, or if it was trying to determine why she'd all of a sudden become so bold. She grew tired of waiting. This presence had nearly scared her friend to death the first night and almost gotten her killed, and she wasn't going to rest until she knew what it was and what it wanted.

"Why don't you show yourself?" Lysette yelled into the darkness.

After a moment of silence, a voice replied from the same direction Lysette felt the presence, "Why should I?"

"Are you afraid to reveal yourself to me? Is that why you hide in the shadows?"

"You are no one to question me."

"Well I think differently," Lysette smugly replied.

"We are all entitled to our opinions."

"I will not let you continue to interfere."

"I am but a mere observer."

"Observer of what? Why are you here?" she wanted answers.

"That is none of your concern," the voice replied.

"The Gods do not take interference lightly."

"How do you know what the Gods take lightly? I do recall a time when you feared what they would do to you for your failure in allowing the chosen one to be turned. You know only of what the Gods tell you. I am sure you do not believe they have trusted you with all of their knowledge."

What the voice said was true; she'd had to face the Gods after Gedeon had confessed to bringing Nicolay across. She'd always thought the Gods withheld information, but she was just the messenger between the two worlds. It was not within her power to question the Gods.

"How do you know of the God's wishes?" Lysette was beginning to think this creature was sent to spy for one side or another.

"Again, I am here as an observer."

"What are you supposed to be observing?"

The presence laughed at her question. "I grow weary of your interrogation."

"Don't you dare walk away!"

Lysette let the anger engulf her. She opened herself up to all of the power bestowed upon her as the Mayan Goddess of Life and Death. She dropped her human form and stood before the creature hiding in the shadows as her true Goddess form. She hovered slightly above the ground, surrounded by an orb of light. Sensing the creature was about to retreat, she thrust her power in all directions. It pierced through the trees and wrapped around the hidden figure. She couldn't see its face clearly, but she now saw where it stood.

"Now, I will ask you again," she slowly but confidently approached the shadow, "Why are you here?"

The figure closed the distance between them, then walked right through her. It continued to walk towards the house, speaking to her as it walked away, "Your power is undoubtedly strong; however, it only affects the living or the dead. You cannot control what I am," it turned around and thrust a wave of power at her. Then it was gone.

The wave of power struck her with a force she'd never before encountered, causing her to gasp for breath. She drew her power back, creating a shield. It was just barely enough to allow her to breath. Lysette feared if this was just a taste of this creature's power, she was in way over her head. There were few if any creatures whose power matched or surpassed hers, save for the Gods. She wondered now if one of them had become a rogue. She'd have to keep closer watch on the events as they unfolded to ensure this creature remained just the messenger that he'd said he was.

CHAPTER THIRTEEN

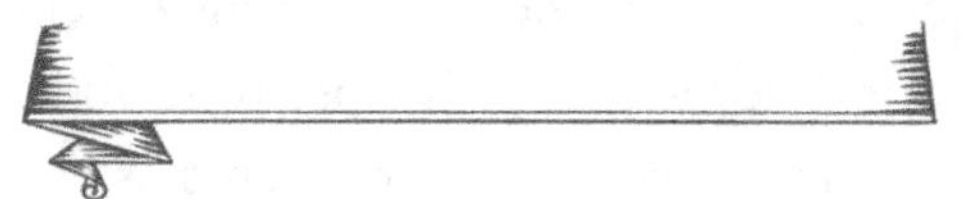

THEY DROVE A RELATIVELY short distance after leaving the plantation. The driver turned right onto the main road and headed towards Savannah. Dakota stared up into the night sky. The stars above twinkled like little lights against the pitch black cloak of night. She thought about asking the driver what their destination was, then decided against it. Tonight was going to be an adventure. She didn't want to ruin the surprise, so she sat quietly thinking about the previous night. She could almost feel Nicolay's arms wrapped around her. The thought of his touch calmed all of her fears. He'd understand her, just as she understood him.

Dakota relaxed as the driver pulled into one of Savannah's many marinas. He pulled in front of a set of docks and stopped the car. Picking up the phone, he placed a call and proceeded to get out. He walked around to the rear passenger door and opened it for her. Offering her his hand, he helped her from the car. By the time he'd closed the door, Nicolay took his last steps from the pier.

"I see you made it safely," he took her hand and placed a light kiss on the back.

Dakota stood there speechless. Before her stood the most gorgeous man she had ever laid eyes on. He'd opted to let his hair loose for the night. It blew lightly in the wind. He reminded her of the men on the front of romance novels, except he had clothes on. All sorts of seductive thoughts crossed her mind and she began to blush.

"Modest. I like that in a woman."

Quickly changing the subject, Dakota asked, "Are we going on a boat ride?"

"If you can call my Bertram a boat, then the answer is yes. Come, the night awaits us."

As he led her to his vessel, she looked at the other boats in the marina with awe. She'd never been this close to so many private yachts in her life. When she was younger, her parents used to bring her and Dayton to the river in Savannah to watch the barges and fishing boats come in and out. She'd imagined there were just as many private boats in Savannah as there were industrial barges, but she'd had no idea there were marinas like this so close to her. She tried to count the boats as they walked past, but after sixty, she gave up the task and just enjoyed the sound of the water lapping gently against the dock as some of the smaller boats headed for the river. Their pace slowed as they approached what she assumed was Nicolay's boat.

"Welcome to one of my homes away from home."

He scooped Dakota into his arms as he walked up the pier and stepped on deck. He lowered her to the deck, holding her tightly in his arms. A shallow breath was all he needed to smell the sweetness of her. The rich aroma of blood and patchouli mixed with the moisture in the air created an intoxicating cocktail that Nicolay knew he'd be fighting to resist all night.

"Ready to spend the night at sea?"

He looked down at her as she smiled back up at him.

"How do you know I don't get sea sick?"

"Well if you do, I guess it just means I'll have to take care of you now, doesn't it?"

"Maybe," giving him a seductive look, Dakota slipped away from his grasp and walked towards the front of the boat.

Nicolay turned and instructed the captain they were ready to go, then he joined Dakota.

"We might want to go below when he speeds up. Wouldn't want you out here soaked all night; or, wait a minute, maybe I would," he said with a devilish grin. The look on his face said he'd actually enjoy having her out there soaking wet. It'd be an excuse to get her out of her clothes.

"Everything's so calm out here," Dakota took one last look at the marina before they headed below deck.

"It is quite peaceful. I try to come out here at least once a week," Nicolay stared out across the bow of the yacht as they turned and headed out to the river, "Not even the gulls are out. I get a lot of thinking done out here on the water."

"What do you think about?" she asked with curiosity in her voice. She'd watched him become more distant, as if caught up in his thoughts.

"Life, love, loneliness," he gently took her hand, "Come, your dinner's getting cold."

He led her to the stairs and she followed him down. Beneath the main deck, the spacious yacht remained amazingly calm. She felt them increasing in speed, but the cabin stayed relatively stable. She looked around, taking the time to adjust to their quaint surroundings.

"What would you like to drink with your dinner?"

"I'm not sure. What am I eating and what do you have?" Dakota had forgotten she'd only had a quick bowl of fruit all day. The hunger snuck up on her at the mention of food.

"You're having baked salmon, black beans and wild rice with fry bread. I have red and white wine, green tea, and I believe there is some soda in the fridge. So what will it be?"

"Red wine," she replied.

"Red wine it is," he proceeded to fill two glasses with it. He handed one to Dakota and then began to prepare a plate for her.

"So, I'm dining alone?"

"Yes and no. I'll be here with you so you'll have company, but I can no longer stomach solid food."

Nicolay intentionally kept his back to her, hoping she didn't ask if he'd fed tonight. He found drinking blood a necessity, not a pleasure, and he didn't want to have to talk about it on their first date. He allowed his mind to wonder for a moment if she'd be sweet like a fruity wine, or strong like merlot. He quickly shook the thought from his mind as he returned to the table.

Dakota closed her eyes as the first bite of salmon melted on her tongue. A soft "ummm" escaped from her throat, drawing Nicolay's attention from her soft lips down to her neck. He smelled the sweet aroma of her. He was almost able to taste the essence flowing through her veins.

Quickly drawing his attention back to the lips, now coated with a sheen of butter, he asked, "What do you think?"

Dakota wasn't quite ready to speak. She took another moment to savor the flavor of the fish against her tongue before allowing the warmth of the food in her mouth to be invaded by the cool cabin air.

"This is wonderful. Please tell me you didn't cook this," she couldn't believe how tender and moist the salmon was. Before he could answer, she broke off another piece and placed it in her mouth.

"Just because I can no longer stomach solid food does not mean I cannot cook," he sounded just a tad bit offended, though he hadn't meant for it to come out that way.

"I didn't mean it like that; it's just, I've never tasted anything so wonderful in my life. If the rest of the meal is as good as the fish, I'm not going to be any good to you after I finish."

She'd thought she would feel awkward eating in front of him, but he'd made her feel comfortable by not staring and by distracting her. The food tasted so good, she was tempted to scoop it all into her mouth at one time. She somehow managed to remember her manners and eat small bites. She took her time, savoring each morsel as the aroma entered her nose and traveled to her other senses, warming her from the inside out.

"Eat as much as you like and enjoy it. It's not often I get to cook for a beautiful woman, and it is nice to know someone appreciates my cooking. If you give me the opportunity, I'll cook for you whenever you like."

"Where'd you learn to cook like this?"

"For a time, I resided in Brazil. I met someone there, a chef, who taught me everything I know about preparing a delicious meal for a special lady."

"Does that mean you speak Portuguese?"

Dakota wanted for so long to travel out of the country, but fear of being in a strange place kept her close to home. She settled for watching documentaries and the Travel Channel to quench her need to explore. Her psychic gift made it very difficult to live in her current state of minimal contact with the outside world, so she didn't even bother with trying to go out to some exotic land. Maybe if things worked out between them, she'd get the chance to travel the world.

"A beleza da rosa pales na comparação à vida em seus olhos a paixãoem sua respiração e o amor em seu coração. Eu prometo-lhe minha vida sempre e somente a morte peça nos."

The words were music to her ears. They rolled from his tongue naturally. He'd have had to live there for quite some time to be able to fluently speak the language without it sounding learned. She even detected the slightest bit of an accent when he spoke.

"Are you going to tell me what you said in English?"

"I said 'the beauty of the rose pales in comparison to the life in your eyes, the passion in your breath, and the love in your heart. I pledge my life to you always and only death will part us.'"

Dakota blushed. She didn't know how to take his last comment. She was so new at dating and this was the first man she'd ever had interest in. She wanted so much to believe him, but she still remembered what Lysette had told her. There were a lot of men out there willing to do anything or say anything to get what they wanted. Dakota decided to just wait and see how much he really meant those words. She still hadn't explained to him her secret, but before the night was over she'd see if he still wanted to be a part of her life.

"Is Portuguese the only other language you speak?"

"*Lo sfarfallamento delle stelle nel ballo del cielo di notte come lelucciole molto piccole nei vostri occhi.*"

"Italian?" Dakota thought she recognized some of the words, but the accent and diction made her sure it was Italian.

"Very good. It means, 'the flickering of the stars in the night sky dance like tiny fireflies in your eyes.'"

Again Dakota blushed. If he kept this up, she'd be as bright as a fire engine before the night was over.

"Any others?"

"Quite a few. What about you?"

"I can speak enough Spanish to get me to a bathroom or the police station; otherwise I am at a complete loss when it comes to other languages. Foreign languages weren't very important to me in high school. I figured what's the point; I never planned on using them, so why learn."

"You've never wanted to visit another country or see the world? You've never wanted to see what other cultures were like?"

"I never said that," she lowered her eyes, "My situation is complicated. It's hard for me to go to public places close to home. I have no idea what would happen if I traveled to some other country."

"And what is it about your situation that makes this so difficult?"

Dakota knew where this was going, and she was glad to finally be able to tell him about her gift. She was prepared to accept his judgment if he decided it was more than he could handle.

"How much further out are we going to go?"

If she was about to reveal her secret, she wanted to be outside among the stars. She'd always found the night comforting and she needed that right now.

"We can stop here if you like."

"That'd be nice."

"Finish your dinner and meet me up on the deck."

Nicolay stood, wine in hand, and disappeared up the stairs. He'd deliberately left her alone, giving her the time and space she needed to gather her thoughts. When he'd asked about her situation, he'd noticed the immediate change in her heart rate and breathing. She was anxious to get this over with, as if she dreaded having to reveal this side of her, but he didn't know why. She seemed so afraid to tell him. And the way she'd looked at him was troubling.

Dakota took a long cleansing breath. This was the moment she had anticipated since she'd left the club last night. Staring down at the little bit of food left on her plate, she no longer had an appetite. Above her was a man whom she had a growing interest in. He too had his own secrets and maybe, just maybe, because of that he'd be more understanding of hers.

CHAPTER FOURTEEN

DAKOTA STEPPED ONTO the deck and searched for Nicolay. He sat on the bow waiting for her. Had it not been for the slight wind causing waves in the water, the yacht would have been completely still in the water. He reached his hand out to her, beckoning her to come to him. Dakota initially hesitated, not sure what to expect. She didn't know why, but something seemed different about him tonight. Maybe it was her fear of his reaction to what she was going to tell him. She took a deep breath and slowly walked over to where he sat.

"I won't bite. I promise."

He wrapped his fingers around hers and drew her close. Gazing down into her beautiful almond shaped brown eyes he almost lost himself. He could smell her, the scent of patchouli, over the smell of the sea. He swung them around so they sat on the bow with her resting comfortably between his legs. She leaned back against his chest taking in what might possibly be their last few moments together.

Nicolay held her close, running his hands up and down her arms. His touch seemed to soothe her and he felt her letting go of her anxiety. He'd let her tell him when she was ready. For now, he'd just enjoy the feel of her body next to his. She fit perfectly in his arms, her body melding perfectly with his. He closed his eyes and inhaled her, internalizing her smell, forcing it to be burned into his memory, so even when she was away he could still be close to her.

She shifted ever so slightly in his lap and he knew the time had come. She was ready to reveal her secret to him and he was prepared to accept anything she thought might tear them apart. He'd never let anything come between him and the one he loved ever again. He'd done that once and the memories still haunted him.

"I'm ready," the words sounded timid, but Dakota knew she was only prolonging the inevitable.

"Then, what is it you wish to share with me?" Nicolay asked.

"I think it will be easier if I show you."

Nicolay looked at her curiously. He'd expected her to just tell him. Now he wondered what it was, that she thought it easier to just show him.

Dakota placed her hands on the cool fiberglass below them. She opened her mind to the images that would, without a doubt reveal themselves to her. She felt the energy moving through her. It swelled deep within her, moving from her head and toes to her center. It then shifted, pouring itself through her veins, traveling up through her shoulders down to her arms and then out through her fingertips. She pushed the power out, knowing it would gather its strength and push its way back into her. Her aura shifted, allowing the portal to reopen and her mind to accept the visions of the past.

Nicolay felt the air around them change. It grew dense, so thick he felt the need to try to cut the air with his hand. Dakota began to gasp for air as if she was suffocating. Then her breathing stabilized and she began to speak to him.

"This yacht has a troubled history. Over there," she pointed to the right side of the bow, "there is an older man, maybe in his late fifties. He's got short blond hair, but it's not natural. He's short and a little pudgy."

The man turned around and then stepped back off of the edge of the boat into the water. Immediately, Dakota screamed.

Nicolay grabbed her. She had almost gotten away from him. She was trying to go to the spot she had pointed to, like she was trying to reach the man her mind saw. He didn't see anything, but he had an idea what was going on. He pulled her back to him, gently rocking her, trying his best to calm her.

"Dakota? Dakota, can you hear me? What is it that you see?"

"He jumped! Oh my God he jumped!" she cried hysterically.

Nicolay tried to calm her. He knew the history of the yacht, knew that one of the previous owners had drowned, but he'd had no idea the man had committed suicide. It was all clear to him now. He understood why her life had been so hard and so isolated. He understood now she must be a touch clairvoyant. If he'd known, he'd never have agreed to let her show him her gift. He cradled her in his arms, making sure no part of her touched the boat. He wanted to protect her, to protect her mind from any other images she may see.

"Dakota. Listen to the sound of my voice. Dakota, can you hear me?"

She slowly responded to him, though she was still crying, "Nicolay?" she looked up at him as if she didn't really recognize him.

"Can you shut them out? The images, can you shut them out?" Nicolay hoped she could, but he was prepared to hold her on the trip back if necessary.

"I, I don't know?" she was beginning to shake uncontrollably. He needed to get her calm or he was afraid she might go into shock.

"Can you try baby? For me, can you try?"

"I-I don't think I can," her head shook frantically.

"Dakota, Dakota listen to me," Nicolay placed both of her palms on his face, "Remember last night. Remember you tried to read me but you couldn't. Concentrate. Try to read me now."

She tried, tried as hard as she could to focus, to shake the image of the man jumping over the side, but she couldn't.

"I can't! I can't!"

She fought him, trying to escape the image. It played over and over again in her mind. He cradled her closer and lifted them both from the bow. As he rushed below, he instructed the captain to get them back as quickly as possible and to notify his driver to be waiting for them on the pier. He knew now what he had to do. He needed to distract her and he had an idea as to how to do it. He just hoped he was right.

Nicolay rushed her to the lower level of the yacht and into the master bedroom. Estimating how far out they had come, he knew it would be at least twenty minutes before they were back at the docks. She may hate him after what he was about to do, but he needed to snap her out of the spiral of memories she'd been sucked into. He sat down on the bed with her still cradled in his arms and quickly but carefully undressed her until all she wore was her bra and panties. She'd calmed down some and she was no longer fighting him. Instead, she just stared out into space. He'd called her name a number of times with no response.

After undressing her, he carried her to the shower and turned the water on. He stepped into the ice cold water fully dressed with her in his arms and she immediately responded. She looked back up at him and really saw him.

Dakota stared into those beautiful auburn eyes of his. She watched his hair beginning to stick to his face as the water weighed it down. She wanted so much to reach up and touch him, but fear held her captive. The memories still lingered in her mind and she wasn't quite ready to risk accidentally touching the walls. She wanted the memory gone, but she wanted even more to kiss Nicolay's lips.

He rested his head on the shower wall and closed his eyes. She felt so good in his arms, and watching the water glisten down her body was making him weak in the knees. He closed his eyes, attempting to calm his lust. He wanted her so much. He wanted to touch her all over, to savor all of her, to be inside of her.

He felt her shift in his arms. She wrapped her arms around his neck and began to pull him down to her. Nicolay kept his eyes closed. He knew if he looked at her he'd lose what little control he had left, and that was not an option. She was vulnerable and he didn't want to rush her. As he felt her warm breath against his lips, he promised himself he'd only allow this one kiss. He needed to do this, but most of all, he felt she needed to do this.

As their lips touched for the first time, Dakota felt a wave of calm surge through her body. She relaxed as Nicolay lowered her to the floor. The shower was small, not designed for more than one person, so they pressed so close to each other she could feel his body stiff against her. She knew what his body wanted, but she was afraid to answer the call. She slowly pulled away from him as a faint sigh escaped her lips.

Nicolay looked down at her and asked, "Are you all right?"

Dakota finally let her eyes open.

"Um hum," was all she could manage. He still held her in his arms, and she could still feel the coolness of his breath against her lips even though they were no longer touching.

"I'm sorry," Dakota said.

"About what? You did nothing wrong. Actually, I am the one who should apologize to you. I knew the history of this yacht. I should have warned you. I had an idea of what your gift was after what happened last night. I never meant for you to have to see that."

"No, I should have just told you. I knew the possibilities of my abilities, and I've seen worse from people. I just didn't expect what I saw. I wanted so much to help him, to save him. Sometimes my mind can't separate memory from reality."

She laid her head against his chest, needing to be close to him but not sure why.

"We should get out of here before you get sick," Nicolay said.

He turned off the water and scooped Dakota back into his arms. As they entered the master bedroom again, Dakota realized she no longer had her clothes on. She looked up at him startled.

"I didn't want you to have to ride back home in wet clothes," he pulled a towel from under the sink and wrapped it around her shoulders, "I'll wait outside while you dress."

Then he exited the room, leaving Dakota standing in the middle it shaken and staring at the closed door. She peeled the wet underwear from her body and dried off. She slipped the sweater over her head and stepped into her slacks. The memories had subsided, but she wasn't sure if touching anything would cause them to come rushing back. After taking a moment to unwrap her hair and use the damp scarf to tie it in a ponytail she called out to Nicolay.

She sat on the bed, her hands resting in her lap. She knew he was standing just on the other side of the door. She could tell he hated to leave her, even if it was for just a few minutes for her to get dressed. He looked worried and she was sure he was still blaming himself for her psychic episode.

He closed the door behind him, keeping his distance. Dakota wasn't sure if it was because of her episode or because of the kiss they'd shared in the shower.

"You're all wet," Dakota commented. She'd been staring at him, watching the water drip from the waves in his hair.

"It is not a problem."

"Still, you shouldn't be walking around in wet clothes. It leaves nothing to the imagination," Dakota smiled deviously at him. She could see his body was still glad to see her even if his mind was focused on making sure she was really all right.

Nicolay turned slightly red as he realized what Dakota was referring to, "If you'll hand me a pair of pants from the closet above your head I am sure I can rectify the situation."

"I'm not sure if it is safe for me to touch anything," Dakota was being extremely careful. She didn't want a replay of the earlier events.

"Sorry. I shouldn't have asked. I'll get it," he reached around her to the small closet cut into the wall next to the bed and pulled out a pair of linen pants, "I'll be right back."

She watched as he entered the bathroom and closed the tiny door behind him. She closed her eyes and tried to remember what it felt like to lay against his cool body. His arms were strong, but he'd held her with such care. She licked her lips, remembering how it had felt when they first came in contact with his. They'd shared a magical moment. She felt a tingling run through her body. Even then, she knew what they would share would be magnificent.

Nicolay stepped from the bathroom in just the dry pair of pants and a towel wrapped around his neck. He'd tried unsuccessfully to towel dry his hair.

"You want me to pull that back for you?" she asked, pointing at the stray locks hung over each shoulder.

"If you don't mind," Nicolay approached her and knelt with his back to her. Dakota gathered all of the stray locks and braided them into one long braid down his back. She hadn't noticed until then how thick his hair was.

"There, all done."

He turned to look up into her beautiful brown eyes, "Thank you. Now, are you sure you are well?"

"Yeah. So now do you understand why I spend so much time away from civilization?"

He nodded, indicating he did truly understand, "May I ask you a question?"

"I guess," she replied.

"Are the images always so troublesome?"

"Sometimes there aren't even memories. Sometimes, I just get a feeling, like if I touch something someone throws in a fit of rage or a child's favorite toy. The objects may contain residue of intense human emotions. That's usually what I pick up on."

"Do you get them all of the time?"

"If I am not protected, yes. Remember Lysette, the girl I came to the club with?" he nodded his confirmation, "Well, she's a witch, really good one if you ask me. She wrote a shielding spell we use when we go out. It usually wears off within twenty-four to forty-eight hours."

"Did you use it tonight?"

"No. We cast it near six last night, so it should last me a few more hours."

Nicolay was curious. He wanted to know as much as possible about Dakota's gift so he wouldn't make the same mistake he'd made tonight, "How long have you known about your gift?"

"As long as I can remember. The images became overwhelming around the age of, I'd say, six. My first years of school were hell until Lysette wrote the spell."

"So how long have you two been using this spell?"

"Since I was about eight or nine I guess."

Nicolay found it interesting that Lysette had been able to write such a powerful spell at such a young age, "And how old was Lysette when she wrote the spell?"

"Umm," Dakota thought for a moment before she answered, "Maybe eleven or twelve. Why?"

"No reason, just curious."

"Well, her mother was a witch and her father came from a long line of medicine men, so she was raised in a house full of worldly magic."

"I see," Nicolay felt the yacht slowing. He figured they must be pulling into the marina, "Ready to go back up top? I think we're back."

"I guess, but I still don't want to touch anything."

"Anything?" he looked saddened by her comment.

Dakota reached her hand out to him as she stood, "Well, almost anything."

CHAPTER FIFTEEN

AS NICOLAY LED DAKOTA up the stairs, the scent of the night wrapped around them. The wind seeped through the pores of Dakota's sweater. Hers nipples hardened as the air rubbed against her unprotected skin. She hovered beneath Nicolay's arm trying to escape the chill. He pulled her closer, covering her head with his arms to protect her from the breeze.

They pulled into the dock and the captain anchored the yacht in its designated place next to a sailboat at the end of the pier.

"My driver is waiting. Would you like for me to escort you back to your home?"

"Is there time?" Dakota asked gazing up at him.

"Yes," he replied.

"Then I think I'd like that very much."

He scooped her up and stepped onto the pier. They walked back to shore in silence. When they reached the car, the driver already had the door open, waiting for them. Nicolay helped her in and then slid in beside her. He instructed the driver to ensure the heat was on and that they'd be returning to the Naverro Plantation.

As they began their journey, Dakota huddled close. Her body and her hair were dry, but she still felt a slight chill from not having on any underwear.

"I guess I should thank you for undressing me before you plunged me into that ice cold water."

"It was my pleasure," she was warm against his chest. Nicolay could smell the slightest scent of patchouli from her hair.

"I'm sure it was. But the fact that you left my underwear on really told me a lot about you tonight."

"Oh really? And what exactly did the gesture say about me?" Nicolay asked.

"For one, that you're considerate. I mean, you could have taken advantage of the situation. You had the perfect excuse to get me out of all of my clothes."

"I do not wish to rush you. I don't want anything to ruin the possibility of us being together. You know, I was afraid I had ruined my chance with you at the club. I'm not sure what it is about you that makes me lose almost all of my control."

"You didn't lose your control tonight," Dakota replied looking up at him.

"No, but I came close, especially when you kissed me. That was a pleasant surprise."

"Can I tell you something?"

"As long as you are not about to tell me to go away, yes."

"I don't think I'll ever be able to tell you to go away."

"Don't be so sure of that. I can be very protective of what I consider mine," he looked away then, not wanting her to see the hurt in his eyes, "I've been told at times I can be a downright tyrant."

He'd had one lover before tell him that. She'd said it to spite him, and he knew it, but he never stopped wondering if there was some underlying truth to what she'd said.

"I could see you being possessive, I mean what man isn't? But a tyrant, never."

"Only time will tell if you'll change your mind. Now, what was it you wanted to tell me?" he placed a gentle kiss on her forehead as he changed the subject.

"Actually, it is a confession."

"Going to reveal a dirty little secret?" Nicolay asked.

"No, but I want you to know the kiss we shared was the most wonderful kiss I have ever experienced. I've never had my breath taken away."

Nicolay pulled her closer to him so her cheek rested right above his heart, "If you'll let me, I can make sure there will be many more breathtaking moments in the future."

"I think I'd like that."

"Then it will be so. I'll make sure of it."

They rode the rest of the way in silence. Dakota took the time to relive the events of the night. She was glad her little episode hadn't scared Nicolay away. He'd gotten the chance to see what happened when she lost all control over her gift. It wasn't quite how she wanted to reveal herself to him, but he'd seen what was probably her worst episode in a long time and he was able to think fast to calm her mind. If he'd been anyone else, he'd have panicked, but because he'd had his own battles to fight, he helped her through what could have been a severely damaging mental episode.

Dakota looked up at him again as they made the turn onto the long stretch of driveway leading up to the house. He really had no idea how grateful she was that he was able to bring her back from the downward spiral she'd felt her mind falling into.

"What are you thinking?" he asked. He'd felt her stir beneath his arms. He'd waited for her to speak when she looked up at him, but when she didn't he'd felt the need to find out what was on her mind.

"You," her face stayed serious.

"What about me?"

"My little secret. At least for now," Dakota replied. As they approached the house, Dakota noticed the light on in her bedroom. "I see Lysette waited up for me."

"She lives with you?"

"Only when she's too lazy to drive home. Actually, now that I think about it, lately she's been too tired just about every night. Maybe I need to start charging her rent," Dakota was joking on the outside, but in the back of her mind she did wonder why lately Lysette had been spending a lot of nights at the Naverro Plantation. She'd have to remember to bring it up tomorrow.

The car pulled to a stop in front of the wooden staircase leading to the front door. Out of habit, Dakota reached for the handle to open the door. Nicolay caught her hand intertwining her fingers with his.

"The driver will get it. Besides, we still do not know if it is safe for you to touch anything unfamiliar."

The driver opened the door and Nicolay slid out. He offered his hand to Dakota and helped her out of the car, making sure she didn't touch anything other than him. He escorted her up the stairs and to the front door.

"Regardless of what happened, I had a really nice time tonight," he was genuine with his words. It had been too long since he'd gone out on anything resembling a date, and he'd never had one as eventful as this one.

"So did I. Will I see you tomorrow night?"

"Yes," Nicolay replied. "Shall I pick you up after dusk?"

"Don't you have to work?"

"My dear, I am the boss. My manager can handle things while I am away. That is what I pay them for."

"Then after dusk will be fine. I'll see you tomorrow night," Dakota wanted to kiss him again, but she was afraid. She'd already asked him out on a date and then kissed him. She thought it inappropriate to do it again. She hoped he could see the longing in her eyes and kiss her.

Nicolay watched the emotions dance across her face. He knew she wanted to kiss him. He tasted her longing. He reached down, drawing her as close as possible to his body. Then, he leaned down and claimed the lips that so desperately called out to him. She tasted of butter and spice and wine. He wanted to suck the flavors from her lips and she offered him the privilege.

He slowly drew away, still savoring the softness of her lips, the warmth of her breath, the hunger lying just below the surface waiting to boil over.

"I should be going," he whispered only inches away from her mouth, "Dawn will be upon us soon."

"I'll be anxiously awaiting your return."

"Make sure you lock the door," Nicolay stepped back, putting a little room between them.

"I will. Goodnight," Dakota leaned back in, wanting to once again taste the softness of his lips, but he pulled her to him, giving her a comforting hug.

"Don't you mean good day?"

Dakota wrapped her arms around his body, holding him close, wanting to be a part of him in ways she could only imagine.

"Good day then," she whispered into his chest.

He released his hold on her and stepped away. She unknowingly tempted him and he needed to put space between them. Regardless, dawn was quickly approaching and he needed to return to the safety of his lair before the first light of day pierced the darkness.

Dakota inserted her key in the door. The sound of the lock echoed through the silence of the night. She pushed the door open and stepped through the threshold. When she turned to close the door she saw Nicolay walking towards the car. He stopped, feeling her watching him and turned.

"I'll be back sooner than you know. Now close and lock the door."

She did just that, leaning with her back to the door, not wanting to see him get into the car and drive away.

As Nicolay approached the car he sensed something powerful in the air. He stopped, taking a moment to scan the area around the house. He searched with his power to detect whatever it was out there. He felt it wrap around something in front of the house, not far from where he stood, but then it was gone and all was calm. He turned back to the house to see if Dakota had been watching him. He was relieved when he saw no sign of her.

"I sensed it too. Whatever it was, it was here when I came to pick her up," the driver said to Nicolay.

He looked back at the man and then slid into the back seat of the car. The driver closed the door and climbed into the driver's seat. Assured that whatever it was was gone, Nicolay instructed the driver to return him to The Apache. Neither spoke a word as he left Dakota behind. Dawn was very near and all Nicolay could do was hope whatever the thing out there was it wouldn't harm her while he was dead to the world.

"SO, HOW WAS YOUR DATE?" Lysette was perched at the top of the stairs, looking down at Dakota as she stood with her back to the door, apparently reliving some special moment she and Nicolay had just shared.

"Damn, can I get in the house good?" she knew Lysette was going to be waiting for her. It was her first date and she knew her friend wanted to know everything. She climbed the staircase and walked right past her.

Dakota had made it only a few steps past her when Lysette spoke, "Didn't you have a bra on when you left here?"

Dakota turned around and rolled her eyes at her, then she continued to the master bedroom. Lysette's footsteps echoed throughout the house as she stomped her way on the hardwood floors to Dakota's bedroom. When she entered the room, Dakota was sitting on the bed playing with Dinner, her pet chinchilla.

"Are you going to answer my question young lady? What happened to your bra?"

Lysette slipped into mother mode without realizing it. She was very protective of Dakota and rightfully so, considering she was the gatekeeper to the realm of all evil. Lysette hadn't yet told her or Dayton of their true purpose in life, and since Dayton was gone, someone needed to make sure Dakota didn't let her wild side overshadow her common sense.

"The same thing that happened to my panties," was the only reply Dakota was going to give her friend.

She wished Lysette and Dayton would stop treating her like she was a two year old. She was a grown woman. Nicolay had seen that tonight, and she had finally realized herself that as a grown woman she wanted the companionship of a man in her life. She needed to start making decisions for herself and stop worrying about what Dayton and Lysette thought. It was time she threw caution to the wind and starting living her life on her own terms, and if her brother and best friend couldn't understand that, then to hell with them.

"Dakota Calise Naverro. I never expected you to become a hoochie after one date," Lysette fumed inside. She did all she could to hide it from Dakota.

Dakota had gone out on her first date and made the biggest mistake of her life, sleeping with a man she knew nothing about. Lysette was nearly heartbroken. She'd tried to protect her as much as she could, encouraging her to become a woman while still keeping her safely under the wing of someone with experience in life, but she never thought her friend would go out and have sex on her first date.

"Are you done judging me?"

Dakota put Dinner down on the bed to let him run around, chasing one of his toys. She watched Lysette run through her assumptions. She was sure her friend envisioned she'd gone out with Nicolay, thought she'd fallen in love and dropped her panties the first chance she'd got. Dakota was hurt that her friend thought so little of her, but at this point she no longer cared. She wanted Lysette to understand how she and Dayton had smothered her for far too long. She'd gotten a taste of real life and she liked it. From now on, she decided she'd make her own decisions. She didn't want to hurt her friend or her brother, but she needed to spread her wings.

"I'm not judging you, I'm just disappointed. I'd hoped you'd wait until you found the right person."

"Disappointed at what? What is it you think I did tonight?" Dakota asked crossing her arms over her chest and giving Lysette the evil eye.

"First you come in here with no bra on, and then tell me your panties are gone too. What am I supposed to think?"

"You're supposed to trust that you, Dayton, and my parents have raised me right and that I'd never sleep with a guy I just met," she laced the words with hurt. Lysette needed to have more faith in her. Dakota had been sheltered all of her life but she had common sense.

"Well if you didn't sleep with him, then where are your bra and panties?" Lysette asked.

"If you're done with your assumptions, I'll tell you."

"Well, by all means madam queen, enlighten me."

"What is it we forgot to do before I left tonight?"

Lysette played through the events of the evening. She remembered getting to the house and sensing something outside. She remembered Dakota getting dressed, being nervous and then leaving. Then it dawned on her what they'd forgotten.

"Oh my. I am so sorry. How could I have let you leave out of here without casting the spell? Did you have an episode?" Lysette had been so preoccupied with getting Dakota on her date so she could confront whatever it was lurking just beyond the house that she'd completely forgotten they needed to recast the shielding spell.

"In a way, yes, but I think the severity of it was due to what I saw more so than my mind being completely unprotected."

"Want to talk about it?" Lysette asked. Dakota usually felt better after she talked about what she saw.

"Not really. I saw something really horrible and I am not ready to relive it."

"That still doesn't explain what happened to your underwear," Lysette crossed her arms over her chest and tapped her foot, indicating she wanted an answer and she wanted it now.

"Well, apparently I got caught in a loop in my mind. All I could see was the image. I tried to fight it, tried my best to push it out, but nothing worked. I felt my mind being drawn under, like I was drowning but not physically."

Dakota turned from her friend. It had been a long time since she'd experienced her mind being sucked under by some force she had no control over. "I could hear Nicolay calling my name but I couldn't respond. I could see him, feel his touch but I was powerless to do anything. I started to slip away from myself. I was being pulled further and further into darkness. He tried to get me to read him but I couldn't. I just couldn't do it. The next thing I knew, I was in his arms in only my underwear in a cold shower."

Dakota plopped back down on the bed, not knowing when she'd first stood and began pacing. The feeling still seemed too real for her. She wrapped her arms around her body, trying to ward off the darkness pushing to resurface from deep within her. She rocked back and forth, cradling herself. Lysette sat next to her, pulling her into a hug, gently rocking them both until she stopped shivering.

"So, he was honorable in his intentions?" Lysette asked after she was sure Dakota had composed herself and was ready to continue.

"Completely," she stood, drawn by the light of the nearly full moon, and made her way to the picture window on the other side of the room, "He was the perfect gentleman, even after I kissed him," Dakota stared out into the night, watching the shadow of a lone owl cross through the solidity of the moon.

"You kissed him?"

"Yes. And it was the most wonderful thing," she raised her hand to her lips and closed her eyes. She could still feel his lips against hers as if he were still there sharing the moment with her. The memory caused her body to react. She felt her nipples hardening and her body tensing with need. She needed him to hold her, to comfort her, to be there with her when she became overwhelmed with the visions.

Lysette decided to give Dakota some time to adjust to the feelings she was experiencing. She remembered what first love felt like and it was the most wonderful feeling in the world. She wanted Dakota to have the time she needed to enjoy the feelings.

"You've had a long night. Try to get some rest. We'll talk more in the morning."

Rising from the bed, Lysette walked to the door. Dakota didn't respond, so she decided to just leave her to her thoughts. She pulled the door closed behind her as she exited the room.

CHAPTER SIXTEEN

DAKOTA WOKE TO THE phone ringing too close to her head. Picking up the receiver, she greeted the person on the other end of the line.

"Hello."

"Lysette keeping you up all night?" the male voice replied.

"Hey Day. Naw, just tired. Had an episode last night." Dakota yawned and stretched as she turned over to gaze out of the window. She watched the sun form a beautiful orange haze through the morning mist as it began its ascent into the early morning sky.

"You wanna talk about it?"

"Not really," Dakota looked at the clock on the nightstand and realized it was almost seven in the morning, which meant it was nearly four in the morning in Seattle.

"You up kinda early aren't you?"

"I couldn't sleep," Dayton paused, sensing what was coming. Dakota always knew what was bothering him, sometimes even before he discovered what it was.

"You felt it didn't you?" Dakota asked. Because she and Dayton were twins, they always seemed to have a mental connection. Whenever she was stressed or had an episode, Dayton was able to feel what was going on in her head. Sometimes he even experienced the same things she experienced.

"You know me too well," he wanted to know what was going on with his sister. For two days she'd been elusive, and with the episode last night he was beginning to worry more and more about her.

"I'm sorry Day. It's no big deal, just touched something I shouldn't have."

"I thought you and Lysette were using the shielding spell."

"We forgot last night," Dakota really didn't want to talk about last night and unless she changed the subject, she was sure Dayton was going to continue to push the issue, "Is that the only reason you called?"

Dayton thought about what she'd just asked him. She was once again avoiding him and he hated when she did that, but what could he do? She was an adult and it was about time he started treating her like one.

"I need you to do me a favor," he replied

"And what might that be?"

"Well since I don't know how much longer I am going to be out here, I need you to feed Coco and Turbo."

"Any critters left?" Dakota asked. She'd had to feed her brother's snakes on a number of occasions. Whenever he and the guys went camping she'd end up with feeding duty.

"No. You're going to have to go to the pet store to get some."

"When's the next time they need to eat?"

"Preferably sometime today. You know how Turbo gets when he's not fed."

"Yeah, just like his owner," Dakota allowed her snicker to escape.

"Oh so what are you saying? I get snippy when I don't eat?"

"Your words, not mine."

"Okay, Okay. I guess you're right. I can be an ass when I haven't eaten."

"Damn straight."

"Whatever. You can call the pet store before you go down there and tell them the critters are for me. They'll probably have them packed up and ready for you when you get there. Remember, Turbo gets the rabbit and Coco gets the two medium sized rats. And don't stare into their little faces. You know what happened last time you stared into one of those cute little furry faces."

"You're never going to let me live that down are you?" Dayton always teased Dakota about the one critter she'd thought too cute to feed to the snakes. They'd named him Dinner, and now he was her little pet.

"Not a chance."

"I guess I can handle that. Anything else?"

"Not that I can think of. Anything going on at the shop I should know about?" Dayton wasn't quite ready to get off of the phone. He missed hearing Dakota's voice and he wanted to feel closer to her for just a few minutes more.

"Wouldn't know. I didn't get the chance to go down there yesterday. I'm going to try to get some work done today after I run your errand."

"And how's Dinner?"

"Are you really concerned about Dinner or are you just trying to keep me on the phone?"

Dayton tried masking his true feelings but Dakota always saw right through him, "I just miss you."

"I know. But you'll be home soon. It's not like I'm going anywhere," Dakota missed him as much as he missed her, but she was glad to have had this time away from him. Especially since she'd met the first man in her life she was attracted to in *that* way.

"How did I ever let you talk me into this trip?"

"You didn't."

"Oh yeah that's right, I was forced into a corner."

"And I am so good at doing that to you. Now go get some sleep. I'll call you if I need you."

"Yes ma'am."

Before Dakota had the chance to reply, she heard the dial tone. Her brother was getting really good at making smart comments to her. She'd have to be quicker with her responses in the future.

Dakota really didn't have time to lie in bed and watch the sun rise, but she just couldn't force herself to get up. She pulled the covers tightly around her body and thought of her night with Nicolay. She'd never imagined she could be so comfortable in a man's arms. Her body melded to him perfectly as if they'd been poured from complementing molds. She couldn't wait to be in his embrace again.

Dakota slipped out of bed and started her day. She drew the sheer curtains back to reveal the most beautiful morning she'd ever witnessed. Since meeting Nicolay, she was more than glad to get her day started. The sooner it started, the sooner it would be over and the sooner she'd see him.

By the time she'd showered and dressed, she smelled breakfast cooking in the kitchen. Now she remembered why she never fussed about Lysette staying the night. If Lysette stayed, breakfast was a guarantee.

"GOOD MORNING DAKOTA," Lysette hadn't even turned around but she felt her friend standing in the kitchen doorway watching her.

"What's for breakfast?"

"The usual: bacon, eggs, French toast and fruit. You hungry?"

"Do you really need to ask?" Dakota took a seat at the kitchen table as Lysette finished cooking their meal.

She placed a plate of food in front of Dakota and then joined her at the table, "Now, you gonna tell me about the rest of your date?"

"There's not much else to tell. After he finally got me back into my right mind, he left me to dress and we came home."

"So what do you think of him?"

"He's a nice guy," she bit into a piece od bacon, her gaze drifting outside.

"Nice guy? All you can say is he's a nice guy?"

"What do you want from me? You want me to fall all over this guy after just one date?"

"No, but you can give me more than just 'he's a nice guy.'"

"Okaaaay..." Dakota replied bashfully, "I really like him. I mean really really like him."

She held a piece of fruit up to her lips but decided against biting into it, "I mean, he had the perfect chance to take advantage of me and he didn't. How many men would have passed up the opportunity?"

"Not many, believe me," Lysette understood her friend's apprehensions. She'd dated a number of men that only wanted one thing. She was glad Dakota had found a respectable one even if he had been dead for centuries.

"I know you've told me not to get my hopes up, but I think he might be the one."

"What makes you say that?"

"I don't know. He just seems to complete me. I feel like I have found a missing piece of myself. His touch alone is calming. It's kind of weird."

"Are you going out with him again?" Lysette already knew the answer. She could see it in Dakota's eyes.

"Yep. We have a date tonight."

"Where are you two going?"

"Ah damn, I forgot to ask."

"Well, I'm sure he'll call. So what do you have planned for the day?"

"Have to go to Savannah to get critters. After that I was going down to the shop. Wanna come?"

"Naw. I'm just gonna hang around here."

Dakota let out a small laugh, "You know, Nicolay asked if you lived with me."

"And what did you tell him?"

"With as much time you spend over here, I should be charging your behind rent."

"You know Dayton wouldn't hear of it."

"Hey, when he's not here I'm in charge."

"So what do I have to do to keep you from charging me rent?"

"Just keep cooking," Dakota swiped the last piece of bacon from her plate as she stood.

"Go start your day. I'll take care of these dishes," Lysette grabbed their plates and placed them in the sink.

"You are such a good friend," Dakota really meant it. Lysette was the best friend anyone could ask for.

"I know. Now go," Lysette shooed Dakota from the kitchen and began to clean the mess she'd made cooking.

CHAPTER SEVENTEEN

DAKOTA PICKED UP THE critters and stared on her way back to the plantation. In her mind she ran through the list of things she needed to do today. She needed to feed Dayton's snakes, she had two projects plus paperwork at the shop she needed to tend to, and she still had to figure out something to do with her hair and what to wear for her date tonight. It was then Dakota really appreciated all of the years she hadn't had time to worry about dating. If she didn't have to worry about her date tonight, she could probably get most of what was on her plate done.

As she passed mile marker sixteen she slowed. It was daytime and she felt safer. She remembered a couple of nights ago when something had jumped out in the road ahead of her in this very spot. She just had to make sure there was nothing strange lurking about. Scanning the area, she didn't see anything unusual. Maybe Lysette had been right, maybe it was just a deer.

Dakota turned onto her gravel driveway and made her way back to the house. She pulled in front of the stairs and got out with the boxes containing the critters in one hand. As she closed the door to the car, a strange feeling came over her. She looked around in all directions but didn't see anything. She had the feeling someone was watching her, but she couldn't figure out where it was coming from.

She quickly made her way to the front door and inserted the key. As she forced the door open, she tossed the box of critters onto the table by the door and slammed the door behind her. The sound of the lock sliding into place was comforting.

"What's your problem?" Lysette asked.

Dakota jumped at the sound of her friend's voice. She knew Lysette was there but her mind was still focusing on the feeling she'd just experience.

"Have you been outside today?" Dakota asked.

"No why?"

"I just got the creepiest feeling, like someone was watching me."

Lysette rushed to the window. Pulling the curtains back, she looked around to see if she saw anyone, "You sure you're not letting your imagination run away with you again?" Lysette continued to stare out the window.

"Ha ha, real funny. I'm going to check the security cameras," Dakota started walking back to the weapons room located on the side of the stairwell opposite the kitchen, "Can you grab that box and take it up to Day's room?"

"What's in it?"

"Dinner for his pets."

Lysette grabbed the box and headed upstairs. She'd forgotten about the security cameras Dayton had installed a couple of years ago. Hopefully Dakota would see someone and they could both figure out what was going on.

Ten minutes later, Lysette entered the weapons room in search of Dakota.

"See anything?"

"Hey come look at this."

She leaned over Dakota's shoulder and stared at the black and white image on the screen. The figure was blurry, but the outlines of the trees and even the car were crystal clear.

"What do you think it is?" Lysette asked.

"Hell if I know. Look," Dakota flipped through five or six other frames that she'd frozen.

Lysette leaned a little closer to get a better look, "It's in all of them. What are the dates on these?"

"The first one was just a few minutes ago. The second and third were from last night and the fourth one was from night before last."

"These are the only out of place images you see?" Lysette needed to be very careful. She hoped the cameras hadn't picked her up last night when she had confronted the creature hiding in the shadows.

"Yeah."

"Print them out and I'll take a closer look. If you want I can take them to a friend who is pretty good with digital pictures. Maybe he can clean them up and we can get a better look. I'll need the log file though."

Dakota popped in a disc and burned a copy of the video. She handed the disc to Lysette and stood, "I've got to go to the shop and get some work done. Can you take care of this and meet me back here around five?"

Lysette looked down at her watch. It was a little after noon. "That's cutting it kind of close. This guy has the top of the line equipment but I am not sure how long it will take to analyze this."

"Well, get what you can and meet me back here."

Lysette followed Dakota out of the room and to the garage door. Dakota tossed the Civic keys to her, "You might need these. I'll take the truck. See you in a few hours."

"Be careful."

"I should be telling you that. Remember, I'm the one carrying the concealed weapon."

Lysette watched as she climbed into the truck. She opened the garage door when Dakota started the engine. Dakota waved goodbye to her and pulled out of the garage, closing the door behind her.

CHAPTER EIGHTEEN

DAKOTA PULLED INTO the parking lot of Paradise, Inc. and shut off the engine. She just shook her head as she watched the hundred ten pound Rottweiler, Shasta, bolt from her spot in the shade to greet her master. As she exited the vehicle, Shasta panted by her side, waiting for her usual greeting of a pat on the head and belly rub.

"What's up you big lug?" Dakota said to her trusted friend.

After giving Shasta her belly rub, Dakota walked into the shop through the open bay doors. Kelsy was working diligently to bolt the handle bars on a motorcycle they needed to deliver by the end of next week. She looked around expecting to see the other two guys she worked with, but instead she saw no one else.

"Hey Kelsy, where are Kelly and Greg?"

"Do you really have to ask?" he shouted back, "They were supposed to be back hours ago with some parts."

Dakota was getting really tired of chasing after those two. The past few weeks they'd both been slacking. Their work was half done, and Dakota had to check behind them to make sure they'd paid attention to the little details. She'd talked to Dayton about it and he'd had a talk with Kelly and Greg, but Dakota knew when Dayton took this trip they'd try her.

"I'll handle them. Need any help?"

"Naw I got this. Some packages were delivered yesterday. They're in the storage room. I didn't know if you needed to inventory them so I just left them sealed."

"Thanks. What time you heading out today?"

"It won't be until late. I need to get this bike finished so I can start on the restoration project Dayton left."

"Cool. And Kelsy?"

"Yes ma'am."

"Thanks for not taking advantage of the situation. I mean, with Dayton gone and me missing work, I just want to let you know I appreciate you being here and working."

"That's what you pay me for."

"All right. Get back to work. And when the Bobsy twins get back, tell them I want to have a few words with them."

Kelsy smiled at her. He knew the few choice words Dakota had for his comrades. There'd be hell to pay, and Kelly and Greg were on the receiving end of the bill.

Dakota spent most of her day doing inventory and balancing the company books. Her little conference with Kelly and Greg had gone quite well as far as she was concerned. They both left her office with scowls, but she knew they wouldn't be coming in late, leaving early, or be missing ever again. Whether they liked it or not, she was the boss, and she didn't take what went on in the shop lightly.

By the time Dakota got to a stopping point on the one project she needed to complete, it was nearly four thirty. She'd almost forgotten she needed to meet Lysette back at the house around five. She was filthy, and she needed time to make herself presentable before Nicolay showed up.

"Kelly!" Dakota called, "Come here for a second."

She didn't sound too happy. Kelsy and Greg both looked at Kelly. They wondered what he'd done now. Dragging his feet, rolling his eyes, and sucking his teeth with each step, Kelly made his way over to where Dakota stood with her arms crossed over her chest.

"You rang?"

"You know what, you can take that attitude and get the hell out of my shop or you can address me respectfully, the choice is yours."

Dakota waited patiently for him to make his decision. She was fed up with his arrogance and disrespectful behavior, and he was about to talk his way out of a job.

Kelly's problem was he didn't know when to quit. He'd push and push and push just to see how far he could get. But this time he was about to push himself into unemployment, and there wasn't going to be anything anyone was going to be able to do about it. Dakota was prepared to fire his behind if it came to that, and she wouldn't lose a wink of sleep over the decision.

Kelly knew she was serious. He was just still upset they'd gotten caught and she'd chewed them out.

"I apologize. What do you need me to do?"

"I need this cover cut tonight. Do you think you can handle that?"

"Yes ma'am."

"And get Greg to help you. I've already marked it. It just needs to be cut."

"Will do. Anything else?"

"Just make sure you both wear gloves. Otherwise, I think that's it," Dakota turned to Kelsy and Greg, "I'm heading out. Anybody need anything before I go?"

They all looked at each other then back at Dakota shaking their heads no. She grabbed her keys and headed out the door. Before she could get to her vehicle, the uneasy feeling crept back into her bones. It crawled under her skin, making her body shiver all over. She closed her eyes, her mind trying to convince itself she was imagining things, but this feeling was too real. Dakota always listened to her intuition, it had never steered her wrong. She looked around but once again saw no sign of anyone. Even Shasta remained in her favorite spot under the oak tree by the front door of the shop.

Instead of getting into the truck, Dakota went back into the shop. The cameras at the house had picked up something, maybe the one at the shop had as well. The security system at the shop was much more sophisticated than the one at the house. Dakota hoped the files here would hold the answer to this growing mystery of who was following her.

She walked right past the guys, not even taking time to acknowledge their concern, and entered the back office. She didn't really have the time to look at the files here, so she decided to just burn another disk and take it back to the house.

Disk in hand, she again bid goodnight to Kelly, Kelsy, and Greg and headed back home.

CHAPTER NINTEEN

Nicolay arrived at the Naverro Plantation just after dusk.

THE HOUSE APPEARED to be empty, and he wondered if Dakota had even made it back home. He rang the doorbell and waited, but there was no answer. As he walked back to the car, the scent of chocolate cigars caught his attention. He followed the intensity of the smell to the roof. He could just make out the outline of a pair of tennis shoes propped up on the gutters.

"What are you doing up here?" Nicolay lowered himself next to Dakota on the roof of the house.

She cut her eyes at him as she took a drag off of her cigar, "I was minding my own business until you showed up."

"Is there something wrong?" though they'd only had two nights together, he didn't understand her displeasure with him.

"I don't appreciate you sending your spies to follow me."

"What are you talking about? I do not have anyone following you."

Dakota tossed a stack of photographs his way. She couldn't believe he was sitting there lying to her. She didn't know him that well, and he damn sure didn't know her. The pictures showed her all she needed to know.

"Recognize the gentleman in the photos?" Dakota took another drag off of the cigar and expelled the smoke through the corner of her mouth.

Nicolay flipped through the pictures. He did recognize the man in the pictures. What he couldn't figure out is why one of his employees was following her.

"Now I am going to ask this just once, why is one of your employees following me?"

"Truthfully, I do not know."

"Bullshit. That's bull and you know it. You know, I thought you were a nice guy," Dakota stood and brushed her pants off. She turned from him and walked towards the tree she'd used to get up to the roof, "But I guess I was wrong."

She jumped off of the roof and disappeared into the branches of the tree. Nicolay walked over to where she had jumped over the side. He'd expected to see her climbing down, but instead she stared back at him, her back against the trunk of the hundred year old oak.

"What do you want me to say? I really do not know why Xavier is following you," Nicolay didn't know what to say or do to make her believe him. Either she did or she didn't, and right now she was too angry to listen. No matter what he said to her, she'd swear he was lying.

"You know, the first night we left the club, I had the feeling someone was following us. I swore I saw something run across my headlights. Never did figure out what it was. When I came home earlier today I got the feeling I was being followed, so I checked the security camera. I couldn't make out the face, so Lysette took the files to one of her friends to enhance them. Then when I went to work I had the same feeling, so I checked the security cameras and there he was," Dakota took the last drag from her chocolate cigar and flung the remains into the night.

"I'd like to find out why he is following you. Please believe me, I have nothing to do with this."

She stared back at him, "How can I? I mean, you seem too good to be true. I haven't had much experience dating and you've done everything right so far. I've heard the dating horror stories, it's just hard for me to believe you don't have some ulterior motive. This guy works for you I find it hard to believe you don't know anything about this."

"Wait, you said the first night when you left the club you had the same feeling. If this was the same person that is in these pictures, then it couldn't have been Xavier. He was still working. He was the last to leave and that was hours after you left," Nicolay explained.

What he said made sense. It only took her and Lysette twenty minutes to get back to the house. If Xavier was still at work, then the man in the pictures couldn't have been him.

"Well if it wasn't him, then who?"

"I do not know." Nicolay reached out to her. She seemed to have calmed down. He hoped she believed him.

"Come, let's go back to the club and see if we can figure this out, together."

Dakota took his hand and allowed him to pull her back to the roof, "So you really didn't have anything to do with whoever this is following me?"

"Afraid not, but we'll find out who it is together. In the meantime, I don't want you going anywhere alone," Nicolay was being cautious. There were too many strange things going on. First the dream, then the feeling something was seeking him out, and now this.

"I can take care of myself."

Before Nicolay had a chance to protest, Dakota's cell phone rang. Checking the caller-ID she realized it was a call from work.

"This had better be good, I'm a little busy," she exclaimed.

"Thank God you're still answering the phone," replied Kelly in an anxious voice, "Uh, we kinda got a problem here."

"What is it?" Dakota asked making sure her irritation was readily known.

"Well you know the Chevy you told us to cut the bed cover for?"

"What did you do?"

"We..."

Dakota heard another voice in the background yelling "We, wasn't no damn we. He fucked up! I ain't have shit to do with that."

"Man, shut up," Kelly replied to the other voice, "Dakota you still there?"

"Yeah, now are you going to tell me what you did?" she asked in a not too friendly voice.

"See what had happened was ..." he began.

"Don't even go there, just spit it out."

"Well, we were going to cut the bed cover, but you know how you always tell us to double check the measurements."

"I left you the exact measurements. I even marked the cover for you so all you had to do was cut it. Please tell me all you did was cut it," Dakota was trying to stay calm. If they had messed this up it was going to take her hours to fix it.

"Uh we cut it but we sort of altered the measurements. I mean we went back," Kelly began talking fast trying to explain, "We just wanted to check the measurements and we thought they were off, so we used ours."

"Damn it, do I have to do everything!" Dakota sucked her teeth. She was livid. She'd told them time and time again she always double checked, sometimes triple checked her measurements. All she asked was that they cut the cover and they couldn't even do that right.

Nicolay wrapped his arms around her waist. She'd been pacing and not realized it. He feared in her anger she may step off of the side of the roof and he couldn't let that happen. She swung at him, it was a natural reaction, but he'd anticipated the swing and ducked. Then she stood completely still. It was then she realized they were still on the roof.

She again spoke to Kelly on the phone, "I'll be down there in a few minutes. Don't fuck anything else up!" and she shut the phone off. Dakota knew they'd be gone by the time she got down there. When she was on the war path, all steered clear.

Nicolay rubbed his hand up and down her spine. Dakota found herself relaxing into his arms. It was amazing how just being in his arms made her problems seem insignificant. The tension and anger just floated from her body. She took in a couple of deep cleansing breaths and looked up at him.

"Feel better?" he asked.

"Surprisingly yes. What did you do to me?" Dakota was suspicious. She'd never felt better. It was as if he'd taken her anger and frustration away.

"Nothing the gentle touch of a man who loves a woman wouldn't be able to do. So do you trust me now?"

"Yes." She said it with no hesitation, "I'm sorry I doubted your intentions."

He placed a gentle kiss on her lips, "No need to apologize. Now, care to share the problem?" his hearing had allowed him to hear both sides of her conversation but he didn't want her to think he was eavesdropping. Besides, he was sure she'd feel even better after she talked about it.

"They fucked up something at the shop. It's going to take me hours to fix this mess. Sorry, I'm going to have to cancel our date."

"Do you mind if I join you?" Nicolay asked. Whether she wanted him to or not he'd make sure she made it to work safely.

"I don't mind, but I'll probably be there long after dawn."

"Don't worry, I'll make it back safely and if you will agree, I'd like to send someone to make sure you get home without incident."

He didn't want to alarm her. She'd had enough of a scare as it was with this guy disguised as Xavier following her. He didn't want her to know this might be more than just a coincidence.

"There's something you're not telling me," Dakota eyed him, attempting to determine what he was hiding.

She sensed there was more going on than Nicolay was revealing. She still didn't know why someone would be following her, but she found it strange this had come to light since she'd first met him. Dakota secretly wondered if the two were related. Maybe he didn't intentionally have anything to do with her being followed, but she believed he was just as suspicious about this as she was.

"I do have some suspicions, but I think it best to not discuss them until I have ruled out additional possibilities."

Dakota studied him, trying to determine if she pushed a little more if he'd tell her what was on his mind. He was genuinely concerned about her, and she was feeling vulnerable without Dayton. She decided to trust her instincts and allow him to ensure her safety. If they were wrong, no harm no foul, but if they were right she'd be glad for any extra help.

CHAPTER TWENTY

THE TRIP TO PARADISE, Inc. was a relatively short one. Dakota pulled in front of the shop and parked. Just as she'd suspected, everyone was long gone.

"Wait here. I have to put Shasta up. I am not sure how she'll react to you."

"Shasta?'

"The guard dog."

Dakota entered the shop and put Shasta in one of the storage rooms. She returned to the front door and opened it for Nicolay.

"Welcome to Paradise," Dakota smiled as she swung the door open.

"Feel free to look around, I've got to get the stuff I need from the storage room in the back," she turned and headed down a hallway, disappearing around a corner.

Nicolay had never seen so many vehicles crammed into so little space. Business must be good if they had this many projects going simultaneously. He walked over to an area that seemed somewhat removed from the rest of the open space. Everything in the area seemed to have its place. Someone was a neat freak and he wondered who.

"Interesting you'd be drawn to my work area," Dakota reentered the bay and approached him.

"So you're the neat freak?"

"I wouldn't exactly consider myself a neat freak, I just don't have people rambling through my tools looking for stuff. My area is off limits to everyone."

"And why is that?"

"My gift of course. I don't want any of the memories the guys who work here harbor. So to cut down on that, everything of mine is off limits. Even when they're working on one of my projects I have strict orders everyone wear gloves."

Dakota pulled back the tarp covering the truck to reveal the mess she now had to clean up. Looking over the damage she knew she'd definitely be here way beyond dawn.

"Ready to see the Maestro at work?" she asked.

"Mind if I use the phone first? I'd like to make the arrangement for your safe return."

"Sure. There's a cordless right behind you."

Nicolay grabbed the phone and stepped outside to make his call. Dakota took the time to mix the fiberglass and attach the support so she could put the cover back together before she had to cut it correctly. By the time Nicolay had returned, she'd already begun applying the first layer of the bonding agent.

Dakota worked tirelessly for hours patching, sanding, drying, and then patching again. Nicolay watched in amazement as she worked to repair the damaged cover. He'd had no idea the amount of work it took to repair a vehicle. By the time she was ready to cut again, they were both covered in dust and dawn was fast approaching.

The sound of the buzzer pulled Dakota's attention from the last bit of sanding.

"Keep working. I'll get it."

She continued sanding, making sure the part she had patched was completely smooth. When she was convinced this part was perfect, she took a minute to rest. This was only the beginning. Now that she'd repaired the damage, she needed to re-measure, remark, re-cut, and bond the correct pieces back together. Her night had been long, but her day was going to be just as long and just as tiring.

She was leaning over the half finished product with her head between her elbows and her hands on the back of her head when Nicolay and his friend returned.

Nicolay knew she had to be tired. She'd been working for hours without rest. He hoped his choice in escorts for her would turn out to be more than just assurance of her safe return home.

"Are you all right?" he asked.

Dakota rubbed her already dirty face with her arm and pinched the bridge of her nose. She needed some air and she needed some sleep and she needed this mess to fix itself.

"You want the truth?"

"Actually, don't answer that. You need to rest."

"Look, I don't have time to rest. I still have to measure again, cut and do the bonding process and I have to have this done by three o'clock."

"Maybe I can help."

Dakota hadn't even taken the time to acknowledge the gentleman who was with Nicolay.

She studied the lean face of the young man. "Don't I know you?" she asked.

"I'm surprised you recognize my face. When we were in school you spent most of your time ignoring me."

"Autour Rashon. I can't believe it. Where the hell have you been hiding?"

"I take it you two know each other."

Autour and Dakota looked at Nicolay and then at each other.

Dakota spoke first, "He was my competition when I was learning to do sheet metal fabrication."

"She always wanted to do things the long and hard way, by hand," Autour replied.

"Yeah but in the end, even with all of that fancy technology, my projects were always better than yours."

"Touché"

"Well then, I'll let you two catch up. I must be getting back. Let him help you okay?" Nicolay felt the sun rising. He needed to leave now to make it safely to his lair before dawn.

"I guess so. Are we still going out tonight?" Dakota asked.

"If you feel up to it, meet me at the club. I'll leave word at the door that I am expecting you. Bring Lysette with you if you like."

"I'll do that."

"So I shall see you later," Nicolay stepped through the open door and disappeared into what was left of the night.

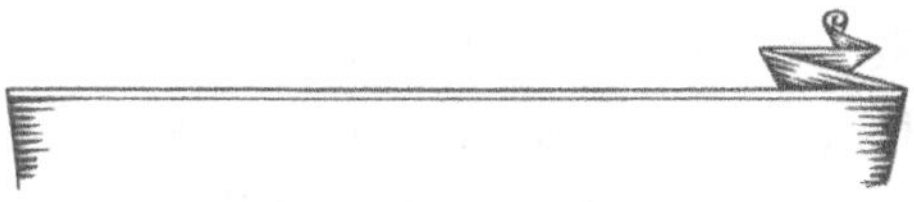

CHAPTER TWENTY-ONE

"So how have you been?" Dakota asked.

"PRETTY GOOD, HOW ABOUT yourself?"

"Can't complain. Business is good. We're making it."

"You know word has it you and Dayton have done quite well for yourselves. By the looks of things I have to agree."

"We do what we can."

"So what are you working on?"

"Cleaning up someone else's mess. I've got to measure the bed cover, cut it, and rebond it so that it fits the Chevy over there."

Autour ran his hand over the center of the cover, the part Dakota had just finished repairing, "Nice work. I guess I should have expected as much from you. You did this all by hand?"

"Yeah and it's taken me all night. I can't afford another mishap."

"My work can't compare to this, but how about we do this. I'll measure and cut it while you go take a nap. Once I'm done I'll complete the first layer of bonding and wake you when it's ready to be sanded. Deal?"

Dakota wasn't sure about trusting this job to someone else. She'd trusted it to her own employees and they'd fucked up. She didn't have the time to repair it again.

"Come on. You know I am capable of measuring and cutting. Besides, in the shape you're in wouldn't you rather have someone who's had some sleep do the tedious work?"

Dakota huffed, "Come on. I'll show you were you can find every-thing you need. You can work over there," she pointed to a vacant workstation on the other side of the bay, "I'll bring you the stuff you'll need for the bonding."

"Still the same old Dakota. You still don't let anyone touch your tools do you?"

"You know me so well."

Dakota walked back to the storeroom to get the materials Autour would need to cut and start the bonding process. When she returned, she dumped everything on the table.

"I'll be in my office when you're done. It's down the hall, the sec-ond door on the right, and in case you need it the bathroom is the first door on the left."

"No working, just sleeping, right?" Autour gave her a stern look.

"Right."

DAKOTA DIDN'T KNOW how long she'd been asleep, but the tapping on her office door dragged her subconscious from the most wonderful dream.

"You can come in."

The door swung open and a dust covered Autour stepped into the office. His face was full of fiberglass dust and his sweat made his shirt stick to his body. The only clean spot was where he'd used goggles to protect his eyes. He reminded her of Pigpen from the Charlie Brown cartoons.

"What are you smiling about?"

"Oh nothing. What time is it?"

"About eleven. I put the cover under the heat lamps. I'm pretty sure it's dry."

Dakota yawned, stretched and stood from the couch in her of-fice, "You made good time."

Autour followed Dakota down the hallway and into the main bay. She took a moment to admire his work. She ran her hand over the grey spot on the bed cover. It was amazingly smooth for him just to have begun the bonding process.

"Did you already sand this?" she asked.

"I figure you wouldn't mind. Did I overstep my boundaries?"

"No. Thanks, you just saved me hours' worth of work."

"Well Nicolay instructed me to keep you happy. Besides, you needed the rest. You were looking pretty bad when I first got here," running his hand over the cover he said, "You could probably get away with just one more layer."

"You gonna help?"

"That's what I'm here for."

The two worked together and completed the second layer in record time. They hung the finished cover under the heat lamps and packed up.

"You following follow me home?" Dakota asked.

"Actually, I was hoping to ride with you. I'm not supposed to leave you alone."

"What do you mean?"

"I am here as your escort and guard. Once we get to your house, I am supposed to keep watch and make sure you're safe until I am relieved or we head to the club."

"So in other words you're here as Nicolay's little spy," Dakota rolled her eyes at him.

"Call it what you want, but Nicolay is concerned about you being followed. I have a feeling there's more going on than he is telling the both of us. Believe me, I've known Nicolay for a few years now and I've never seen him this concerned about anything."

"Any ideas what's going on?" Dakota asked.

"Not a clue. But many of the employees of The Apache have reported having these strange feelings. Something big is brewing, but none of us know what it is."

"Well, let me let Shasta out and we can go," Dakota was ready to go home and take a long bath. The nap had done her good and with Autour's help, she now had an additional three hours she hadn't planned on.

"I'll meet you outside," he stepped through the door and closed it behind him.

Dakota went back to the storage room and let Shasta out. She shut off all of the lights and closed the front door behind her. She armed the alarm using the remote and joined Autour in front of her truck.

"Something wrong?" even though she asked, she didn't need to. She too felt whatever it was that seemed to have Autour's attention.

"I'm not sure. Let's just get out of here," Autour replied.

They jumped into the truck and Dakota sped off down the path behind the building that led to the house.

"Where are you going?" Autour was confused. The main road was in the opposite direction.

Dakota smiled over at him.

"Shortcut. The property is split between the shop, the drag strip, and the house. Day and I own it all. We've got all kind of paths running back here through the woods."

"Leave it to the Naverro children to have cut their own private roads."

Autour stared out of the window, watching the branches of the trees. He so wanted to be out there in the woods, running free, but Nicolay had given him a job to do and he had no choice but to do it.

In less than five minutes Dakota was pulling into the back door of the garage. Dayton had convinced her they needed doors on both sides so when they came up the back they didn't have to circle the house to pull in. It also made it easier to leave, since they could just pull straight through.

"Here we are."

"Nice. How long have you two lived out here?"

"Forever. We were born and raised here," Dakota replied as they exited the garage and entered the house.

"Does anyone besides you two even know this place exists?"

Autour took his time to admire the old house. It was still in immaculate condition. He didn't know how the two of them kept it looking so nice. He did notice some places near the rear where the screen in the veranda was torn and the house would need a new coat of paint in another year or so, but other than that it looked to be perfectly preserved.

"You two live out here alone?"

"Yep, except for the occasional friend staying over it's just me and Day," Dakota tossed her keys, laid her pistol on the kitchen counter, and pressed the button on the answering machine.

"Want something to drink?" she asked as the first of the three messages began to play.

"No, I'm good. I'm going to look around the outside of the house if you don't mind."

"Go ahead. I'll unlock the front door."

"Just wait for me to ring the bell before you open it," as he stepped out of the kitchen through the garage the last message began to play.

"Hey Dakota, it's Lysette. Let me know what your plans are for tonight. I'll be back around five. If you need to reach me hit me up on my cell. Love ya."

Then the phone went dead.

Dakota just shook her head. How was she going to explain Autour to Lysette? Her house hadn't seen this many men since the last time Dayton had invited the guys from the shop to come watch a game. Now she had another to explain.

Dakota watched as Autour systematically checked the perimeter. She noticed he seemed to be using all of his senses to check the area. He sniffed the air, then rubbed his nose and hands over the trees. She found his behavior rather odd and wondered what he was doing.

Dakota unlocked and opened the front door. Immediately Autour turned to face her.

"You spying on me now?" he asked.

"No. Just curious. What are you doing?"

"Let me finish checking out the area and I'll explain. Stay close to the house. I think something has been out here."

"Any idea what?"

"Nothing I recognize," he stepped further into the trees lining the driveway. When he was nearly out of her sight, he turned and came back, "Whatever it was went out that way."

"How do you know?"

"Long story. How about this, you go get cleaned up, I'll make us something to eat, and I'll tell you about it over late lunch."

"That sounds good. Think you can find your way around my kitchen?"

"I think I can manage it."

They stepped through the door and secured it behind them.

"Then I'll see you in few," Dakota began to ascend the stairs.

"Anything in particular you want to eat?"

"Nope. You have free reign. Make yourself at home," she yelled back at him as she reached the middle of the staircase.

Autour watched as she climbed the stairs. He regretted never telling her he was in love with her. Now he'd missed his chance, she was involved with the most powerful creature in these parts and his friend. As she reached the top stair, Autour turned and made his way to the kitchen.

CHAPTER TWENTY-TWO

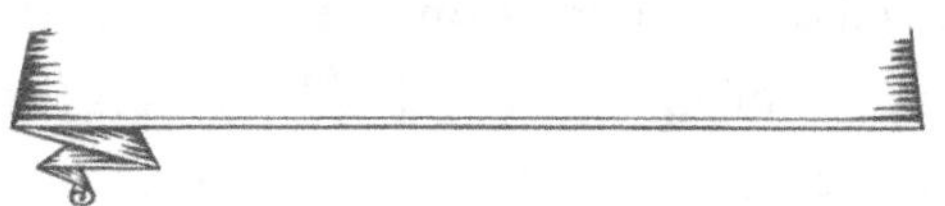

DAKOTA TOOK A LONG hot bath. Oddly enough, Autour rambling through her kitchen, the sound of a male voice echoing through the halls gave her comfort. The house was old, so after she'd turned the water off she'd been able to her Autour in the kitchen singing. He did have a nice voice. She'd have to remember to tell him that.

When she was clean and relaxed, she dried off, put on a thin layer of lotion and threw on a tee shirt and some jeans. She still needed to decide what she was wearing tonight, but she had plenty of time for that later. She was looking forward to catching up with Autour. He had some secret to reveal, she was sure of it, and she was ready to find out what it was.

It didn't take her long to find him. He was perched in front of the television flipping channels.

"Find everything you need?"

"Sure did. Your food's in the microwave."

Dakota retrieved her plate and joined him in the living room, "I didn't even know we had tuna in the house," she said as she bit into the soft tortilla wrap he'd made.

"Why do I believe that?"

Shrugging her shoulders Dakota replied, "I don't know. Why do you?"

"I'm going to leave that alone. So I guess you want me to answer your question."

"That's up to you. We've been out of each other's lives for years. You don't owe me an explanation for anything."

"I appreciate you giving me an out, but I think you should know."

"Know what?"

Autour clicked off the television. He didn't want any distraction, "Like you said, we've been out of each other's lives for years, and a lot has happened in that time. The biggest thing is that I am now a shape shifter."

Dakota couldn't believe her ears. First she'd fallen in love with a vampire, and now she'd been sent a shifter as a bodyguard.

"Is that why Nicolay chose you to guard me?" Dakota continued to eat as they talked.

"I think that was part of the decision, that and my mechanic background. Guess he figured if anyone could help you get done faster it was me."

"So let me get this straight, you're some sort of werewolf or something?" she didn't mean to gawk at him, but she didn't know what else to do.

"Not exactly. I was infected by a Eurasian lynx."

"So every full moon you turn into a monster?"

"I'm not a monster, Dakota. I'm still human most of the time. And the moon doesn't control my changes. I can change at will or refuse to change at all, although the latter takes much concentration and energy."

"Wow," was all she could say.

"You okay with this? I mean, if you want I can just wait outside."

"Why would you say that?"

"I don't know. I just figured you'd be freaked out."

"P-lease. As long as you don't go wild and destroy my house or something you're fine I'm cool with it. Besides, you know I've always kept an open mind. I try my best not to judge people by what's on the outside."

"Man, you took it better than I thought."

"Hey, what can I say? Plus, if Nicolay trusts you to keep me safe, then I trust you too."

"So we're good?"

"Yep, we're good," Dakota took the last bite of her sandwich and stood. She was on her way to the kitchen to dispose of her plate when the doorbell rang.

"You expecting company?" Autour asked.

"Yeah, it's probably Lysette."

"Lysette, your best friend Lysette," he hadn't heard that name in who knows when.

"The one and the same."

"Mind if I get it then?" he said with a devilish smile.

"Be my guest. I'm going to put these dishes in the sink."

Autour opened the door and scooped the young lady standing there into his arms. He swung her around, not giving her a chance to protest until he was good and ready to let her go. When he finally put her down, he stepped back to get a good look at her.

"You haven't changed a bit," he said.

It took a moment for Lysette to comprehend what had just happened and what this guy answering Dakota's door had said to her. She studied the face of the gentleman, but was drawn immediately to his eyes. She stepped back, not sure she was seeing what she thought she was seeing.

"What's wrong Lysette, cat got your tongue?"

"Your eyes. I can see the forest in your eyes," she stuttered.

Autour squeezed his eyes shut and then opened them again.

"Better?"

"Yes. Now who are you, how do you know my name, and why are you answering Dakota's door?"

"Hey Lysette," before Autour had a chance to answer her questions Dakota stuck her head around him, "Don't you remember Autour? He went to school with me. Remember his best friend was the date from hell?"

Lysette took another look at the young man. He did seem vaguely familiar. Now that she thought about it, he seemed really familiar. She studied his face a little longer. He looked almost the same, except his face had filled out and his eyes had changed.

"Yeah, I do remember you. How have you been?" Lysette was a little suspicious. Neither of them had explained why he was here. She didn't like it one bit.

"I've been okay, and just so you know, I am only here at Nicolay's request."

"How'd you know I was wondering why you were here?"

"Come on Lysette, it's written all over you face," he turned then and went back into the living room to flip channels.

Lysette stepped though the doorway into the house, "What is he?" she asked Dakota.

"Not my secret to tell. If you want to know, ask him," Dakota turned and proceeded to climb the stairs to start getting ready for her date.

Once upstairs, she went back into the bathroom and tried to figure out what to do with her hair. She'd already decided on an outfit for her rendezvous, so this was her only task now.

"So what's the plan for tonight?" Lysette asked as she entered Dakota's bedroom.

"We've been invited to join Nicolay at the club."

"Really now? Then I'm glad I brought some club wear with me. Autour coming too?"

"Yeah, we're all headed to the same place," Dakota said it with an attitude. Why was Lysette asking such stupid questions? How else was he supposed to get there? There wasn't another car outside and she surely wasn't going to loan one of hers to a virtual stranger.

"Oh, someone's touchy touchy. What gives?"

"I don't know. Tired I guess. I had to work most of the night and I haven't had a chance to catch up on my sleep."

"You sure that's all it is?" Lysette raised an eyebrow.

"Well, that and I can't get Nicolay out of my mind. I have to admit, I kinda had a dirty dream about him while I was napping at the shop."

"So what's wrong with that? When's the last time you had a man in your life other than Dayton?"

"Come to think of it, I can't remember. I don't think I've really ever had a man other than Dayton in my life."

"Dakota's got a crush. Dakota's got a crush!" Lysette loved teasing her friend.

"Stop acting like a school girl. It doesn't become you."

"Yeah. Whatever. So which ride are we taking tonight?"

"Uh...yeah...ride," Dakota stumbled over her words, not sure how to break the news to her friend that she would not be able ride with her.

"I'm not going to like this am I?" Lysette sounded worried, but she would give her friend the benefit of the doubt.

"Small change in tonight's plan. Uh, you can't ride with me to the club tonight."

"Why?" not what Lysette had expected to hear, but she wanted a good excuse to tell her friend she was out of her mind if she thought she was going to let her go to the club alone.

"I'm riding the bike."

"The bike? Out in the middle of the night? Alone? I don't think so."

"Look, it really doesn't matter what you think. I have been riding that bike alone for five years now. I can handle it. Plus, I want Mr. Right to know the real me, not the prissy me you turned me into for the past couple of nights."

Dakota sighed. She was tired of having to explain to everyone the real her. She liked being a "biker chick." She liked designing cars and motorcycles. She never minded getting dirty during the fabrication process, and she was going to make sure tonight that Nicolay knew the whole package he was getting.

"Ok. Ok," Lysette conceded, "I guess that means you won't be wearing the outfit I picked out."

She lifted up a very slinky number from the bed. Dakota hadn't even noticed the fire engine red dress with a very low cut top. It reeked of cheap and sleazy. Dakota already knew she would be the envy of the club with Nicolay on her arm. She didn't need to make it worse by appearing to be the cheapest thing in the place. Plus, she had other ideas for the night.

"No, but I think you'll agree the outfit I picked out will do just fine."

"Oh really, well this I gotta see."

Dakota stepped into her bathroom to dress. Thirty minutes later, she stepped out and Lysette could not believe her eyes. Her girl looked great.

"So? What do you think?"

Lysette sat there speechless. Standing before her in more leather than she believed anyone in this town owned was Dakota. Instead of shortening her hair, she had added more tracks and pulled it all back into a ponytail that ended halfway down her back. The all black ensemble complimented her Champaign complexion perfectly. The leather pants fit just enough to show off her girl's figure without making her believe she had to hold her breath to pull the pants up. The leather vest appeared to be simple enough, until Dakota spun around and Lysette realized the sides were tied up with crisscross straps. She knew then Dakota couldn't have been wearing a bra, but the vest didn't give any other indications of that fact. Lastly, she noticed that her five foot three friend appeared to be much taller than usual. Dakota saw her looking at her feet and she raised her pant leg enough to show the five inch stiletto heeled boots she so comfortably sported.

"Are you going to say something or just stare at me like I just appeared out of thin air?" with hands on hips, Dakota waited for her friend's reply.

"I really don't know what to say. I do know this, your new man had better watch out. When you show up to the club on that bike of yours and in that outfit, every man, and probably some women, in the city is going to be after you."

They both had a big laugh, but somehow Lysette thought head turning was the reaction Dakota was going for. She was usually a sort of extremist, but in a good way.

"So what am I driving?"

"That all depends. You're coming home alone, so I assume you won't want to drive Dayton's bike. That leaves the Civic or the El Camino. Your choice."

"Guess I'll take the Civic. I have been brushing up on my straight shift driving for an occasion just like this."

"Are you ever going to get your car fixed?" Dakota fussed with her hair, making sure it was secure under a bandana.

"Soon as the money's right."

"Go get dressed. I'll wait for you then we can head out together."

"Guess this means Autour is riding with me?" Lysette stood and sashayed across the room.

"You got it. Now go."

While Lysette dressed, Dakota applied a little eyeliner, eye shadow, and a tad bit of gold lip-gloss. As she applied her makeup, she thought of what this night could mean. True, she had just met this guy, so she really didn't know what to expect. On the other hand, he seemed interested and willing to accept her for who she was.

"I'll be done in a minute," Lysette yelled down the stairs.

Dakota was sitting with Autour on the couch, waiting for Lysette. When she finally made it down the stairs, Dakota grabbed her Springfield Armory Ultra-Compact P1911-A1, her shoulder harness, and her leather motorcycle suit jacket and headed for the front door.

"What's the plan for tonight?" Lysette asked.

Dakota knew what Lysette was getting at, but she was not falling for it. "Tonight, we meet at the club. I find Nicolay and have my date. You stay out of my business and out of my way."

Lysette gave Dakota the evil eye, but she knew sooner or later her friend was going to draw the line. She couldn't protect her forever. Besides, it was her plan to go clubbing that started all this. She took one last look at Dakota and shook her head. She was grown now and had to learn about life and love on her own. Lysette wanted to spare her friend some of the heartache she'd endured herself, but some lessons were learned from sheer experience. She just hoped this guy would not take advantage of Dakota's innocence. Actually, in her own way, Lysette was going to make it abundantly clear that if he hurt Dakota, he would pay gravely.

Autour stayed as far out of their conversation as he could, but he couldn't help admiring the two beautiful women standing in front of him.

Dakota stared at Lysette before she asked, "What are you thinking?"

The twang in her voice let Lysette know she was not playing. Dakota could almost see all of the thoughts running through that head of Lysette's and she didn't like it one bit, and she was going to make sure her friend knew it.

Lysette put her hands up as a sign of peace, "I know. You're an adult and I am going to stay out of your business. But that doesn't mean I have to like it. I'll respect your wishes and steer clear of the two of you, but be forewarned, he hurts you and there will be hell to pay."

"I hear you loud and clear, but at least give him the benefit of the doubt. I mean, yeah he seemed to be full of charm and all of that, but there's something more. I just can't put my finger on it. It's almost as if he was hurt before and is treading very carefully as to not make the same mistake. But enough of analyzing this whole thing, we are both going out tonight to have fun, and that is that."

Dakota didn't really believe that, but she didn't want to talk about this anymore. It was just after sunset and she wanted as much time with Nicolay as she could get. There were so many unanswered questions, and she wanted to learn a little more about him before dawn forced their separation.

"Ready?" Dakota asked Lysette.

"Ready."

With that, Dakota threw the Civic keys to Lysette and all three of them headed for the garage.

CHAPTER TWENTY-THREE

LYSETTE AND DAKOTA got separated on the way to the club, mostly because Dakota decided to be daring and run every red light, swerve between every stopped car, and disobey the law every chance she got.

"I'm going to kill her."

Autour just laughed at Lysette's frustration. She'd always been uptight when it came to Dakota.

Lysette was definitely going to give that girl a piece of her mind when she got to the club. That is, if her friend didn't scare her to death or kill herself before they both got there. By the time they pulled up, she was fuming. Dakota nonchalantly sat the bike, strategically parked way too close to the door of the club, with a grin on her face.

"What in the hell do you think you were doing out there? You could have been killed driving like that. I swear I don't know what has gotten into you. Since Dayton has been gone you have lost your mind. Your brother is going to hear about this. Now, Miss Missy, what do you have to say for yourself?"

"I am so not having this conversation with you," Dakota turned and walked past the long line straight to the door.

It took Lysette a moment to collect herself. She had to keep telling herself that Dakota was grown and could take care of herself, but the way she was just driving out there put huge doubts in Lysette's mind. She decided to drop the issue for now. She'd have a long heart to heart with Dakota about not giving other people heart attacks with her antics later.

By the time Lysette joined her, Dakota was leaning on a tinted glass window of the club with her arms crossed and a smirk on her face, waiting for her.

"Your panties still in a bunch because of my driving?" she laughed under her breath.

"I came to the club to meet a new friend and have some fun. I am not going there with you," Lysette rolled her eyes. Dakota wanted to toy with her tonight and she refused to get sucked into the little game.

Autour walked past them into the club as the guard moved the velvet rope to let them in. Dakota gave Lysette a dirty look, wanting so much for her to say something else. They chose to put their differences in opinion to the side for now and headed into the club.

Before Dakota could get into the club completely, she was grabbed from behind, swung around and kissed more passionately than she had ever been kissed. She was taken aback by the tenderness of the embrace. It took her a moment to realize she hadn't even had the time to glimpse the face of her captor. Her gentleman suitor slowly pulled away but she could still feel the sexual tension holding heavily between them. Her lips quivered with desire not to end the kiss. She heard her friend giggling beside her.

"Go ahead. Open your eyes. He's real," Lysette said with a Cheshire cat smile on her face.

Dakota gave the woman the dirtiest look she could. She secretly hoped Nicolay hadn't seen the sneer but at the moment she didn't care. She closed her eyes again and turned back towards Nicolay. She wanted to savor the feeling of being in his arms just a moment longer. She wanted to live in the moment, experience the way he made her feel, even without the visual. Then she heard him confirm he'd felt the same thing she did.

"I agree. I hadn't expected it to be that incredible either. I have been anxiously awaiting your arrival. I am glad you reciprocated instead of slapping me silly. Although any touch from you would warm my heart."

Dakota couldn't help but laugh. She finally opened her eyes to gaze upon Nicolay. She could not believe this magnificent man had just kissed her.

"I'll leave you two alone to get more acclimated. Don't do anything I wouldn't do," Lysette slipped her way through the crowd to find Mr. Right Now leaving the two love birds to their nesting.

Dakota took a moment to take in the suave outfit of her new friend. Linen was definitely a good choice of fabric for him. She rubbed her hands over his broad shoulders, feeling the way the button down shirt hugged the muscles. The way the linen pants flowed down to his feet... she had to bite her bottom lip to distract her mind from the naughty thoughts the image gave her.

"Now that your friend has deserted us, based on your attire, I do not believe you planned for us to spend this evening dancing."

"Now you've got the idea. But what you're wearing will never work for what I have planned. Please tell me you have a change of clothes somewhere in this place."

"Let us proceed to my office. I am sure I have something that can accommodate your plans," Nicolay gently grasped Dakota's hand and led her through the crowd. As they walked the length of the club the crowd parted, and just as quickly as their path was made it was swallowed again.

Dakota noticed the envious and spiteful sneers from the women as they weaved a path through the club. She paid it no attention. She had what she had come to the club for, this caramel Adonis on her arm.

The doorway to the office was set off to one side, its position masked by one of the many drapes covering the walls. It was strategically hidden so that no one would mistake it for a restroom door.

Nicolay guided her into the office and shut the door. Instantly, they were engulfed in silence. The walls were painted the red orange color of sunrise. A maple veneer desk with a matching pen and pencil set sat in front of one wall. The executive style leather chair behind it was the only dark piece of furniture in the room. The tan couch laid cattycornered to the end wall and the two matching chairs faced the desk. He'd tossed pillows of all sorts everywhere, but the paintings were the most amazing Dakota had ever seen.

On each wall a mural of some sort depicting a sunrise or sunset hung. Dakota walked over to the largest one on the wall furthest from the door. As she gazed upon the painting, it seemed familiar, as if she had been to the exact spot. She could just barely make out the outline of a person on the beach. They appeared to be taking a picture of the eye-catching event as if it may be their last sunset. In the bottom right corner, she noticed a collection of seashells. They appeared to spell out the letters NC.

Dakota heard Nicolay approaching from behind. She realized this was the first time she'd been able to hear him closing the distance between them. All of the times before, he was just there. He reached around her laying his chin on her shoulder. She relaxed her body against him. She felt at home in his arms.

"Beautiful isn't it," he remarked.

"Yes, it is."

"But not as beautiful as you," Nicolay inhaled her scent. He wanted so much to share his world with her. He wanted tonight to be special and he'd do whatever it took to make it perfect.

"So what is the plan for the night?" He asked.

Dakota turned her head and glanced at him, "No linen. A tee shirt and jeans would be ideal if you have them. Actually," she glanced down at her outfit, "I think I am a little overdressed for what's on my mind right now. We have to make a stop anyway so I'll have a chance to change."

"I think I can handle that. Would you prefer to wait here or join me in my chambers?" Nicolay could not believe he was offering to show Dakota where he slept. He knew how dangerous this was, but he couldn't help but trust her. He didn't know why, he just knew that he did.

Dakota looked around. The only door appeared to be the one they had entered the office from. She wondered where the other entrance was. She figured it must be hidden behind one of the floor length paintings hung from the walls.

"Do you think it's safe for me to know where you sleep?"

"Maybe not, but that doesn't mean I won't show you. It is your choice."

She looked him in the eyes, having no fear he'd enchant her, "Sure."

He led her to the one half empty wall, "Press your hand to it," he instructed.

Dakota did as he asked. She reached for the wall, expecting her hand to pass right through it. She was sure it was some kind of illusion. Instead, though, the wall was solid. The texture appeared to be similar to that of cinder blocks. She ran her hand along the wall up to the place where the painting hung. It was completely solid.

Dakota then moved to the other side. The walls on each side were completely impassible. She felt for a loose block or some indication of a switch that would cause the wall to move, but all in vain. There was nothing.

Nicolay walked close enough behind Dakota that his presence could not be denied. He then touched the wall, and immediately it became transparent. There was still the faint outline of the wall that was there before, but Dakota could clearly see the room on the other side. She was sure it was a hologram. One minute, she is feeling a wall that is without a doubt solid, the next she is looking straight through it.

"How did you do that?'

"Baby I wish I knew. I have been trying to figure that out for five hundred years."

"Only five hundred? I thought you said you've been the undead for six hundred years."

"The first one hundred years as a Vampyre I lay in my coffin in denial. Shall we?" he gestured her forward.

"How do we get through?"

"We just walk through it."

Dakota reached out and this time her hand did go through the wall.

"Amazing."

"Come. I do not wish to waste a moment more. You know my time is limited."

Dakota followed Nicolay through the image on the wall. When she got all of the way through, she turned. She could see the room she'd just walked out of in front of her now. Nicolay walked to an armoire and opened the double doors. He pulled out a pair of jeans and a black tee shirt. As he turned around to gaze upon Dakota, he really noticed the skintight leather pants that fit her behind just right. He wished she had taken her jacket off. Just as the thought crossed his mind, she began to lower her jacket.

She turned slowly, the jacket still making its path down her body, to meet his gaze. She felt him staring at her and she wanted him to get a good glimpse of the straps that held the top in place.

"Kinda hot in here," she smiled deviously and he knew it was for his benefit. Just as she completed her turn to face him, the jacket slipped from her hands and dropped to the floor. His eyes followed its path. He followed the line of her body from the tips of her boots up her body to her plump, wanting lips. He glanced from her face to the pistol hung at her side.

"That for me?"

Dakota looked confused. She had not a clue what he was talking about. When he motioned to her side she realized what his comment referred to. Dakota had forgotten about the Springfield. She was so used to it, it had practically become a part of her. Most of the time she never knew it was there until she needed it.

"I wasn't going to use it on you. But I did ride all the way down here alone. A girl's gotta protect herself."

"If you say so. You are welcome to stay while I dress," he could see in her eyes her heart wanted to, "but I would not be offended if you returned to the other side of the wall. But know this, once you cross back over, you will not be able to change your mind and come back in. For reasons beyond my control, the door becomes one way depending on the side I am on."

"I'll stay."

"I'm glad."

Nicolay turned and walked back to the chair he had laid his clothes across. He slowly began to unbutton the linen shirt he was wearing. He kept his back turned to Dakota as he moved. The motions seemed all too natural for him. Dakota stared at his back, watching each smooth movement with amazement. He slowly slid the shirt off of his shoulders and then down his arms. This was the first time she noticed all of the tattoos. She wandered if they were the reason he always wore long sleeves. As he turned to face her, she observed that there were tattoos on most of his body.

"I meant to ask you about your body art the other night," she commented.

"Actually, I don't think the markings could be considered body art. I've had most of these since I was a child. It is remarkable how as I grew, they didn't distort. The woman who found me on her doorstep didn't know what they meant. I have been told over many years they are Native American symbols, possibly of Aztec or Mayan origin. I suppose they tell who I am. Unfortunately, I've run into dead ends trying to find out anything definite. I have had enough on my mind for these last hundreds of years, so the meaning of the markings has not been a priority on my list. Besides, if what everyone says about my kind is true, then I have all of eternity to trace their meaning."

"How old were you when you became a vampire?"

"Just barely twenty-seven."

He reached for the belt and unbuckled it. He then unbuttoned his pants and slowly slid out of them so that he stood before her in a pair of silk boxers. He took care as to not wrinkle the outfit. He gently placed it on the chair next to his jeans and tee shirt. There were elaborate tattoos down both of his legs. He was tattooed over eighty percent of his body. He stepped into his jeans and pulled them up. He watched Dakota's eyes as she watched him dress. He could see the lust in them, but he would not comment on it. Now was not the time. He put on some socks and a pair of tennis shoes and then grabbed the tee shirt.

"Acceptable for our night out?"

"Perfect."

"Then shall we?" as he slid the tee shirt over his head, he gestured for Dakota to precede him through wall.

She walked through and expected Nicolay to be right behind her. When she turned around, all she saw was the brick wall. She touched it, and once again it was solid. She hadn't believed what he had said earlier about the door being one-way depending on which side he was on.

Suddenly, she felt coolness on the palm of her hand. As she attempted to pull her hand back, Nicolay's fingers wrapped around hers. Apparently, he had been watching her from the other side. He stepped through the wall as if it wasn't there.

"After you," he spoke, the words rolling from his lips.

He opened the office door and allowed her to go through. They made their way to the bar so she could tell Lysette that she was leaving and he could instruct the club manager what to do in his absence. With all loose ends tied up, they exited the club.

"Based upon your attire, I take it our chariot is the one over there attracting so much attention?"

Dakota hadn't expected her bike to be so interesting to onlookers, but she wasn't totally surprised. If they thought the bike was interesting, she could only imagine the reaction the large crowd was going to have when they approached. No time like the present to see.

They walked up to the bike and the crowd spread like wildflowers. Most of the women were taken aback by Nicolay, while the men were trying to understand what Dakota was doing with the vampire. Needless to say, they all stepped aside and allowed them to mount the bike.

"Where are we off to?"

"Paradise."

"Paradise? Your job?"

"No, just wait and see," Dakota started the bike with one fierce kick-start and they headed out.

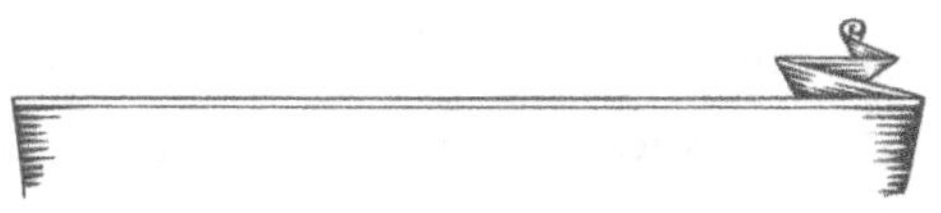

CHAPTER TWENTY-FOUR

TWENTY MILES DOWN THE highway they turned off the main road onto a side street. Although large oak trees lined the narrow road, it was easily passable by the motorcycle. They drove another ten minutes until they reached what appeared to be Paradise, Inc. This was the first time Nicolay had come to the shop from the main road. Dakota circled the building and parked next to the back door.

"You want to come in?"

"I'm not sure?" he teased.

"I won't hurt you. Scouts honor," she held up her three fingers, promise sign of a good little Girl Scout.

"If you say so," he smiled down at her watching the deviousness dance in her eyes, "I figured you'd have had enough of work for one day."

"Actually, I need to change clothes. Another change of plans," Dakota cut off the motor, and with Nicolay's gentlemanly help she got off of the bike.

She opened the door and disarmed the alarm. She rubbed Shasta on the head and led her to one of the back offices. Coming around to one of the bay doors, she pushed the automatic opener. The huge metal door creaked on its chains as it rolled itself up above their heads. Only the bay door's gate with the insignia Paradise, Inc. in steel separated Dakota and Nicolay.

Lifting the gate, Nicolay followed Dakota into the bay. Car parts, motorcycle parts, blue prints, power tools, anything and everything you would need to build a car or a bike were still scattered about. Dakota turned and walked towards one of the offices. She always kept a spare set of clothes in the shop. Things usually got a little messy when they were working. She had been a victim of an oil spill a time or two, plus getting dirty was the nature of their business, so she learned to always be prepared.

"Where are you going?" Nicolay stopped in the center of the shop. He scanned the area, quickly shaking off an uneasy feeling.

"To change, of course."

"Mind if I join you?"

None too quickly she replied, "Yes, I do. Just because you are comfortable undressing in front of me doesn't mean I feel the same way."

"And yet I have kissed you, told you my deepest darkest secret, and endangered my life by revealing my main lair."

"Your problem, not mine. Besides, you've gotten me out of my clothes once and been a gentleman; I don't want to press my luck."

Her comment cut him to the quick; she still didn't fully trust him, but he understood all the same. This was all still new, and he even had to admit that seeing her changing wasn't such a great idea.

"Can't blame a guy for trying."

Dakota closed the door to the office. Nicolay took this time to look around the shop. He noticed this time a little corner behind Dakota's work area that definitely had a woman's touch. The walls were lavender with a darker purple trim around the edges. There were two large paintings hung on the wall just behind the desk. He knew this was where Dakota did her paperwork. He wanted to touch everything she had touched. He approached the area, admiring the choice of colors in the paintings.

He ran his fingers over her chair, then her desk, and then the picture frame placed on the corner. He wondered who the guy in the picture was. She and the guy looked so much alike it was unnerving.

He had to be her brother. The guy appeared to be close to the same age, if not a year or two older, as he had pegged Dakota to be in her mid-twenties, although, being a gentleman, he would never ask a lady her age.

He lowered his body into the chair, amazed at how the leather molded to the shape of his body. It was a sign of good quality. As he picked up the picture, he couldn't help but notice the dimple in Dakota's chin when she smiled. He hadn't noticed it in the darkness of the club or on their first date, although he had excellent eyesight. He traced her outline with his finger, wondering what was going through her mind when the picture was taken. He was so engrossed in looking at the photograph he hadn't heard her come into the room. She'd walked right past him and he hadn't even noticed. The only reason he knew she was there was because he could feel her warm breath against his neck. She leaned over his shoulder to look at the picture.

In the most seductive voice he could muster he spoke, "You really shouldn't sneak up on a vampire like that."

"And you really should pay more attention to your surroundings in a strange place."

Nicolay turned his head just enough to kiss Dakota on the cheek. He didn't want to press his luck with her either. As far as he knew, she had a gun pointed at the back of his head.

"I'll remember that little tidbit. Who's the gentleman in the picture?"

Dakota detected a little jealousy in his voice, "My twin brother. His name's Dayton."

"Twins. So that explains the uncanny resemblance."

"No denying we're family."

"So, is this where our adventure ends?"

"Of course not. And if you're finished snooping, we can go."

"Snooping, me, why I never. If you had allowed me to watch you change, then I wouldn't have been looking around. Plus, you are the one who suggested I snoop as you call it."

"Ok, you've got me there. Ready to go?"

"With you, anytime."

Dakota pulled the bike they had ridden in on into the hanger. She pointed to a Tahoe parked in front of the open hanger door, indicating they would be taking it.

"Get in so I can let Shasta out."

Nicolay did as instructed. As the office door swung open Shasta took one look at Dakota and rolled over to have her belly rubbed.

"You are so spoiled," was all Dakota could say as she reached down. She rubbed Shasta's belly, then walked toward the truck. Shasta didn't even appear to notice Nicolay in the passenger's side as she walked in the other direction towards the office Dakota had changed in.

Dakota climbed into the truck and started it up. The loudness of the exhaust startled Nicolay and he nearly hit his head on the roof turning around to see what the noise was. Dakota laughed. She didn't think anything could startle a vampire. That moment was priceless and she knew that would be a memory she'd forever hold of him.

"What is that noise?"

"You've never heard a dual exhaust system?"

"Only on a motorcycle."

She just shook her head, "You have been so deprived. Guess you're in for a big surprise when we get to our final destination," The smile on her face said it all. She was enjoying every minute of teasing him.

"And where is that?"

"You'll just have to wait and see, won't you."

CHAPTER TWENTY-FIVE

THEY TURNED OFF OF the main road about a mile from Paradise and proceeded down a wooded dirt path. Dakota came to a stop at what appeared to be an abandoned campground. She jumped out of the vehicle as excited as a schoolgirl whose first crush finally noticed her. She swung open the rear double doors and was pulling the mounted ramps out of their slots before Nicolay exited the truck.

"What are you doing?"

"What? What are you talking about?" his question had her confused. Then, looking at Nicolay, she thought, he was probably just as confused by her actions as she was about his question.

"Sorry, I just love to come to this place and I can't wait a minute more. Now, are you going to just stand there and gawk at me like I am crazy, or are you going to help?"

"What do you want me to do?"

"Pull the other ramp out and help me unload the four-wheeler."

"How many more vehicles are we going to take tonight?"

"Don't start," the scowl on her face said it all. He was treading on thin ice.

"Uncle?"

The one word made her laugh. At least one of them hadn't lost their sense of humor.

Riding on the back of the four-wheeler gave Nicolay another chance to wrap his arms around this beautiful woman and he savored every moment of the ride. When she came to a screeching halt in

161

a clearing not far from the campground, he was disappointed. He didn't want to release her.

"You can let go now," she said in her sexiest voice.

Nicolay slowly unlocked his arms from around her waist to allow her to get off the vehicle.

"Come on. I have something to show you."

It was only ten at night. They had plenty of time. He didn't see what her rush was. She led him to a row of trees and came to a halt before taking one step further into the cluster. She turned him to face her and grasped both of his hands.

"Now, close your eyes and listen."

He did as he was told. At first, he didn't hear anything out of the ordinary. He could hear the sounds of owls, crickets, and the other creatures of the night, but as those sounds became white noise, he could faintly make out what sounded like automobile engines.

Dakota stared at him as he attempted to decipher all of the sounds of the night. She watched his facial expressions as he recognized each sound and then dismissed it. She knew the moment he acknowledged the sound she wanted him to hear. She studied his face as he listened more intently, questioned the reverberation in his mind and then reassured himself that he was hearing what he thought he was hearing. Just as he was about to speak, she silenced him with a kiss.

"Let me grab the blanket and I'll be ready," she ran the few steps back to the four-wheeler, grabbed the blanket they'd strapped to the back, and skipped her way back.

"Ready?" she asked.

He nodded his confirmation. Blanket in hand, Nicolay swept Dakota off of her feet. She lay cradled in his arms like an infant. She gestured with her head through the gathering of trees. As he stepped through them, Nicolay could only admire the smile on Dakota's face. On the other side was a different kind of paradise than she had shown him earlier. The sea of monkey grass swallowed his feet. The clearing was moonlit and breathtaking. Exploring the surroundings, one would swear someone had come out in the middle of the woods and landscaped this clearing. Even in the middle of the night, he could only admire God's handy work.

"Put me down and I'll show you what I brought you here to see."

He slowly and reluctantly lowered her to the ground. She snatched up is arm and dragged him to what appeared to be the top of a hill.

"Look," she pointed below them.

"I think I have seen it all. A drag strip in the middle of the woods?"

"Actually, we're standing in the middle of the woods. The strip is at the back end of my family's property. We took the long way here because it's easier at night. It used to be a landing strip for the crop duster my great grandfather used over the fields. Paradise is at the far end of the property. Another mile or so down the road is the main house. So, I get the best of all of my loves on one plot of land."

"Your family owns all of this?"

"Yes, when my great grandfather inherited this he knew he wanted to remain here and raise his family. The place was just far enough from town for privacy, but close enough that if we needed help we could get it. It passed down to my grandfather, then to my father, and now to Dayton and me."

"So you've never considered leaving this place to move to the city?"

"I'm a country girl. I like the privacy this place offers. I like to be able to do what I want with my yard. I like to sleep with my windows and doors open and not have to worry about someone coming in to attack me or steal from me. Most people don't even realize there's a house back here, much less the shop and the strip. Our clients don't even know about this place. They usually tell us what they want and we deliver the end product to their door. This is the Naverro's small part of paradise, and I wouldn't change it for the world."

The passion in her eyes as she spoke of her love for this place was enough to engulf even the fiercest of opponents. Nicolay knew in that moment he would love Dakota for a lifetime. He would never wish upon her the curse he bore, but he would love her unconditionally as long as she would let him. She completed him. She was his *Tehya Aquene*, his precious peace, and he intended to let her know just how he felt.

Without giving his mind the time to refute what his heart had already embraced he encircled her waist, turned her to face him and kissed her. The exchange between them was earth moving. At that moment, time stood still. The kiss intensified to the point where Nicolay felt he would explode. He reluctantly pulled away from her lips so she could breath. He could feel her chest rising and falling with each breath. He could hear her pulse quickening like that of humming bird.

"That...was...incredible..." she managed as she gasped for air.

"I so desire to make love to you, but I will not do anything you do not wish of me."

Dakota stared at him. He's just read her mind, "You know what I want right now?" she said, sounding seductive and devious all in the same breath. She lowered her head, almost as if in shame.

Nicolay refused to allow her to do this without being completely sure it was what she really wanted. He had to be certain this was her decision and she would not regret having made love to him the next morning. He raised her chin so she would look him directly in the eye to say the words he hoped would roll from her lips.

"Your wish is my command."

After a slight moment of hesitation, she spoke, "I want you to make love to me."

There was no hesitation on his part, only a comforting embrace as he whispered in her ear, "As you wish."

Now that he had been given permission to do what he had been yearning to do all night, he wanted to take pleasure in every movement. He wanted her to know that what he was about to do would be just as she asked. He would not have sex with her. He would not screw her or fuck her. He would make love to her for as long as they both could enjoy it.

He retrieved the blanket and spread it across a level section of the plateau. Kneeling on the blanket, he offered his hand to coerce her to come to him. She extended her hand to him. He wrapped her fingers in his and slowly pulled her to the blanket.

He never took his eyes off of her. He sensed her hesitation, but he wasn't sure what was causing it. She seemed very confident in her decision a moment ago. Maybe she was having second thoughts? He decided to give her another way out if she chose it.

"As much as I want this, remember, you can tell me to stop at any time. I won't hold it against you."

Her eyes became misty at the realization that he really wanted to make love to her, but if at any time she had doubts, he was gentleman enough to adhere to her wishes. She raised her hand to his jaw and traced the line with her index finger.

"Thank you," as the words exited her mouth she cradled his face in her hands and kissed him.

Reassured that she really wanted to allow him to make love to her, Nicolay responded to her kiss by drawing her close. He traced her back with his hands while his mouth explored the nape of her neck. He wanted to taste every inch of her body. He gently kissed her forehead and traced her eyebrows with his tongue. He placed baby kisses on each of her eyelids while tracing circles down her spine. He paid special attention to the spot at the tip of her nose as he took a moment to massage it with his tongue. He placed precious kisses starting at each cheek and working his way down her jaw line on each side. He licked at the corners of her mouth and then took her bottom lip between his lips and gently sucked.

Her body quivered with need to have him, all of him. But his actions made it clear he would not be rushed. As she tried to kiss him, he evaded her attempts and moved to the line of her neck. He licked the spot where the major vein ran just below the surface of flesh. She could feel his fangs extend as he sucked gently between her neck and shoulder. Her pulse quickened and he could taste the fear in her perspiration.

"I will not feed from you without your permission," he assured her.

In that moment her entire being relaxed. She hadn't known the thought of him taking blood from her had made her so tense. It was then she really began to let herself go and let her body truly enjoy all of the pleasure Nicolay bestowed upon it.

As his tongue traveled down her collarbone, he slowly raised her tee shirt. He kissed down each side and around to her stomach, intentionally avoiding her breasts. Sliding his hands under the shirt on her back, his tongue darted in and out of her belly button. As he raised the shirt and her arms over her head, his kisses progressed up her belly. When the shirt reached the tip of her fingers and he pulled it over her hands to drop it to the ground, his mouth encircled her left breast and he began to knead the nipple with his tongue. The sensation made Dakota release a sigh of enjoyment.

Nicolay watched the pleasure flow across her face as she closed her eyes and fully concentrated on enjoying these new sensations. He took notice as her nipples become tiny pebbles between his fangs. He caressed the line under each breast as he alternated between the left and the right.

As much as he was enjoying pleasuring her, Nicolay knew there were other erogenous zones he wanted to tend to. He carefully released her nipple as to not nick her with his fangs and traced is tongue back down her stomach. He paid close attention to the reactions of her body in order to give her as much pleasure as he could. Tonight would be about pleasing her and nothing else.

Wrapping his arms around her waist, Nicolay laid back on the blanked pulling her down on top of him. The sudden movement surprised her, but she fully trusted Nicolay. He flipped them over so she lay on her back with him above her. Immediately he picked up where he'd left off. He planted butterfly kisses on each of her hipbones and then proceeded to unbutton her pants with his teeth. She could feel his cool breath on her lower stomach as he performed this task. He slid is arm under her just enough to lift her as he slid her pants down.

"No underwear. Why am I not surprised?"

She smiled deviously and continued to enjoy his teasing and pleasing of her body.

As quickly as he was taken aback by her not having on panties, he returned to his mission of giving her the best night of lovemaking she had ever had. He continued on his journey, kissing each thigh while sliding her pants down and then eventually off. He worked his way down her left leg to her knee, calf, ankle and eventually each toe on her beautiful foot. He massaged the arch of her foot while he sucked each toe. He watched her face, and was glad to see her enjoying this little game he was playing with her body. He had to keep telling himself though, that the best was yet to come. He slowly licked his way up her right leg to her thigh. He nibbled at her bikini line and then little by little parted her legs.

Dakota was in no way prepared for the sensations she felt as he licked and sucked her sex like a baby feeding from its mother's breast. Her entire body tingled and she felt herself squirming from the pleasure.

Nicolay took much pleasure in pleasing her, but he was not quite ready to bring her to orgasm. When he sensed she was about to reach her peak, he lowered the intensity of the sucking motion and slowly rolled her sex around his tongue. He did this until she begged him to make love to her.

Dakota grabbed at his shirt and pulled him up to her lips as fast as she could. While kissing him as intently as she could, she whispered, "I can't take much more of this teasing. I want you. I want you now. Please make love to me."

Each word made Nicolay desire her more and more. He would answer her plea by making the sweetest love he had ever made. She pulled his tee shirt over his head and threw it to the wind. While he kissed her lips, cheeks, eyes, forehead, she unbuttoned his pants and slid them down his legs with her foot. Although she had never done this before, undressing him came easy.

Her need was so great that all she could think of was getting his clothes off so she could feel him uninhibited. He pulled her body close to him and positioned himself between her legs. He looked into her eyes, lowered his lips to meet hers, and slowly inched inside of her body. He hadn't meant to hurt her, but the minute he got halfway inside of her, along with the slightest indication of pain on her face, he smelled blood. He knew then she had been a virgin and she had offered him the one gift that was hers to give once in a lifetime.

Nicolay continued the slow rhythm until her body adjusted to him being inside of it. Her body then began to respond with its own rhythm, increasing the pace. Once again, just as he had prolonged her orgasm before, when he felt her about to explode he slowed the pace.

At times, he would completely exit her body only to thrust his sex back into her. He could appreciate the expressions on her face as he continued to pleasure her. As much as he wanted to do this all night, he knew, with this being her first time, he needed for her to truly understand and experience her first orgasm.

He held her tight and whispered in her ear, "Are you ready to experience another kind of paradise?" though she was nearly out of breath, he could make out a distinct yes from her lips, "And will you allow me to take just a little blood to enhance the experience even more? I promise, it will not hurt," she groaned her agreement, "Then welcome to paradise."

He increased the rhythm of their love making a little at a time until Dakota's body responded in sync with his. When she reached the point of no return, her body tensed. As the experience of orgasm hit her like a freight train, she held on to Nicolay, digging her nails into his back. He could feel her sex pulsing around him, squeezing and pulling at his sex almost to the point of orgasm. As she drew blood from is back, so did he from her neck. The bite was painless, but it intensified her orgasm, and it brought him to climax with her.

At that moment, time stood still. The sensations she felt lingered on as Nicolay released his bite and collapsed on top of her. She had never felt anything like what she was experiencing. Her entire body was relaxed and tingling. She was numb, but it was the most wonderful, euphoric sensation. She felt Nicolay roll her onto her side and spoon with her. He wrapped her in his arms and just held her.

"Don't try to talk, just enjoy the aftershocks."

At first, she didn't understand, but as she began to really focus on what she was feeling, she could feel the tremors emitting from her body. She did enjoy the feeling, but she was glad he was holding her. She felt safe in his arms, which meant she could let her mind rest and just enjoy the feeling. As the tiny earthquakes receded, he kissed her neck. He could already see the puncture wounds healing, another one of his secrets.

She intertwined her fingers with his and spoke, "That was like nothing I have ever experienced."

"I am glad you enjoyed it. Considering it was your first time, I wasn't sure you would. Most people don't their first time out."

"How'd you know?"

"I am a vampire. I smelled the blood when I, how do you say deflowered you."

Dakota was a little embarrassed that he could smell the blood from such a private area of her body, but she would get over that. She just wanted to lie there a little longer and enjoy being in his arms. She had just had a life altering experience with this man she barely knew, but for some reason, it didn't matter. It was as if they were meant to be. That he was the missing part of her.

Nicolay rolled on his back and rolled her over to her other side so that her left arm lay sprawled over his stomach. He kissed her on the top of her head and willed her to sleep.

The next thing she knew, light kisses on her ear coaxed her from her slumber; the sound of Nicolay whispering that she had to get up pulled at her mind even more. Nicolay didn't like how pale she appeared. Noticing how weak she was, he feared he'd taken too much blood.

"Can you sit up?" he watched as she tried, "I apologize. I've taken too much. We have two choices," he said, "You can let me carry you back to the truck and drive you home, or you can take a small amount of my blood to help offset what I took."

Dakota thought for a moment. She wasn't sure about taking his blood. She didn't know what affect having his blood would have on her or her gift. She wasn't too comfortable with the other option either. If he carried her, they would have to leave the four-wheeler out here all night.

"How much would I have to take?"

"Just a little. A drop or two of my blood would be equivalent to about a pint of blood from a transfusion. The effects of you taking my blood would be minimal. You would gain some extra strength for a few days. The decision is yours."

"So what do I need to do?"

Nicolay nicked his finger and offered it to her. She licked the metallic tasting fluid and instantly started to feel better.

"Give it a moment or two, and then try to sit up again. We must hurry though. Dawn approaches and I am far from any of my resting places."

As Dakota waited on the blood to take effect, she asked, "Do you have to have a coffin to sleep in or will just a dark place do?"

"Before I began to sleep in the club, I just slept underground. I didn't have a coffin then. Why, do you have a suggestion?"

"I think I may. At the house, there's a room my brother used to use as a dark room when he was going through his paparazzi faze. The place is light tight. No one has been in there for years. The place is practically empty. We have a fold away bed we store in the basement. You are welcome to use it. It's my way of saying thank you for showing me the most wonderful night of my life."

"Only if you are sure."

"I'm sure."

After two tries, Dakota managed to stand and comfortably walk to the four-wheeler. She decided to let Nicolay drive, using her new found strength to hold him tightly around the waist. Once back at the truck, she sat in the passenger seat while Nicolay loaded the all-terrain vehicle in the Tahoe and closed the doors. He opened the driver's door and climbed in. The movement appeared awkward for him. It made him appear to be more mortal. She laughed under her breath; she knew that he had never ridden in a vehicle this high up from the ground.

"Anything else?"

"Not that I can think of," Dakota replied.

"Then we're off," starting the engine, Nicolay headed in the direction they'd come.

CHAPTER TWENTY-SIX

NICOLAY DROVE CAREFULLY back to Dakota's house. He had not anticipated what they had done. She had made his life complete in the last few hours. How could he ever go back to the way things were? He knew he never wanted to go back to being without her. But he also knew the reality of their situation. He was a vampire, a creature damned to eternal life. She on the other hand, was mortal and would age and eventually die. He would never wish his situation on anyone, and he would not be responsible for her eternal damnation. He would not think of that now. He cleared his mind of all thoughts of the future. He just wanted to be here, right now, with her.

He pulled into the circular driveway and parked just in front of the stairs. He glanced around at his Nubian queen. He'd imagined this moment for centuries. Now that it was here, he was at a loss. She was all he'd imagined, feminine enough to nourish his heart but strong enough to hold her own. She'd spent most of her life being herself, not the someone she was expected to be. The traditional nine to five job she'd tossed to the wind. Frilly pink dresses and manicured nails were replaced by tight leather and a pistol. Dakota was a real woman and he loved her.

There she was, sleeping like a baby. He just wanted to hold her and keep her safe, forever. She was so warm, so alive. He could still taste her, feel her body bonding with his, their bodies filled with ecstasy as they reached their peak. What he wouldn't give to relive the last few hours.

He sighed. There would be many more times. For now, she needed to rest. Fate was so cruel to bring her into his life now. All he could do was enjoy the time they did have together. He would make the most of every moment.

He opened his door and walked around to the passenger side. Hovering over her, he stood in silence. She almost didn't seem real. Quietly he opened the door, hoping not to wake her. He just couldn't get enough of her beauty. Goosebumps formed on her arms and he knew it was time for him to get her into the house. Couldn't have his *Tehya Aquene* sick, even though he knew the effects of his blood would protect her. Still, he didn't want to risk it.

He reached over her body and unfastened the seatbelt. She gave a slight moan as his arm brushed her breast. Immediately his eyes were drawn to the sight of her nipple hardening. They beckoned to him, summoning him to take them in his mouth and suckle. He resisted the urge, the hunger for her body. She needed to rest and he was going to make sure she did.

He slowly raised her body from the seat, careful not to bump her head, and held her close to his chest. His heart began to beat in sync with hers. He hadn't had a heart beat in a long time, and the feeling was weird and wonderful all at the same time. He caught a whiff of her, the scent of patchouli filling his nostrils, making him drunk with need. He needed to get into the house before he lost control.

Nicolay slowly and carefully ascended the staircase. He tried the door, and just as he had suspected, it was unlocked. As much as he hated to, he'd have to wake her. One of the few facts about vampires that was actually true was that they could not enter anyone's sanctuary without being invited. Although he had heard of one case where a very old vampire had been able to do this, his years nowhere near matched those of the exception.

Nicolay nuzzled Dakota's ear, just below the lobe. As she stirred in her sleep he whispered, "I cannot enter without your invitation."

Half asleep, half-awake she responded, "You can come in."
Nicolay entered the doorway.

"Thank you my love," he again whispered, "Now sleep."

The sound of his voice hypnotized her. Dakota's eyelids once again became weights, and before she knew it she was asleep.

Nicolay looked around the house in amazement. Standing in front of him was a plantation styled staircase that split at the top. How was he going to know which bedroom was hers? He really didn't want to wake her again, then he thought about it: *just follow your nose.*

He buried his nose in her hair and drew in her scent. He really didn't need to smell her hair, her scent was all over him, but he refused to pass up an opportunity to get closer to her. He then followed the scent up the stairs and down the right hallway. The bouquet that was Dakota filled the air. He hoped the intoxicating aroma of his *Tehya Aquene* would lead him in the right direction. He needed to find her room and fast or he was going to take her right there. He followed the scent to the last room on the right. When he opened the door, he knew he had found the right place.

The room was painted a soft gold color. The centerpiece of the room was a cherry wood four-poster bed covered in teddy bears. The spread was gold with small lilac flowers forming triangular patterns throughout. The curtains had been drawn, and a single lamp on the nightstand was the only source of light. It cast a soft glow against the wall. She had pictures of herself and Dayton on the nightstand and on the other side, a vase of fresh tulips sat on a table by the window.

He slowly lowered Dakota's body onto the king size bed. He untied her shoes, slipped them off, and placed them in the closet. He rustled through the drawers of the dresser and located a matching sleep set. Undressing her, he once again admired her beauty. He dressed her in the nightclothes and pulled her close into his arms. He laid her body against his chest and held her, listening to her pulse and her breathing. He drank in her scent and blanketed her in his power.

As she shuddered in her sleep, he whispered, "Sleep my love," and she did just that.

Nicolay got up from the bed a short time before dawn. He needed to locate his resting place for the night. After searching all of the obvious doorways, he noticed a small entrance under the right side of the staircase. He entered the archway and located the door he was looking for. He pulled the folding bed into the large room and closed the door behind him. As he prepared for his rest, he whispered, "Sleep my love, I shall see you in the night."

Then, he was dead for the day.

CHAPTER TWENTY-SEVEN

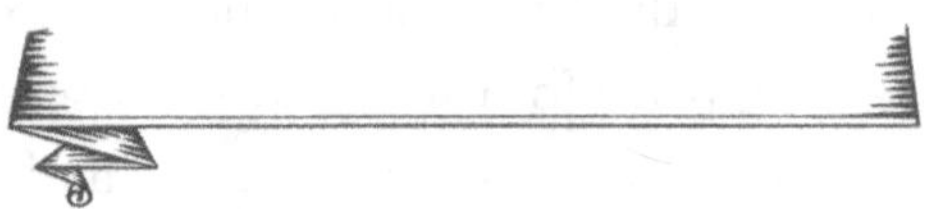

DAKOTA DIDN'T RECALL getting out of the car last night or getting into her bed. She lay still for a moment, trying to force her mind to replay the events of the previous night. Some parts, like those of her and Nicolay making love, were as vivid as the sunlight beaming through her window. Others, like how she had gotten undressed and into bed, eluded her. She then remembered Nicolay nudging her awake to give him permission to enter her home. Everything after that was a blur. She was sure he had undressed her and put her to bed. It felt strange to wake up after a night like last night without her lover by her side.

"My lover," Dakota rolled the syllables around her tongue. She could not believe she had given up her virginity just a few hours ago. She did not regret what they had done last night. And for once in a very long time, she was happy.

She looked at the clock and realized she had been asleep for almost nine hours. She was turning into a hibernating bear. It was time to get up, but she didn't want to. She took a few more minutes to explore her body to see if anything felt different.

Her friends had told her the first time would be painful, but she didn't remember any pain. All she remembered was Nicolay whispering, "*Welcome to Paradise*," in her ear. It had felt like paradise, every bit of the encounter. Even the moment he fed from her felt like paradise. She knew he'd bitten her, but she couldn't feel any fang marks.

Her skin felt smooth and sultry every place she touched. She wondered if that was because she had drunk from him.

Finally dragging her body out of bed, she drew a bath in the old claw foot tub, opened all of the blinds in the room, and slid into the comfort of the warm water. It soothed her soul and allowed her time to evaluate all she'd experienced. In just three nights, she had seen her brother off to the other side of the United States, fallen in love with a vampire, and become a woman in the true sense. For once, things in her life seemed uncomplicated.

Dakota enjoyed how simple her home was. Home and Paradise, Inc. were among the few places she could go and not have to worry about touching things and picking up left over images of people long past. She and Dayton had strict rules in the shop that no one touch anything in their areas. Most of their friends knew their secrets and abided by the rules. Because of this, they rarely entertained at the house. She wondered if Dayton would know that Nicolay had stayed there when he returned. She hadn't picked up anything from touching him, but she wasn't sure the differences in their abilities wouldn't allow Dayton to pick something up.

Dakota could hear the phone ringing in the other room. She was beginning to prune, so she decided to get out of the tub, but she would not run for the phone. No, on this day, she would take her time in everything she did, just as Nicolay had taken his time in making love to her last night. As she dried her body off, she noticed a slight stiffness in her legs, but otherwise she felt magnificent. As she entered the master bedroom, she took a seat in the Queen Anne chair by the nightstand and pressed the play button on the answering machine.

"Hey, sis. Guess you and Lysette are out on the town. I see she's turning you into a little night owl. Just wanted to let you know that I'll be back early. I'm catching a flight Sunday night. I've got a ride from the

airport so you don't have to come and get me. Well, don't party too much while I'm gone. Miss you. Love you. 11:4pm."

Dakota thought, *At least he didn't call in the middle of the night to check on me like a normal brother would.* The next message began to play.

"Figured you'd be home by now. Girl, call me when you get in. I hope your night was as exciting as mine. You've got to tell me all of the juicy details. Call me. 3:16am."

Mustn't forget to call her back, Dakota thought.

"That was your last un-played message," the machine exclaimed.

Dakota looked at the clock. It was one in the afternoon on a Saturday. She thought about going into the shop, but decided against it. Then she realized in all of the excitement of last night, she hadn't eaten dinner. *Definitely Italian food.* Although she had planned to return long before lover boy awoke, she decided to leave him a little love letter just in case she didn't make it back in time.

She sealed the note in an envelope, sprayed it with the perfume she was wearing last night, sealed it with a kiss, and slid it under the door to the darkroom. Fear of allowing light in kept her from sneaking a peek, so she settled for pressing her head to the door and attempting to read the room. Nothing... not that she was surprised.

"Sleep tight," she whispered to the door.

Grabbing her car keys and opening the garage door, she realized that Nicolay had parked outside. Closing the door again, she exited the house through the front. She had her back turned to the driveway while she locked up. She felt a sting on the back of her neck, reached to feel what had bitten her, and everything went black.

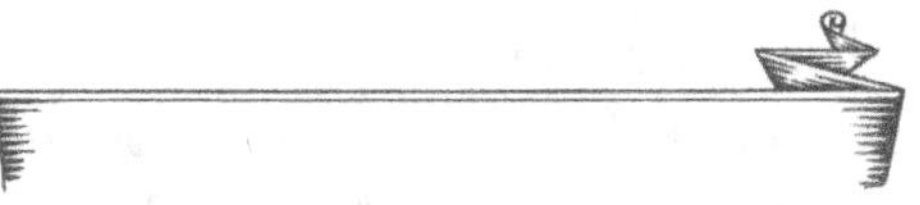

CHAPTER TWENTY-EIGHT

NICOLAY AWOKE TO THE smell of Dakota's perfume, patchouli. He glanced around the room. No sign of her. He followed the scent to an envelope that had obviously been slipped under the door. He waved it under his nose. The perfume was intoxicating, just as it had been on her the night before. He couldn't wait to hold her in his arms again. He wanted so badly to make love to her again. He opened the letter and read:

Dear Nicolay,

I had an amazing time last night. I woke up this morning invigorated. Hope you enjoyed it as much as I did. I hope you will have some time tonight to spare. I know your life is busy, and I don't want to crowd you. There are still some things I would like to explain to you, like that first night we met. I fully intend to return before you arise from your slumber, but if I miss you, I will definitely see you at the club tonight.

With all my love,

Kota

"With all my love," he repeated the phrase three more times. Each time he spoke those four little words, his mind swam with emotions. He wanted to proclaim to the world he loved her. Needing to see her smiling face right now, he opened the door and called out to her.

"Kota, Kota...My *Tehya Aquene*!"

No answer. He searched each room of the house, even Dayton's room. No Dakota. He checked outside the window and saw that the Tahoe was still in the driveway. Maybe she had another car in the garage, or maybe her friend came and got her. He checked the garage, but no other vehicle was there. Finally, he chose to leave. He left a note pinned to her closet door saying he would meet her at the club.

DAKOTA CAME TO IN DARKNESS. Initially, she thought she was dreaming, then she realized her hands were bound above her head and her legs felt like they were attached to a wall. She was still disorientated, and the fact that she was blindfolded didn't make things any better. She tried to get her bearings, but it was nearly impossible. She took a moment to calm down and tried to remember what had happened.

She took a deep breath and concentrated. The events of the last couple of days flowed through her mind like a motion picture. Her seeing her brother off from the airport, the two nights at the club, making love with Nicolay, the bubble bath, and leaving the note for her lover. All of the events seemed crystal clear except leaving the house. She remembered being hungry and heading out to grab Italian food. Then, everything had gone blank. Someone had drugged her, and she didn't have an inkling as to who or why.

Dakota ran all of Paradise's clients through her head. They had had some clients upset with them when they couldn't pay and Paradise took possession of their vehicles, but she couldn't believe someone would kidnap her over that. She didn't have any enemies as far as she knew, and neither did her brother or any of their friends. The only thing that had changed in her life was meeting Nicolay. She contemplated for a second, then realized that unless he had hired someone, he could not be responsible for her kidnapping. It had occurred in broad daylight. She played all sorts of scenarios through her head, but each lead to the same conclusion. She didn't know where she was or who had kidnapped her.

"Focus. Stay calm and focus," she kept telling herself.

What did she know about the situation? She couldn't see, so she didn't know if she was alone. Her hands were bound above her and her legs were bound below her. Based on the position of her chest and the solid coldness against her back, she was hanging from a wall rather than standing with her hands attached to it. The place had a musty, moldy smell, and there was dampness to the air. If she reached with her fingers she could feel the chains that attached her to the wall. Listening intently, she made out a faint voice, but it was too far away for her to hear the conversation. She couldn't make out what the person was saying, but she only heard one voice. Whoever it was must have been talking on the phone.

Lastly, she was still fully clothed, a plus if she escaped. That was the extent of the deduction she could accomplish with her other senses. She closed her eyes and tried to read the room. She placed the back of her hands against the wall. Nothing. Wherever she was had not had human contact in a very long time.

Dakota had to make some decisions, and fast. First she had to decide if she wanted to let her captor know she was awake. Maybe her captor had left her alone, or maybe she had been left with a guard whom she could convince to let her go. Was she willing to take that risk?

"Well, here goes nothing," she whispered, "Hello, is anyone out there?"

No response. Not sure if that was a good or bad thing, Dakota had to think of something else. But what?

AFTER CALLING THE CLUB to let Xavier know he would be in later, Nicolay took a detour from Dakota's house to one of his homes of hibernation to feed. He always kept a warm tank of blood stashed for occasions such as this. Since he was dead to the world during the day, he took some time to reflect on the events that had occurred over the last couple of days.

His life, or afterlife that is, had become complete in a matter of three days. So much had changed in so little time. He had never imagined he would be a victim of love at first sight. Here he was now, head over heels in love with a woman who accepted him for who and what he was. All of the time he spent in hiding, sure he would never find love, and in less than seventy-two hours he was ready to commit his life to a woman he barely knew. She had him hook, line, and sinker, and he would do anything in the world to keep her happy.

Things were happening so fast, but for once in his life, he was okay with that. He actually felt happy, a feeling he had longed for over hundreds of years. He'd had his share of women, but none had ever fired his loins as this one had.

Nicolay wanted to do something really special for Dakota tonight. He thought about it and came up with just the thing. But he had to hurry; there was much preparation needed and very little time. First stop, the flower shop. He needed two-dozen roses. One dozen to give to his love, the other to spread in the bath he was going to draw for her. Next, he needed bubble bath, massage oil, and candles. Lastly, fresh towels, a linen table cloth, soft music, and incense to set the mood. Nicolay planned to pamper his *Tehya Aquene* like she had never been pampered before. There was no time to waste. He packed up his silk boxers and robe, an extra robe for Dakota, and the fluffiest towels he had, then he headed for the stores.

NICOLAY GLIDED PAST the line at the entrance to the club. He hadn't come in the front in a long time. He searched the crowd, hoping to catch a glance of his queen, but to no avail. His hopes became shards as he reached the entryway. Roses in hand, Nicolay entered the club. He made his way to the bar where he observed Xavier making cocktails.

"Where ya been, boss?"

"Had some business to tend to. Seen the lovely lady I left with last night? She said she would meet me here. I didn't see her vehicle out front, but I thought her friend may have driven."

"No boss, haven't see her tonight. I'll keep an eye out for her. Pretty busy tonight though. She may be out in the crowd somewhere and we just haven't spotted her yet."

"Well, when she gets here ring me in the office. Don't tell her I am here and don't let her hear you make the call. I want to surprise her."

"Got it, boss. Will do. Is she the one that all of the stuff is for?" Xavier hadn't seen Nicolay ever bring a woman tangerine roses.

"Yes, but like I said, it's a surprise. I know you can keep a secret," Nicolay winked at Xaverier

"Sure can, boss."

Xavier proceeded to turn and grab a bottle of Captain Morgan rum from the top shelf of the bar while Nicolay turned to scan the crowd. He really had expected Dakota to beat him to the club. He searched intently, but there was no sign of her.

"I'll be in my office."

"Sure thing, boss."

"Why do you continue to call me boss? We've been friends for years now, you can call me Nicolay."

"Can't, boss," Xavier gave Nicolay a look of reassurance. They'd had this discussion before and it always ended the same. Xavier had too much respect for Nicolay as his boss to refer to him by a name other than his full proper name or title. After some coercion, they finally agreed boss would be appropriate. Plus, Nicolay's name was meant to be spoken by royalty, and it felt awkward for him, a country field hand turned bartender, to say it.

"I'll leave it alone, but that doesn't mean I understand it."

Shaking his head in disbelief, Nicolay proceeded to his office, packages in hand to prepare for the arrival of his *Tehya Aquene*. Making his way through the crowd, he attracted more attention than he really wanted to. He'd remember next time he was going to deliver roses to a woman to come in through the back door. After being stalked, groped, and all out handled in the most embarrassing ways possible, Nicolay made it to the hallway where his office was located.

As he approached his office door, he noticed something was not quite right. His door always remained closed and locked. Before he and Dakota had left for the night, he made sure the door was secured. A vampire could never be too careful. Even his most trusted friend didn't have a key to his office, yet here he was standing in front of an office door that was slightly ajar. A soft glow emerged from below the door. Someone had been in his office.

He carefully placed the items he had brought with him on the table that stood by his door. He forcefully opened it, making sure it hit the wall to ensure no one was behind it. The room was in total disarray. The desk and chairs had been flipped. Holes had been knocked in the walls and ceiling. The rugs had been shredded, the floor dug out in places. Whoever it was had even torn the tailored curtains from the walls. But all he could comprehend at that moment was his paintings. The paintings he had worked so long and so hard on, the paintings that were his refuge when all seemed lost, they had been forcefully ripped from the walls and pieces lay strewn across the floor. He fell to his knees, overwhelmed by the destruction of his paintings. The paintings of the sunsets were all he had left to remember the world he was no longer a part of.

"Someone will pay for this. Someone will pay dearly for this."

As he held the tattered pieces of his memories, he became more and more enraged. Who would dare violate him like this? Who would bring upon himself the wrath of the unknown? Humans had only heard make-believe stories of what vampires were capable of. He didn't know who and he didn't know why, but someone would meet his maker for this abhorrent act. The rage built in him moment by moment. He had forgotten all about his plans for tonight. All that mattered in that moment was someone had to answer for this, this abomination his office had become.

"*Xavier*!" Nicolay shrieked, his emotion apparent in his voice.

Xavier heard the bellow of his name. He glanced around at the crowd, but it appeared that only he had heard the call over the volume of the music. Xavier grabbed one of the waitresses and instructed her to watch the bar while he went to see the boss. He tossed the dishtowel to her and quickly made his way through the crowd to the hallway of offices. As he approached the single open office door, Nicolay stood in the doorway like a giant with what appeared to be pieces of the wall painting in his hand. The abyss his eyes had become was far from a good sign.

All Xavier could ask was, "What happened?"

Nicolay looked at his friend. He was so angered; he needed to take a moment to calm himself before he hurt someone. He counted to ten although it felt like ten thousand. Before he spoke, he turned and took one more look at the shambles. He couldn't turn back around and show the disappointment now masking his face. Even after all of these years perfecting the art of hiding his emotions, some were just too strong for him to cloak. As calmly as he could, he finally spoke. Anger, disappointment, but mostly hurt and sadness apparent in his voice, he could only manage a few words, but they were a few important words.

"You have no idea who did this?"

Nicolay was concerned that the one person who always knew what was going on had no clue. He thought this was suspicious, but then dismissed the idea, because he knew his friend too well. If he'd had anything to do with what had happened to his office, Nicolay believed that he would be able to tell.

"No, boss. I haven't even been down here. When I got here, the alcohol was being delivered. By the time that was done and inventoried, I had just enough time to set the bar up, take the chairs off the table, and divide the money pickup for the registers. Plus, you made sure no one had a key to the office," Xavier took a good look at what was left of the molding around the door. The wood was splintered in a number of places, "Apparently, whoever wanted in didn't care much about using a doorknob or having a key."

In all of the distress, Nicolay had not noticed that there was forced entry. He had assumed whoever did this had used a key.

"What do you think they were looking for?" Xavier asked.

The club had been in business for a few months now, and many of the patrons came just to see if they could catch a glimpse of the owner. The club made decent money, and especially so since the owner was breathtakingly gorgeous and also a vampire. Women flocked to the establishment like flies to honey, and the men would follow hoping to catch some unexpected lonely lady after she was devastated by the vamp turning her down.

Money was a possibility, but Nicolay had other ideas of what the vandals had been looking for. True, he could dismiss the holes in the walls as a perpetrator looking for a safe, but inside, he knew what they were really looking for. The more he thought about it, the more the motive became apparent. Someone wanted to know the location of his main lair. Many of the employees had seem him enter the office before closing, but no one had ever seen him leave. Maybe last night they took the opportunity to see if they could find his lair while he was out with Dakota. The question now was who.

"What is it boss?"

Xavier placed his hand on Nicolay's shoulder to get his attention. His boss had been pondering something, and Xavier was hoping he would want to share what was on his mind for a change. Lately, they had grown further and further apart. There were times when he and Nicolay would talk hours on end, but as of late he had become somewhat of a recluse. Now was not the time for him to keep anything inside. Someone was out to get him.

Nicolay turned and looked at his trusted friend. How could he have ever doubted him? He was ashamed he'd even thought Xavier had had anything to do with the destruction. What did puzzle him though, was there was no sign of forced entry from any of the other doors. He had instructed Xavier to activate the alarm to the club if he had not returned by closing time.

"Was anything out of place when you came in this evening?"

"Come to think of it, the lock on the outside of one of the backdoors was undone. I thought maybe I missed it last night. But the alarm was armed last night and when I came in, there was no indication it had been set off anytime during the night. I am pretty sure only you and I know the code to the alarm, but I can't guarantee that. As careful as I try, it is possible someone may have seen me activate or deactivate the system. Sometimes I'll walk the female employees to their cars when it is really late or we've had some creepy customers. It's possible one of them may have seen me enter the code," Xavier scanned the damage, shaking his head in disbelief.

"So what now, boss?"

"Leave me. When Dakota shows up, call me and I'll come out to meet her. No reason to alarm her that anything has occurred."

As Xavier turned and retreated down the hallway, Nicolay just stared at the destruction. He wanted to cry, but crying wouldn't bring his paintings back. He grabbed the discarded items from the nightstand, entered the office, and closed the door behind him. He'd clean this mess up later. For now, he would retreat to his lair and wait. The damage to the wall had not mattered. It was almost as if his lair lay in a parallel dimension. They could tear the wall down completely, but would find nothing. He was the key, and without him, no one would find his home.

As the hours passed, Nicolay's concern for Dakota escalated. Dakota had promised to meet him at the club, but up until this point, she was nowhere to be found. Dawn was fast approaching and all sorts of situations played over in his mind. He convinced himself that maybe she had gotten caught up with her friend. He would try not to worry. He made one last desperate call to her home hoping she'd overslept, but all he got was her answering machine. He chose not to leave a message. Just as he hung up the phone, the sun crept above the horizon and he allowed a troublesome sleep to engulf him.

CHAPTER TWENTY – NINE

DAKOTA DIDN'T REMEMBER blanking out again, but when she came to she heard the voices of two people talking in another room. She listened intently and if she concentrated, she could make out the conversation.

"Master, we have the girl. He will be ours soon enough."

"Did you locate his lair?" the very powerful and arrogant voice asked.

Dakota could tell the other person greatly feared this one. The voice alone gave her goose bumps. She promised herself she never wanted to meet the owner of a voice like that.

"No, master, we searched the office but we couldn't find anything."

"We have searched for this one for centuries, do not let him escape."

"No master, we will not fail you and soon you will once again walk the earth."

Dakota didn't recognize the voices, but she took note of the conversation. Apparently someone had kidnapped her to get to someone else. She listened harder, hoping to gain more information on her captor as well as why she was taken.

"I have waited far too long to return to the realm of the living. My patience grows thin."

"We have left a message for him. He loves this one, he will come for her."

"How can you be so sure of this?"

"We have watched him over these years and he has never been in love. But now, this one human will be his undoing."

"Make sure that she is. After I have what I seek, she is yours to do with as you please."

"Thank you, most gracious master."

Then silence. *This is getting creepy*, Dakota thought. The only men in her life were Dayton and Nicolay. She couldn't think of a soul that would want to hurt her brother. On the other hand, she still knew so little about Nicolay and here she was, her life endangered, she assumed, because of him.

"I'm really going to have to reconsider this dating thing," she whispered under her breath.

"So I see you're awake."

Dakota jumped, not realizing she was no longer alone. She wondered how much of what she had just said the person had heard.

"Fear not, you will not be harmed unless we do not get what we want," the man's voice said.

"And what is it that you want?"

Dakota hoped by keeping him talking she could stall until she could get more information out of him or figure out how to escape. She figured, the more she knew the better. Hopefully she would be able to use the information to her advantage.

"It is not what we want. It is who. Your little boy toy has eluded us long enough and with your help, unwillingly or not, he will soon be where he belongs."

"And where is that?"

"That is of no concern to you."

"So why kidnap me? What are you going to accomplish? Since it seems you have been following him around, you should know he and I just met. I am not as confident as you that he will risk his life for me," although Dakota had just spoken the words, she in no way believed them. She knew Nicolay would risk his life to save her. She just hoped her captor would believe otherwise.

"*Au contraire* my dear, I think that is all the more reason to come to your rescue. The guilt of something happening to you would eat at his conscience. Just as you have carefully observed him, we have been doing so for centuries. We know him a lot better than you do. Probably a lot better than he knows himself."

"So once you have him, what happens to me?" Dakota already knew the answer to this question. She had overheard enough of the conversation in the other room to know he'd get her once they had Nicolay. She needed to know for sure what he had planned for her. If he planned on killing her anyway, she may as well try to save herself as quickly as possible instead of waiting and hoping Nicolay would come to her rescue.

"Well, my dear," he stepped close enough to run his finger down her cheek. She was no threat to him tied up and blindfolded. Plus, she was just a mere human girl, and no match for his kind, "I plan to have a little fun with you. I'll try to make it as enjoyable as possible for you, but ultimately, you will serve me in any and every way possible. I have big plans for the both of us. Would you like to hear some of them?"

Arrogant son of a bitch. He was so sure of himself, but Dakota knew something he didn't know. She would keep her little secret for now.

Her captor waited patiently for her to decide if she wanted the graphic details of what he planned for her. He knew he'd get the most enjoyment out of the torture he planned for her, and he had so much planned for her, but he would make sure she was fully aware of all he planned to do. He wanted her body so bad he could taste it, but he had to be patient. If Nicolay thought anything had happened to her, he would definitely not accept the gracious offer of his master. They had waited and planned far too long for this.

No, he could wait. It wouldn't be long now. Dusk was fast approaching and after no word from his *Tehya Aquene* he would surely come looking for her. The time was drawing near, and he had to prepare. But before he did, he was going to have a little fun.

"You seem to be having trouble with the question. I'll give you a few moments more. I must go, but believe me, I shall return. Then the fun will really begin."

Dakota didn't like the way he said that. She was sure now that whether he admitted it or not, she would not enjoy anything he had planned for her. She was also more certain that eventually, he would kill her.

"Think Dakota. Think. There has to be a way to contact someone," as she spoke the last words, she smiled.

Instead of no options, she now had two. The question now was, could she pull it off? The first, she was pretty sure she could accomplish. Although they had never tried from this distance, she and Dayton had always had a mental connection. It used to be embarrassing sometimes when she would be thinking naughty thoughts about some guy and then realize Dayton was reading her mind. As they'd grown, they agreed on a clear set of rules pertaining to reading the other's thoughts.

The second option was a spell Lysette had taught her. They had only used it once, right after she had written it, just to see if it would work. It had worked, and it about freaked them both and Dayton out. She remembered the incantation, but she was missing two vital elements they'd used to cast the spell.

Time was running out. She could hear footsteps fast approaching. She had to make a call and fast. She decided to try to contact Dayton first, then, if that didn't work, she would try the spell. She would have to make do with what she had to try to cast it. She wasn't sure it would work, but she was fresh out of ideas.

Dakota stilled herself. Concentrating on her breathing, she found a peaceful place in her head. She saw herself sitting in the white space. She closed her eyes. Quietly, but confidently she called Dayton's name in her mind.

"Dayyyy-ton, Dayyy-ton. Dayton, its Dakota, I need you to hear me," then, she waited. She sat there for what seemed like an eternity. Even in her mind, she could feel the cool wind of Dayton answering her summons.

"You've only called me like this once. If you have resorted to speaking to me in your mind, something is terribly wrong."

Dayton seemed confused and worried. His sister did not take sharing her mind lightly. She had to be in a life or death situation to resort to opening herself up to this type of invasion.

Dakota had to remain calm. If she began to panic, she might lose the connection.

"Listen to me Day, I've been kidnapped. I have no idea where I am. There isn't much time. I need you to get a message to a friend that he's in danger. I'm not sure how I'm going to get out of this, but I need to make sure he understands the situation."

"You're scaring me now, Kota, what's going on?"

Dayton was trying to remain as calm as he could. He had only been gone a few days but apparently much had happened. He needed to know how much and fast.

"I don't have time to tell you everything. You have to get a message to a friend. It could mean life or death for the both of us. You gotta understand, I want to tell you everything, but I can hear someone coming."

"But—"

Dakota cut him off, "There are no buts, just listen to me." The footsteps were getting closer. She had to hurry or this wouldn't work.

"Contact Lysette; tell her I've been kidnapped. Tell her to find Nicolay. Whoever these people are, they want him and plan to use me to get him. I know as little about my situation as you do. She knows she won't be able to contact Nicolay until after dusk."

"But it's after dusk now."

"Even better, now listen, you have to trust Nicolay. He will do whatever it takes to make sure I come back safe. He may be a stranger to you, but I trust him with my life, just as I trust you will relay this message. I'll try to get as much information as I can out of my captor, but until then, Nicolay must know what's going on. Hopefully, he'll have more of an idea who wants him than I have right now. He may also know where I am."

"Then what? Are we just supposed to wait around for you to escape or for me to lose my connection with you after you are dead to do something?"

Dakota heard the frustration in her brother's voice, "Listen, I know you're frustrated, but you have to trust me on this. I have a plan. I also think my captor has left some sort of indication he has me. I overheard a conversation and apparently they are setting some sort of trap for Nicolay."

"You mean there is more than one?"

"I don't know yet, I heard at least two voices, but I've only talked to one person. Now look, some strange things may happen tonight. Just remember I am always with you. Now go; and hurry. I'm counting on you, Day."

Dakota severed her connection with Dayton, and none too quickly. As she returned to her body, her captor entered the room.

CHAPTER THIRTY

NICOLAY'S WORRY JOLTED him out of his slumber. Something wasn't right. It wasn't quite dusk yet. He still felt the sun beating on the walls around him. By the time he quickly showered and dressed, the sun had made its final descent below the horizon.

He needed to see Dakota and he needed to get to her as quickly as possible. As he walked through the wall, he was reminded of the horrible events of the previous night. He'd requested nothing be touched. He wanted to try to save at least one of the paintings, so he decided to clean up the mess himself. He'd planned on doing it last night, but was so overwhelmed by not seeing Dakota and trying to figure out who had done this and why, dawn had snuck up on him.

As he entered the club, the weeknight bartender, Kaida, greeted him. Nicolay had rescued her from a cruel and unforgiving master nearly a century ago. She had endured enough torture and hate for more than one lifetime. Ultimately, he had aided her in releasing all of her kind from their master. Her master had deserved the death Nicolay had given him. They both made sure he would never harm another of her kind again.

"Something's happened," instinctively she knew.

Kaida and Nicolay had been friends since the day he had rescued her. She had watched Nicolay struggle with many aspects of what he was for many years now. The one thing she knew was he hated feeding off of others. Over the years she'd helped him through this dilemma. He had fed from her many times. A strange relationship theirs was, but she committed to never look at him as anything more than her boss and a friend.

"First you feed, then we'll talk about what happened," she offered her wrist to him.

Kaida had been through this before with Nicolay. He would exit his office pale and look like his heart had been ripped from his chest, but he had never looked this bad. Something was terribly wrong and she desired to find out what it was.

He couldn't even look at her while he fed. This beautiful woman standing in front of him, offering her sustenance to him so that he may thrive, and he couldn't look at her. He felt so ashamed, not because he was feeding from Kaida, but because he should be on his way to find his true love. Instead, he was here, feeding off of his dear friend.

"Get that out of your head. You know you have to have nourishment. Stop kicking yourself about it. You know I don't mind. It's been too many years and we've been through this too many times. I accept who and what you are just as you have done for me. The least I can do to repay you for saving me is to offer you a meal."

Nicolay finally opened his eyes and looked up at Kaida. She so understood him. He never understood how she could just let him feed off of her. He hated doing it, but she insisted and he always felt better after having her blood.

The taste of her blood was different from that of Dakota's. Kaida's blood was sweet, almost sugar like, and ran thick. Dakota's blood ran like water, almost as if she was anemic, and it had a slight metallic taste to it. However, Dakota's blood was human, Kaida's was not. Nicolay took the last drop of his meal and released Kaids's arm. He drew in a deep breath and licked the remaining droplets of blood from his fangs.

He sighed, then spoke, "A lot has happened in the past couple of days." He knew he could confide in her and he felt slightly better talking to a woman about his problems than to a man. He figured that is why he hadn't told Xavier about what had happened with Dakota.

Kaida listened intently as Nicolay relived the past few days. His last words were, "I am in love with her, and want her with me always, but I fear I have scared her away and I do not know what to do."

"Have you tried calling her?"

"Yes. No answer," he looked like a wounded puppy. "I fear I came on too strong and now she may be lost to me forever. Then, with all this mess going on with my office being ransacked, I don't know what to think anymore."

Kaida placed her arms around him and gave him a motherly hug. He was on the brink of tears and she couldn't stand to see him like this. She knew they had to do something, and she had just the thing.

"First, you are not about to cry. Pull yourself together and listen," Nicolay looked up at her with the saddest puppy dog eyes she had ever seen, "Based on what you've told me, you may be worrying for nothing. You say you know where she lives, right?" He nodded his agreement, "Then, I think we'll pay her a little visit. Let me call someone to cover the bar and then we'll be off."

She stood, turned, and walked to the phone behind the bar. Nicolay watched each movement with wonderment. She was so beautiful and in complete control of her life. Far from what was going on with him at the moment. His life had spiraled out of control so easily.

He thought back to the time he had first seen her. Her captor dragged her down the street with a leash around her neck like some disobedient animal. He had hated the man with a passion the moment he'd laid a hand on Kaida's beautiful face. Even with him dragging her down the street on the leash, she fought with every ounce of her being, defying his every beck and call.

Kaida returned to him, hand outstretched, waiting for him to return the gesture, "Shall we?"

"Before we go," he wrapped his arms around her, "I just want to say thank you. Thank you for caring. Thank you for listening. Thank you for being my friend."

"You're welcome," she returned his hug, "Now, let's go. I want to meet the woman who finally nabbed your heart."

She had a giant Kool-Aid smile on her face and Nicolay could only laugh.

"What's so funny?" Kaida asked.

"Why, you of course."

"I'm going to let that slide. So, are you flying or should I?"

"I'll fly," Nicolay replied, "Wouldn't want to cause mass hysteria around here now would you?" it was his turn to show off a huge smile.

"Look, you're going to get enough of these cheap laughs at my expense."

Nicolay knew she was kidding, but she had left herself open for that last one.

"Let's get going." He lightly grasped her hand and off they went. She wasn't much of a burden flying, mainly because he was energized from drinking from her, but also because she had as much experience flying as he did. True, in her natural state, she flew quite differently than a vampire, but her motions were no less graceful.

IT DIDN'T TAKE LONG for them to arrive at the house. He remembered Dakota saying she left the doors unlocked most of the time, them living out in the middle of nowhere and all, so he'd left the door unlocked last night. There were no signs of life in the house, which was the first thing to worry him. The Tahoe appeared to be in the exact spot he'd left it when they returned from the clearing the other night.

"Place looks lived in but deserted," Kaida observed as he lowered them both to the ground, "Sure she is home?"

"No, and the place looks just as I left it last night. That worries me."

"Does it look like the vehicle's been moved?" she heard the worry in his voice. The abandoned look of the place was not helping. Kaida wanted more clues before she came to the same conclusion she was sure Nicolay had come to.

"Doesn't look like it, but better safe than sorry. Let's take a look," Nicolay approached the vehicle with ease. As he opened the driver side door, the first thing he noticed was the pistol Dakota had been carrying sitting on the middle console. He remembered leaving it in the truck when he scooped her out of it. He was sure if she went somewhere she would have taken it with her. That it lay there on the console was a very bad sign.

"Hood cold?" he asked.

Kaida checked around the automobile to see if she saw any signs of struggle or anything out of place. Everything around the truck appeared to be copasetic. She then proceeded to the front of the vehicle from the side opposite that of Nicolay to feel the hood.

"Cold as a day old corpse. No offense. This puppy hasn't moved all day," not a reassuring sign, "Does she have another car?"

"None taken, and yes, she has many but I don't know if she had any others at the house. When I rose last night, she was already gone. She left a note telling me she would meet me at the club. She never showed up. I'd initially dismissed it as something had come up, and I hoped I hadn't scared her away, but now I am beginning to suspect something has happened to her."

The despair was once again rising in his voice. Kaida had to keep him calm and thinking positive until they had a sure indication something had actually happened. She looked at her friend. He had such a soft heart and he didn't deserve to have his emotions walked all over like this. Kaida vowed if this woman were just avoiding him, she would pay dearly.

"We don't know that yet. Is the house open?"

Stay focused on the task at hand. If she kept his mind on looking for clues, maybe something would show that Dakota had some emergency to tend to.

They cautiously approached the house. As they reached the path leading to the stairs, Kaida grabbed Nicolay by the arm and stopped him.

Speaking lightly just in case someone was listening she asked, "What's that?"

"What?" he hadn't seen what it was she had motioned at.

"Shhh. There, on the side of the step. Something shiny. Can't quite make it out at this distance."

Nicolay walked around to one side of the massive staircase and picked up the discarded item. He stood for a moment, frozen to the spot, unable to move, stricken with grief, sadness, but most of all fear. He looked almost like a garden statue standing there so still.

"Now I know something is wrong."

"What is it?"

"The keys to the house and the vehicle."

The revelation made Kaida just as worried. As she approached him for a closer look, coming closer and closer to the house, she froze. She sniffed the air and scanned the surrounding area.

Nicolay noticed the sudden change in posture and awareness in Kaida. It caused him to be more alert of their surroundings as well. He mirrored her actions and scanned the area, although he was not quite sure what he was looking for.

After being sure they were alone, she sniffed the air again and spoke, "Do you smell that?"

Nicolay smelled the air; all he could detect was the pine from the trees.

"Smell what?"

Kaida sniffed again and followed the trail. It led to the woods. She followed it as far as she could, but it just dropped off, as if the creature had just vanished. Kaida turned back towards the house and followed the scent up the stairs. She opened the door and once again, the scent dropped off. Whatever had been here had not entered the house. She sniffed the air just inside of the house.

"Patchouli?" she asked as she turned to Nicolay.

"Dakota's scent," he replied.

"Now, we should worry," she sighed heavily and shook her head. She dreaded telling him what she had smelled, but she knew he had to know, and she had to be the one to tell him.

"I smell, how do you say," Kaida took a minute to seek out the correct word, "an *Ahpuch*."

"A what?"

"*Ahpuch, O'Yamma, Supay*," there really was no real English translation for what she had smelled.

"*Supay*? *Supay*. Where have I heard that before?" Nicolay thought long and hard. He knew that word, "Think. Think."

He scanned his memories but came up with nothing. Just as he was about to give up, it dawned on him.

"Oh no. It can't be. *Supay*. I know where I have heard that before. If we're dealing with what you say, we are going to need help, and lots of it. A devil, I never thought I'd ever cross paths with one."

"Trust me, it won't be a pleasurable experience. And if he has your woman, then she is in more trouble than we are. Let's go in the house. There isn't much we can do standing here. We need a plan, and fast."

They entered the house. Nicolay did a quick walk through just to make sure Dakota wasn't there. A silly reassurance, but something he needed at the moment. Plus, he wanted to make sure he hadn't missed any clues telling them who this devil was and where it had taken Dakota.

"I just don't understand it," Nicolay was getting frustrated and fed up. He couldn't think of one reason anyone would want to kidnap Dakota, "Who would want to kidnap her and why?"

He wanted answers and he wanted them now. Kaida saw the flames in Nicolay's eyes. She knew he was on the brink of losing it. She had to do something, and fast. She started to piece together all of the information they had collected. They'd all been sensing something not too friendly lurking about, he meets and falls in love with a beautiful woman, he returns to his office to find it ransacked, she breaks a date, now she's missing. Her keys are dropped by the stairs, the weapon that was her second skin is left, and it all comes together with the scent of a devil.

Kaida turned troubled eyes to Nicolay, "Her kidnapper doesn't want her. He wants you. I don't know why but I am sure of it."

"You mean I am the reason Dakota is in danger? I'm the reason her brother and her friends may never see her again? I'm the reason the woman I love may now be fighting for her life?"

That was it, the last straw, Nicolay finally lost it. He grabbed the first thing he saw, the living room table, and threw it. It shattered upon impact with the wall. Kaida tackled him and pinned him to the floor. True, he was a vampire who was on an emotional rampage, but she had her own secret to supernatural strength. She slapped him one good time and he froze.

Rage burning in his eyes, he snarled at her but he dared not try to attack. He could have taken her, but that wasn't the point, he had lost control and that would not bring Dakota back. They had to come up with a plan, and his losing control wasn't going to help anything.

"I apologize. I did not mean to do that. It will not happen again."

"Make sure that it doesn't. I don't think your lady friend would take kindly to returning to a home that had been redecorated by a raging vamp," Kaida was serious, and she was sure the look on her face told Nicolay she meant business and that they were wasting precious time, "Now, if you are going to act like a civilized vampire, I'll let you up."

Nicolay agreed. She climbed off of him and waved him to the couch. She was glad her night vision was perfect, otherwise she would never have found the chair sitting across from the couch. "Now, take a moment to compose yourself and then we will come up with a plan.

They sat in darkness and silence for what seemed like an eternity. Nicolay stared blankly into space while Kaida closed her eyes and meditated. She always found that meditation helped her think. They were both so engrossed in their thoughts; they didn't hear the front door open.

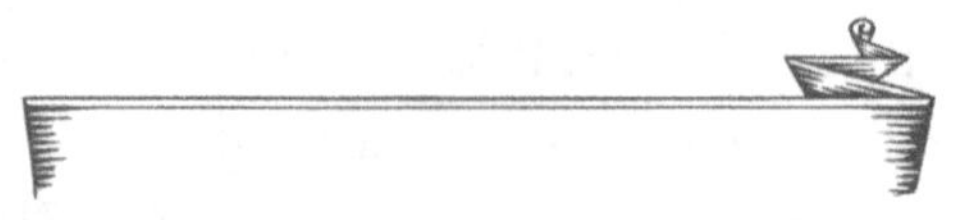

CHAPTER THIRTY-ONE

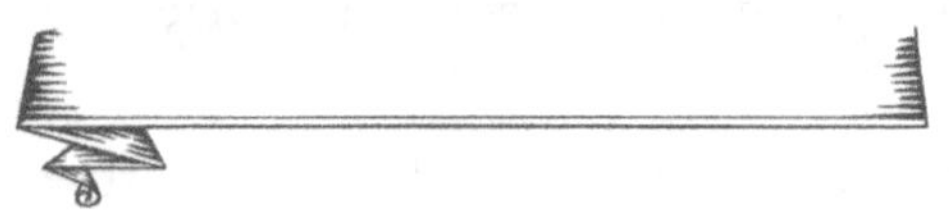

DAYTON PUT HIS KEY in the front door. He had planned to surprise Dakota, but instead she was the one with the surprise for him. He was about to enter the house when her calling his name caught his attention. After looking around for her, he realized she was calling him in his head. She had dropped a bomb on him and he had to act fast. He didn't know who Nicolay was, but after all of this was over, he was going to have a long talk with Dakota, Lysette, and this Nicolay.

Dayton entered the house, hastily dropping his bag in the middle of the entrance. As he walked to the phone to call Lysette he noticed a silhouette in the living room and a strange smell in the house. The scent was putrid and like nothing he'd ever smelled before. He immediately reached for his gun.

Evidently, whoever this was in their house hadn't heard him come in. Dayton crept up behind the shadow and pointed the gun to the back of his head. There was strange smell coming from the figure. If Dayton hadn't known any better he'd have sworn the figure was a rotting corpse.

"You've got about 30 seconds to tell me what the hell you are doing in my house."

"I am sorry we must meet under these circumstances, but I fear something has happened to someone we both love."

Nicolay was surprisingly calm. Kaida was thankful for that. Apparently, the guy with the gun hadn't seen her slip out of the chair and back against the wall in the shadows. There were advantages to her heightened hearing and her ability to move swiftly, unnoticed. She slowly circled behind the stranger. She would not attack him though, until she knew his intentions.

"Ok, so now I know why you are here, but that still doesn't tell me who you are."

"My name is Nicolay, and the young lady standing behind you is Kaida."

"Behind me?'

Just as Dayton turned, Kaida grabbed the arm with the gun and twisted it behind his back. She quickly disarmed him, then let him go. It was two against one and the speed at which she was able to neutralize him had definitely shaken him up.

"We mean no harm. You must be Dayton. Once again, I am sorry we must meet under these dire circumstances, but I fear your sister has been kidnapped."

Dayton lowered his head before he spoke, "I know. I've spoken with her."

Nicolay was immediately on his feet, peering down at Dayton. Even his five foot six frame was overshadowed by the power emitting from the six foot three vamp. Dayton didn't know how in the world this guy had moved so fast. One second he was on the couch, and the next he was towering over him. Just as Nicolay was about to lift Dayton off of his feet, Lysette walked in.

"What the hell is going on here?" she was furious. First, Dakota had been ignoring her, now she walks in on what appeared to be an altercation between her brother and her new boyfriend.

"Nicolay, don't you dare lay a hand on him or you will have to answer to me personally."

"Actually, he'll have to answer to the both of us."

In her haste to keep Dayton safe, she hadn't noticed the young lady standing on the other side of the living room. She glared at the woman, but Kaida kept her attention on Nicolay.

"Fine, what did Dakota say," Nicolay calmed himself once again. He was really going to have to control his emotions better. It was just he had never been in love like this before, and love was making him do some irrational things.

"What are you two talking about? Who is she," Lysette gestured towards Kaida, "and where is Dakota?"

Lysette had no idea what was going on. She knew she'd been trying to call Dakota since yesterday, but she just thought her friend had just gotten busy or was sleeping with the ringer off. All of these people seemed to believe something had happened to her.

"Well? Is anybody going to answer me?"

Kaida broke the silence, "My name is Kaida, and based on the little tidbit Dayton just dropped, I would say something really bad has happened to your friend."

"I don't understand?" Lysette was even more confused.

"If the two boys over there will calm down, I think Dayton has something to tell us. Boys?" Kaida used her most motherly tone to tell the guys the time to fight was not now, "Nicolay, let us not have a repeat of earlier. Take a seat and let Dayton tell us what he knows."

Nicolay glowered at Kaida but he did what was asked of him. Besides, they were getting nowhere with the staring match.

"After you."

"How about we sit down at the same time. You take the couch, I'll take the chair."

Dayton proceeded to step backwards and move to the chair. He never once turned his back to Nicolay. Lysette took a seat at one end of the couch, Kaida sat at the other end which left Nicolay sitting between the two women.

As Dayton sat in the chair, he noticed the coffee table was missing.

"What happened to the coffee table?"

Kaida decided to answer this time, "You don't want to know. Now, you said you had spoken with Dakota. Please enlighten us."

They all sat patiently, waiting on him to collect his thoughts. After a couple of minutes he began to tell them what she had said. He informed them of what little he knew, telling them Dakota thought someone was using her to get to Nicolay. She was going to see how much information she could get out of her captor, and they should wait for her to relay some sort of message.

Dayton looked around the room at all of the faces, "So now what?"

Leave it to Kaida to be the logical one, "Now, we search the house, go back over the car and yard to make sure we didn't miss anything, and we wait."

"I agree," that coming from Lysette was reassuring.

The men were ready to tear the world apart looking for a needle in a haystack. They had to be rational about this. At least retracing Dakota's last few steps would give them something to do other than sit here and twiddle their thumbs.

"Plus, I have an idea of what Dakota may do, but I won't know until it happens," they all looked at Lysette, "Don't ask. It's just a magical gut feeling."

Everyone in this room had their secrets; she planned to keep hers as long as possible. If they didn't tell, neither would she.

"Well, let's get to it. Dayton, you take the house. If you see anything out of place, let someone know. Nicolay, since you were the last one in the truck, check it out. After you finish there, take the woods. Kaida, if you don't mind, can you come with me? I may need your help outside around the staircase. Anything suspicious, yell. We'll meet back here after we're done."

Everyone got up and started on their tasks. They were all glad to have one person there who could be objective and take charge. They were running on pure emotion, and that was never a good thing in a situation like this.

CHAPTER THIRTY-TWO

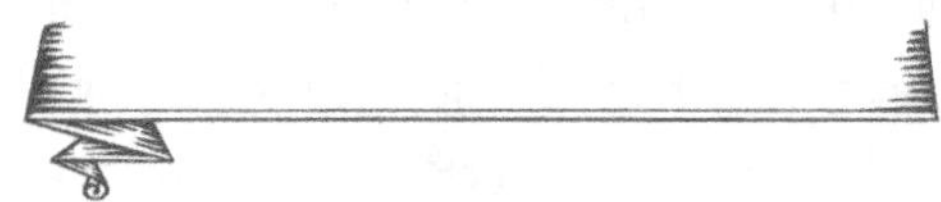

DAKOTA HEARD HER CAPTOR enter the room. She had severed her link with Dayton just in time. She already knew what she had to do. Now, she just needed to get him close enough to enact her plan.

"Now, where were we?"

"I think you were about to tell me why you kidnapped me," Dakota attempted to sound confident, keeping the quiver in her voice under control.

"Kidnap is such an ugly word. Let us just say I have borrowed you for the time being. If your friend cooperates, then no harm will come to you."

"So why do you want Nicolay?"

The more she knew about her situation, the better off she would be. True, she didn't know much about Nicolay, but she knew he wouldn't hurt a fly. She couldn't figure out why anyone would want him. Maybe he wasn't who she thought he was. No, she couldn't and wouldn't think like that. He was as much in the dark on this situation as she was. Or at least she hoped.

Her captor sighed, apparently growing tired of explaining things. Maybe if she saw who he was, she would understand. He took a moment and stepped closer to her. He carefully untied her blindfold and lowered it from her eyes.

It took Dakota a moment to realize what he was doing. Now she knew he was arrogant, either that or extremely stupid. After a minute or two, her eyes adjusted to the light. She knew she was in a cave, but not much else. The walls were bare, except for her hanging from one. There were no windows and no doors. Through the open entryway appeared a hallway lit by torches.

The only light in the room came from a torch placed in a crevice on the wall furthest from her. The surfaces of the walls were smooth, like they had been carved by water. The floor was wet. There had to be a spring in the caves not far from where she was. Because she was suspended from the wall, she hadn't noticed the water.

Her captor stood in the middle of the room facing away from her, oblivious to the pool of water he was standing in. His silhouette seemed familiar to her, but she couldn't quite place it. She studied him, watched his body move as he breathed. The movement seemed unnatural, like he was in a body that wasn't his. Finally he turned to face her, and she did recognize the face.

"Xavier."

His name was the only word she could force from her lips. Her brow furrowed. She couldn't figure out what he would have against Nicolay. They appeared to be friends from what she had seen at the club. What could Nicolay have done that was so terrible he would want revenge? Not only that, what could be so terrible he had to resort to kidnapping her in order to get what he wanted out of Nicolay? She was paralyzed with emotion, so many thoughts racing through her mind. Now that she knew who she was up against, what could she do?

"Nice of you to remember me. Most of his women don't even notice me, much less remember my name."

"You sound bitter," she replied smugly.

"Bitter I am, but not for the reasons you think."

"Must be hard living in the shadow of a vampire?" she wanted to get a reason behind him wanting revenge on Nicolay. Apparently, there was much more going on between the two men than she had thought.

"Not as hard as one would think. He has his secrets, I have mine. Trust me, I know him better than he knows himself. He will be much happier once he accepts my master's offer and joins us."

The words were spoken with malevolence. Whatever it was his master had planned for Nicolay could not be worse than the torture he had endured over all of these centuries, but he hoped so. Banished to this world to suffer for failure was as harsh a punishment as he had ever experienced. He would not fail again, not after his master had so graciously given him the opportunity to redeem himself. Nicolay would be turned over and then he would be free of this place. The time could not come soon enough.

"So why me, why now? I'm sure you've had ample opportunities to persuade him to come to your side of whatever this is. Why now? Please, make me understand."

Xavier came to stand in front of Dakota. He admired her strength, her defiance of the inevitable. He did want to make her understand. There was so much to explain, and she, a mere mortal, could not possibly comprehend the extent of what her dear Nicolay was.

She was so beautiful, and yet she seemed to care so much about Nicolay even though they had just met. Humans, he would never understand them. Once someone had lived as long as he had, little things like love no longer mattered. It was survival of the fittest, and survived he had.

"Why do you care for him so?"

The question caught Dakota off guard. She thought about it for a moment, and she wasn't sure. One thing she was sure of though, she had just seen the weakness she was looking for in her captor and she planned to take full advantage of it.

"I'm not sure. He seemed so troubled when I met him. He had lived so long but had been deprived of so much. I guess it was instinct that had me wanting to comfort him, to take all of the pain away, to show him the world the way it should be. And yet, when he kissed me, my body became a roaring fire burning out of control. I don't know any other way to explain it."

"I see," he turned to her, his face so solemn, so full of hurt and need.

He was so close she could smell him. His scent was strange. She didn't know if it was the musk of the cave or him, but the stench was horrible. She had to take short breaths to keep from vomiting. Now was her chance. The thought of kissing him repulsed her, but she feared death more.

She licked her lips and stared into his eyes. She saw centuries of loneliness in their depths. She truly wanted to fill the pools with love and understanding, but she also saw the need of power. The root of all evil was in this one. She would do what she had to do to escape, but that didn't mean she had to like it.

She slowly closed her eyes and parted her lips. She could feel him lean in closer to her, his warm foul breath reaching out and filling her nostrils. She would not look at him when she did this. She'd allow him to kiss her, but she'd feel nothing. As his tongue invaded her mouth, she nearly gagged. She played with the foul serpent until she could stand it no longer. Then, before he had a chance to react, she bit down on his tongue, drawing blood and tearing a small piece from it as he snatched his head back from her.

"You bitch!" he shrieked as he wiped the blood streaming from mouth.

Dakota gave a wicked laugh. It sounded like the laugh of the devil himself. She looked up at Xavier and smiled, "Ah ah ah, didn't your mother teach you any manners? It's not nice to call people names," the words exited Dakota's mouth with confidence. She now had what she needed to make the spell work. She didn't have the stones, she didn't have the herbs, but she had flesh and blood and nothing was more powerful.

"I see I have underestimated you. Believe me, it will not happen again."

Those were the last words he spoke before he exited the room. Dakota took this time to do what needed to be done. She swallowed the foul piece of flesh and the blood, then she repeated the incantation, trusting and hoping it would work.

"With dark return a bitter fog
A name be knowenst to all doth call
Light I call behold a fright
Thy will be done I sacrifice
Flesh I give
Blood remain
All be known speak his name."

Then she fell into silence. It was done. All she could do now was wait and hope someone heard her plea for help.

CHAPTER THIRTY-THREE

KAIDA AND LYSETTE SEARCHED the bushes around the house looking for any indication of a struggle, anything that may give them a clue as to what had happened to Dakota.

"What is that smell?" the smell was beginning to overwhelm Lysette.

Kaida looked pleased, "So you smell it too? What are you?"

"Yes, I smelled it when I first arrived at the house. And I do not understand what you mean by what am I?"

"Your senses are strong, more so than any mere human's. Dayton didn't notice the smell. Not even Nicolay noticed it, and yet you did," Kaida was very still and very serious. Lysette was not who she was pretending to be and Kaida knew it. The look in her eyes made Lysette know it as well.

"What I am is of no consequence," if anyone should be asking questions, it should be her, not this stranger. Kaida had intruded on their lives not the other way around. Lysette tried to remain civil, but she was beginning to get suspicious of Kaida.

"Oh, but I think it is," Kaida was not going to let her get out of answering the question that easily.

"Well, since you want secrets, you tell me what you are and I'll tell you what I am," two could play that game. Just as Kaida had detected she was not human, Lysette had tasted Kaida's magic years before. She wasn't quite sure how Kaida had been able to hide the scent outside, but the smell lingered around her every waking moment.

"Fair enough," Kaida accepted the give and take between them. She didn't expect Lysette to admit her secret without her wanting something in return, "The meaning of my name tells what I am."

This was all of the information she planned to divulge until Lysette admitted what she was.

"Riddles will get you everything and nothing. Besides, I knew what you were eons ago. Have you ever wondered what Nicolay was doing in Japan the day your master decided to be especially cruel to you?" Lysette smiled. She watched Kaida remember the day Nicolay rescued her from that tyrant.

"We sent him to you. The one we had watching over him had been attacked. He was badly wounded and we couldn't risk another of our lives. You were the obvious choice to replace our watcher, my dear."

"Who sent him to me, and why me?" Kaida remembered Nicolay telling her he wasn't sure why he felt the need to come to Japan at the very moment she was in need of help. He thought it a strange coincidence, but he had no other explanation. If what Lysette had said was true, then he had been sent there to free her... but why then, why not sooner?

"I was sent to ensure the safety of Dayton and Dakota. I couldn't be in two places at once. We needed someone strong to keep Nicolay. We had no doubt he would be able to save you and we knew he would befriend you. We had no fear he would become romantically involved with you because we had already contacted his true mate."

"First, how'd you know what I was thinking? Second, how come I was never told of this? What would have happened if I had decided I had paid my debt to him and left?"

"We have many abilities, telepathy one of them, although out of respect some of us choose to temper our usage. We thought it best you not know. The longer you were kept in the dark, the safer you would be. Preparations were put in place in the case you left, but we were confident, sure you would follow him, just as you did."

Lysette grew disenchanted of this conversation. She couldn't tell Kaida much more.

"Look, we knew sooner or later Nicolay would find the others. He doesn't know it yet, but he is very important to the survival of all of our kind as well as the mortals. Dayton and Dakota do not know their roles in this either, and I need to keep it that way until they are ready to understand and accept what they are."

"So what are they?" Kaida wanted to know what they were facing.

"It's best you not know. I've already told you too much and possibly endangered your life as well. But we must find Dakota before it's too late."

"I'll accept that for now, but I don't have to be happy with it. Still, you haven't answered my question," Kaida was determined she was going to get the answer out of Lysette if it was the last thing she did, "I did reveal my secret even if you already knew what I was."

Lysette sighed. She hoped to be able to resolve this without having to disclose what she was. Guess she didn't have much of a choice.

"In short, I am magic. We all are in our own ways. Nicolay's magic animates him, the dead, to react as if he were alive. Dayton's and Dakota's magic allows them to see and hear all of life and death. My magic, just as yours, allows me to keep a human form."

"Bullshit. Anyway, we're short on time so know this, you have a lot of explaining to do after all of this is over."

"As you wish, but be careful what you wish for, you just may get it," this one was going to be trouble. She would deal with her when the time was right.

"So now what?" Kaida asked, pulling the other woman out of her thoughts.

They both scanned the area one last time and proceeded back into the house. Dayton sat on the couch staring out the window, eyes glazed over. He was probably taking this the hardest. Dakota was his sister and he had sworn to protect her. Now here he was, no clue as to where to find her.

"Hey, you haven't failed her," Lysette took a moment to comfort her friend. Kaida glared at her, but she quickly dismissed the look and continued to comfort Dayton, "We're going to find her and she'll be home safe and sound before you know it."

As much as she wanted to believe that, she knew better. If they were dealing with a devil, it could only mean things were going to get worse.

On the verge of tears, Dayton pointed towards the end table before he spoke. Nicolay entered the room a moment before Dayton said the words, "I found it on the table by the front door. She would never go anywhere without it."

At that moment, Nicolay knew Dayton was referring to the Springfield that Dakota carried. He had brought it in earlier when they had checked the Tahoe. For a few moments, he had forgotten she didn't have the gun. Now, with the reminder, he worried more about her.

Lysette took the seat next to Dayton. She held him in her arms as a mother would a wounded child. Nicolay took the chair across from them. Kaida stared out into the night through the bay window to the right of them.

The tension in the air was so thick you could cut through it. They were all very still. Each person dealing with his or her own scenarios running through their minds. What had they missed? What could they have done differently? What should they do now? No one dared look at another. Each and every one of them felt helpless and hopeless and at a complete loss as to where to go from here.

KAIDA WAS THE FIRST to notice the change in the room. Something magic entered the space they occupied. It wasn't magic like what she had felt when Lysette had entered, but it was strong, very strong. It made her skin crawl, and she had to rub her arms to rid them of the eerie feeling.

Just as she turned around to see if anyone else had noticed, Lysette raised her head from the back of the sofa. Her eyes opened wide. Dayton jumped and backed as quickly as possible to the wall, trying to get as far away from Lysette as he could.

Nicolay observed Lysette as the magic surrounded her. Just as Kaida had sensed it, he too had noticed it as it seeped into the room. He snarled at the magic as it pushed against him. He tasted the air and it was thick and musty. Then he smelled it, he smelled her. Somehow Dakota had been able to send them a message. The room was filling with her, her magic. When the scent of patchouli became nearly intoxicating for him, he turned to Lysette, noticing her eyes. The color of her eyes had changed from chestnut brown to a deep aqua color. Her eyes were no longer hers, they belonged to whatever this magic was being shared among them.

Lysette began to recite the incantation she had taught Dakota. As she spoke the words, Dakota's voice filled the room.

"With dark returns a bitter fog
A name be knownst to all doth call"

Before she could get the next line out, the magic reached out and enveloped Dayton, and he began to recite the words with Lysette.

"Light I call behold a fright
Thy will be done I sacrifice"

Then the magic reached out to Nicolay. There was so much of it in the room it nearly strangled Kaida. She watched, paralyzed, as the magic grabbed a hold of Nicolay. He continued with the spell along with the others, but unlike them, his voice and his eyes were his own.

"Flesh I give
Blood remain
All be known speak his name."

Just as the magic had entered, it dissipated. Finally able to breath, Kaida gasped for air, not quite able to get as much as her body desired. When she had caught her breath she screamed.

She turned to them, "What the hell was that?" she demanded, her voice full of fear, "Somebody better start explaining and start explaining quick."

Lysette slowly came to herself. She turned to Dayton to see if the effects were wearing off. The last time they had done the spell, it had taken nearly half an hour for him to return to normal. She was glad to see he too was following suit, quickly regaining his eye color and his own voice. His power and control was growing with maturity. Soon he would be ready for what was to come for him.

Kaida turned and ran to Nicolay. She called his name over and over, trying to get him to snap out of what ever had possessed them. Kaida became frantic when Nicolay did not respond to her pleas.

"What have you done to him? Why won't he answer?" Kaida lowered her face into the palms of her hands and began to cry.

Lysette calmly raised her right hand out to Kaida before she spoke, "Come to me, my child, and I will explain."

As Lysette spoke the words, she sent a calm, warm wave of magic out to Kaida. She still had much to learn, and soon she would know the truth. They'd hidden enough, hoping this would be resolved before they needed to pull Kaida in. But things hadn't worked out quite as planned.

As the magic washed over her, a sense of peace fell upon her, allowing her to quickly regain her composure. She sat down on the couch next to Lysette, noticing the look of fear of Dayton's face.

Though fear remained with him, he appeared as relaxed as she had ever seen him. All of this was so strange.

Lysette reached out to Dayton and he took her hand. She pulled him down onto the couch with them. She needed them both to understand what had just happened. She was pretty sure Dayton knew, they had been through this before, but she knew Kaida had not a clue.

"Please," Kaida's voice quivered, "please tell me what just happened. Please tell me Nicolay will be all right. He's all I have."

Lysette knew better than this, but now was neither the time nor the place to discuss Kaida's place in this world. She took a deep breath and began to explain.

"Years ago, I convinced Dakota to let me write a spell of protection for her. She, as well as Dayton, possess psychic gifts. Dakota's seemed to be more prominent and she had less control over it, so the spell made things easier for her to live a comparably normal day to day life.

"We use the spell almost every day to make it possible for her to go out and explore the world without her having to worry about the side effects of her gift. She is clairvoyant, so she picks up residual images from everything she touches. The spell worked so well, when I approached her with the call spell, she wanted to try it immediately. We did, but we didn't realize the spell connected us all, she, Dayton and me. We nearly scared Dayton to death the first time we tried it."

"Yeah, they almost gave me a heart attack. I was glad I was alone, though. Imagine if I had been out with my friends and all of a sudden Dakota's voice started coming out of my mouth." Dayton smiled able to look at the brighter side of the situation since he had experienced it before.

Lysette continued with her explanation, "The spell was designed to connect Dakota with me any time she was in danger. We assumed because she and Dayton were twins and their gifts were so similar, that's why he got pulled into it. I'm not sure though why Nicolay was pulled into it this time. The only thing I can think of is they have become closer than I realized."

"What do you mean by that?" Dayton wanted to know more about his sister getting closer to a man who was a complete stranger to both of them.

"Calm down, it's nothing like what you're thinking. I'm not sure, but I believe that sometime within the last couple of days she has shared blood with him."

Things were starting to make sense to Kaida now, but there was still one lingering question, "Why then has he not shaken the spell as you two have?"

"Actually, the spell takes control of Dayton and me. It did not control Nicolay in the same way. Did you notice anything different between us and him?"

"Yes, his eyes didn't change like yours did. And even though he spoke the words in perfect unison with you two, his voice was his own."

"Then his attachment to the spell is probably related to something they have shared. The spell is not the reason he is not responding. I believe he's gone to her."

"What do you mean he's gone to her?"

"Before the hold of the spell was severed, he spoke to me. He said he needed to go to her. Apparently, after the effect of the spell, he realized he could touch her mind. So instead of allowing the spell to be the end of his connection with her, he used it as a way to travel to her."

"You mean to tell me his mind is not in his body, but rather in Dakota's," disbelief filled Kaida's voice.

"That's exactly what I am saying. Nicolay has denied what he is for so long he doesn't know or trust his own power. There were many gifts bestowed upon him when he became the undead, but until now, he has never had the need to use any of them. Most vamps discover their particular gifts because they need them for protection. Master vampires such as Nicolay tend to be very possessive and territorial. His power alone may have been enough to keep any other from challenging him. In a sense, that may have crippled him. The power he exudes has always been his protection; therefore, he has never tested the waters of his full potential. One of his gifts must be some other form of telepathy that allows him to separate from his physical form. It must create some sort of bridge with another or at least with those he has chosen to share a small portion of the gift with. Since the spell strengthened his powers, he was able to literally separate his mind from his body and join Dakota in hers."

"This is all too weird," Dayton shook his head.

"I know, my little one. There is much to learn and we have little time, and that is partly my fault. I just hope he can figure out where she is," Lysette's worry was written all over her face, "Good luck, Nicolay, and God speed."

CHAPTER THIRTY-FOUR

NICOLAY WOKE TO BRIGHTNESS as he stood in the middle of an all white room. He took a moment to gather his thoughts and tried to remember how he had gotten here. He remembered the spell, and feeling Dakota's mind reach out to him. He recalled reaching back to her, and the next thing he knew he was being pulled into an abyss. Then he regained consciousness here.

"Am I in Dakota's mind?" as he spoke the words, the echo returned to him.

"Only one way to find out. Dakota?" no answer, "Dakota? Are you here?"

Out of nowhere, she appeared. One minute there was emptiness, the next she was just there standing in front of him. The minute he saw her he ran to wrap his arms around her.

"You had me so worried," he buried his nose in her hair taking in a whiff of the patchouli scent that was forever her. "Where are we?" Nicolay asked, still not comprehending the fact that he was in her mind.

"We're sharing one mind," Dakota could see the confusion on his face, "I am not sure myself how it is possible for you to be here. The only other person who has ever been able to invade my thoughts was Dayton and even with him, I usually go to him. I can't recall a time he has come to me. What are you doing here?"

They didn't have much time. Whenever she was in the quiet place in her head, she left her body vulnerable. She couldn't afford to do that. Not with Xavier watching over her.

Just as she was about to speak, she was snatched out of the quiet place and violently forced back into her body by a searing pain. She screamed the minute her mind connected with her body. The pain came from her stomach. She felt her shirt becoming heavy with blood. He had cut her and from the feel of it, the cut was fairly deep.

"Nice of you to join me. I couldn't let you miss all of the fun, and what better way to get your attention than good old pain."

Dakota didn't like the laughter in his voice. Things were about to take a turn for the worse.

"My friends are coming for me. Then we'll see who has the last laugh," he wasn't convinced, and in actuality she wasn't either.

"Well my dear, that is all part of the plan. When your dear sweet Nicolay arrives, he will either surrender to the dark side or watch his precious little lady die. And if you die it will be all his fault," Xavier stood in front of her, licking the blood off of the dagger he had sliced her open with, "But until then, I am going to have a little fun with you. Since you seem to like dishing out pain, we're going to see how much pain you can take."

She didn't like the sound of that. She had to get back to Nicolay and warn him, but she was afraid to leave her body.

Xavier watched the emotions cross her face and quickly dismissed them as fear.

"You have much to fear, my dear. It's unfortunate that Nicolay will never again be able to share your body. However, I promise I'll make this as painful as possible," he grabbed a hand full of her hair and snatched her head back against the wall. He then began kissing and licking down her neck, ensuring his arm was as far away from her mouth as possible.

He stopped only long enough say, "I plan on making you scream, and I promise it will not be a scream of pleasure," he ripped her shirt and began to kiss down from her neck to her breasts.

NICOLAY DIDN'T KNOW what had happened. Just as quickly as Dakota had appeared, she was gone. He calmly called her back to him. At first, she fought him, trying to hold on to her body. Eventually, though, she weakened and once again she was there in his arms. This time, she looked horrified.

"My love, what has happened?"

All she could do was collapse and cry. Her weeping tore at his heart. What had happened in the few moments she was gone? He needed answers. Answers only this weeping maiden in his arms held.

"Dakota listen to me," he ran his fingers through her hair, massaging her scalp, hoping to calm her down, "You must tell me what has happened."

Slowly, she regained control. When she'd gained her composure enough to speak, she answered, "He's going to rape me and then he's going to kill me."

She stuttered, trying to prevent the sobs from creeping into her throat and escaping.

Now he knew why she was horrified; she had just been introduced to the world of intimate pleasure. He would not permit Xavier to ruin that for her. He held Dakota tightly and slowly began to rock her.

"Shhhh, my dear," he whispered in her ear, "Sleep. Sleep," he used the ever slightest bit of his power to coerce her into sleep. Soon, she was asleep in her mind.

Nicolay imagined a king sized bed for her and it appeared.

"I'm beginning to like this," he gently placed her on the bed. He dared not disturb her. She had been through too much already. He placed a light kiss on her forehead and decided he would pay the dear Xavier a visit.

Concentrate, Nicolay. You have to concentrate, he urged himself on. He could do this. He then imagined himself in Dakota's body and he was there, watching every move his dear friend was making. How could Xavier do this to him? Nicolay trusted him with is life. How could things have gotten so bad between them he would resort to kidnapping and raping his lover?

Nicolay stepped from the place on the wall where Dakota still hung. He was there and then he wasn't there. He stood there, watching his friend defile his lover's body. How had he let this happen to his angel? He dared not speak, unsure if Xavier knew he was there. He didn't want to alarm him, at least not yet.

XAVIER CONTINUED TAKING pleasure in Dakota's body, disappointed she had passed out. He wanted her to hate this as much as he was going to enjoy it, but there would be other times. He planned on making sure of that.

After removing what was left of her shirt and her bra, he took a moment to admire the perfection of her breasts. He took one in each hand and gently massaged them. They were full and proportionate to the rest of her body, and were nearly identical in shape and weight. He ran his thumb over the nipple of her right breast and it began to swell. Even in her current state of unconsciousness her body responded to his touch.

Xavier then leaned down and ran his tongue around the areola of the other breast. He was enjoyed watching the involuntary reactions of Dakota's body. As the nipple on that side hardened, he wrapped is lips around it, biting gently. He then began to suckle her breast one at a time until her nipples were so hard they felt like little pebbles on his tongue.

Xavier lifted her body from the stake she had been hung from, though he left her hands and her feet bound in case she came to and fought him. He was definitely going enjoying himself. He laid her limp body on the table. For the first time in a long time, Xavier was able to take his time.

He usually took whatever it was he wanted. So many times he had to beat his victims. It happened so often he'd convinced himself it was all part of the game. It would be different this time. He didn't have to worry about fighting his victim. Her body would be relaxed and take him in. She would do whatever he wanted her to.

He unzipped her jeans and unrolled them from her body. He tossed her shoes aside, unbound her legs, and pulled the jeans completely off. He felt the need to touch her everywhere, proceeding to explore all of her body. Her flesh felt like butter under his tongue, each touch making him need her more and more until his body burned with desire.

He had had enough of taking his time. He would have his way with her now. He ripped her panties from her body and mounted her. Unconscious or not, he would have her right here and right now, and there was nothing her poor little Nicolay could do about it.

First, though he need to remove his clothing. He felt the need to be next to her, uninhibited. He then slid his hands between her legs and felt her body as it prepared for him. With each stroke his fingers made, she became wetter.

Finally he entered her. She was warm around his member. Her body formed a glove around his. She was so tight and yet so wet. He began a rhythm, pumping in and out of her body as fast as he could. She just lay there, oblivious to what was happening with and to her body. He pulled her body to his, holding onto her, and when the ecstasy hit him, so did Nicolay.

EACH MOMENT NICOLAY stood there watching Xavier his anger grew. He watched, paralyzed, as Xavier undressed his beauty. He tried to reach out to grab Xavier and toss him far away from her, but each time he seemed to pass through them both. He watched helplessly as Xavier entered Dakota's body, sharing the place only he had been allowed to touch. He turned from them, not able to witness anymore. But he could still hear them, the sound of Xavier defiling her body and the smell of sex in the air.

Rage bubbled through Nicolay's veins, threatening to erupt like a volcano. He had never asked anything of Xavier. Even after he had saved the man's life, he never asked for repayment.

"But this, this is how you repay my kindness? I should have let you die when I had the chance," fury was the only emotion occupying Nicolay's body. He merged all of his power and all of his strength, turned once again to face them. He tackled Xavier, throwing his body into the far wall and rendering him helpless, unconscious.

Nicolay went to his dear *Tehya Aquene*. He reached for her, but once again, his touch moved through her and the table. How could he have let this happen to her? He had promised to protect her and he had failed miserably. He knew time was short, so he took one more look at Dakota's body, saddened he could do nothing for her, but relieved that her mind had been at rest during the ordeal. He would make sure she never had to live the details of what Xavier had done to her.

Nicolay then turned his attention to the task at hand. He needed to figure out where she was being held. He examined the room. He hadn't noticed the water before. The walls of this room had been cut not by the likes of man, but the years of Mother Nature's ultimate tool. She was definitely in some sort of cave but where was the question. He glanced around at her one last time. As much as he hated to leave her body there with Xavier, he didn't have much of a choice.

Exiting the room via the arch in the wall, Nicolay walked aimlessly from corridor to corridor. This entire place had been carved out by nature. The walls were smooth, definitely the work of rivers long past. He reached an impasse, not sure what to do. As far as he knew he was walking in circles. He could wander in this place for years and never figure out how to get out. Then he heard the voice.

"Nicolay, trust your instinct and your power. You are a creature of the night. You cannot always rely on human perception. Remember you are vampire."

He understood what the voice told him. He didn't know how or why, but there was someone on his side.

Nicolay stopped thinking with his mind and began to feel his way through the tunnels with his power. The magic filled the pathways, pushing out on the walls. It spread like a virus until it broke free from the prison. He followed the flow of magic until he too was free of the labyrinth.

"I know this place," he spoke to no one. He smelled the water in the air and heard the river as it took its final plunge over the cliffs. He then wondered if Dakota had ever explored all of her family's property. He remembered hearing the falls the night they watched the races. He heard them, although he wasn't sure she did. The falls were not far from the spot they had stood, but they had to pass them coming from Paradise, Inc.

He knew then he'd be able to lead everyone to where Dakota was being held. *But why here? What is so special about this place?* Nicolay looked around him. He didn't see anything in particular indicating why Xavier had brought her here. As long as he had known him, Nicolay couldn't recall a time when his friend had traveled out of the city. Why would he come this far out into the woods? It just didn't make sense. None of this did.

One good thing had come out of this though; he knew where Dakota was being held. He needed to get back to the others and devise a plan. There wasn't much time. He wasn't sure if Xavier knew it was him who had knocked him unconscious. He hoped he could get back to Dakota in time.

With all of his power, Nicolay retraced his way back through the tunnels to Dakota. As he entered the chamber she was being held in, he noticed Xavier still lay in a pile on the floor. He walked over to Dakota's body and gently traced the bridge of her nose.

He kissed her lips whispering, "We will come for you, my dear. Soon, you will be in my arms again," he then laid back down into her body and reentered her mind.

She lay there, just as he had left her, sleeping peacefully in his bed. He longed for her to be there, to be safe. He didn't know why this was happening, but he would protect her as best he could from any additional harm. He knelt beside the bed. Not wanting to wake her, he whispered, "Sleep my dear. When I return, you shall be safe."

Then he was gone from her mind and back in his own body.

CHAPTER THIRTY-FIVE

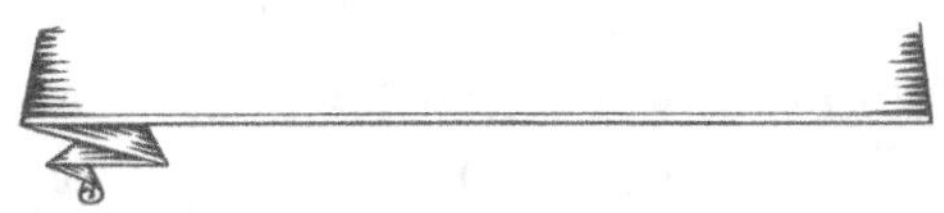

"WHAT'S HAPPENING TO him?" Kaida was worried. They had been watching over Nicolay's body for what seemed like hours. His body lay still, unmoving, unresponsive. Then suddenly it began to fade as if he was trying to bring his body to the place where his mind had gone. The corpse jerked violently, then, once again became deathly still.

Lysette didn't want to alarm the others, so she calmly said, "He knows what he is doing. It takes a lot of power for him to remain with Dakota. The best we can do is make sure nothing happens to his body. I've never witnessed this, but there has been at least one other so powerful he could transport his body to wherever or whenever he wanted it to go."

She had never seen anything like this before and she had lived a number of centuries herself. What was happening to Nicolay's body was new to her. He must have been fighting, but who or what she didn't know.

They all needed to remember Nicolay was strong. No one, not even in seclusion, could survive for as long as he had without being strong and careful. Kaida had to accept the fact that he was a grown man and he knew what he was doing. Still, it scared her to death knowing his mind was somewhere other than here.

Lysette excused herself. She had to get to Nicolay, but she couldn't do it with Dayton and Kaida so close. She went into the hall bathroom, closing the door behind her. From the looks of it, this bathroom had been added at least a hundred or so years after the house had been built. Though she knew it was there, she'd never been in it so she didn't know for sure. The house was definitely a plantation house, but the Naverro family had made many upgrades over the years.

The hall bathroom was painted a soft pink, Mrs. Naverro's favorite color. Fluffy pink towels hung from a towel rack next to the white and gold-clawed foot tub. A pedestal sink stood a foot or so from the door, but it was the smell of patchouli that gave the place a feel of home. Dakota must use this bathroom sometimes. It smelled just like her.

Lysette pulled the chair from under the vanity and sat comfortably on the soft cushion. She reached out first to Nicolay's body. She felt the cold that was ever a part of him. She explored his mind, looking for the connection that allowed him to return to his body. When she touched it, she felt him. She saw him wandering in darkness. Because he was a vampire, he saw perfectly in the dark, and because she was in his mind she saw the walls of the caves just as well as he did. She felt him searching, trying to figure out where he was. He needed to stop searching with his eyes and start searching with his power. She then spoke to him, telling him what he needed to do.

"Nicolay, trust your instinct and your power. You are a creature of the night. You cannot always rely on human perception. Remember, you are a vampire."

She felt him, and she knew the moment he recognized her. She had done all she could do, now it was up to him. Lysette returned to the living room to wait, and wait they did.

"Do you mind?" Dayton's pacing was beginning to annoy Kaida. She turned to face Lysette, "What's taking so long? Why hasn't he come back?" she was about at her whit's end.

Lysette reassured them both that Nicolay was working as fast as he could. He would return soon. She'd felt him reaching out with his power searching for the entrance. She'd felt the enclosure, the dampness in the air. He was learning quickly. The more he learned, the better off they would all be.

Suddenly, Nicolay's body stood. He jerked, his body thrown from side to side. Then he collapsed. Lysette, Dayton, and Kaida all looked at each other. Kaida went to him; she held his head in her lap. Lysette knelt beside him just as he spoke.

"It hurts."

Lysette looked at Kaida, then back at Nicolay, "I know. The first time is always the hardest. Plus, you did it the hard way, forcing yourself into her mind. When she's open to you, it doesn't take nearly as much energy. When we have time, I will teach you. Right now we have other things to tend to."

Nicolay knew she was right, "Dawn approaches."

They didn't have much time. Nicolay was old, he probably didn't have to sleep until dusk, but what he had done tonight had taken a lot out of him. He needed to rest. If he didn't, he would be of no use to them tomorrow night.

Lysette turned to Dayton, "Is there somewhere he can sleep? We've got to get him out of the light. He's weak and his lair is too far from here."

"Wait a minute, how do you know where his lair is?" Kaida wanted answers, knowing Nicolay was very protective of his lair. Even she didn't know where it was located.

"She's been in my mind. We've shared much, she and I," his voice was shallow, weak.

"Look, I'll explain later. Right now we need to find a place for him to rest," agitated, Lysette looked at Dayton, "Where?"

He thought for a moment. All of the upstairs bedrooms had sheer curtains; Dakota always changed them during the summer. She liked the light. It was nearing fall, but he hadn't had a chance to get to storage to get the heavier ones. The rooms in the other wing were all empty. They had stripped the windows years ago.

Nicolay interrupted Dayton's train of thought, "Dark...room," were the only words he managed.

Dawn was pressed against the walls. They had to hurry. He didn't know how much strength he had left. He was sure it wasn't enough to walk. Someone would have to carry him.

"Darkroom? What is he talking about?" Lysette had stayed in the house many times over the years, but she had never seen this darkroom.

"The darkroom. I guess it would work," Dayton hurried to a door under the staircase.

"I didn't know there was a room there."

"Yeah, dad made the storage area into a darkroom when I was about fifteen. I used to develop my pictures in there. It hasn't been used in ages."

As he opened the door, he was surprised by what he saw. He then gave a look so evil at Nicolay that he was sure the man felt his eyes piercing daggers into his heart.

"I'll explain that later. Quickly, I can feel my skin beginning to burn."

Not wanting to give away her super strength, Kaida motioned Dayton to them. Dayton grabbed Nicolay under his arms while Lysette and Kaida each grabbed a leg. They carried him to the darkroom and laid him on the bed. Dayton quickly exited, wanting to get as far away from the vampire as possible.

Nicolay had just enough strength to turn his head to face Kaida, "Please leave me with Lysette, I need to talk to her."

Kaida was skeptical, but she agreed, "I'll call the club and make the arrangements for tomorrow night. I guess neither of us will be in. I'll stay close. I'm sure Dayton won't mind me spending the day here.

If you need me, you only need to call," Kaida gave one last glance to Nicolay and Lysette and then left the room.

"Close the door, please," he used a little of his remaining energy to light the two candles he had brought into the room the last time he'd slept there.

Lysette closed the door, the illumination behind surprising her. Assured no light entered the room from the outside, she closed the little distance between them.

"She is hurt, and I fear she will be hurt even more if we leave her there."

"Where is she?"

"Near."

"I know you're weak. Tell me what you can, but don't force yourself. I have an idea of what we are dealing with. She'll be safe until tomorrow night. The evil we are dealing with is nocturnal, just as you are. It will sleep during the day. Now tell me."

Nicolay laid his head back, and began to relive the last few hours.

"The place she is in is not far from here. I can hear the river as it plunges to its death. It is not far from a place she took me. The first night she took me to a place not far from Paradise. She said the property belonged to her family. We watched her friend's race. She is there in a cave. There are trees everywhere. No path for a vehicle to enter. I do not know how Xavier got her there, but she is deep underground. Follow the patchouli."

Then he was gone, pulled into the dark sleep that would entrap him for hours.

"Xavier?" Lysette was sure he was mistaken. What would Xavier want with Dakota? She had sensed a dark evil, but she was sure Xavier wouldn't, no, couldn't be working with it. When they'd met, he'd seemed nice enough. Usually she picked up on negativity coming from people. Negative energy gravitated around evil, but there wasn't any around Xavier.

Lysette slid out of the door letting as little light in as possible. She found Kaida and Dayton sitting at the kitchen table, staring out of the bay window, watching the sunrise. They both looked like they'd been through a torture chamber. Without rest, they'd be no good tonight. Tonight they would fight an evil none of them had ever known. Tonight was a blue moon, and any and everything was possible.

"Hey, you two," their heads turned simultaneously as if someone had pulled a string attached to both, "Nicolay is resting and Dakota is safe for now."

"How can you be so sure?" Dayton was skeptical.

Lysette sighed. If what Nicolay had said was correct, Dakota would be safe until dark. Instead of explaining, she addressed a simple question to Dayton to distract them, "Do you know where there's a waterfall around here?"

He thought for a moment, "Yeah. My father talked about one on the other end of the property, the side that's undeveloped, but I haven't been there in forever. I am pretty sure Kota's never been there. Why do you ask?"

"Nicolay mentioned something of a place where you can hear the river plunging to its death. Do you have a map showing where we can find it?"

"I'll look," he quickly dismissed himself to look for the maps.

Lysette sat by Kaida, who had turned back to the window, "What are you thinking?"

"I have known Nicolay for three centuries. He saved my life, but I can't help but wonder if your people hadn't sent him to me where would I be? What would have happened to my people? Would we still be held in captivity by that tyrant?"

Lysette understood the turmoil Kaida now faced. All of this time, she'd thought luck had brought Nicolay into her life. Now, to know her release was all part of someone's master plan...she really should have kept that to herself. She owed Kaida an apology, a big one.

She turned to Kaida, "Does it really matter at this point? Think of all you and Nicolay have been through. Would you trade any of it? If you could go back to that day, knowing what you know now, would you keep him from saving you?"

"Guess not," Kaida still didn't feel any better. She would have to ask Nicolay about that day when all of this was over.

"So now what?"

"Just as Nicolay is doing, we rest. We will be facing an evil unknown to any of us. There are some things I must tend to in preparation. I'll explain everything once Nicolay arises. He is old, so he will awaken before true sunset. That will give us some time."

Lysette got up and began making a pot of tea. She would lace it with her own special blend of magic so Dayton and Kaida would rest peacefully, at least for a little while.

"We need to make sure all of these windows are covered before he awakens. I don't want to waste any time."

"Got it," Dayton returned with a survey of the property and a map, "We should be able to figure out where the waterfall is with these."

"Thanks, Day," Lysette handed them both a cup of tea, "Now drink."

None of them had realized how thirsty they were. Lysette made sure she put enough magic in the tea to make them sleep at least three or four hours. That would give her time to try to contact Xavier and her people. They were going to need a lot of help tonight. The fate of the world as they knew it could be in their hands.

Lysette watched Kaida and Dayton as the tea began to take effect.

"I'm going to try to get some rest. I guess the adrenaline of the night has worn off. You're both welcome to stay; there are plenty of empty rooms. Lysette knows where to find everything," Dayton stifled a yawn and exited the kitchen in search of his bed.

"It would do us all some good to get some rest," Lysette eyed Kaida. The tea was taking a little longer to take effect, but she could see her growing drowsy, "Do you plan on staying?"

Kaida turned from watching the sunrise.

"I don't have much of a choice. Guess there is no reason for you to drop me off at home to have to come back and get me," it was a weak excuse at best. In truth, Kaida didn't plan on leaving Nicolay alone with two strangers. He had protected her once, now she'd return the favor.

"Well, I'll show you to one of the guest rooms. I'll have to get you some linen," Lysette rose to exit the kitchen when Kaida stopped her.

"Don't worry about it, just bring me a blanket. I'll crash on the couch. I've never slept in a strange bed and I don't intend to start now."

"You are a most loyal friend," Lysette left to get the blankets. She knew Kaida wanted to stay as close to Nicolay as possible. She couldn't blame her though; Nicolay had trusted his body to two strangers, something no vampire should ever do. She'd have to have a talk with her dear Nicolay when all of this was over.

Climbing the staircase, Lysette took a moment to admire the paintings hung on the walls on either side of her. There was a picture of the original plantation owner at the very bottom of the stairs. Lysette never figured out why the Naverro family never removed the portrait. They said many times he had been kind to the family, but to keep a picture of the slave master in the home was beyond her.

The second portrait was that of Dakota's great great grandfather, Thaddeus Naverro. He looked to be a very distinguished gentleman. Hard lines from years of work in the fields gave his features character. His gentle smile gave way to a soft heart. Dayton and Dakota spoke highly of all of their family members, but most of all, their "granddad

Thad" as they called him. Lysette smiled to herself. The Naverro family had been through a lot over the generations, and yet they remained strong. *Probably why they are the chosen ones.*

The third portrait was a family portrait of the next generation. To the left was Dakota's great grandfather Louis and next to him was his wife Patricia. Their children, Thaddeus, Michael, Mary, and Clarence sat at their feet. Thaddeus, who had been named for his grandfather, was the youngest and had the most striking resemblance to his grandfather. All of the others had taken features from their mother's side of the family.

Halfway up the staircase hung the portrait of Theodore Naverro, Esquire. Theo, Thaddeus's only son, had been the most traveled of the family. He had met his wife Gwendolyn, a gypsy woman, in Belize while on vacation. The years he had owned and run the plantation had been profitable ones and he traveled often. Gwendolyn spent to her heart's content and bore only two children, twins, Dayton and Dakota.

At the top of the staircase hung the largest portrait of them all. This portrait was of the most recent generation of the family Naverro. Standing tall and firm, Theodore Naverro showed not a drop of mercy to strangers, but was as gentle as a mother hen when it came to is only daughter, Dakota. He loved his daughter so.

Their mother, Gwendolyn was strict but fair. She ensured both Dayton and Dakota grew up with the proper training in being a lady and gentleman. What had happened to them had been a tragedy. No one should have died in that manner.

Lysette sighed. Dayton and Dakota's childhood had been filled with history and magic. Now, that magic could condemn them all to an eternity in hell. She dreaded having to tell them all they needed to know. She dreaded even more that it might already be too late for Dakota. No. Lysette shook her head. She had to think positive. Dakota was going to be alright.

She grabbed the blankets from the linen closet at the end of the hall and descended the stairs. She found Kaida stretched out, fast asleep on the couch. Covering her with the blankets, careful not to wake her, Lysette slipped out the front door determined to find Xavier.

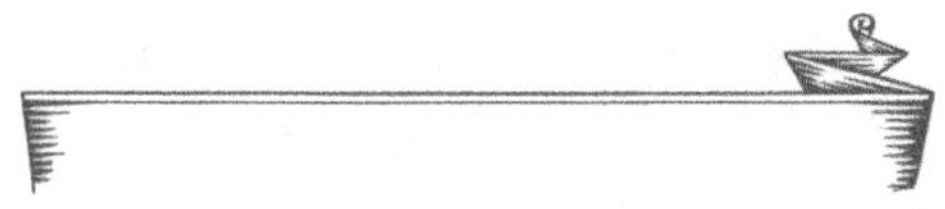

CHAPTER THIRTY-SIX

LYSETTE ENTERED THE west wing of the Naverro Plantation house through what had once been the servants' entrance. Although the wing had not been occupied by mortals for years long past, she wandered the halls aimlessly sometimes for hours to clear her head. The walkways were eerily quiet at times, and that quiet is what she sought right now. She walked from room to room, admiring the structure, appreciating it for what it truly was, a marvel beyond comprehension.

She came to the place where the verandah had been etched away by years of neglect. She ran her hand over the screening and stepped through. Instead of appearing on the outside of the plantation house, she entered another realm. She stretched, shedding her mortal disguise, freeing her body of its confines. It was nice to be home.

As Lysette walked to the opening of El Castillo of Xunantunich, the animals of her home greeted her. She knelt, bowing her head to show respect to the Harpy Eagle that forever watched over the temple entrance. All creatures here respected each other. They were all separate and yet one in the same. She knew soon the Margay and Ocelot of the region would be waking. She had not seen her animal friends in centuries and longed to stroke their soft fur and scratch behind their ears. Though very shy around humans, the Margay had become her best companions. Their extremely large tiger eyes and secretive ways were ideal for keeping unwanted visitors at bay in the darkest hours of night.

She reentered the temple to prepare. As she walked past each wall, the torch, dormant for hundreds of years, burst to life. She walked to the stone alter that dominated the upper room of the temple. Here is where it had all began. Placing her palm flat on the surface, she was drawn back centuries to the day everything changed.

"We have to get out of the rain!"

Running towards the temple for shelter, the man and his pregnant wife took refuge in the first place they had come to. Neither had expected to be caught out in a tropical storm, but here they were when the skies opened up and began to cry a sigh of relief. The altar was the only place to sit in the old temple. The woman, frantically panting, attempting to catch her breath, found her body aching. Excruciating pain filled her lower body and she collapsed, overcome with the torture her unborn child had bestowed upon her.

"You should not be here," a voice scolded from a distance, the figure taking form from the shadows, "You do not belong here. This is a sacred place only for those who are worthy."

The man and woman didn't have any other place to go. The baby was coming and he or she was coming now.

"Please, I fear my wife has just gone into labor. My child cannot be brought into this world out in the rain," the man pleaded with the stranger, his fear stricken eyes filling with tears as he watched his wife endure so much pain.

"She cannot be here," the stranger grew more agitated.

The man wondered what was so wrong with them taking shelter... Before he could finish the thought, his wife let out a wail of a thousand mothers before her. It was too late. Before the stranger could escort them out of the temple, the baby came. All of the years she had spent there, guarding the temple, preventing evil from again rising from the depths of hell, and she had failed.

Lysette slowly pulled her hands away from the altar. As she did, the memory faded into oblivion. All of those years ago and yet the memory was as vivid as the rays of the setting sun that beat against the temple walls. She could still smell the mist that remained after the birth of the gatekeeper.

Lysette sighed. She had kept the secret for far too long. Now, it may have cost them all their lives. One detail, though, gnawed at her. In all of her years in the temple, the inhabitants of the villages had not gone there. No one dared venture so far into the jungle. How had they found it?

Although she didn't want to believe it, in her heart she knew. *He* had sent them, shown them the way, then tickled the heavens above until they burst, showering their joy and pain over this world.

"Nothing I can do about it now."

She continued to inspect the remains of the temple. The magic she had cast had kept the place fairly intact. She recited the inscription on the wall, lightly pressing some stones while avoiding others. When she had circled the altar completely, a portion of the wall shifted and revealed a passageway. She carefully descended the circular stairway, recalling the steps were stone and not all of them had been cut to the same size. Just before she reached each torch, the flame smoldered and then burned brightly.

Time had been kind to her humble abode. Paintings of places and people long past hung from the stone walls. The small chest she had purchased from the orient nearly two centuries ago rested in a corner above a rug one of the villagers had made many moons before. She sat on her bed, the pillow top stuffed with the down of thousands of geese. Laying her head on the pillow, she stared at the mural on the ceiling.

Her image stared back at her. The artist, a then ten year old Mayan boy, had captured her likeness exactly. In the picture she stood at the peak of the temple, peering down at the village below, hovering over the villagers like an over protective mother. She had kept them safe for so long, and yet, they were oblivious to the knowledge that here on their ground, evil slept, waiting patiently for her to make one tiny mistake.

She had done just that. From that day forward, she vowed she would protect this world if it was the last thing she did. The reality of it was, it might be the last thing she ever did. If they failed tonight, the world's fate will be sealed. The greatest of all evil will once again roam freely through this world. She took one last long look at the painting. The time had come, she must prepare, but first, she needed to find Xavier.

Lysette called to him, "Xavier, Xavier," her voice floating on the wind, traveling through time and space beckoning to him. She felt him in her mind, sleeping, but not the sleep of his kind. Something was not as it should be. Lysette's magic was old and allowed her to probe his mind, trying to gain an understanding of what had happened to him. His mind was lethargic, unusual for a creature of his power. Few had been able to get close enough to subdue a Phoenix. She couldn't see him. He was weak, so his magic couldn't help her. She sniffed the air around him and got the answer she so searched for.

"Roses," the word snapped her out of the trance. His kind was vulnerable to one thing and one thing only: roses. She had been convinced earlier that Xavier had not been capable of kidnapping Dakota. This only confirmed her suspicions. Now the question was, had someone used mind control so it would look like he had kidnapped Dakota, or had someone drugged him, then stolen his human form to commit the crime?

Lysette contemplated attempting to decide how much of this she should tell everyone else. They all had enough to worry about. Nicolay and Kaida knew Xavier well enough to be able to pick out an imposter. At least she hoped they did. It made her wonder why Nicolay hadn't detected that the person he thought was raping Dakota really wasn't his friend. She'd have to ask him when all of this was over. For now, she would keep this new information to herself, at least until she was sure it needed to be revealed.

Raising the lid on the hundred year old trunk at the foot of her bed, she stared down at Nicolay's belongings. For centuries her kind had prepared for his birth. They watched him grow up, fully aware of his destiny. They did not interfere, for to do so would change the course of the future and not necessarily in their favor. Eventually the time would come. They all knew it. The only thing to do was to keep watch and wait. Why that had been the decision, no one amongst them was willing to share, but once the decision had been made it was law, and no one dared break it.

She pulled the ritual dressings from the trunk, lifting them to her nostrils, inhaling the scent long lost in the world she now lived. She remembered it all just like it was yesterday.

The villagers greeted the new arrival with cheerfulness. Little did they know they were welcoming the Chac-Xib-Chac into their village. The new child, seed of Cimi and Xaman Ek, was what the villagers referred to as the Ah Ahzah Cab, the Awakener. As the offspring of the God of Death and the God of the Portal at the center of the night sky, he was destined to become the keeper of the night. His Mayan family named him Itzam Yeh, bringer of magic, but they had no idea of how fitting the name would be or the power that had just been unleashed into the world.

The moment the child had been born, Lysette returned to the council to relay the news. Although she was filled with terror, the council showed no ill feelings. They assured her that there had been nothing she could have done. The council had been aware of the couple roaming deep into the forbidden area of the jungle. They only waited patiently while fate took its course. Her news had not come unexpected.

Lysette was then informed of her true purpose. All of these years she had believed she had been summoned to the temple to guard it, to keep the chosen one from being born, but she then realized why as Cuaxolotl,

Goddess of Life and Death, the temple had become her home. She was drawn here to protect the chosen one. Chac-Xib-Chac was much more important on earth than he had been in the heavens. She needed to ensure his life until the time death came to seize him.

It had not all made sense then. She had been sure the council was going to punish her for failing, but quite the opposite; she had been entrusted with the most important task of all. Protecting Chac-Xib-Chac was her new mission. She was to deliver him to the Tansi, of the Hopi. Then she was to find the others.

Just as before, Lysette had been given as little information as possible. She always felt the council knew more than they ever told, but who was she to question them? She took her orders and returned to the village in search of the Chac-Xib-Chac.

She returned to the village in her human form, disguised by the floral cloak. She did not come there often, only when things weren't what they should be. Whenever she did, the villagers hid as if their lives depended on it. The villagers always feared her. She never meant any harm, but they saw her as the guardian of the forbidden temple, so they only associated her with evil. She wished it had not been that way. She'd so wanted to play with the children. She watched as they'd tried to come out of the houses. Their mothers ushered them to the back of the house for protection, far away from the cloaked figure.

The village was empty when she returned. Though night was hours away, the sky was black. She followed the glow of torches to observe the crowd gathered around one home. She knew he was there and she had to get to him fast. As she approached the mob, they parted, each running for cover as they realized who she was. By the time she reached the door, she stood alone.

With all of the commotion outside gone, the residents opened the door. They knew who she was, and why she had come. They quietly wrapped the baby in a blanket and handed him to her. She then turned and disappeared into the night.

"Reminiscing, my dear Cuaxolotl?"

Lysette knew the voice. Without answering his question she replied, "What are you doing here?"

"I am only here to help. As much as you hate to admit it, you need me."

He was right. They had tried to fight this battle many times before, but they always needed him.

"You have come now. Why?"

"The time approaches, the Great Evil One will try to make his entrance tonight under the blue moon. The portal will open and we must be waiting."

Lysette fought the urge to go to him, to love him once again. She could not, would not succumb to loving him. They had been through this time and time again with devastating effects for the both of them. She had tried many times to destroy this one, Nicolay's maker, only to fail and remain in love with him. To face him now, the need to be with him so great it caused her heart to ache, would be detrimental to all they needed to accomplish.

"I know you still love me. I can feel it in you," the man said.

"But you know we can never be," she sounded disappointed even to herself. What he'd said was true, she did still love him. She'd always love him. Even when she'd tried to kill him it was out of love.

"So you say. It is your choice. I will not interfere with you and the other. You lust after him, but you do not love him. One day you will realize it is only me you love, and I will be waiting," with stillness only he, a vampire, could manage, her former lover was gone. The air didn't move. He was just gone.

Lysette lowered her head fighting back the tears. *How could I have thought he would not come?* He was always there. She needed to talk to him, she just didn't know how. She didn't know how to reach out to him. She'd blamed him all of these years for crossing the line.

How could she tell him now she understood why he'd done it, that it was okay?

You know how to reach me. You have only to call.

She knew the voice was in her head. They had always been able to communicate with each other in their minds. She wanted to call to him, wanted his arms wrapped around her body. She wanted so much to look up into those dark brown eyes of his and lose herself. It had been so long since she'd touched him, felt his cool skin beneath her fingertips.

Taking in a deep breath and slowly blowing it out she did what her heart and mind beckoned her to do. She spoke his name. "Gedeon."

I am here, my queen. The voice again in her mind. *Come, join me outside of the temple.*

Gedeon hated the temple with a passion. He always felt he should have been the chosen one. He had taken the life of the *Chac-Xib-Chac,* bringing him over, with hopes he had destroyed whatever magic made him the most sacred of the gatekeepers. However, Gedeon had only succeeded in completing the cycle. When he vowed to destroy Nicolay, his one true love turned on him. He allowed Nicolay to live only to pacify his love, Lysette. She never forgave him for the threat. She still believed he had a vendetta against Nicolay. In a way he did, but it was for a different reason now.

Gedeon hated being here, so close to her and being denied the only thing he cherished in the world. He'd spent most of his thousand years searching for true love. Traveling the world, he met women and men of all ages, races, and creeds. Many had at one time caught his fancy and he remained with those for centuries, only to grow weary and begin his search once again. The lands of Spain and Germany, cities such as London and Paris, exotic places like Madagascar, Australia, Brazil, and the beaches of St. Croix he'd searched heedlessly until he came here to Belize. He had all but given up until he had stumbled upon a quaint little village. Discovering the secret room in the temple had been his blessing and his curse.

There she lay; adorned in the most beautiful garments he had ever seen. She slept quietly, peacefully until she sensed he was there. Upon awakening, the air became thick with magic. She was not his kind, but she was powerful. More powerful than anything he had come across in all of his years as a vampire. She spoke to him in his mind, something only the one who had made him had been able to do. In that small gesture, he had finally found love, embraced it, lived and breathed it, only to have it ripped away far too soon. He admitted his decision to bestow the dark curse upon Nicolay had been hasty, but he had done it in a moment of jealous rage. Now he lived every night with the consequences, as terrible as they may be.

"Come my queen, I await you at the foot of the temple," this time he spoke the words aloud. They floated from the foot of the temple up through the night. He had no doubt she had heard them.

Lysette was torn. She love Gedeon, had always loved him, but she had failed in letting Nicolay be born and he had failed her by bestowing the curse of vampirism upon him. In six centuries she had not forgiven him. She sighed. No longer able to deny her feelings, she went to him. Not sure of what the future held, she was tired of being alone and this may be the end of all of them. She refused to have this end without Gedeon knowing that she forgave him and she loved him. Besides, he had been considerate enough to come to her first instead of just intruding in Nicolay's life once again. Bad blood was destined to remain between them, but sooner or later they needed to put their differences aside for the good of all. They'd cross that path when they got to it. For now she needed to speak her piece.

Night was upon them. The Harpy Eagle that protected the temple by day soon parted to hunt for the night. The Ocelot nervously circled the base of the temple, while the eyes of the Margay shone brightly in the moonlit sky. All of the animals were curious as to why after all of this time, the inhabitants of the temple had returned.

Lysette searched the night sky. They didn't have much time. She still needed to prepare and she needed to get back to the others. She also had the painstaking task of informing Nicolay that Gedeon had returned.

"I am here, my love," once again in her human form she stood just inches away from him. It still it felt like miles. She had taken the first step. Now, everything was in fate's hands.

Gedeon turned, reaching for her, but not wanting to rush her. If she was to truly love him again, if she really was going to forgive him, he wanted her to know he planned to be there no matter how long it took. He'd learned patience over the years and now was going to be the time it would be tested.

He opened his arms to her and she collapsed into them, tears streaming down her face. She released the centuries of pain with one troublesome wail. All of the years of anger, hurt, disappointment, but mostly loneliness came pouring from her heart. She had denied herself love far too long. After all of this was over, she vowed to spend some time making things right with Gedeon.

Gedeon stroked Lysette's back, rocking her tenderly as she released all she'd kept inside for all of this time. He had mourned the loss of their relationship, their love, but holding her there in that moment he realized she never had.

"Always the strong one. It's okay to let it out."

And she did, over and over again. The sadness flowed through the jungle in waves. The animals were completely in tune with her pain. They joined in, filling the air with a cadence of sorrow. Then all was still. The time for mourning had past. Now in his arms he held the future.

He hugged her to him, filling her with his love. "I have loved you always. Even when I thought it was not possible to love you, I loved you. Whether we are together or apart, I will always love you," he rested his chin in her hair, "We have been apart far too long, let us not repeat the past, but start anew."

He promised himself then he would never let her go. Even if she rejected him, he would always be there to protect her whether she knew it or not. Gedeon was sure that soon things would be right between them.

Lysette lay in his arms, the last of the pain slowly dissipating. She pulled away from him, just enough to look him in the eyes.

"I love you," were the only words she could manage.

Gedeon leaned down and claimed the lips of his one true love. The passion danced around them, their power merging and exploding in a wave of ecstasy that left them both overwhelmed and speechless. The wave of passion, magic, and power raced through them out into the surrounding jungle. Then all was again quiet. No words needed to be spoken between them, the love they felt was mutual and each knew it.

"We don't have much time. I must prepare," Lysette hated to leave his embrace, but the fate of the world lay in their hands tonight and they could not afford to be distracted.

"I shall wait for you where the river plunges to its end," Gedeon claimed her lips one last time in a feverish attempt to sate his hunger for her affection. Then he was gone.

She collapsed on the bottom stair of the temple. She had once again confessed her love to Gedeon. Not sure how she really felt about that decision, she stood and made her way back to the temple entrance. He spoke to her once again in her mind.

"I will not rush you, my love. Just knowing that you love me is enough to sustain me for the next hundred centuries if it must. Always remember, I love you no matter what."

Then the connection was gone.

She entered the temple with a smile. His love had washed over her, cleansed her of the sorrow and the loneliness. If tonight was her last night amongst the living, just knowing he still loved her would be enough for her to accept death with open arms.

Remaining in human form, Lysette gathered everything they needed for tonight. She placed all of the items in a bag and returned to the trunk to get one last item. She searched the trunk, removing a silk cloak and the second Mayan Book of the Dead before she came to the item she was looking for. Carefully removing the woven coverings, the dagger that belonged to Nicolay lay in her hands.

The blade of the dagger was six inches long and adorned with jade. The markings on the butt were the same as the temple walls. Each picture represented his lineage. He had come to this world many times before, but never as strong as he was now. If he didn't believe in reincarnation, when the dagger was reunited with the book he would. Lysette wrapped the dagger once again and placed it in the bag. She would only give it to him if he needed it during the battle. If not, she'd return it after they were all safe.

Taking one last look around her home, Lysette placed the hood of her cloak over her head and ascended the stairs. She sealed the door to the secret chamber and walked to the temple entrance. Once there, with a wave of her hand, she was once again in the west wing of the Naverro plantation house.

CHAPTER THIRTY-SEVEN

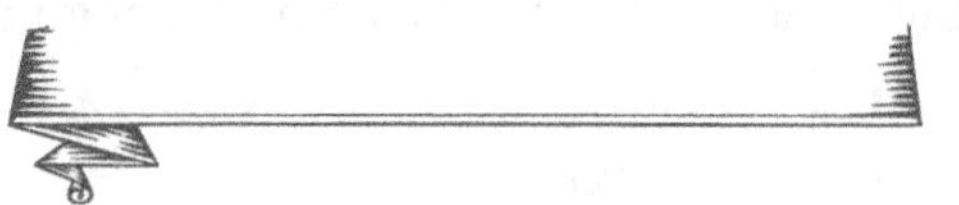

NICOLAY WOKE BEFORE sunset sensing something was wrong. It was too quiet in the house. He wondered where everyone was. Using his power, he chose to seek out the answer. He felt Kaida sitting at the foot of the stairs just on the other side of the darkroom door. He sensed her turning towards him. She must have felt him searching for her. Dayton was still upstairs in bed. He too was stirring. Nicolay was sure he would be waking soon. He wondered what Lysette had done to them?

Stretching his power to the other parts of the house, he searched for Lysette, but she wasn't there. He searched all of the rooms with his power, but he could not sense her. Just as he was drawing the magic back, she was there, her life-force appearing out of nowhere.

"How did she do that?" he was sure he had just searched through that same room and she wasn't there, and now she was.

"Kaida, is it safe for me to leave the darkness?"

Kaida heard Nicolay in her mind.

"Yes. I've closed the curtains. They're fully lined so you should be safe."

Nicolay cautiously opened the door to the darkroom. She had told the truth, the only light came from the candles on the mantle and end tables and the lamp in the corner of the living room.

He turned to his friend. She sat on the bottom stair hunched over with her arms crossed over her knees.

"Guarding me?" he smiled at her.

"You might say that. When I woke up, it was nearly dusk. I searched the house, but I didn't find Lysette. I even checked in on you to make sure she hadn't staked you while we slept. I'm not sure what she did to us. Dayton is upstairs still sleeping. The last thing I remember was drinking some tea. I don't even remember going to the couch, but when I awoke, there I was," she shrugged her shoulders. She really didn't recall much after drinking the tea.

"Lysette is here. I am not sure how, but when I searched the house with my power, initially I did not sense her. Then, there she was. I can't explain it. She approaches," he gestured to the top of the stairs on the opposite side from where they both knew Dayton slept.

"Find what you were looking for?" Lysette tried to be cheerful. She'd felt Nicolay searching for her. It was easy for her to hide from his power. She was just as powerful as he, if not more. She knew he was going to be angry with her, but she also knew curiosity would get the best of him and she had prepared to explain her actions.

"Where have you been?"

Lysette heard the anger in his voice. She needed to tread lightly.

"Why, home of course. We have a big night ahead of us and I needed to prepare," Lysette brought bad news and the last thing she planned to do was deliver it to an angry vampire. She retreated to the kitchen, putting on a pot of water to boil and grabbing a box of chamomile tea from one of the cabinets. She proceeded to pull down three coffee mugs, the sugar and honey and a diffuser from the other cabinets. Placing all of the items on a tray, she waited for the water to boil.

"How do I tell him?" she spoke the words aloud.

"How are you going to tell me what?" Nicolay entered the kitchen alone. Kaida had gone upstairs to try to wake Dayton. He assumed she had been talking about him when she asked the question.

She turned from him to busy her hands in order to gather her courage. She removed the whistling tea kettle from the stove and quickly started a cup of tea for herself. She needed something to calm her nerves. This was not going to be easy and she now regretted the moment Gedeon had stepped back into her life.

Growing weary of the secrecy, Nicolay asked, "What are you keeping from us?" the evasiveness was going to stop and it was going to stop now.

Lysette fought back tears, hearing the anger and irritation in his voice. She had kept so much from him for so long. Now, it was all catching up with her. A single, lonely tear fell from her eyes. She didn't want to hurt him, but he had to know. If they just showed up at the falls and he saw Gedeon there waiting, it would be an all out war between the two. How to make him understand that was her plight.

Lysette turned to him, pain in her eyes. What she was about to tell him would make or break tonight. Regardless of their feeling towards each other, they all needed Gedeon to defeat this evil. She took one last deep cleansing breath and spoke.

"Gedeon is here," were the only words she could muster. No additional explanation, no reasoning why, just that he was here.

She waited for Nicolay's reaction, prepared herself for the worst, but there was only stillness. She was sure he had retreated into himself, pondering what to do about Gedeon. She'd almost relaxed hoping he had accepted that the one who made him had returned. Then she saw it, the rage. His eyes became like ice staring back at her. She watched as his fangs lengthened and as much as some part of her desired to run, she stood her ground. Any moment now he would decide to let her live or kill her, and she was ready for anything he threw her way. Not having any fight left in her, she was prepared for her fate. If she allowed him to take her life now, the world was surely doomed, but she didn't care. The secrets she harbored ate away at her day in and day out. She was tired of it all. What was the point?

The rage consumed Nicolay. All he knew in that moment was that this one was going to die. As he grabbed her, tilting her neck sideways, preparing to drink her dry, Kaida stormed in.

"Nicolay! *No!*" his rage had bled into the house, burning, growing like a wild fire. She rushed down the stairs hoping she reached them in time.

Hearing her voice snapped him out of the fit of rage long enough to toss Lysette aside like a rag doll. Her body hit the wall with a thud. She crawled as far away from them both as quickly as she possibly could, shaken from the force of her human body hitting the wall. He looked at her, realizing what he had just done, seeing in her eyes the fear and pain he'd just caused her. Then he was gone.

Lysette began to cry uncontrollably. She didn't have any broken bones, but for the first time in her life, she knew fear. She truly hadn't expected him to attack her. She was just the messenger. She had to make sure this never got back to Gedeon. If it did, she could only imagine what would happen.

Kaida approached her with caution. By the look on her face, she had never been as close to death's door as she had been just a minute ago.

"You have to promise me you will never speak of what just happened here. You have to find him and make him promise. Make him promise!" her voice began to rise, "Promise me!" Lysette grabbed at Kaida like she was a lifeline, "Promise me!" She grew more and more hysterical, "Promise me!"

Finally Kaida agreed only to calm the woman. She needed to find Nicolay, but Lysette needed her more. She cradled Lysette in her arms until despair and exhaustion pulled her under and she passed out.

Kaida tried time and time again to wake her. One minute Lysette was sobbing uncontrollably in her arms, the next she lay as still as death. She finally called out to Dayton, hoping with all hope he'd hear her.

When Dayton entered the kitchen, he didn't know what to think. Kaida had rushed out of the room sure that something was going on downstairs. He was still trying the shake the effects of the tea. By the time he was fully awake, he heard Kaida yelling his name. Now, standing in the doorway with Lysette and Kaida on the floor, he didn't know what to think.

"I-i-is sh-she?" he stuttered not sure if the woman was dead or alive.

"She's alive, but she just had the scare of a lifetime. I need you to take care of her. I must find Nicolay," this was not good. She felt bad for Lysette. Kaida didn't know what she could have said to Nicolay to cause him to attack her like that.

The anger began to grow in Dayton, "Where is the bastard? I'll kill him for hurting her."

"I don't know. Look, we don't have much time. I am not sure what happened here but I have to find him. He is our only hope in getting your sister back."

Kaida was surprised at herself. She too now felt responsible for Dakota's safe return. Her first thought, when Nicolay had told her that the girl was missing, was good riddance, but not now. She knew if anything happened to Dakota, Nicolay would never forgive himself. She hated to see him with someone else, but she wanted him to be happy. If helping him save this girl would keep him happy, then she would help.

Dayton knelt and scooped Lysette from Kaida's arms.

"Lay her down and place a cool rag on her head. If you have any smelling salts, that should wake her up. If not, just keep calling her name. She just passed out so she could come to at any moment," Kaida gave one more look at Lysette lying in Dayton's arms, "I'll be back as soon as I can."

She then left in search of Nicolay.

XAVIER BEGAN TO WORRY. He'd hung Dakota's lifeless body back on the wall, but she had not come to since last night. Though he spent his days in hiding, his kind did not have to sleep by day. He didn't know what had hit him last night. One moment he was enjoying her body, the next he was coming to on the floor. No one knew of this place, he was sure of it, and yet someone or something had apparently attacked him.

He turned to admire Dakota's body once again. He saw why Nicolay had fallen in love with her. She was stunning. Her body though should have been the last thing on his mind. The Dark One was returning to realm of the living tonight. He had much to do before the time arose. Dusk was approaching and Nicolay was coming for her, he was sure of it.

"Well, we anticipate your arrival, my dear Nicolay, and yours too, Gedeon."

Xavier sensed Gedeon's return. He'd made the one who had made Gedeon thousands of years ago, and a thousand years ago Gedeon had turned on his maker. Tonight, well, tonight was payback. He planned to have his ultimate revenge on the only one who dared attempt to destroy one of his line. Xavier had waited a very long time for this night. Tonight, his victory would be his greatest revenge.

CHAPTER THIRTY-EIGHT

NICOLAY PACED IN HIS office like a caged tiger. He hadn't succumbed to his anger and lost control in centuries. He hadn't meant to hurt Lysette. She was only the messenger.

"Gedeon!! Why did you send her to do your dirty work?!"

Kaida stood outside of the unrepaired office door to The Apache waiting for Nicolay to calm down. She listened as he took out his frustration on the office furniture. The club was in full swing and with all of the noise upstairs, no one heard what was going on in the back offices. When she thought it safe, she entered.

"He sent her to test you and you failed miserably."

Nicolay stopped, her words biting at his conscience. She was right. He owed Lysette an apology. She had tried to warn him, nothing more nothing less. In return, he had almost taken her life. He collapsed in the leather executive chair, tilting his head back.

"How is she?"

"She passed out."

"Did I hurt her badly?" he asked, more concerned now. He hadn't meant to throw her against the wall. He just needed to get her away from him as fast as possible and tossing her seemed easy.

"I left her in Dayton's care. I think the fear caused her to pass out more than her being hurt. She seems strong. I think she'll be okay. What about you? What happened in there?"

"I let my hatred get the best of me. It will not happen again."

"It's not me you have to convince. Remember, we do not have much time. When you're ready, you'll know where to find us."

That said Kaida left Nicolay to his thoughts. She'd heard the Gedeon story enough to know why Nicolay had attacked Lysette. Gedeon had forced the curse upon Nicolay, and he never forgot. He vowed to kill him if the chance ever arrived, and that was something that he had to live with.

Nicolay understood what Kaida said. He needed to apologize to Lysette. But would she forgive him? He had hurt her, not just physically but mentally, and right now he needed to regain her trust. He entered his lair feeling the need to be in his own home. Drawn to the armoire, he removed the book with the pictures of his life. If he died tonight, he needed to be reminded one last time of his past. Although he didn't understand it, he felt connected to the book.

The pages were exactly as he remembered them. He flipped each page, admiring the craftsmanship of the artist. As he reached the last page that had been drawn on, Gedeon stared back at him, changing him from mortal to monster.

Shaking his head, he was about to close the book, but something urged him to turn the page. He was sure the next page was empty as it always had been, but he needed to see it, just one last time.

He turned the page only to find the paper was not empty. He turned page after page. Pages that had been blank before now held images, images of the events of his life. He flipped back to the first new drawing. He stood in "The Commons," a quaint little club in Japan. Kaida was there, bound by a collar and leash to her old master. He turned the page. He stood before her, removing the collar, freeing her from her former master.

He proceeded to the next page. The image depicted the day he had met Xavier. He was still a new vampire, and sometimes the hunger overwhelmed him. Xavier had crossed his path becoming the latest victim in his quest to satisfy the hunger for blood. He had only taken a small amount of Xavier's blood, but the hunger was gone. Xavier turned to him and smiled, then he was gone. They had been reunited only recently, when he had opened the club.

Nicolay almost cried when he turned to the next page. It was a picture of Dakota sitting alone at a table in the bar, bathed in the moonlight. It was the first moment he knew he had to meet her and become part of her life. He had to get her back.

The pages that followed he didn't understand. One was the image of a circle with four figures standing across from each other as if they were the four corners of the world. One stood alone in the middle of the circle. The next page appeared to be a drawing of him, but instead of one of him, there were two. It didn't make sense but he didn't have the time to be worried about it. He needed to get back to the others so they could save Dakota.

KAIDA RETURNED TO THE plantation house. She lightly knocked on the front door and waited for Dayton to open it. She marveled at the house while she waited. It was well kept. The front of the house appeared to have just gotten a new coat of white paint. The navy shutters accented the stature of the massive pillars surrounding the front entrance.

Kaida turned at the sound of the door opening, "How is she?"

Dayton stepped outside and pulled the door up behind him, "She's still a little shaken and mad as all hell, but nothing appears to be broken. Did you find Nicolay?"

"Yeah. He is truly sorry for what he did. He will nurse his anger and join us shortly," Kaida believed every word she told Dayton, "How do you think she'll react to his return?"

"I'm not sure. Knowing her though, she'll be able to put this aside for the time being, at least until we get Dakota back. Lysette is strong. She has always been able to put the important things first. She took the attack personally, but Dakota's safety is more important to her than her feelings. After this is over though, I don't know."

Kaida stared out into the night. Why was Gedeon here? And how did Lysette know Gedeon? Kaida wanted answers, but after what had happened, she wasn't sure Lysette was ready to give them to her.

"I'm going to go talk to her. Can you give us some time?"

"Sure, I'll leave you two to your girl talk. When is Nicolay returning?"

"Dayton," she drew out his name, warning him, "We need to stay focused on getting Dakota back. We all have to put our personal feelings aside for now. Do you understand me?"

Dayton looked at Kaida. Who was she to be ordering him around, even if she spoke the truth? She didn't know a thing about the relationship between him, Dakota, and Lysette, and she had no right to be talking to him like she was.

She asked again, "Understood?"

"Understood," he wanted so badly to make Nicolay pay for what he had done to Lysette, but he could wait. When all of this was over, he and Nicolay had a score to settle.

LYSETTE STARED OUT the bay window in the kitchen, a mug of chamomile tea laced with magic in hand.

"Stupid Stupid Stupid."

How naive she had been to think Nicolay would just accept the news that Gedeon had returned. She expected him to be angry, but not to attack her. She filed that little piece of knowledge away for safe keeping. She refused to make the same mistake twice.

Lysette had underestimated Nicolay's power. Although he had not killed in centuries, he was strong, stronger than she had anticipated. He'd use every ounce of that strength tonight. Tonight, they faced the greatest of all evil, the devil himself.

Fear swept over her again. Gedeon was going to have a fit. She had to make sure everyone knew that what had happened here was to remain unspoken. Lysette had seen what happened to others who crossed Gedeon. It was never a pretty sight. Those he let live wished for death, those who died pleaded for mercy until the very end.

"How do you feel?" Lysette hadn't heard Kaida come into the kitchen.

"All right I guess, considering I was attacked by an angry vampire."

"He's really sorry about what happened. I've never seen him lose control like that, but his anger towards Gedeon runs deep."

"I know. I should have known. I don't know what made me think he'd accept that Gedeon was here."

"Why is Gedeon here?" here was Kaida's chance to get answers. She didn't know how Lysette and Gedeon knew each other. Hopefully Lysette would open up to her.

"Are you asking for you or for him?"

"Actually both. I've heard Nicolay's side of the story, but I get the feeling you know Gedeon personally. I just want to make sure there will be no conflict with him here."

Lysette snickered at the thought. A conflict with Gedeon being here was an understatement. She was more concerned about him and Nicolay killing each other than him being a distraction to her.

"Gedeon and I have a history laced with turmoil. He's here to help and as much as I hate to say it, we need him," Lysette was starting to sound like Gedeon, "Look, I'm not sure we can defeat our enemy tonight, even with his help. However, I am positive we don't have a chance without him. We must choose the lesser of two evils and Gedeon is just that."

Kaida agreed, "So? Care to share any of the details about Gedeon? You know, girl to girl?"

Lysette was amused; however she was not about to share any of her life with Gedeon with anyone. The time held too many bad memories and now was neither the time nor the place to discuss it.

"I'd rather not," she turned back to gaze out the window, "Where's Dayton?"

"Outside. I'll go get him. We need to go over the maps and come up with the plan for tonight. Nicolay should be here soon," Kaida waited for her reaction.

"When he arrives, send him to me. He and I have some unfinished business."

Lysette sounded awfully calm, but Kaida left the kitchen in search of Dayton. She found him outside at the bottom of the staircase leading to the front door. Before him Nicolay paced.

CHAPTER THIRTY-NINE

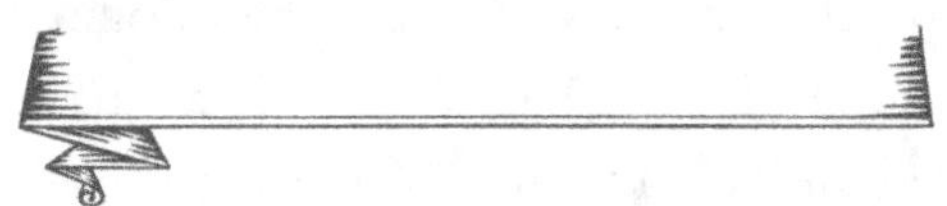

"I FEEL LIKE I AM WATCHING a tennis match," Dayton'e eyes followed Nicolay's steps through the gravel walkway.

"I hate it when he gets like this. Nicolay! Stop pacing!" Nicolay's pacing was a bad sign.

He snapped out of his trance to look at Kaida. The question was written all over his face.

"She wants to see you. Alone."

"You sure that's a good idea?" Dayton asked. Those two alone might not be the best idea. He loved Lysette as a sister and Nicolay had hurt her once. He was not going to allow it happen a second time.

"It's her choice. She asked me to send him to her."

Kaida observed Nicolay. She didn't see a hint of anger left in him. She hoped he had accepted that Gedeon was here. She wasn't sure he would agree they needed his help, but what choice did they have? Lysette seemed to know what she was talking about. Maybe she had dealt with this evil before.

Nicolay faced Dayton, "I promise not to lay a hand on her pretty little face," he'd have to make this up to Dayton. If he didn't smooth things over, Dakota might be lost to him forever.

"Just know we'll be in the other room and if I so much as think she is in trouble I'm coming in," Dayton was as serious as he had ever been. He hadn't quite figured out how he might handle a vampire, but he'd think of something.

"Agreed."

They all entered the house. Kaida and Dayton sat at the dining room table and spread the maps out. Nicolay approached the kitchen door with caution. He knew he had hurt Dakota's best friend and he needed to correct the faux pas. What he had done should be unforgivable; he just hoped Lysette had it in her heart to understand.

As he entered, he called to her, "You wanted to see me?"

She had changed clothes while he was gone. She stood before him, her back turned, covered from head to toe in white. The silk pants fit nicely around her waist and billowed ever so slightly around her legs. The silk tunic complimented her pale complexion. Her feet were bare save for tattoos. Her ankles and wrists were surrounded by bands of jade. She had drawn a silk cloak over her head and there was a glow about her... power surrounded her. She was showing more of her true form to him.

"I misjudged your power. For that I apologize."

That voice, where had he heard that voice before? "No need to apologize, it is I who owe you an apology. I never meant to hurt you. I do not know what came over me."

She interrupted him before he had the opportunity to say another word, "Rage came over you, but what is done is done. We have more pressing matters to tend to," she turned to face him.

"It's you," Nicolay refused to believe his eyes. The minute he saw her hands he knew it was her. He thought the tattoos on her feet seemed familiar, "But how?"

"I know you've opened the book, have you not yet figured it out?" Lysette felt his curiosity earlier when he opened the book. The book was a part of her, just as the dagger was.

"But, but how? You, in the dream, and here now?"

"Shh, my child. I will explain in due time. For now I have another gift for you," she reached under the cloak and handed him something wrapped in animal skin. She'd decided that whether he needed it tonight or not, it was his and now was the right time to return it to him.

He reached out taking the object from her hands. Whatever it was, it was heavy. He slowly unwrapped the animal skin to reveal a dagger. It was the same dagger pictured in the book. The jade handle fit perfectly in his hand as if it had been fashioned for him.

"It is yours. I am only returning it to its rightful owner. It has been kept safe for centuries until you were ready to receive it."

"Why are you giving this to me now?"

"Because time draws near my child, and I do not know if I will get another opportunity to return it to you."

"What am I supposed to do with it?"

"Sadly, I do not know. It was sent to me for protection. Only you know what you must do with it."

He toyed with the dagger in his hands, tossing it from one hand to the other. It felt familiar to him like he held a missing a piece of himself. He still couldn't understand all of the markings. He studied each picture and it finally hit him. He stretched out his right arm and placed the dagger parallel to it. The pictures matched up perfectly.

Lysette watched Nicolay as he became reacquainted with the weapon. Sooner or later he'd figure out the dagger was once a part of him, just as the book was. He was coming into his own, but not fast enough.

"What do the markings mean?" he spoke to Lysette, but was still comparing the markings with the ones on his body.

"The dagger unlocks the magic."

"What do you mean by unlock?"

"As I said, I do not know the full history or purpose, only that it is some sort of key."

"So now what?" they had lost precious time with the events of earlier in the night.

"Now, we go and plan, and meet up with Gedeon."

In all of the excitement with the dagger, the thought of seeing Gedeon again had slipped Nicolay's mind, "Why is he here?"

Lysette had anticipated the question, and she answered it as best she could, "He is here because he is always here. There is still much you do not understand. Come, let's join the others and I will explain what it is you need to know," she then turned, reclaiming her full human form, and exited the kitchen.

Nicolay stared in awe. One minute, she was a glowing orb of light covered by tattoos and the most beautiful material he had ever laid eyes on, the next she was a mere mortal, the tattoos and jewelry gone. He wondered if Dakota knew what Lysette really was. Had she ever seen her in true form? After taking another moment to process all he had seen and been told, he followed Lysette's lead and joined the others in the dining room.

CHAPTER FOURTY

"NICE OF YOU TO JOIN us."

Kaida's smart remark was taken without comment. Only she turned to face Nicolay as he entered the room. Lysette and Dayton hovered over the maps. They had pinpointed the exact location of the falls as well as a set of caves that ran underneath. Dayton drew a path with his finger on the map.

"There's a path here running from the street to the falls. Dakota didn't know about it, but me and the guys used to go hunting through that part of the woods. Nicolay, if you take Kaida with you, you probably won't have any problems getting there, but Lysette and I will need the four wheeler. "

"That's not a problem. It's in the back of the Tahoe," Nicolay replied.

"And how do you know that?" Dayton asked.

"Long story, and we don't have time for it right now."

"Gedeon will meet us here," Lysette indicated the top of the falls.

"Are you going to explain why he is here now?" Nicolay asked although he was sure Kaida had asked the same question.

"Yes, Nicolay," her tone expressing her irritation, "I'll tell you why he's here."

Lysette took a moment to collect her thoughts. She walked to the window, turning her back to everyone. She relived this moment again and again in her head, remembering that whenever true evil threatened to walk the earth, Gedeon was always there, his power saving the day. She finally spoke.

"When the Great Evil comes, it is always in darkness. The Great Evil feeds off of the darkness and all that comes with it. Most mortals are afraid of the dark and rightfully so. Fear makes The Great Evil grow stronger. For thousands of years, Aurek was the keeper of the darkness. His curse was to forever walk the darkness, keeping The Great Evil from finding and opening the portals to this world. When Aurek disappeared, Gedeon took the place of his maker. That is, until you were born," she turned, pointing at Nicolay.

"Gedeon's power had been unmatched until then. He was solely responsible for the lives of all creatures, both mortal and magic, on earth. But in all of that, he didn't have the power to open or close the portals to the realm of death. All he could do was distract The Great Evil, keeping it from finding the portals."

"But why has The Great Evil come now, here?" Nicolay knew what The Great Evil was, but there were other pieces of the puzzle that still remained to be seen.

"Think about it. Wars waged over oil, people killing each other over money, territory, even shoes. Man has gotten so caught up in the belief that he controls everything, but all he has succeeded in accomplishing is making The Great Evil stronger."

"That doesn't explain why he's here," Dayton and Kaida had been thinking the same thing. They listened intently as Lysette explained why the Naverro's land was chosen to harbor the portal.

"It has been said that the portals to the realm of death were re-opened when the greatest of all wrongs occurred. American soil is filled with mass graves of Native Americans and slaves that suffered and died at the hands of other men. Each one of those graves has the potential to harbor a portal. This place was probably chosen, one, because you all were here," she pointed to Nicolay and Dayton, "Two, because of a mass grave of some sort located on this land and three, because these lands have twice the tragedy as some of the others, making the portals more susceptible to tampering. These grounds may have originally been sacred to the Native Americans, but eventually numerous slaves lost their lives here."

As Lysette spoke, she felt the sorrow of all of the centuries of death that plagued the land just below the surface. The land itself was awakening beneath them. She was sure it would be soon that the Great Evil would attempt to open one of those graves. She was also sure the Naverro family didn't know the full history of the place the plantation stood on. She felt the restless spirits of those who suffered and died at the hands of the immigrants as well as the plantation owners.

"Dayton, didn't you and Dakota always say you felt a special connection to this place? Like it was home to you for more reasons than the fact that you grew up here."

"Yeah. When the rest of our family left to head North, Dakota and I couldn't bear the thought of leaving."

"That is because you are a part of this land, just as it is a part of you. And you, Nicolay, do you know why you were drawn here to open The Apache?"

"No. I mean, I wanted a change of scenery and what better place to start over than in the South?" Nicolay didn't see what this had to do with everything.

"But there is more to it than that. The land called to you didn't it? The power drew you to this place whether you realize it or not. The Great Evil had already begun to plan. In the end, the need for good to fight evil will overcome us all. Each of us plays an intricate part in the balance between good and evil. Some of us do not yet know what part we play, but ultimately, the truth will be unveiled and all will be as it should."

"Ok. Ok. I think we all get it. What's the plan for tonight?" Kaida was becoming more and more anxious.

Lysette had already thought this through, "First I have to locate the portal. Since Dakota is being held near the falls, I think it's safe to assume the portal is nearby. If she is just a pawn to lure Nicolay to the portal, it makes sense."

"You still believe someone or something is using Dakota as a decoy?" Dayton rambled through his mind again and again trying to figure out who would take his sister.

"Yes, I think that is why Xavier has taken her."

Dayton didn't know who Xavier was or how he and Dakota had met. He thought it was time to ask. Everyone else appeared to already have the answers.

"So, who is Xavier and what do we know about him?"

"I'll answer that. I think if anyone knows him I do."

Lysette was relieved that Nicolay wanted to address the question. She was sure the person Dakota thought was Xavier wasn't really him. The spell only worked as well as the caster's belief. If this thing disguised itself as Xavier, she was sure that is why the name was the result of the spell. But she wasn't ready to reveal what she knew. They needed to focus on getting Dakota back and closing the portal. She would worry about getting Xavier back later.

"Xavier works in my club. I thought of him as my friend, but after what I witnessed, I am very much reconsidering my decision. I would have trusted him with my life. Now, I don't know what to think."

"What did you see last night?" Lysette was worried. If Nicolay really believed who he saw last night was Xavier, maybe she needed to reveal what she knew.

Nicolay glanced over at Dayton. He wasn't sure what kind of reaction he was going to have at finding out his sister had been raped. Dayton's eyes flicked back and forth between Lysette and Nicolay, waiting for the answer.

Lysette observed the concern on Nicolay's face. He must have witnessed something terrible happening last night. She thought long and hard, scenarios of torture and brutality sifting through her mind. Then, what he saw last night hit her like a freight train. She wasn't sure whether it was her thought or his, but she saw the image of Xavier on top of Dakota's body, defiling her, stealing her innocence. Her face grew deathly pale at the thought of the horror. Of all of the things he could have done to her, why that, why did he have to steal her innocence?

Dakota always said she was saving herself for her soul mate. Lysette played along; knowing that she hadn't been pure for centuries. Now Dakota would never have the chance to freely give the gift of her innocence away.

Nicolay again entered Lysette's mind. He had shown her what he had seen. He listened to her thoughts and he needed to assure her Dakota had no recollection of what had happened to her body last night. Lysette's memories of the conversations she and Dakota had about their virginity wrapped around him. He heard each thought as clear as the crickets in the clearing the night he had first made love to Dakota. He smiled when she thought of Dakota giving her virginity to her soul mate. He was fortunate enough to have received the gift before all of this happened.

Finally, Nicolay spoke to Lysette in her mind.

"Listen, there are some things you need to know."

"How can you do this? Even Gedeon can't talk to me here unless I will it so."

"I'm not sure, but we don't have time to discuss that. Dakota doesn't know everything that happened to her body last night. When I went to her, Xavier was just beginning to fondle her. She was so distraught that I put her mind to sleep. He may have raped her body, but I separated the two. She may feel some of the after effect when she awakens, but she will have no memory of the events."

"So, when will she wake?"

"When we come for her. I will wake her mind once we are closer."

"Wait."

Nicolay started to pull away from her mind, but she stopped him. She decided he deserved to know that they might not be dealing with Xavier, but with some other evil.

"We may not be dealing with Xavier."

"What do you mean?"

"Today, while you rested, I searched for him. I found his mind, but it was dormant. I tried to call to him, to get some sign of recognition, but there was nothing. Because he and I do not share a bond, I only had access to touch his mind, not open it."

"So what are you saying?"

"I'm saying that the Xavier that you know does not know anything about what is going on."

Then, she shut him out of her mind.

"You two did the mind talking thing again didn't you? What are you hiding?" Dayton didn't like being kept in the dark. They had kept enough from him. He was growing irritated with all of the secrecy.

"Dayton," Lysette addressed him calmly. He trusted her judgment. They had been like family for years, "I think it is best for right now you not know what he saw last night. I promise when all of this is over, I'll explain everything."

He didn't like the answer she gave, but he accepted it. Lysette always tried to protect him and Dakota. Her decision was in his best interest and the thought was comforting.

They went over the maps and the plans again, ensuring no stone was left unturned. Lysette would prepare the site so they could close the portal as quickly as possible. She hinted that there would be others there to help. She was sure The Great Evil was going to send his minions to attack them so escaping wouldn't be easy, but Lysette was already prepared for that.

Kaida's responsibility was to get Dakota and bring her to her place, then she would take her place and they would close the portal. Nicolay would go to Dakota and keep her mind at rest until Kaida arrived to rescue her body. Dayton would remain with Lysette at all times.

"Everyone know what they are supposed to do?" Lysette glanced at each of them. She hoped everyone understood the severity of any mistake tonight.

They all nodded in agreement.

"Well then, let's get this show on the road."

They picked up their belongings and headed for the door. Kaida and Nicolay lagged behind. They agreed they didn't need to ride with Lysette and Dayton, and they would meet them in the clearing.

"What did you see last night?"

Nicolay knew Kaida was going to ask, "You don't want to know."

The look on his face saying it all, Kaida agreed and dropped the subject.

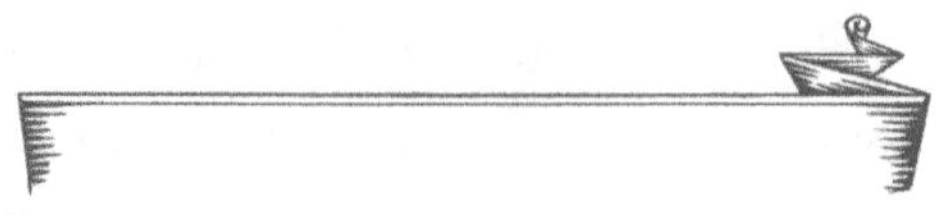

CHAPTER FORTY-ONE

NICOLAY AND KAIDA ENTERED the clearing near the top of the falls. Kaida looked over the side of the falls with amazement as the water plunged over the edge. She closed her eyes, bathing in the cool mist against her face. This place reminded her of home. Her lair was safely hidden at the foot of the one hundred and twenty-two foot Nachi Falls. How she missed her home.

Nicolay watched Kaida as she took in their surroundings. She was beautiful with her long auburn hair draping like a curtain over her shoulder. Her complexion could be compared only to the richest caramel. In her human form, she was five feet tall, but her attitude more than made up for her lack of height. She was confident, sometimes even borderline arrogant, but that was who she was and she never apologized for it. He didn't know if it was her beauty or his hunger that drew him to her tonight.

Kaida caught him staring at her, or through her that is.

"What are you thinking?" she saw the bloodlust in his eyes. His fangs were showing. He hadn't fed tonight. In the end, no matter how much he fought her, he would feed from her. He needed her magic tonight and she'd offer it to him freely.

Embarrassed, Nicolay replied, "Do you want the truth?"

"I already know the truth, but I want to hear it from you," She needed him to say the words. He needed to say the words. When it all boiled down to it, destiny brought them together. If it was just for the purpose of her sharing her blood, her magic with him, then so be it. She'd accepted that fact a long time ago.

"You know you're beautiful, right?"

"Don't," his comment hurt more than it helped, "Like I said I already know the truth. You need to feed from me, don't you? Say it! Say it! Why can't you just say it?" she was yelling now, her anger growing.

"Because he still holds on to the mortal ways. He still has not accepted what he truly is."

They followed the voice and watched as the stranger stepped from the woods. Kaida regarded the stranger with disdain. She didn't appreciate his eavesdropping.

Gedeon sensed her unease, "Save your strength, you'll need it to fight the evil we face tonight," he stepped into the open part of the clearing to join them.

Kaida considered the stranger closely. He wore all black, as did Nicolay that night. He was tall and of a medium build. A long braid, bound by leather, hung over his right shoulder. He kept his eyes hidden from them with the brim of his hat. If she didn't know any better, she'd have called him a bounty hunter. His outfit, the battle ax peeking over his shoulder, and his demeanor fit the bill perfectly. But there was something else, a mysteriousness about him she just couldn't place.

"So, am I correct in my observation?" Gedeon was being his usual smug self.

"You should know. You made me what I am against my will," anger masked Nicolay's voice. He addressed Gedeon as if it were just the two of them in the clearing.

"Tame your anger young one, we have bigger enemies to face tonight. Always remember, just as I made you, I can destroy you."

"You sound pretty sure of yourself. We have not crossed paths for many centuries now. Are you truly this confident, or are you becoming an arrogant fool in your old age?"

"Watch your tongue or it shall be the death of you. Always remember with age comes power for a vampire."

Lysette and Dayton entered the clearing. She had hoped to arrive before Gedeon revealed himself, but so much for wishful thinking.

"Enough of this bickering. I will not have you two fighting. At least not until we have Dakota back and the portal is secured," Lysette stared at the two of them, warning them she was not going to let them jeopardize this mission.

"Now, if the two of you can't play nice, one of you will have to leave. Gedeon, I have had about enough of your games, leave Nicolay be. Nicolay, don't let him push your buttons. Remember we're all here to ensure Dakota's safe return and to keep The Great Evil from walking the earth again. Have I made myself clear?"

"Perfectly, my love," Gedeon turned to face Lysette. She was even more beautiful when she was angry.

Lysette turned to face Nicolay, "I know you have not fed. We need you at your best tonight. Come, you can feed from me."

"No! I will not allow this. He cannot feed from you," now Gedeon was the angry one.

"He can feed from me," Kaida spoke softly. She didn't want to startle anyone. They were all on edge tonight. Apparently, everyone had forgotten she was standing there.

She watched the possessiveness fill Gedeon's movements. He was tense, his hands opening and closing, trying to control the urge to grab Lysette and take her away.

"As you wish," Nicolay approached Kaida.

"Not here. Over there," she gestured to a spot on the other side of the clearing.

She didn't feel comfortable being close to two vamps while one fed from her. She knew Lysette could keep Gedeon in check, she had just witnessed that first hand. Still, it wasn't enough. She wanted to be as far away from him as possible. Plus, other than when he was sleeping, Nicolay was most vulnerable when he was feeding. She didn't want to give Gedeon that kind of advantage.

Nicolay followed Kaida to a spot near a large oak tree.

"Let's get this over with," she wanted this done so they could get back to the task at hand.

"You know, you don't have to do this."

She quieted him by placing her fingertips over his lips, "In my own way, yes I do."

She tilted her head sideways, exposing her neck. She usually only let him feed from her wrist, but tonight was special. Offering to let him feed from her neck was her way of letting him know that she trusted him with her life.

Nicolay brushed one stray curl from her neck. He smelled the crimson river flowing through her veins. He watched her pulse beneath the flesh of her neck; her heart beat beckoned him like the Siren's song. He felt his fangs fully lengthen.

Carefully pulling her into his arms, he pierced her skin, savoring the taste of her. She released a soft whimper, and then the ecstasy of the bite overwhelmed her.

Although she was not human, the effects of the bite were still euphoric. He drank from her, their hearts beating in unison. He could drink from her until the hunger was satisfied and she would have no ill effects. He slowly drew back from her, licking the two marks on her neck to close the wounds. He ran his tongue over his fangs, tasting the last drops of her.

"I wondered if you were trying to take it all," Kaida smiled up at him. She had enjoyed it as much as he had. Maybe that's why she still let him feed from her from time to time. Sometimes, she forgot how amazing it could be for the donor.

"Making jokes are we? I take it I did not take too much then," he held her tight, "Thank you," he wanted her to really know he appreciated her willingly allowing him to feed from her, "I'll never forget what you have done for me."

Kaida relaxed, allowing her head to fall against his chest. It felt right to be held by him, even though he was destined to be with Dakota. He may one day love her, but Dakota was his soul mate. She let out a breath and pulled back from his embrace.

"We'd better get back before someone comes looking for us," she grabbed his hand and started walking back to the others when he pulled her back to him.

He looked into her eyes before he spoke, cradling her chin in his hands, "You do realize that no matter what happens tonight, you will always remain near and dear to my heart. I may not love you the way you want me to, but that doesn't mean I don't love you. You are my family, and I do what has to be done to protect that which is mine. Understand?"

Kaida regarded him in a new light. He had never truly expressed how he felt about her. She had told him on a number of occasions how she felt, but he always kept his feelings inside. With the words he had just spoken, she knew if ever she needed him, if it was in his power, he'd be there.

"I understand."

He placed the most gentle of kisses on each of her cheeks and then grasped her hand, leading the way back to the others.

CHAPTER FORTY-TWO

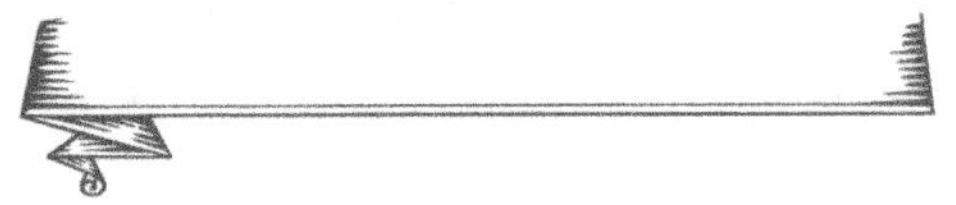

IN THE CLEARING, THEY found Lysette marking the trees with a white powder. She had drawn a Wotan's cross on the ground. Dayton sat off to the side, next to the falls. He appeared to be meditating. Nicolay wondered if he was trying to communicate with Dakota. When they had first arrived he had probed the area. He searched for any indication that she was stirring. Her mind was still at rest, just as he had left it. He went to her, stood by the bed in her mind. Spoke softly to her that he was coming for her. She would awaken soon, sensing they were near.

"The portal will open. There is a gathering of negative energy radiating from this spot, more so than anywhere else in the clearing. Come everyone, the time draws near."

"What about Dakota?" Nicolay needed to get to her.

"Kaida will have to get her. We'll need her in order to seal the portal. With Gedeon's help, I think we can hold the evil off until everyone takes their rightful places."

Lysette pointed to each spot, instructing each person as to where to stand and what to do, "Nicolay, did you bring the dagger?"

He unsheathed the dagger and handed it to her. Lysette placed it in the center of the circle, the place where Dakota would stand.

"Chevoya, Come!"

They all looked at each other, each face asking the same question of the others. Who was Lysette talking to? Then they appeared, one by one from the darkness, creatures of all sorts, creatures most of them had never laid eyes upon, creatures of myths and fairytales. Unicorns and faeries, wereanimals of all kinds, werewolves, wereleopards, ghosts and ghouls, all there to fight the evil threatening to destroy their homes and existence.

"We are here, my queen, and we come bearing gifts," Chevoya quickly turned to two others and indicated they should bring the prisoners forward.

"We found these three lurking in the woods."

Lysette walked up to each one. They all reeked of magic. She gave a hearty laugh. Turning away from them she instructed, "Let them go. They are hers. They mean us no harm."

Chevoya's men released the prisoners. They scurried to their queen.

Kaida turned to Lysette, "How did you know?"

"As I told you at the house, your kind reeks of magic. You may be able to hide behind a human form, but magic knows magic. You shouldn't have told them to come. They are in grave danger here."

One of the men stepped forward, speaking for the others, "She didn't tell us to come. We sensed she was not happy and came on our own."

"It's okay," Kaida assured them.

"Your numbers are few. If you do not wish your kind to become extinct, I suggest you send them away," Lysette spoke directly to Kaida, dismissing the human male standing in front of her.

"She is the last female of our kind. If she dies, we become extinct anyway."

Kaida rested her hand on the arm of the man defending her honor. She turned him to face her, "That's not exactly true."

She turned from them, ashamed she had kept this secret for so long, "There are two others, sisters of mine if you may. Callisto and Sakura lay dormant in a secret chamber in our lair. If anything should happen to me, one of them will awaken to take my place. They are both young and fertile. The chosen ones will bed them and repopulate the world with our kind."

"But how can this be?"

"There's no time to explain. Go and take the others with you. If either Callisto or Sakura awakens, then I shall not return," Kaida knew he understood her. Should one of the others awaken, she had met her death, "Go. Now!"

She turned from them, not able to bear to watch them leave. Her lover was among them. The eldest, Tatsu had been with her since she had awakened. He had been her chosen one, but they never got the chance to mate. She was captured not far from the lair after sneaking out for a midnight stroll. He had warned her not to go out at night alone, but she had ignored his warnings. She was young then, but she was lucky enough to have lived to learn from the mistake. They had tried for centuries to rescue her and each time they arrived, she sent them away, afraid they too would be captured. When Nicolay finally rescued her, they all became forever indebted to him. She had been with him ever since.

Tatsu knew Kaida had feelings for Nicolay. In the end though, he knew she would make the right decision to ensure their kind lived on. Eventually she would return to him, they would mate, and a new generation would be brought into the world. Faced with losing her permanently, he refused to just walk away.

The three men looked at each other. They had no choice. Their queen had given them an order and they had to follow it.

"The others will go, but I will not," it was time Tatsu put his foot down. Life without her had been hard, but he knew she was out there. Now, if she died, he knew he couldn't live without her. He was her mate and he could never be the chosen one for another.

Kaida looked to Lysette for guidance. She nodded her agreement, confirming that he could stay if the others agreed to leave. She faced the others, "So be it."

The others stared at Nicolay. One of them spoke, "Take care of the both of them," then they took flight, leaving their queen and her mate behind.

"Anyone else have anything to tell us? Speak now or forever hold your peace," Lysette glanced around at the crowd. Every creature, living and dead, stood among them completely sure of their purpose.

"Okay people. We've only got thirty minutes 'til midnight. Let's do this."

Lysette instructed the creatures to form a larger circle around the circle of trees she had marked earlier. This would keep them far enough away from their circle to not interrupt the magic, but have them shielded from all sides.

"Kaida, are you ready?" Lysette looked her over one last time. She had the most important job of all. She had to get Dakota's body.

"As ready as I'll ever be."

Nicolay instructed her on the path to take through the cave. The entrance was just on the other side of the falls.

"If ever in doubt, follow the patchouli," Dakota's scent was strong. If he smelled it, he knew Kaida could.

Kaida then went to her task, Tatsu following close behind to protect the one he loved. Lysette, Dayton, and Nicolay took their places at each point of the cross. Gedeon hovered above them, watching from each angle.

"Now what do we do?" Dayton was nervous. The fate of the world depended on things going off without a hitch.

"Now we wait," Lysette replied.

Dayton took this time to meditate. Lysette spoke to the others with her magic, encouraging them to be strong. Soon she had to start the incantation to seal the portal. She already felt the presence of evil magic pushing to the surface beneath her feet.

Nicolay became statue still. He wondered where Xavier was in all of this. There had been enough of a commotion on the surface to wake the dead, and yet, he hadn't shown his face. Something wasn't right. He went to Dakota; he needed to wake her so she could tell him if Xavier was close by.

Lysette watched as Nicolay's mind left his body to join Dakota. "Good luck my young one."

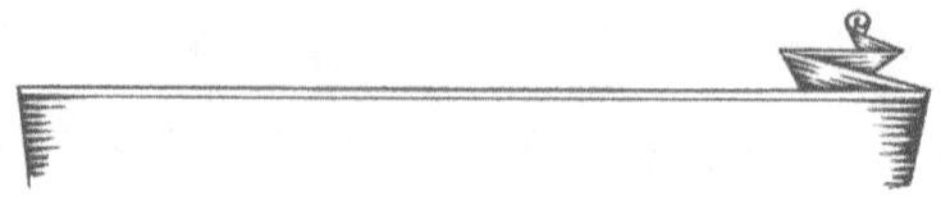

CHAPTER FORTY-THREE

KAIDA AND TATSU ENTERED the cave. The air, thick with humidity, nearly choked the life out of them both. It took a moment but they eventually adjusted to the change. Deeper and deeper into the cavern they traveled. Though their night vision was as good as any vampire's, they relied on their sense of smell to guide them.

Nicolay was right. Dakota's scent filled the cavern. Even with the moisture in the air, the scent was unmistakably hers. Some other scent still hung in the air. The place smelled of death. And the further into the caves they traveled, the more the stench overpowered the distinctive scent of Dakota.

Backs pressed against the wall, Kaida and Tatsu reached the entrance to the room Nicolay spoke of. Only the smell of patchouli lingered in the air. Who or what ever had kidnapped Dakota was long gone.

Kaida entered the room, only to be met with the most horrible sight she had ever seen. Dakota's nearly nude body hung from a sconce. Before the scream exited her mouth, Tatsu covered it with his hand. They still had to be careful. They hadn't seen or sensed anyone in the caverns, but that didn't mean they were alone.

Tatsu quickly turned Kaida away so she didn't have to witness the sight of Dakota's body. Although they did not know each other, he was sure it was difficult for any woman to see another woman's body abused the way Dakota's body had been abused. The sight was hard enough for him to comprehend, so he knew it had to be tearing Kaida up inside.

Tatsu contemplated the best way to get Dakota's body out without hurting her. Every part of her body had some sort of injury to it. Welts covered both sides of her face. One eye appeared to be swollen shut. Someone had taken a razor sharp blade to her stomach, slicing her like a piece of meat. Dried blood covered both of her legs and by the bruising on the inside of her thighs, no one had to tell them she had been raped.

"I'll get her down."

"No! Don't touch her!" Kaida yelled at him pulling away. "Don't ever touch her!"

Tatsu didn't take Kaida's reaction personally. He understood Kaida's need to do this. In a way, it was a relief. He wasn't sure how Dakota would react if she came to in his arms.

Kaida calmed herself enough to assure Tatsu she could get Dakota. He took his shirt off and handed it to her. "I'll leave you two alone." He left the room to give them some privacy and to keep watch by the door.

NICOLAY STOOD OVER Dakota in her mind. She was beautiful when she was sleeping. He so wanted to just scoop her up and run away with her. He hated that anything had happened to her. Thinking about it, he wasn't sure if he wanted her to remember any of last night. He was confident that while her mind rested she hadn't experienced any of the torture her body endured. Somewhere in her mind the experience remained, sealed behind a door. He had the ability to easily erase all recollection of yesterday's events and for a moment he considered finding that door and doing just that. But one thing he'd learned about Dakota made him hesitate. If he did erase her memories, she may hate him. Instead he decided to let things be and allow her to make the decision about her memories. Taking one last look at the sleeping image in her mind, he stepped away from her and touched the place that connected him her body. He needed to know its condition before he woke her.

Concentrating, he again found himself standing in the room they had been in last night. Blood covered the table. Dakota's body once again hung from one of the walls. He searched the room, looking for any sign of Xavier. Evaluating the surroundings, Nicolay stepped from Dakota's body. He glided to the entranceway and checked down each side of the hallway. He heard Kaida and Tatsu approaching. Soon, they'd be here to collect Dakota.

"The sooner the better," he whispered to himself.

Assured he was alone, he turned to see the horror of his *Tehya Aquene's* body. He reached out to her, wanting to cradle her and heal all of her wounds. He vowed Xavier would pay for what he had done.

Nicolay decided then that he would wait for the last possible moment to wake her. If he woke her too soon, her mind would endure the torture of the journey from the caves to the surface. He'd stay with her in her mind until they brought her to the surface. Then, he would wake her. He hoped Kaida understood him not telling her what he witnessed last night. Now though, after seeing what Xavier had done to Dakota's body, he kind of wished he had.

Standing by the doorway he waited. Visions of the pain he'd inflict on Xavier danced through his head. Nicolay's word was as good as gold and yet, Dakota's body hung behind him, a reminder of how he had failed her.

"I will make this up to you, my love. I promise. And those who have done this to you will suffer my wrath."

As Nicolay approached the tattered body that hung from the wall, a muffled scream halted him. He turned to see Kaida standing in the door with a male's hand covering her mouth. Her pain stricken eyes pierced through his heart. Now he really wished he had warned her. What was done was done. He stepped back into Dakota's body and mind. Scooping her into his arms, he cradled her to him, rocking her slowly, tenderly. They lay on the bed in her mind, sharing a moment Dakota would never recall, and he was just fine with that.

KAIDA TOOK BABY STEPS, getting closer and closer to Dakota's body. How dare anyone do this to another creature, human or otherwise? She thought back to all she endured as a slave. Her master had been a tyrant, but never had she been treated as Dakota had. All of the sorrow of the world filled Kaida in that moment.

She reached out, fear filling her every muscle, to touch Dakota's chin. Nicolay assured them he'd wake her when they came for her. She hoped he knew the extent of Dakota's injuries and saved her from the pain of the journey back to the surface.

"Dakota?" Kaida whispered softly to her, hoping not to get a response.

All was quiet. She was sure Dakota was alive. Kaida checked her pulse and breathing before removing her from the wall. Placing her body on the blood covered table she removed the shackles from her wrists and ankles with a wave of her hand. Slowly drawing the tee shirt over her head, Kaida covered her as best she could with the little she had.

They needed to get her healed, and soon. Looking around, the room showed sure signs that someone had lost a lot of blood and based on the cuts on Dakota's body, it was probably her. When she came too, she'd be weak. Kaida just hoped Dakota had enough strength to help them close the portal. Kaida scooped Dakota's body into her arms, cradling her, being as gentle as possible.

Tatsu stood at the door, his back turned to them. He heard her approaching and turned.

"You okay?"

"No. Let's get this over with."

They retraced their steps through the caverns walking side by side. With each step, Kaida heard Dakota's breathing growing shallow, a sign that she may have had some trauma to her lungs.

The roar of the falls became louder and louder, echoing like thunder around them. When they reached the entrance Kaida hesitated.

"What's wrong?" Tatsu saw worry in her eyes.

"I'm not sure how Nicolay and Dayton are going to react when they see her."

Tatsu positioned himself behind Kaida, just enough for her to lean back against his chest, "We don't have much of a choice. Plus, the sooner we get this done, the sooner she can rest."

"I know."

So many thoughts entered Kaida's mind. Nicolay's anger was a force to be reckoned with, but he wanted what was best for Dakota. She was more concerned with Dayton's reaction. She hoped he could see past Dakota's injuries and be thankful that at least she was still alive.

Kaida made a move to exit the cave when she heard the sounds of battle surrounded them. Screeches and screams filled the air as those tossed over the falls plunged to their deaths. They smelled blood in the air. They needed to get to the inner circle and fast.

Kaida looked over at Tatsu. Apparently, he heard the battling as well. He changed form, grabbed her and Dakota and flew them over the battlefield. Greeted by Gedeon in midflight, he escorted them to the inner circle as quickly as possible, fending off any demon that breached the outer circle and threatened them.

Once safely across the battlefield, Tatsu lowered them into the inner circle and again took flight with Gedeon to help the others.

CHAPTER FORTY-FOUR

IN THE INNER CIRCLE, all was quiet. Lysette, Nicolay, and Dayton each stood in their places on the Wotan's cross. Lysette observed the fear and sorrow on Kaida's face. Then, her eyes dropped to gaze upon Dakota cradled in the woman's arms. Her mind would not comprehend what her eyes saw.

She didn't know how long she stared at Dakota's body before she looked up but when she did, the horror almost overwhelmed her. Lysette shook her head, trying to erase the image that was burned into her mind. She didn't have time to process what she saw, she only knew that they had to close the portal and they had to close it now.

Lifting her eyes to Kaida once again she spoke, "Place her in the center of the cross," she then turned to Nicolay, "Wake her."

He did as he was told, never taking his eyes off of Dakota. He entered her mind and slowly nudged her awake, "My *Tehya Aquene*, come back to us my dear. It is time. We need you."

Dakota's eyes fluttered open and she smiled, gazing into Nicolay's handsome face, "Where are we?"

"Still in your mind. The Great Evil approaches and we need your help to close the portal."

"Great Evil? Portal? What are you talking about?" Dakota was confused. The last thing she remembered was Nicolay holding her, they were in her mind, then drowsiness overwhelmed her and she slept.

"Your mind has been asleep. I don't have time to explain. The others are waiting for us," he wanted so much to warn her of the condition of her body. He took a deep breath and asked, "Are you ready?"

"What about my body? And Xavier?" Dakota remembered what Xavier had been doing to her before Nicolay put her mind to sleep. She feared how she would feel when he returned her mind to her body.

"I will be honest with you; your body is badly bruised and you've been cut up pretty bad. The fate of the world is in our hands baby, and I need you to be strong," he held Dakota's face in his hands, gazing down at her, "Can you do that for me? Can you be strong, at least until we can save the world?"

How could she deny him? "Yes."

As he released her, her mind returned to her body. She was immediately aware of the damage her body had endured. Dakota regained her feet and turned around. She saw her brother, staring wide eyed right at her, a look of terror on his face.

"I must look like shit," she spoke lightly to him.

Turning around a little more, she saw Lysette. She appeared pale, like she had just seen a ghost. Continuing in her circle she laid her gaze upon Nicolay. He was as handsome as ever. He bowed at the waist, showing his respect for her. Lastly, as she completed the circle, a stranger stood before her.

She pointed at Kaida and, as politely as she could, asked, "Who are you?"

Nicolay answered the question knowing that no one else had it in them to, "She is Kaida. She works for me. She is the one who saved your body."

Dakota's eyes never left Kaida, "Is that true?"

Kaida could only nod her agreement.

"Then thank you. I know you didn't have to do that."

Lysette interrupted the introduction, "We must work quickly. There is only a moment before midnight," she instructed Dakota as to what she needed to do.

With each person now in their place, Dakota turned to face Nicolay. The living and the dead, humans and magic, surrounded her on all sides. She picked up the dagger that lay by her foot and then she felt it, the magic welling up inside of her.

Lysette yelled, "Now! You must do it now!"

Although no one had told her, Dakota inherently knew what she needed to do. She sliced her wrist and allowed the blood to drip to the ground. She tossed the dagger to Nicolay and he did the same. They each repeated the ritual, first Kaida, then Lysette, and lastly Dayton. He initially hesitated, but after seeking assurance in Dakota's face he too sliced his arm, completing the circle of magic.

They all spoke in unison as the ground around them began to separate.

"Death before us
Life behind
By shedding of blood
This portal we bind"

"*No!*" was the only sound to be heard before a white light reached from each of them, passing through Dakota and into the heavens. Then the light returned through them to the realms below. The fighting around them halted and demons burst into flames, dropping to the ground to become piles of ash.

The other creatures who had come to help stared in amazement. None had ever seen anything like this before. The light was beautiful as it still surrounded the inner circle. Then, just as quickly as it had come, it dissipated.

CHAPTER FORTY-FIVE

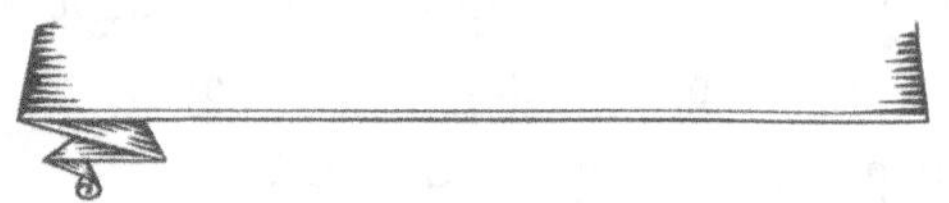

THEY ALL COLLAPSED, save for Nicolay. Though weak, Dakota's instincts told her she had to check on everyone. She lifted her body from the ground, gaining a kneeling position. She turned, barely able to see Dayton trying to compose himself on the ground.

"Day...?"

Dayton looked up at his sister, "I'm good...just drained. What just happened?"

"I don't know?" and Dakota truly didn't. She didn't even know how she knew what words to speak. She felt as if something else possessed her body, using her as a medium.

"What about the others?" the clearing was cloaked in darkness as if the moon had retreated from the sky the moment the light passed through them. They both looked around. Then Dakota spotted what looked like Lysette a few steps away. She looked strange, like her body was covered in something.

Just as Dakota began to crawl towards her, Gedeon stepped from the shadows and knelt beside Lysette.

"How is she?"

Gedeon glanced over at Dakota, "She is very weak. I haven't seen her lose control over her human form in centuries."

"Human form? Centuries? What are you talking about?"

Gedeon gave her a strange look and then spoke, "She hasn't told you, has she?"

"Told me what?"

"It is not my place to reveal her secret. I will take care of her. Go tend to the others," with that he scooped Lysette into his arms and carried her closer to the falls for privacy.

"Secret? Centuries? What is he talking about?" she whispered the words to no one in particular but an answer came from her left side, the side Kaida had been on. Dakota turned her head, only to see a long figure lying on its side. The figure slowly raised its head and Dakota nearly screamed.

"You're... you're a dragon."

Kaida answered, her voice still remaining the same as it had been in human form, "Yes, that is what you humans call my kind."

"But, I thought dragons were only creatures of myths and legends?"

Tatsu, also in dragon form, landed slightly behind Kaida. She looked over her shoulder just to make sure it was him. He nuzzled up behind her and stroked her scales with one of his claws. She smiled back at him, a strange sight for Dakota to see. She had always thought dragons were fictional creatures. Yet, lying here before her, were two.

Tatsu spoke, "We like to keep it that way. Humans fear us. They want to kill us or put us in cages to be displayed in zoos. Our kind does not do well in captivity. We were born to be free, so we have hidden ourselves among you, as have many of the other creatures of human myths and fairytales," Tatsu smiled, seemingly proud of himself. Dayton and Dakota would be the only humans to ever know their secret.

Dakota shook her head, not believing all that she had seen tonight. However, the one person she needed to see, the one person who called to every part of her being, was nowhere in sight. She called out to him in her mind and he spoke for all to hear.

"I am here, but I fear we are not alone," his comment brought everyone's attention to him.

"What do you mean? We closed the portal in time didn't we?" Dakota was sure The Great Evil, whatever it was, had been stopped before it had the chance to escape.

"I believe so, but there is something or someone else lurking about."

"But..," and before Dakota could get the rest of the sentence out, something grabbed Nicolay from behind and thrust a stake into his chest.

Dakota screamed, her agony passing through the woods, drowning in the distance. With Lysette still in his arms, Gedeon appeared next to Dakota trying to determine what all of the commotion was about. Pointing, so Gedeon knew why she was hysterical, Dakota saw a glimpse of fang as the creature bit into Nicolay's neck, attempting to drain the life from him. As much as she tried, she could not turn from the horror. Her mind would not believe what her eyes saw.

Nicolay let out a laugh the devil himself would have been proud of. Then, as calmly as she had ever seen anyone being attacked be, he grabbed the creature by the neck and swung it over his shoulder. Holding it with one hand, the feet dangled loosely above the ground, he snapped Xavier's neck and proceeded to rip the body in half. He held the halves of Xavier's body to each side and then tossed the pieces in opposite directions. Nicolay then pulled the stake from his heart and as it inched out of his chest, the hole closed behind it.

They all stared in amazement. Dakota shook her head, trying to decipher what she had just witnessed. She was sure she had seen the stake come all the way through and yet, Nicolay was still standing before them, unfazed.

"How can this be?" Gedeon was just as surprised as everyone else. No vampire in the history of man had ever been staked and survived.

"It can be because I will it so."

Everyone's heads turned, following the sound of the voice. They all watched in awe as Nicolay stepped from the trees behind them and into the clearing. Heads turned back and forth as if they were watching a tennis match, none of them believing their eyes.

Nicolay walked to his mirror image and the two stood side by side. He faced the image and raised his palms. The image imitated his every move. He pressed his palm to the image and then through the image. They all watched in amazement as Nicolay's hand passed through. Then, with a wave of his hand, the duplicate disappeared.

CHAPTER FORTY-SIX

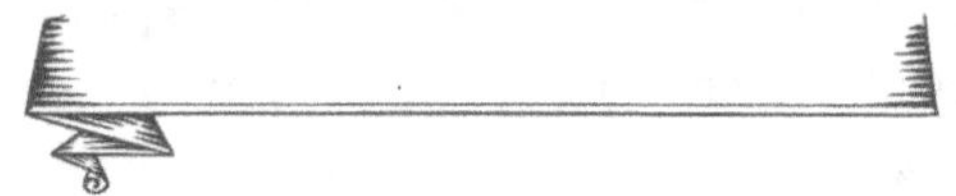

LYSETTE GRINNED, SMILING as proud as any mother whose child had come into his own and become a man. Nicolay was truly learning the extent of his power, for none before him received the gift of duplicity. She hoped with the revelation, he'd accept the gift bestowed upon him. She could only admire him from afar; scared if she went to him, tried to touch him, the moment would shatter like glass. It was in that moment she knew why Nicolay was the chosen one, why Gedeon had only been given a part of the power, but Nicolay had received it all. It took her back to the day Gedeon informed her of what he had done.

Sitting at the iron laced window in the large medieval castle, Lysette gazed out into her garden. Gedeon promised her he'd be home tonight. She watched anxiously as the sun descended beyond the horizon. Gedeon would be waking soon from the dark slumber that trapped him by day. As the last flicker of light disappeared like a star shedding its last light, she rose from the chair preparing to meet her love.

It had been three weeks since she had last seen him. When they parted, it had not been under the best of circumstances. Another argument over Nicolay Constantine caused her to lash out at him, vowing that if anything happened to Nicolay, there would be hell to pay. She knew he would never harm Nicolay. Not because it was the right thing to do, but because he had promised her.

She pushed open the heavy doors and ran towards the entrance to the garden. She looked in every direction, turning in circles trying to find him. She knew he would not disappoint her. So where was he?

Gedeon stood in the distance admiring his one true love. Since the first time he had laid eyes on her, he had loved her. She was all he'd dreamed she would be. But in the back of his mind, all of that was about to come to an end. He had promised to spend tonight with her for he knew it would be their last.

He watched her, the disappointment now filling her face. He had prolonged the inevitable for long enough. It had to be done, and it had to be done tonight. Tonight, he would deliver the news of what he had done. He had already prepared himself for her reaction, for her anger and disappointment. Tonight, he would break her heart and in return, she would break his.

Lysette lowered her head. She didn't want to believe he wasn't coming, but now she wasn't so sure. Their time together was already limited, the sun stealing him away from her at dawn, so she was sure as soon as night fell he would be there. So where was he?

Just as she began to lose all hope, she felt his arms wrap around her waist.

Elated she asked, "Where have you been hiding?"

"Nowhere and everywhere, but none of that matters now, I am here," he quickly turned her around and gazed into her eyes. She was even more breathtaking up close. He wanted to enjoy these last few hours with her, sharing her, drinking her in, her sight, her smell, all of her. He brushed the slightest kiss upon her lips and then intertwining his fingers with hers he lead them to the garden.

Lysette's Garden of Eden was as breathtakingly beautiful by moonlight as it was by sunlight. During the daylight hours, this is where she spent most of her time. She made sure there were no weeds destroying its beauty. She'd decide which of the flowers she'd pick and bring into the house. But sometimes, well, sometimes she just came to the garden to sit and enjoy the view. Whenever she was homesick, longing for her dear sweet Belize, the garden comforted her, surrounding her with the feeling of home.

The garden was also their lover's paradise. She and Gedeon spent hours there walking, not a word spoken between them. Being together in their special place was enough. She planned never to leave it.

Gedeon remained silent, burdened with his thoughts. How was he going to tell her what he had done? They'd had many arguments over Nicolay, but none like the last. When he stormed out of the house, his fury as fierce as that of a madman, he'd had no intention of following her orders. How dare she forbid him from doing anything? He was a grown man, a thousand year old vampire, not her child. The last words she had spoken to him rang in his head.

"If you so much as harm one hair on Nicolay's head, I swear to you I will leave and you will suffer for all eternity."

Gedeon was furious. Sometimes she would sit for hours in the parlor, that damn book in her lap, staring at the picture of the baby. She had never forgiven herself for allowing him to be born and she had spent the last twenty-seven years ensuring his safety. Well, Gedeon was getting damn tired of it.

She had stormed out after speaking those words to him, slamming their bedroom door behind her. He waited and waited, sure she would return to apologize for speaking to him in such a manner, but she didn't. He frantically searched every room in the house only to come up with nothing. He returned to the bedroom, the full moon beckoning him to the window. He looked down into the garden and there she was, head in her hands crying for Nicolay. Well, he'd had enough of this mess. He was tired of it and he planned to do something about it. With that last thought, he disappeared into the night in search of his revenge.

It had taken him only an hour to find her dear Nicolay and only a few moments for the deed to be done. He'd thought about taking it all, leaving him dead on the street, but for some reason he just couldn't do it, so he made the decision, and brought Nicolay across.

He was paralyzed with fear the moment he realized what he'd just done. It wasn't just the fact that he'd gone against Lysette's orders, it was that in all of the time they had been together, this was the only thing she had ever asked of him. All she ever wanted was to make sure he never brought Nicolay across, and he had done just that.

He hid the body in one of the farmhouses, making sure it would not be exposed to any light. He planned to return the next night to face him, to find out what bond he had to Lysette, but when he returned, Nicolay was gone.

It took Gedeon three weeks to gain enough courage to face Lysette. Three weeks to convince himself this was not a dream, that he had done the unforgivable in her eyes. Three weeks to realize he would lose his one true love forever. He finally faced the fact that Lysette had to be told, and he had to be the one to tell her.

Now having her close to him, knowing the secret he harbored, he didn't know how he was going to tell her. Sooner or later, she was going to find out and he thought it best she heard it from him. He led her to a bench in the part of the garden where the iris was always in bloom.

"I have something to tell you," sorrow filled his voice.

Lysette glanced up at him. He had been unusually quiet during their walk. Initially, she was sure it had something to do with the fight they had a few weeks ago. She had long gotten over that, knowing he wouldn't do anything to jeopardize their relationship. But now, with the sorrow in his voice, she wasn't so sure anymore.

"Please, sit," he gestured for her to sit on the bench and she did.

"What's wrong? What's all this about?" Lysette was confused. She had never seen Gedeon look so sad.

He pulled her into his arms, wanting to hold her, rock her, and be with her one last time before it was all taken away.

"You know I love you, right?"

Lysette thought that a strange question, "Of course I know that, but I have the feeling you are questioning that same thing?"

"And you know I would never do anything to intentionally hurt you or us, right?"

"Gedeon, what happened?" Lysette was still clueless as to what he was getting at.

He thought about telling her a lie, making up something, but before he could think of anything the words fell from his mouth.

"I brought Nicolay over."

She gasped and all of the color drained from her body. She frantically shook her head in disbelief. The only thing she had ever asked of him is that he let Nicolay be and he had broken his promise. She began to beat on his chest, first in anger, then in fear. He really had no idea of the ramification of his actions, the kind of power he had released into the world. The potential death and destruction that now faced them all.

She was sobbing uncontrollably by then and he reached for her.

Quickly drawing away in anger, with hurt and sorrow on her face, she yelled at him, "Don't touch me! Don't ever touch me again!"

Then she ran. She ran as fast as she could to the house, her wails trailing behind her, piercing his heart.

Gedeon stared out into the night. Dawn was fast approaching. He considered just sitting there and waiting. Waiting for the sun to warm his cold body until it burst into flames. But he couldn't do that. That would be the easy way out. He vowed to make this mistake up to her if it took him all of eternity. Then he retreated to his lair for the dark slumber to pull him under, make him forget the look on her face the moment he had broken her heart.

Coming back from her memory, she gazed into his face. Seeing all of the love he had harbored for her for so many centuries, she knew she could no longer deny him.

Lysette gazed out amongst the few creatures that remained after the battle. None of them had any idea of the danger they had just faced. But her gaze always returned to Nicolay. He seemed so at peace with all that had just happened. She decided not to ruin it for him, to give him more time to adjust to all he had learned over the last couple of days.

Gedeon watched as emotion overwhelmed Lysette. A smile inched its way across her face until she looked like a Cheshire cat.

"What are you so ecstatic about?"

Lysette took a quick look at Gedeon, wishing she had hidden her glee a little better. She opted not to tell him the truth, not believing he was ready to accept it, so she chose a simple half truth.

"I'm just happy things turned out for the best."

Gedeon carefully considered her explanation. He didn't believe a word of it, but he'd accept it for now. It seemed she finally realized they were meant to be together and he didn't want to jeopardize that.

NICOLAY WATCHED AS Lysette recognized what Gedeon felt for her. He knew the feeling Gedeon was experiencing holding the love of his life in his arms. He felt the same way about Dakota.

"Nicolay, I believe you have someone to tend to," Lysette gestured toward Dakota who now lay on her side on the ground.

He was right beside her in the blink of an eye, lifting her limp body and pulling her close. Even after all she had been through, she was still the most beautiful creature he had ever laid eyes on. He whispered in her ear, "My *Tehya Aquene* come back to me."

Her eyes slowly opened. She smiled weakly at him, only having enough strength to keep her eyes open for a moment, and then the darkness overtook her dragging her into the abyss.

Nicolay pressed her to his chest listening, intently to her heartbeat. He smelled the crimson river flowing through her body. The flow, now weak from her loss of blood, no longer brought the need to feed from her. The rhythm of her heart was slow, her breathing shallow. She needed rest, and lots of it, but most of all, she needed him.

He addressed Dayton to assure him that he would take good care of her.

"She is badly hurt, but I can save her. She needs rest and I'll make sure rest is what she gets. I shall return her to you by daylight in five days," he turned to Gedeon and then to Tatsu, "Take good care of them," then he was gone.

Dayton turned to Lysette, not knowing what to do, "He said he could save her. What did he mean by that?"

Lysette suspected he was thinking that Nicolay was going to bring her over. Although Lysette knew sooner or later it was destined to happen, tonight would not be that night. She whispered to Gedeon for him to put her down and after a moment's hesitation he did. She grabbed Dayton's hand and led him to the edge of the falls. Pulling him down beside her, she prepared to reassure him that his sister would be home and well soon.

"First, let me clarify, she will not return to you as a vampire. He meant he would take her home, his home, and my real home. You see, we are not from this place, and much of what he needs to heal her is in the jungles of South America. He will heal her physical wounds, her mind and her spirit.

"She has been through a lot these last couple of days and the trauma has surely affected all of her. They will have to make some tough decisions about what she should remember, but they have to make those decisions. She is his just as he is hers. Do you understand that?"

"I guess so. But I just don't get any of this. Why is this happening to us? She's all I've got and I can't bear to lose her."

Lysette hugged Dayton, knowing they'd all been through hell and lived to tell about it, "Because we are all the chosen ones. When Nicolay returns with Dakota, I'll explain it all. I promise. So, are we ok?"

He stared into her eyes one last time. Assured she had told him the truth he agreed, "Yeah. Can I ask you something?"

Lysette saw the concern in Dayton's eyes, "Sure."

He looked out into the trees as he spoke, "When you first met Nicolay, did you know what he was?"

"Why do you ask?"

"I asked first."

"Dayton," Lysette patted him on the knee, "Answer my question and I promise I'll answer yours."

"Well, when I first came into the house the night I got back from Seattle I smelled something funny, like rotten meat. Then I saw a silhouette in the living room. It was pitch black in there and there is no way I should have been able to see him."

"Did you know what he was?" Lysette asked.

"Oddly enough yeah, I think I did."

"And what do you think this means?"

"Hell if I know," Dayton turned to face her and asked, "How did I know he was there and how did I know what he was?"

"Well, to answer your question of me, yes, I knew what he was, but it is for a reason very different from yours."

"What's happening to me? Is this another psychic gift that I didn't know about?" Dayton's frustration mounted. It had taken him years to learn to control his clairaudience. He wasn't sure if he'd have the same luck controlling this. The urge to seek out Nicolay had been overwhelming, and if this was any indication of what he would face in the future he didn't know if he could handle it.

"Yes and no. Let me ask you this, how much do you and Dakota really know about your father's family?"

Dayton thought for a moment before answering, "Not much, just the slave stories about how this land got to be ours. Other than that, we don't know anything about that side of the family. Why?"

"Not to bring up bad memories, but there has always been one part of your parent's accident that didn't sit right with me. I found it strange that your father's head had been cut from his body. The coroner never gave an exact account of what may have caused the head to be severed. With all that has happened in the past few days, it makes me wonder," it was her turn to stare out into the clearing.

"Wonder about what?" he still didn't understand what Lysette was trying to tell him.

"Dayton," she let out a small sigh before continuing, "Did your mother ever tell you the story of Dhampir?"

"Dom what?"

"Dhampir."

"No, not that I can think of. What is it?" she'd piqued his curiosity.

"More like a who is it? A Dhampir is by blood and nature a vampire hunter. They were said to be the children of a vampire who had not yet turned and his mortal wife. Your mother was a gypsy was she not?"

"Yes. It's her side of the family that we believe Dakota and I got our gifts."

"In gypsy folklore, Dhampir were important people in the community. I think she may have been drawn to your father because he too was a Dhampir."

"But if our father was Dhampir, then what does that mean for me and Dakota?"

"For Dakota it may not mean anything, but for you it means everything. The powers of Dhampir are usually passed down only on the male side, although I have seen at least one other case where a female Dhampir was born. Your father may have been Dhampir and never have known, or he may have just kept the secret hoping you'd never be exposed to a vampire and you could live a normal life. But the possibility that he may never have come in contact with a vampire are probable, so he may never have realized what he was."

"I still don't understand."

"As long as there have been vampires, there have been hunters. Some chose the profession because of their hatred of vampires, others because of revenge, and still others because of gifts that made tracking and killing vampires easy. But there was a special kind, one who was born into the world for the sole purpose of hunting the vampire. It is rare for a Dhampir to be born, but when one is, if his development of skill is not hindered, he will seek out and destroy vampires."

"So what are you saying?"

"I've watched you for years Dayton. Your fascination with weapons, your protectiveness of things that are just. Every movement of your body, the fluidness of your muscles, even the fact that you're extremely double jointed point to you being Dhampir."

"Is that why I felt the undying urge to just kill Nicolay when I first met him?"

Lysette glanced back at him. She hadn't realized how lucky Nicolay had been. If Kaida hadn't been there or Dayton had already understood his purpose, they might have all been doomed.

"Yes."

"And could I have?"

Lysette lowered her eyes, "I'm not sure."

"So is there anything else I need to know?" Dayton still sensed Lysette was not giving him all of the information. She'd given him enough to think about, but if she wanted to share more, he'd gladly welcome the information. Know Lysette the way he did he assumed she'd keep some things to herself.

"Not right now. Dakota needs to know this as well and I don't want to have to repeat the whole story twice. When she's better, I'll explain it to you both."

Dayton stood and offered his hand to aid her in getting up, "Shall we go join the others?"

"I think that'd be best," Lysette led him back to the others.

"One more question."

"What is it?"

"How come everyone has somebody and I get to go home alone?"

Lysette tried to tell if he was serious or joking. She threw her arm over his shoulder and ruffled his hair a little bit, "Your time will come. Actually, I have already met your soul mate and she is quite interesting. I think she will make you very happy though if what I suspect is true, there will be some details that need to be worked out," that said, Lysette dropped his hand.

"Oh, so you just gonna' leave me hangin' like that? I'm gonna remember that," he said, smiling at her.

"Sure am. Now, why don't you go join the others, I'll be there in a minute."

"You sure?"

"Yeah."

Dayton took one last look at Lysette and then turned and began making his way back to the main part of the clearing.

The others had been waiting patiently for Lysette and Dayton to return so they could go home and get some rest. As Dayton approached the clearing alone Gedeon asked, "Where's Lysette?"

Dayton gesture that she was still back where they'd talked, "If I didn't know better, I'd swear something was up with her. She said she join us in a minute."

Gedeon let out a sigh, "As much as she may want to be alone, she shouldn't be right now."

"You know what's wrong?"

"I'm not sure. You guys go ahead. I'll make sure she makes it back to the house."

Gedeon left the others standing in the clearing staring at each other. He slowly made his way back to where Lysette had taken Dayton. He heard her attempting to control the sobs for fear she'd begin to wail as some pain unknown to him engulfed her. Her tears hurt him to his core. She'd only cried like this once before, and he'd been the cause of her anguish. He promised he'd never let it happen again, that she'd never experience the pain he'd caused her again; yet here she was, trapped beneath the unyielding sorrow and he had no idea why.

Gedeon kept his distance until the sobs intensified and the sight of her in so much pain became unbearable. Then he went to her, not sure if she'd accept the comfort he offered. She allowed him to wrap his arms around her and pull her close. The tears continued to fall, leaving salty trails down each of her cheeks. He rocked her slowly until her wails turned to a light sniffle.

Lysette looked up at him knowing he was waiting for her to make the first move. Centuries as a vampire had taught him patience and he'd give her as much time as she needed without pushing. But Lysette needed to tell him. He and Nicolay both needed to know why tonight had been so important. This wasn't over, it was just the beginning, and Lysette was sure he didn't realize the significance of them having to close the portal. She pulled away and he let her go. She couldn't be in his arms when she said what was on her mind.

Standing in front of the falls, her back to him, she spoke, "Do you know what tonight means?"

Gedeon didn't try to go to her. She'd pulled away for a reason and he'd respect her need for space.

"It means I have failed. If I hadn't failed, the Great Evil wouldn't have found the portal."

"No. Don't blame yourself. It's really not your fault. Let me ask you this," Lysette took in a deep breath and slowly exhaled, "in all of your years, have you ever seen a portal open?"

"No."

"Have you never wondered why?"

"For a time I did, but I just assumed the Great Evil had been following me. I'd tried my best to avoid areas that might harbor a portal. Is there something else I should know?"

"When you took over the responsibility of the gates, it was because the one who made you had disappeared," Lysette wrapped her arms around her body.

"I remember."

"We didn't know for sure if he was dead or alive, so you acted as if you had the sole responsibility of ensuring the portals remained closed."

"What are you getting at?"

"Did you know that Aurek was the key?"

Gedeon raised an eyebrow, "What do you mean the key?"

"Remember when I told you the only way to keep the Great Evil from returning was to keep him away from the portals? Well, for your purposes, that was true. You are one of the chosen, but in order to open or close a portal, you need the help of others. Aurek was a key. He possessed all of the powers to open and close the gates at will. I have only seen the gift bestowed upon two others."

"What are you saying?"

"I think that somehow, from somewhere, Aurek was still keeping the gates sealed. Even if the Great Evil hadn't been following you, if it had found one of the portals, it wouldn't have been able to use it."

"Why are you telling me this?"

"Because I believe I have lost one of my children. If we hadn't closed that portal, the world would now be doomed. The only way the portal could have been opened is if Aurek has joined the other side or has met his death."

"So is that why I was drawn to the portal this time instead of repelled by it."

"Maybe."

"And what does this mean?"

"A couple of things I think. One, that all of the portals are currently vulnerable," Lysette stopped there. Here was the moment she so dreaded. She stared off into the mist created by the falls. She wanted to hold on to the secret for just a moment more. She was sure Gedeon would not take the news well.

"What is the other thing Lysette?"

She turned to face him. She'd look him in the face when she said the words, he deserved that much, "There is a new key." She watched as the anger grew in Gedeon, hoping he wouldn't make her say the words though she was prepared if that is what he wanted.

"Let me guess, it's Nicolay."

"I believe so."

It was his turn to turn from her. He'd suspected there was some other untold bond between Lysette and Nicolay, and now he understood. If anything happened to Aurek, she'd have to find Nicolay to teach him how to keep the portals closed. That was just the way things were meant to be. Gedeon realized whether he liked it or not, once again, Nicolay would have to become a part of their lives. He couldn't blame anyone but himself. If he hadn't brought Nicolay across, none of this would be happening.

"So where does this leave us?" he asked.

"What do you mean?"

"I cannot live the way we used to live. I can't just sit around while you worry about him all of the time. I won't put myself through that torture again."

Lysette reached out to him. She'd had no idea of what she'd been doing to him. She hadn't even thought about him when she was worrying about Nicolay. She'd done so much wrong by him and now she wanted to make things right.

"How come you never said anything?" she turned him around to face her. Lysette tried but couldn't recall one time Gedeon had said anything about how her moods were affecting him.

"Would you have been ready to listen?"

"I guess not," his comment hurt, but what he said was true. "But with your help, we can make things different this time."

Lysette was going to leave the decision up to him. He was the one who had made all of the sacrifices before and she wouldn't hold it against him if he decided that them being together was too hard. She wanted the chance to make it up to him, but only if he was willing to give it a try.

After a short contemplation Gedeon responded, "I know it's not going to be easy, but I'm willing to give it a try if you are."

Lysette pulled Gedeon into a hug. They held each other until it was nearly dawn.

"You'd better get going, it'll be dawn soon."

"So will I see you tonight?"

"Actually, can you give me a couple of nights? I have something I need to tend to."

"Something like what?" Gedeon gave her a curious look.

"I don't want to talk about it until I know for sure. Can you just trust my judgment this time?"

"Don't I always?"

"Yeah I guess you do. So you'll wait until I summon you?"

"If that is what the lady wishes then so be it," Gedeon leaned down a placed a kiss on her lips, "Do you need me to escort you back to the house?"

"No, I can make it back."

They stood there staring at each other, neither quite ready to leave the other behind.

"I'll be waiting for your summons."

"I won't keep you waiting long. I promise."

"Then I bid you good day m'lady," He bowed at the waste and began walking away from her.

"Gedeon."

He stopped and turned back to her, "Yes?"

"I love you," Lysette wanted to make sure he knew. She hadn't said the words to him in far too long and she wanted him to know that she still felt the same way.

"Music to my ears. I love you too. Remember, I'll be waiting," and then he was gone.

CHAPTER FORTY-SEVEN

IT'D BEEN TWO NIGHTS since they'd saved the world and they all still looked like they'd been dragged through the pits of hell. Everyone had rested and physically recuperated from the draining task of closing the portal. So why was it that each of them, Kaida, Tatsu, Dayton, and Lysette felt like they had failed?

Kaida lay on the couch, her head resting in Tatsu's lap. Tatsu did his best to comfort her. He'd watched her each night as the sun would set, and each night at dusk the tears began to fall. He knew she was reliving the moment she'd seen Dakota's body hanging from the wall in the cave. That one image brought back the torture she'd endured while she too had been held captive. He wanted so much to take her pain away, to make things better, but only time could accomplish that.

Even in their own pain, they'd all tried unsuccessfully to comfort Dayton. He shied away as much as possible, shielding himself from any reassurance any of them may have had to offer. For the past two nights he'd stood in front of the bay window staring out into the night. He'd only be comforted when his sister was returned.

They all now had their own personal battles to fight and it was eating away at all of them. Although they ate, both Kaida and Tatsu unknowingly filled the room with sadness. Dayton hadn't eaten in two days and it was beginning to show. His face was thinning and Lysette feared if this continued he'd pass out. She had to do something, the question was, what?

"Kaida. May I speak with you in private?" Lysette asked.

Kaida turned to face Lysette, wondering what could be on her mind. She then looked up at Tatsu, silently asking if it was ok. He nodded his reassurance and urged her join their new friend.

Kaida followed Lysette out the back door into the adjacent orchard. She wanted to make sure they were far enough away from the house to not be heard.

"I cannot allow this continue," Lysette said.

"What are you talking about?"

Lysette was so tired of people asking her that, "Dayton's not eating and growing weaker by the minute, and whether you know it or not, your sadness is choking the life out of us all."

She hadn't meant to sound harsh, but she didn't know any other way to say it.

Kaida lowered her head, "I apologize. I had no idea you could feel it."

"We all can. I want to ask something of you, but I will only do it if you fully agree."

"What is it?" Kaida asked.

"I want your permission to drug you all in a way."

"Why are you asking me?" Kaida was on the verge of yelling, "You should be asking all of us, not just me," the anger began to surface in her.

"I know Dayton will not agree, but if he continues like this I'm not sure what will happen. His health is at stake and I am prepared to take the blame from him. I know he'll understand I did what I did because it was in the best interest of all of us; however, I cannot make the decision for you."

"What is it that you plan to do?"

"I want to make you two sleep. I need to check on Nicolay and Dakota but I don't want to raise any suspicions as to my whereabouts."

"You know where they are?"

"I am pretty sure he has taken them home," Lysette turned from Kaida. She wasn't going to tell her anymore and she didn't want to see the anger in her eyes if she had to refuse to give more information.

"So you just want to put us to sleep, like you did before with the tea."

Lysette released a breath she hadn't realized she was holding, "Yes. That is all I ask."

"And what about Tatsu?" Kaida didn't want to be left in the house vulnerable. She still considered this place strange and she wasn't prepared to be drugged with no one watching over them.

"I will leave him untouched to watch over you both. I think his mood will change once you are asleep."

"And what if he starts asking questions?"

"I'll explain to him what I have done, let him know that you two need the rest."

"Then for myself, I agree. But I will not speak for Dayton," Kaida replied.

"And I would not ask you to. Please send Tatsu out to me."

Kaida turned and reentered the house to seek Tatsu. Lysette sat on the marble bench, her head in her hands. She tried without success to rub away the headache beginning behind her eyes. She felt a cool breeze against her cheek and turned to find Gedeon standing beside her.

"It's dangerous for you to be here."

"I only came to check on you," Gedeon had already spent a lifetime without her, he didn't plan on that happening again.

"I'm fine. Now please, go before something happens," Lysette's voice held the slightest bit of panic. It was enough though to have Gedeon concerned.

"What could possibly happen?"

"There is a Dhampir near. Please, I don't have time to explain. Just go. Now!"

Gedeon followed her orders just as Tatsu came running out the house behind Dayton. Dayton looked around and sniffed the air, trying to follow the scent. It was the same smell he'd smelled before when he'd first found Nicolay in the house.

"Dayton come, you too Tatsu," Lysette beckoned them to her.

"I smelled it again. That rotten meat smell," Dayton said.

"I apologize. Gedeon was here."

"So I am what you said I am," Dayton sounded disturbed by the revelation. He looked saddened. He dealt with so much all of his life. Now there was one more stone added to the pile, one more "gift" to tend to.

"Yes my child, you are Dhampir, but it is nothing to be ashamed of. How did it feel?"

"Strange. It's like I knew there was a vampire near. The smell was overwhelming. I was drawn to it, had to follow it."

"Anything else?" Lysette asked.

"Blood. I wanted blood."

Lysette wrapped her arms around him. She slowly rocked them back and forth. She covered him with her magic, comforted him with her touch, then she reached into his mind and willed him sleep. Dayton's head rested against her shoulder. When she was sure he was asleep, she waved Tatsu over to them.

"What did you do to him?" Tatsu asked.

"He will sleep, at least until I return. Can you help me get him back into the house?"

Tatsu lifted Dayton from her arms and tossed him over one shoulder. Before he turned to return to the house he asked, "Where are you going?"

"To see a friend. Kaida should be asleep as well. She gave me permission to use the sleep spell. Please watch over them. I shall return shortly."

Tatsu nodded his acknowledgement and walked back into the house. He laid Dayton's limp body in one of the chairs and covered him with a blanket. He did the same for Kaida, then slipped into kitchen to let them rest.

CHAPTER FORTY-EIGHT

LYSETTE STEPPED THROUGH the veranda of the Naverro Plantation house and into the temple El Castillo. Dakota's body lay quietly on the altar in the middle of the upper chamber. She seemed to be resting peacefully. Her wrist had been wrapped in white cloth while the rest of her body was covered by a blood red silk sheet.

Lysette hesitated to go to her, not wanting to wake her from her sleep. She knelt beside her friend, ashamed. She'd failed her, broken the promise to keep her safe. Lysette fought the tears. She managed for a while not to cry, but soon, the tears began to stream down her cheeks.

"I am so sorry," Lysette covered Dakota's hand with her own. Never had she imagined things would get this bad, "I never meant for any of this to happen. I should have told you everything sooner," she was sobbing uncontrollably now, "There is so much you should have known, so much you should still know. I hope you can find it in your heart to forgive me."

"She already has."

Lysette quickly gathered herself, "I didn't know you were there."

"I know," he walked to the temple entrance, keeping his back to her so he didn't have to witness her tears.

"She understands why you kept your secrets. I, however, do not."

"How do you know she understands?" Lysette asked.

"She can hear you, she just cannot physically respond."

"What have you done to her? Why can't she respond?" it was clear by her voice she was angry.

"You have no right to be angry with me. I have done nothing to her she has not specifically requested of me. She asked that I make it so she'd heal faster so I've made it so she is somewhat separated from her body. If you listen you can hear her. She is speaking to you," he stepped through the opening and disappeared into the night.

"Dakota?" Lysette spoke her name in her mind.

"I'm here. I heard what you said and I really do understand."

"You're not angry with me?"

"At first yes, I just couldn't believe you'd keep such secrets. I'm not angry anymore though. I know you wanted so much for Dayton and I to lead normal lives. You did it to protect us, and because of you I've had the opportunity to live a wonderful life."

"I regret so much not telling you about all of this," Lysette again knelt beside Dakota's body.

"Don't. I know things are different now and they always will be, but we all play with the hands we're dealt. Nicolay understands that as well, he's just having a difficult time accepting things the way they are. He'll realize soon that he needs to move forward, just as he decided he was tired of hiding and accepted that he is a vampire."

"You were always the optimist."

"So I've heard. So how's Dayton?"

Dakota had been able to feel Dayton's distress, but she needed to focus all of her energies on healing herself. She wanted so much to go to him, to let him know she was getting better. She was too weak though. Dakota was glad Lysette had come so she could find out how her brother was really doing.

"Not too well. He won't eat, he hasn't been to work, and he just stares out that damn window all day and night. He blames himself for all of this. He keeps saying if he'd hadn't gone on that trip you'd be home and safe. I finally used the sleeping spell. Both he and Kaida should be resting comfortably back at the house. Tatsu is watching over them."

"Well, you know how he is. I'll always be his little sister and he'll always feel responsible for me. I think the timing of all of this is his real problem. The first time we are apart and the world almost comes to an end. It's a lot for anyone to have to deal with. It'll get better. Besides, I may be home sooner than you think?"

"What do you mean?"

"From what Nicolay tells me, my body is almost healed. I won't have to be here much longer."

"And what about your mind?" Lysette asked. She was curious. Nicolay had rushed out so she hadn't had the opportunity to ask if he'd given Dakota her memories of that night.

"If you mean my memories, Nicolay reluctantly gave them back. It was hard to deal with at first. I think I have come to terms with what has happened to my body. You know I try my best not to dwell in the past. What is done is done. I can't change it so why let it ruin my life. We are all here only a short period of time so we have to make the best of things."

"You always knew how to make the most out of any situation. Still, I am sorry you never got the chance to freely give yourself to your soul mate," Lysette was more heart broken about Dakota's virginity being stolen than Dakota seemed to be. Giving oneself to another was sacred, and now her friend would never know the true bonding the first time created between two people.

"Don't be sorry. I did get the chance to give myself freely," Dakota replied.

Lysette looked at Dakota's body, not believing what she'd just said to her mind.

"What's the matter, cat got your tongue?" Dakota was taking great pleasure in surprising her best friend.

"You mean?"

"Yes that is exactly what I mean. I never got the chance to tell you about our last date. I made love for the first time with Nicolay and it was the most wonderful experience."

"Well you're just full of surprises aren't you? You'll have to tell me all about it once you're better."

"Actually I have one more surprise for you?"

Lysette was curious what this other surprise was, "And what's that?"

"You know, for a long time my mother didn't want to have children. She and my father had been very careful taking any and all precautions to make sure she didn't conceive. They'd gotten good at it, watching the calendar, playing things safe until one night. It had been the one night when the air outside was just right and a light mist floated down from the sky. It was a perfect night for lovers and they'd made the most of it. Mama was sure the timing was off so she let papa have his way with her. She said the night had been magical and she never regretted it. A couple of weeks later she realized she was pregnant and their world would soon be changing," Dakota became quiet thinking about her mother and how she had told her the story of when she knew she was going to have a baby.

"You ok?" Lysette asked. She'd been quiet for too long.

"Yeah. You know why they tried so much to avoid having children?"

"No."

"They knew something," Dakota hesitated again before she continued, "Have you ever looked at my brother, I mean really looked at him?"

"What do you mean?"

"Have you ever noticed Dayton's smile?"

Lysette thought about the question, "It's been a long time since I've seen Dayton smile."

"But when he used to smile, did you notice anything special about his smile?"

Lysette thought a little harder. She was trying to figure out what Dakota was getting at. She thought back to the last time she'd seen Dayton smile. It had been nearly three years ago. She studied the memory trying to focus on his smile. Then it clicked in her mind. The fangs, Dakota was talking about the fangs. If she didn't known any better, she'd swear Dayton had a permanent set of fangs. Lysette put two and two together and realized what it was Dakota was telling her.

"You know, don't you," Lysette didn't know whether to be surprised or angry.

"I've known for a long time what my brother is," Dakota gave Lysette a chance to comprehend what she'd just said before she continued, "Our father died before he had the chance to tell Dayton he too was Dhampir. I promised Mama I wouldn't tell and in all of these years I never have."

Lysette was truly speechless. She couldn't believe Dakota had kept this big of a secret from Dayton, much less from her, "So you know the story?"

"Yes. One night when we were thirteen I heard Mama and Papa arguing over it. Papa was sure Dayton was showing the signs. When they saw me, they knew I had heard what he'd said. They made me promise not to tell."

"Do you know who the first was? Do you know how rare it is for a Dhampir to be born, much less pass the gift on down through multiple generations?"

"Thaddeus was the first conceived and yes, I know how rare this is. Mama wasn't sure it was true, but Papa was sure. He said Dayton left the mark on the weapons. Because he was also Dhampir, Papa could see the energy signatures left on any weapon Dayton touched. He also said I left the signatures but not nearly as strong as Dayton's."

Dakota had kept this secret too long and it was time they all revealed everything. Dakota also feared when she and Nicolay returned, if Dayton's gift had truly been awakened, things could go terribly wrong really fast.

"Does he know yet?"

"Yes, but I don't think he understands."

"Papa left something for him. He said it would help Dayton understand his gift and his purpose. I'll give it to him when I return. I think it will help him come to terms with his new found gift," Dakota was feeling weak again. The use of her telepathy was draining her energy, "I'm tired. Go to Nicolay, he is waiting for you. Be honest with him and try to understand things from his point of view. I know you two have a lot of catching up to do."

"I'll try," Lysette replied.

"Before you go, let me ask you one more question."

"Shoot."

"You knew, didn't you?"

"What do you mean?"

"The night you took me to the club, you knew he'd be there. You brought us together didn't you?"

"I only aided in getting you two in the same place. The rest was fate's doing. Now you need to save your strength. Rest well," Lysette stood taking one last look at her friend's body.

"I will." Dakota slowly slipped back into the quiet place Nicolay had created for her in her mind. He and Lysette had a lot of catching up to do and they needed their privacy. Dakota thought it a shame it took all of this to get them back together, but what was done was done. The place around her became quiet and she slowly let sleep take her under.

CHAPTER FORTY-NINE

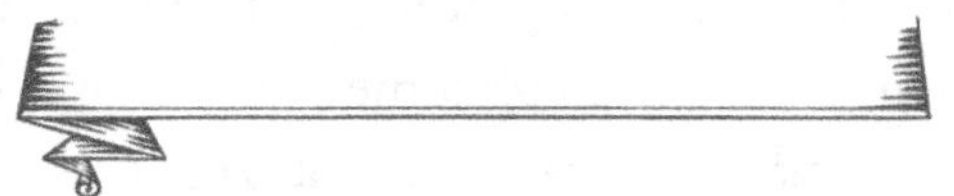

LYSETTE FOUND NICOLAY at the foot of the temple surrounded by the margay. Above them, the Harpy Eagle circled, watching tensely as the two figures below were reunited. She stepped from the top of the temple and found herself standing in front of him. He looked pale, like he hadn't fed for the couple of nights he'd watched over Dakota's body.

"How is she doing, really?" Lysette asked.

Nicolay refused to look at her. He was still furious she'd hidden so much dire information from Dakota. It had almost gotten her killed and Nicolay was not yet ready to let Lysette forget that.

"She's doing better than I expected. Her body is healing much faster than I anticipated. She should be completely healed by sunset tomorrow," he answered her question and that was all. He feared if he continued, he'd hurt her feelings.

"Nicolay, look at me."

He refused. She reached for him but he pulled further away from her, "Why are you so angry with me? I figured Dakota would be, but not you."

Lysette didn't understand the source of his anger. She'd wronged Dakota and Dayton, that much was true, but she'd spent her entire life trying to protect him. She'd sacrificed her happiness for centuries, remained alone for just as long because of him, and this is how he repaid her.

He glowered at her, not believing she didn't understand his anger.

"How can you say that? You knew all along didn't you?" before he could stop, it all came pouring out, "Why didn't you tell them? How could you just leave them out there totally vulnerable? You knew they were the keepers, that's why you stayed with them all of these years. Why didn't you tell them? Why didn't you warn them? Why didn't you prepare them for what was to come? I just don't get you!"

"Oh, so you think this was easy for me, that this was all about me don't you? You think I wanted to keep this secret? You think I liked knowing sooner or later death was going to come for them? You have no idea the decisions I have had to make regarding them," Lysette was furious now. How dare he accuse her of hiding the truth for selfish reasons, "Let me tell you something, I gave up everything for you and I gave them the same courtesy. I tried my best to make sure they lived as normal lives as possible while they still had the chance. You know, when Gedeon told me what he had done, that he had brought you across, everything I had worked for to protect you went down the drain. I had to change my focus and find the others because I knew they'd need me more than you did.

"When I did find them, they were both unknowingly fighting their gifts. Neither could function well enough to lead normal lives, much less prepare to save the world. They had to accept and learn to control their gifts before they'd be ready to use them. And apparently we've all had our secrets. Hell, I just found out myself that Dayton is Dhampir."

The words stopped Lysette's ranting. She hadn't meant to tell Nicolay like this. She wanted him to understand she made the best decisions she could and she wasn't ashamed of it. He needed to know because if it ever came down to it, Dayton had the ability to kill him, but she didn't mean for it to come out like this.

"What did you just say?" Nicolay asked.

Lysette took in a deep breath and slowly released it. She wished she hadn't said that. Well the cat was out the bag so she might as well tell him.

"The night Dayton discovered you and Kaida in the house I thought I saw something. Kaida had his weapon, but there was a distinctive energy signature left on it, the signature only Dhampir would leave. I still wasn't sure but at the falls, when he and I talked, he told me about the smell, and him sensing and seeing you in the living room. It was pitch black in there Nicolay, he never should have been able to see you, but he could. That made me even more suspicious. But, a few moments ago Dakota confirmed it all," Lysette hated this. She hated having to tell him all of this, "She says she has known for quite some time that Dayton was Dhampir. She said he is a third generation. Dhampirs are rare, but I have never met a third generation. This gift in him is strong, but I think his hesitation was merely because it was his first experience with a vampire."

"His inexperience had nothing to do with it. He couldn't have taken both Kaida and I," Nicolay seemed sure of this.

"Not true. If had he fully understood what he was, not even Kaida could have kept him from killing you."

"The weapons of mere mortals cannot hurt me. Even if he'd had silver bullets in it he would not have been able to kill me," Nicolay just stared at her not sure why he was having to explain this. She knew the only way to kill his kind was by taking the head and the heart. Even with the gun, Dayton wouldn't have had enough ammunition to finish the job. Silver burned but it wasn't a killer.

"Don't you know the full extent of a Dhampir's gifts?" Lysette asked him. If he was acting like this he couldn't have fully understood the capabilities of a Dhampir.

"You make it sound like I am missing something. Am I?"

"Dhampir have the unique ability to enchant any weapon. He could kill you with a fork if he so chose."

Nicolay stared at her in disbelief. She had to be wrong but deep inside he knew she wasn't. He'd been naive thinking Dayton couldn't have harmed him. The thought that Dayton could have really killed him began to sink in. How stupid could he have been? He'd have to be careful around Dayton next time, that is if there was a next time.

"So what does this mean?"

"I'm not sure yet. I tried to explain to Dayton what he is but he still doesn't understand it all. Dakota says their father left something for him that might help him to understand. He is growing stronger every minute. His senses are heightening as we speak. Before I came here, Gedeon came by the house. The visit triggered a reaction in Dayton even though Gedeon and I were outside and Dayton was in the house. I think his contact with you and Gedeon has fully awakened the gift. His controls have been diminished. I'll need to help him get it under control and fast. I can create a spell that will help him but it will only be a temporary fix. It may take months for him to be able to fully control the urges on his own. There's really no way of knowing."

"Then go and work as quickly as you can. Dakota will be healed soon. She'll want to go home."

"We shall anxiously await her return. I'll let Dayton know she is doing well."

"You do that. Before you go can I ask you something else?" Nicolay wanted to know how much of what had gone on Lysette really knew. She'd kept a lot of secrets from a lot of people for a long time. Nicolay thought it was time for all of the secrecy to end and he wanted to make sure she knew it.

"Shoot," Lysette was sure she knew where this was going. She too was ready to end the secrecy but she'd humor him and his tactics to get her to talk.

"How much about Dakota and I did you know beforehand?"

"Enough."

"What's that suppose to mean?" she was doing it again, being evasive, and Nicolay was tired of the games.

"What do you want me to say?"

"I want you to tell me the truth, the whole truth. Is that too much to ask?"

"You want to know the truth?"

"Yes."

"I knew when you first came here. I knew that you'd be drawn here and that you'd be drawn to her. I just had to find a way for you two to find each other."

"So you knew I'd be in the club that night?"

"Yes, I made sure of it."

"So you were the one calling out to me?"

"I only did it because the time was nearing. Just as you sensed the Great Evil, so did I. I knew then you two needed to find each other. You need each other and fate has made it so you'll weather anything thrown at you."

Nicolay turned to look back up at the temple. Above him was his second chance at love, he just hoped she'd still have him after all of this was over and she had time to really accept what he was.

"Don't worry. She'll love you for all eternity."

"How do you know?"

"If you ever get the chance, ask Gedeon," Lysette turned to open a portal back to the house when Nicolay stopped her one last time.

"Lysette, one more question."

"What is it?"

"Will it be safe for me to bring her back?" Nicolay was concerned. If Dayton had reacted to Gedeon being outside of the house, there was no telling how he'd react to him bringing Dakota back.

"Yes, I'll see to it," then she turned and stepped virtually through the base of the temple.

CHAPTER FIFTY

DAYTON PACED BACK AND forth in the living room. It had been three nights since his world had changed. He'd rested well the night before after Lysette had cast her spell. He wasn't angry with her. He was actually glad she'd done it. He'd felt a lot better today after the rest.

Nicolay said he would return Dakota in five days, meaning they still had two more nights before Dakota would be home. This waiting was driving him crazy.

"Dayton, come sit down. You're starting to remind me of Nicolay," Kaida chided. He did look like the pacing vamp, but she was only kidding. Watching him actually reminded her very much of Nicolay and for the first time she realized she missed his pacing.

Nicolay and Dakota had been nowhere to be seen for the last couple of days. Other than that, things were back to a relatively normal state. The real Xavier had been found unconscious in the storeroom in the back of the club, bound, gagged and surrounded by roses. Lysette knew what the roses were for, but she didn't care to share that little tidbit with anyone. Xavier seemed happy enough to keep the explanation to himself as well.

So here they were, Kaida, Lysette, Dayton, and Tatsu gathered around the Naverro living room, waiting. Gedeon had agreed to meet them at the house by nightfall, which would be soon. When Lysette had returned from her visit she'd cast a shielding spell over Dayton's sleeping body. She hoped it would hold but she wouldn't know until Gedeon showed up.

The sound of a yawn drew Dayton's attention to the top of the staircase. When his eyes finally focused on the figure dressed in all white he let out a sign of relief. Dakota stood at the top of the stairs, appearing like an angel looking down upon them.

"Dakota?" he asked. His mind was having a hard time comprehending that it was her. He'd expected to have to wait a few more days. He just wouldn't get his hopes up even though in his heart he knew it was really her.

Everyone in the room turned and watched as she descended the stairs. They'd expected her to return in two days, not today. She was radiant. All of the cuts were healed. Not even the slightest scar remained. She was dressed in all white silk. Lysette recognized the garment, it was the same one she had used on a number of occasions when healing the sick, but it looked absolutely ravishing on Dakota. White always seemed to make the patients feel better and it definitely made Dakota look like an angel.

"But...but how?" Dayton stuttered the words.

"After talking with Lysette, Nicolay brought me home last night. He stayed with me until dawn, then retreated to the darkroom. He's been sleeping right under your noses and you didn't even know it. Didn't anybody check my room?"

"Well no. We thought Nicolay would have you with him in his lair," Dayton was gleaming now, so happy to see his sister and yet so afraid to touch her.

They all sat there, gawking at her in disbelief as the last light of the sun escaped past the horizon fleeing from the darkness of night. Then, their heads all jerked towards the sound of the door to the darkroom opening.

"I do not yet have a bed in my lair and I thought she might be more comfortable in her own bed," Nicolay glided behind Dakota, wrapping his arms around her waist. She leaned back, her body molding perfectly to his.

"So, how do you feel?" he whispered in her ear.

"Like a million bucks," she whispered back to him.

Nicolay raised a brow to that, but the smile on her face said it all.

She was happy to be alive and happy to be in his arms. But most of all, she was happy he had given her all of her memories. The first night had been hard for her, she relieved all of the pain and torture the demon disguised as Xavier had put her body through. But the next night and last night had been wonderful. Nicolay had showed her true love. He'd held her, nurtured her, and shared blood with her. Then, he spread a soothing cream over her whole body. Even in the most private of places. It smelled of vanilla and mangos. He then wrapped her body in silk and tucked her in bed. Kissing her gently on the forehead, he willed her to sleep.

She dreamed of him and woke to his name on her lips. He had left her a note, telling her he was dreaming of her just below. He had laid out the white silk outfit for her and she dressed quickly knowing he would be downstairs waiting for her, just as everyone else would be.

The doorbell rang, bringing everyone out of his or her thoughts. Dakota turned to face Nicolay and then she looked back over at Dayton. She knew who stood behind the door. He could not enter without an invitation. She studied Dayton for a moment to determine if he was having any reaction to Nicolay being there or Gedeon on the other side of the door. He seemed calm enough and she wondered what Lysette had done to him.

"You may invite him in if you wish," Nicolay had had enough time to think about his past and the gifts Gedeon had bestowed upon him. Plus, after what had happened, he was sure Gedeon was no longer a threat to him, for he was the stronger of the two.

"Dayton, you ok?" Dakota asked.

"Why do you ask? Who's at the door?"

"Gedeon," she replied.

"How do you know?" Dayton asked.

"I just do."

Dayton then turned to Lysette, "Is that who's on the other side of the door?"

"Yes," short, simple, straight to the point.

"What'd you do to me now?" Dayton knew he should be having a reaction to both Nicolay and Gedeon, but for some reason he wasn't.

"Just a shielding spell. It's kind of like the one I use with Dakota."

"Then I guess it's safe. But you are going to get enough of doing things to me without my knowledge."

Dakota walked to the door. Turning the lock, she pulled the door open. Standing before her was the second most powerful vampire in the world, but he could not enter, could not pass without her permission. He bowed and waited for her to decide if he was welcome in her home.

She read his mind and smiled when he thought how beautiful she was and how lucky Nicolay was to have her.

"Well, since you feel that way, you are welcome in my home. Please come in."

Gedeon smiled, a little embarrassed that she had read his mind, "Don't tell me you can read my thoughts, too."

"I've shared blood with one you've made. It has strengthened my psychic abilities."

"Then I'll be forced to guard my thoughts against you too."

"As you wish, but, I would never use any of it against you," Dakota smiled and made her way back over to Nicolay.

Gedeon spotted Lysette and made his way over to her. He cradled her face in his palms and kissed her. She nearly melted in his embrace.

Dakota returned to Nicolay's open arms. She looked around the room at all of her family, both old and new, and smiled.

"Ok, you two. Either break it up or get a room," Dayton was getting jealous, "Not everyone here has a date you know, and I wouldn't want to be standing outside of this orgy for all of the money in the world."

They all burst out laughing, finding the extreme humor in what Dayton had just said.

"Ok," Lysette addressed them all. "Come and sit down, I have much to tell you all."

And she did. Lysette told them all she knew, hoping to prepare them for their lives ahead.

Author Bio

Author Aziza Sphinx has enjoyed the written word since she was a child. Exposed to literature at an early age she has always had a love for the written and spoken word. The books lining the numerous shelves in her home pay homage to her love of all types of literature. A native of Georgia, she spent many years writing song lyrics to instrumentals provided by her many friends in the music industry. This love of lyrics ultimately led her to completing a Bachelor of Science in Music industry at Georgia State University. Deciding that writing song lyrics wasn't enough, in July of 2004 she ventured into the realms of fantasy, beginning the first book in the Naverro Vampire tales and since has continued to weave tale after tale of challenges for her most beloved characters, Nicolay and Dakota. Her love of creating magical worlds led her to become a charter member of Indigo Ink, a distinguished writers' group in Atlanta.

For more information on Aziza Sphinx
and her alter ego Ana'Gia Wright visit:
www.authoranagiawright.com
anagia@authoranagiawight.com

Don't miss out!

Click the button below and you can sign up to receive emails whenever Aziza Sphinx publishes a new book. There's no charge and no obligation.

https://books2read.com/r/B-A-ASQE-EYLO

BOOKS 2 READ

Connecting independent readers to independent writers.